GOLD 1 BOOK 2

RIPPLE

FOREST WELLS

To James Montenegro;
A talent taken far too soon. Missed, but never forgotten.

And to the victims of 9/11.
Without whom this book, and this author, would not exist.

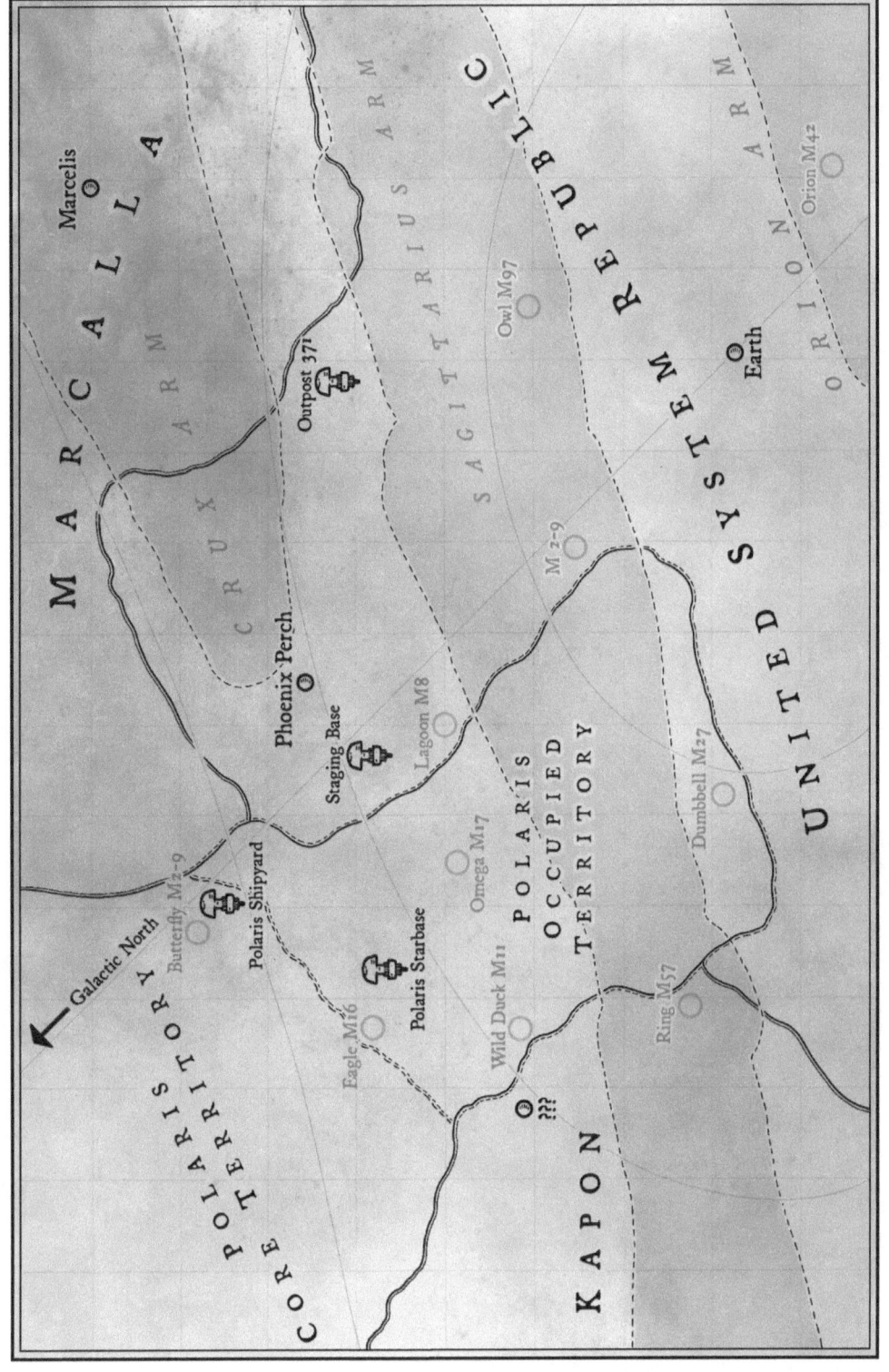

Copyright © Forest Wells 2026

Credits:

Cover art by: Royz

https://www.artstation.com/royzsecondaccount

Cover and interior design by : Miblart

Editors:

Charlie Knight http://cknightwrites.com/

Edge of the World Editing https://www.fiverr.com/share/yp8yE0

CONTENTS

PART 1: THIS FAR, NO FARTHER

CHAPTER 1: PHOENIX BURNING 1

CHAPTER 2: ASHES 20

CHAPTER 3: RETURN TO FORM 56

CHAPTER 4: FROM ONE FRYING PAN TO ANOTHER 86

CHAPTER 5: SECOND CONTACT 103

CHAPTER 6: THE MORE THINGS CHANGE 141

CHAPTER 7: ONE IF BY LAND, TWO IF BY SEA 152

CHAPTER 8: HOMEFIELD ADVANTAGE 163

CHAPTER 9: BUNKER HILL 177

PART 2: AS THE STARS MOVE ABOVE, STILL I SHALL HOLD MY PLACE AMONG THEM, WHEREVER IT MAY BE.

CHAPTER 10: WILD HOLDRENS 203

CHAPTER 11: ENEMY OF MY ENEMY 241

CHAPTER 12: FINAL MISSION 264

CHAPTER 13: YOUR SHOE, MY SIZE THREE PAW 290

CHAPTER 14: ...THE MORE THEY STAY THE SAME 308

PART 3: NO MATTER THE COST

CHAPTER 15: A VIOLENT HOUSE CALL........................ 337

CHAPTER 16: A FUNNY THING HAPPENED
ON THE WAY TO THE TARGET 362

CHAPTER 17: YES, IT CAN GET WORSE 405

CHAPTER 18: THE SEEDS WE SOW 414

CHAPTER 19: CAESAR'S PALACE................................ 423

CHAPTER 20: I SHOULDN'T HAVE ASKED 438

CHAPTER 21: CHAINS OF COMMAND 451

CHAPTER 22: HUNTERS 467

CHAPTER 23: THE GATES OF VALHALLA 478

CHAPTER 24: MY LIFE FOR THE PACK 499

GLOSSARY OF TERMS... 525

ACKNOWLEDGEMENTS 530

OTHER BOOKS BY FOREST WELLS

GOLD 1 SERIES:

"Fog of War"

OTHER NOVELS:

"Luna, The Lone Wolf"
"Blood of An Alpha"

RIPPLE

RIPPLE

RIPPLE:

NOUN:

a small wave on the surface of water.

VERB:

to (cause to) move in small waves.

MILITARY BREVITY CODE:

Two or more munitions released or fired in close succession, usually from the same source.

PART 1:
THIS FAR, NO FARTHER

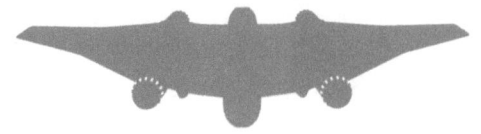

CHAPTER 1

PHOENIX BURNING

Major Yarain shook her head after a wide yawn. It was almost a comment in and of itself from the fox-like holdren; as if it might express everything running through her mind. *I don't understand.* Sundale, her most recent litter and the only one she could reach, wasn't acting like a holdren at all. His wounds had been terrible, but they were healing. A holdren in such a state usually sought out the pack for protection and support. Instead, he had shunned her. No, even less than that.

She'd been in that corridor outside his quarters every minute she could be while off duty. She'd tried to get his attention for the first two days, but it had gotten her nowhere. Since then, she'd just laid on the blue-colored metal floor, tucked tight next to one of the support beams along the similarly tinted walls of the carrier. She kept her ears up and all three tails laid loosely beside her, trying to create a sense of stability for him to find.

Yet every time Sundale came out, he utterly ignored her. Nothing Yarain did even got a turn of an ear. Not a single bark or whimper or word or glow of her rust-red tail tips drew any reaction. She'd tried showing up naked so he could see her full coat. She had taken great care to get it clean that day so the dull orange touching the back of her neck, shoulders, and back stood out against the sandy gold primary color. Her white underside almost reflected on the floor, and the small flecks of dark grey on her face and throat helped to highlight the dark grey that covered the entire tip of her muzzle. She was a beacon of natural holdren, a first mother—what humans would incorrectly call an "alpha female"—claiming that space for her pack to inhabit in safety, yet he walked by like she wasn't there. Meanwhile, she had to face a reprimand for being out of uniform despite the I.C.V. *Alamo* being near the front lines.

I don't understand.

Why would Sundale shun her when he needed her the most? What did Polaris do to him while he was their POW? Why did he want to be alone? What had happened to her cub? The questions came, never with any hope of an answer. Without any input from Sundale, the best she could do was be there if—no, *when*—he snapped out of it.

Yarain heard familiar footsteps behind her. She turned an ear to note his presence but otherwise held her vigil.

"I'm not leaving, Jason," she said. Her voice was always soft and gentle, which apparently left humans expecting a British accent that wasn't there.

A sigh suggested her comment had failed to stop the conversation. "Yarain, this has got to stop. You're doing him no good by being here, and frankly, it's starting to worry me."

Yarain did not let her gaze waver from Sundale's door. "My duties and performance have not suffered."

"It's *you* I'm worried about, Major. What good is this if he won't respond?"

"Someone has to be here when he returns to us."

Lieutenant Colonel Jason Harlem knelt beside her. He was a thin man, some would say too thin to serve, with a narrow face and dark brown hair and eyes that complemented his fair, smooth features. Like her, he wore a deep-blue uniform with a silver sash made of three beveled lines. The "shield" of Interstar, three shooting stars in front of a star-field background, lay on his chest. The emblem of the Gold Group, their fighter unit, sat proudly on their arms. It was a gold and black tricorn design with the longer lower tip outlined in black with seven stars. The group motto, name, and designation were emblazoned on tiny banners over this lower section.

But their uniforms had a number of differences, too. For one thing, he kept his combat knife on his back so he could reach it with either hand, and he was never, ever, without it or his sidearm if he had a choice, whereas she still had her sidearm only because of regulations. He also had a pin on his rank tabs of a falcon with spread wings, and she only had two wings with two mini suns between them. Their specialty tabs around their name and rank plates above the shield were also different, most notably the Passive Operation Systems Navigator or "POSN tab," on hers. Both had socks tucked against their uniforms that could auto-deploy for decompression, except Yarain's uniform stopped at the first joint on each limb and left her tails exposed. So long as her paws weren't in danger, Command allowed her to leave them bare so she could remain comfortable and retain her full mobility. Jason, like all humans, wore full long sleeves and black boots.

After he failed to find the right words, Jason put his hand on her back in comfort. "You sure he will? I talked with Simon before Intelligence got a hold of him. The things Sundale endured... Let's just say Simon's father is going to be facing a few war crimes when this is all over. I get the feeling he didn't tell me everything, and I'm not sure I want to hear it. We might have lost Sundale."

Yarain glared at him, ears perking as her hackles fluffed a touch. She half barked a word as her throat couldn't quite separate her native barks from spoken words. "He's **NOT** dead."

Jason huffed with a shake of his head. "In a way, he might be. That kind of torture can change a person—or a holdren. It can turn them into someone completely different. Yarain, I don't want to give up either. I'm still asking God to bring him back to us every night. But I think we must face the chance that the Sundale we know died on that station. We may have to get to know each other all over again."

"And where does that leave me?"

Jason's hand fell off her while the other floated across his face, looking for a spot to induce thought or relieve stress. It soon settled in his lap as he looked away in search of an answer.

After another sigh, he rose while pinching the bridge of his nose. "I don't know. I don't know."

Yarain held her gaze on Jason, though her hackles and ears softened. "I won't abandon him."

"Even if it means wasting away in this corridor?"

"**YES**," she ruffed.

Jason almost growled, cursed under his breath, and then faced her with a hand on his hip. "Yarain, I know he's your cub, but somehow, someway, you have got to find a way to—"

Alarms and the lighting shifting to blue cut Jason off. The Personal Artificial Intelligence Combat Computer Assistant, or PAICCA, barked details in his usual, steady tone.

"General quarters! General quarters! All hands to battle stations. Set condition one! *Enterprise* carrier group engaged with Polaris forces at Phoenix Perch—prepare to assist."

Jason blew out his frustration, but when he looked at Yarain, he was calm and collected. A look she knew all too well. His "internal switch" that kept his emotions in check during combat had fully flipped. "Come on, Major. We've got work . . ."

He trailed off as Yarain had already begun to shift into her finesse form at the first alarm. By the time PAICCA finished his announcement, she had changed from standing three feet tall at her shoulder to about seven feet tall not counting her ears. Her hind legs grew larger while her front paws had become hands that still remained largely paw-like, including pads and claws. While it wasn't quite Jason's switch, the effect was the same. She had a job to do. It was time to do it. Anything else would have to wait until later.

"In Sundale's stead," she said with a growl.

Jason nodded approval before squeezing into the nearest lift with half a dozen other members of the Gold Group.

"Why Phoenix Perch?" one soldier asked. "There's nothing there of value, no strategic importance. Why attack it?"

"Didn't you hear?" Jason said. "It's the *Enterprise* carrier group. That ship carries not just her own legacy but that of every ship of her name throughout history. Taking her out would be a big blow to morale. I doubt the colony had anything to do with the attack."

"Then the colony itself should be safe," another soldier said. "Everything military is in orbit, starports included. The surface is all civilian."

"Small favors, assuming you're right. If not, they'll wish they'd never heard of me."

"You don't really think—"

"Think about what they did to Sundale, then ask that question again."

An uncomfortable silence that spoke volumes fell on the lift.

When the doors opened, the riders moved in one group toward the shaft-shaped hangar at a steady, if hurried, pace. Once inside, they split off for their G-21 Scorn heavy fighters. Each one was a brick-red ship with a rounded nose and bevel down the middle, with the main weapons and systems occupying the sides of the central fuselage. This "central block" sat between matching engine nacelles that had a sensor cone in the front and a twin-Gatling plasmoid-cannon turret on top. The wings added only a small amount to its profile, though they held the primary heat sinks. The group and Interstar insignias were painted proudly on the hull. An X1 beside it marked Yarain and Jason's ship.

Yarain and Jason headed for Gold 1 hip-to-hip amid a flurry of other crews doing the same. The only thing that slowed them down was the last-minute movements of ships and munitions as the carrier prepared to unleash her fighters on the enemy. Most were G-21 Scorns, but there were a few Phantom squads scattered among the hangar. These were really little more than a large cockpit pod in the middle of two smaller pods attached by thick struts. Though fragile by comparison, even Scorns couldn't match their agility, and their upgraded Gatling cannons made up for a lot.

They found that Captain Hars Gilnt had once again beaten them to their fighter. *Does she sleep in the hangar?* She was a young, tall, stiff-standing woman of Asian heritage with silk-smooth black hair. With Sundale still recovering, she had continued to serve as Gold 1's Active Engagement Systems Officer—AESO for short, or sometimes, "second seat."

Gilnt waited until they were in easy earshot to give her report. Only imminent combat prevented another picture-perfect salute. "The ship's prepped and ready, sir. Magazine is fully loaded; standard weapon configuration is in use."

For the first time since she'd taken over for Sundale as AESO, Gilnt spoke more like a dog barking. She also had a stark, acrid scent about her that spoke of a tension Yarain had never found on her before. Stranger still, it had a weight to it that, for a second, had Yarain's tails on the verge of waving in uneasiness. If it weren't for Jason's calm aura, she might have lost herself in trying to understand why. As it was, she waited for Jason to take the lead as she knew he would, though one ear stayed trained on Captain Gilnt.

"Very good, Captain," Jason said. "Take your station. Yarain, if you'll take yours, please."

"Yes, sir," both said.

Yarain filed through the rear hatch of the fighter behind Gilnt and took her station behind Jason on the right. While the cockpit of a Scorn was small, it still had enough room for a person to stand between the second and third seat stations. Tiny cabinets on the walls held personal gear, and the smallest toilet possible, known as the bucket, sat to Yarain's right. Jason, of course, slipped into the pilot seat as smooth as putting on a slipper.

As her displays hummed to life, Yarain buckled in, and then proceeded down the pre-flight checklist. Here, she could let herself be lost in the hunt. Her instincts wound through her training and experience, forcing her to focus harder than most on getting things right. Energy coursed through her, but she never felt her heart. It was smooth motion after smooth motion as she collected mission and navigation details, processed data from the group, and prepared for combat like she had a thousand times before.

Yarain had just finished pre-flight when the carrier group's commanding officer, Rear Admiral Mason Redding, came over her com-link with specific orders. His tone remained even, but Yarain heard a weight to it few humans would catch.

"We've lost contact with the *Enterprise* and the colony. We have no further information on enemy numbers or location. All fighters are to prepare for a Charlie-two launch. Green and Blue Groups will engage enemy fighters along with Squash and Tagger squads. All other strike craft will cover the carrier group. Be ready for additional orders upon our arrival. Admiral Redding out."

Yarain relayed those orders, to which Jason sighed. "Sounds like we may be too late," he said. "There may be little or nothing left of our base by the time we get there."

"Which means," Captain Gilnt said, "the enemy may get away, too. If their target's destroyed, they'll have no reason to stay."

"Let's hope we're wrong, on both counts. I don't intend to let anyone slip through the cracks today."

Nor do I, Yarain added silently.

With all systems checked and ready to go, the three of them went back and forth for a few minutes, fine-tuning the group's deployment while they waited to arrive. They'd just begun discussions about how far they should let themselves be drawn from the fleet when a repeating alarm sounded in the hangar. Red lights in the ceiling began flashing as well, announcing to all that launch was imminent. The flight staff cleared the area around the landing pads as fighters began to hover over them.

Yarain double-checked the available intel as an almost invisible shield layer rippled over Gold 1's hull. Getting nothing more than best guesses on enemy numbers, she put her focus on her target screen, her hands statue still on her controls. The only thing moving was her waving tails as she sat in preparation for the hunt.

That and her voice to start a common ritual before combat. "First Called."

Gilnt continued the group motto: "Final Star."

Jason finished it, "We hold the line."

After an eternity passed by, the hangar doors opened. The second the doors were fully open, running lights turned green and ushered the fighters out. Every ship moved at once, blasting into the stars at full combat speed seconds after the *Alamo* had dropped out of hyper-light.

Streams of fighters melded into clouds and formations as the groups and squads formed up. They were joined by clusters of point defense drones, which were little more than two Gatling cannons stuffed between tiny engine nacelles under a thin veil of armor. Yarain's sensor screen tracked every friendly with ease while exact enemy locations proved less certain. Gilnt tried to get a better reading, but the enemy E.C.M. was too strong at this range.

Through her targeting screen, Yarain could see a planet very much like Earth to starboard despite the many ships, drones, and fighters in the area. As the Green and Blue Groups moved to join the battleships and cruisers at the lead of the carrier group, the Gold Group was splitting into a wide-range formation to cover the space between the front line and the carrier. Drones from the *Alamo* merged with them in preparation to defend the carrier group.

Yarain was checking her message screen for any updates when a frantic cry came over the comms that drew all life out of her.

"They're attacking the colony!"

Captain Gilnt soon announced the same and more. All that remained of Interstar's forces were burning hulks and clouds of debris. Yet the enemy fleet, instead of leaving in victory, was in low orbit firing on the colony below. Yarain turned her turret to look at the planet and found a surface pocketed with the orange glow of fire where the central city should be. There was a solid block of flame on the outskirts of the city glowing like a fresh scar on the surface.

Jason turned to Yarain, but she held up a finger as Admiral Redding was on the line with new orders.

This time, his voice was hard with controlled anger. "All forces disregard original orders and attack! Stop them by any means necessary! Keep your heads, but take. Them. *Down*!"

"Orders rescinded," she said. "All units, defend the colony at all costs."

Jason turned forward halfway through her report. "That's what I wanted to hear. Gold Group, form up and follow me!"

The fleet, fighters and all, pushed their engines to full acceleration toward the enemy ships. Orders came to keep the fleet together, but otherwise, the mass of ships had one thing on their minds:

Terminate!

The enemy fleet, now caught between a planet and Interstar, turned at an angle in retreat. Clearly, they hoped to avoid combat long enough to warp away. Interstar would have none of it. Yarain received an engagement angle to intercept them long before they got the chance. With one button, she sent the course to Jason's screen and kept the feed active so any updates to it would automatically be sent to him.

"Not sure it'll be enough," Jason said. "We'll get some of them, but some will get their hyper-light cores to full spin before we can stop them."

"I'm not seeing a better course, Jason," Yarain said. "Any other angle would mean a longer intercept time."

"I wonder if it would be worth it to try some long-range—"

"*NEW* contact! Bearing 350 by 2. It's . . . Jason, it's the *Enterprise*."

Yarain could see her decloaking in the distance almost directly in the path of the Polaris forces. She was the same class of carrier as the *Alamo*, a long-boxed hull that came to a point at the bow, though the *Enterprise* had been updated with very tiny wings to hold heat sinks away from the main hull while the Alamo had not. However, the *Enterprise's* long tube-like hangars lining the sides on the back quarter of the ship were either missing or heavily damaged. Some hull breaches along the main hull were still burning, which spoke volumes about her damage. How she'd managed to cloak in the middle of the battle was likely a story for the ages, assuming anyone lived to tell it.

Seconds after the *Enterprise* appeared, a priority message arrived on her screen. "Jason, I'm getting a message from the *Enterprise*. 'We'll ground them. Bury them.'"

Yarain could hear Jason's recoil in his voice. "What? What could that mean?"

"I don't know. Admiral Redding is—"

She got cut off by Gilnt's alert. "Sir! Hyper-light coils are offline. Auto-shutdown. No malfunction detected."

"They have a jammer on board," Jason said. "There's no running now."

"That may not be a good thing, sir," Captain Gilnt said. "I have a large force of enemy fighters heading for the *Enterprise*. With the damage she's taken, there's no way she'll survive."

Jason hit the open comms to give orders directly. "Gold Group, turn for the *Enterprise*. Cover at all costs. Yarain, I need details of their status before we arrive. Inform Admiral Redding of our intent."

"Copy that," Yarain said.

She went to work, requesting a link with the *Enterprise* while sending a simple message to the *Alamo* detailing their current plan. The *Alamo* instantly confirmed and promised assistance. Yarain got on with the *Enterprise* at almost the same moment.

"Good to see you Gold Group," a tired male voice said, "but I don't think there's anything you can do for us. There's very little left to save."

"What's your combat status?" Yarain said.

"'Shoot me' sign."

Cute and not helpful. "Do you have any offensive or defensive systems remaining?"

"Weapons are minimal, point defense is gone, we have no craft to our name, and what shield generators remain are at critical heat."

"Stand by." Yarain looked at Jason. "Jason, they have nothing left to fight with, and shield generators are critical."

His response came without emotion: "Ride 'em till they burn up. We'll do the rest."

"*Enterprise*, maintain shields for as long as possible. Gold Group will cover you."

"Negative! You're too outnumbered!"

"Never stopped us before."

The *Enterprise* didn't respond further.

Oddly enough, while some part of her knew it was a giant risk, the soldier within told that part to shove it. The *Enterprise* was the only thing keeping the enemy from escaping. Further, saving such a storied ship would be worth it for morale, especially after losing the rest of the fleet.

Besides, she'd lost too much already. After weeks of not being able to avenge her cub, she was about to get her chance.

The Gold Group pulled away from the fleet to ensure they got to the *Enterprise* before the enemy fighters. Captain Gilnt confirmed a flight of fifty Polaris fighters, which they now knew were called Comet-class heavy fighters. No doubt their answer to the Scorn, though not as well designed. While it had twin-barreled turrets on the side of a shoe-shaped hull, most of the weapons were on wings on the top near the back. The engines were tight to the hull at this junction point, and they didn't have the Scorn's Gatling cannons or thick shielding. That said, recent history had proven they could be a real threat.

"Barrage wall, prepare to engage," Jason ordered.

The group formed a spread-out wall of fighters, meshing their ranges so that their field of fire was all the same. Yarain made sure the links were stable so no ship was out of position while also coordinating approaching reinforcements. The *Enterprise* fired a few token shots from her main guns, but she had exactly two barrels operational, and these fired too slowly to catch fighters. The enemy fighters continued their charge, returning fire the moment they came into range.

Their mistake was ignoring the help.

"Mow 'em down!" Jason said.

The Gold Group fired a full barrage into the teeth of the enemy squadrons. The focused fire erased four fighters from existence and sent nearly half of their shields flaring heavily. Additional fire appeared, announcing the arrival of the Blue Group right on Gold Group's tails. The enemy scattered to avoid the barrage, which claimed another half dozen when their pilots panicked and collided to make them easy prey or the *Enterprise* got a lucky shot.

Not much of an answer, Yarain thought as she fired her turret on one target that had lost her shields. A pair of missiles went through the hole Yarain made in the armor, turning the damaged Comet into a fireball. *Fitting.* She went looking for another target and found the enemy fighters all turning into the advancing Scorns. Many were aiming directly for Gold 1.

Jason went on group wide again, "scatter and engage. Watch for focus."

The Gold Group fractured in every direction like they'd done tens of thousands of times in training to confuse the enemy while covering anyone who found themselves being focused on. The enemy fighters tried to follow them, almost colliding with each other and doing little overall damage all the while finding members of the Blue Group nipping at their heels. Yarain kept watch on comms and her passive screen for any allies that found themselves under too much fire. Then the members of the Gold Group turned on the nearest target and fired every cannon they had. The result was a burst of shield flaring and a few explosions that cast a brief glow into Gold 1's cockpit.

Jason sifted through the mess to settle on a single target. The moment he got on their six, Yarain turned her turret and fired. Her streams followed them as they tried to evade around the wrecks of their comrades. Jason kept them on target, allowing Yarain to deliver several bursts of fire onto the enemy fighter. When she started striking armor, the enemy fighter flipped over and turned toward them. Yarain and Gilnt focused a steady stream of fire directly onto the enemy cockpit. With the enemy shields already thinned, the combined turret and main cannon fire ripped through their minimal front armor. After the first rounds got through, the enemy bucked wildly up and away, right into another Comet fighter. The collision sent the second ship tumbling long enough for members of the Blue Group to finish her off.

"That works," Jason said. "Who's next?"

He flipped Gold 1 over to find what was left of the enemy running for their lives, followed by the still-firing Blue Group. The capital ships had held their course, but with their HL drives rendered useless, they too were running. Yarain glanced at the chatter for an update. Her screen noted a few Gold Group fighters had taken critical damage but also noted those that couldn't disengage had managed a full survival ejection.

"We're down four fighters, Jason," she said. "No casualties reported, but Seventh Squad is down their top two. Six other fighters report damage but are still combat capable."

"We'll be fine." His words were heavy, but confident. "We're staying together anyway. Gold Group, continue pursuit!"

Just as she sent a quick note for the group to remain a single unit, she saw the *Alamo* had sent updated intercept courses to prevent escape. Polaris wasn't getting away this time.

Soon after the chase began, Yarain's attention was drawn to orders being sent personally from Admiral Redding. *This can't be good.*

"Stand down, Gold Group," he said. "I need you to cover the *Berlin* and the *Alamo*. We need to start search and rescue operations as well as provide cover for the *Enterprise*."

Jason's going to love this. Yarain almost lost her first word in a ruff. "**STAND** down, Jason. We've been ordered to cover the *Alamo* and *Berlin* while they provide support for the colony and *Enterprise*."

"You've gotta be kidding me." Her ears turned back in a slight cringe when she saw a channel opened to the *Alamo*. "Gold 1 to Admiral Redding. Sir, with respect, I'd rather—"

Admiral Redding's voice came back heavy, but left zero room for debate. "You and everyone else in the fleet, Colonel. That's why I want you to stay put. We have a colony *and* a carrier that need our help. With our fleet chasing theirs, I need a Scorn Group I can trust to take charge up here while I oversee search and rescue efforts in two places. I need the best, and that's you. The *Berlin* will be supporting the *Enterprise* while the *Alamo* will head to support the colony. Keep everyone in line and keep us safe. We'll do the rest. Admiral Redding out."

Jason sighed an almost Holdren growl, then motioned for Yarain to relay the orders. "Odds and evens. I don't care how."

Yarain gave a soft growl of annoyance but like Jason, she surrendered to her orders. "Gold Group, fall back. Even fighters, cover the *Berlin* and *Enterprise*; odd fighters, cover the *Alamo*. We've been ordered to cover them during recovery efforts. *No* questions. Keep them safe while they search for survivors. Stand by for further orders as required."

Yarain set the channel to standby as Jason led his half of the group to a low synchronous orbit over the main city. The *Alamo* flew even lower under them as shuttles and transports flowed from her to the planet below. Other transports, some big enough for multiple ground vehicles, were coming from the main fleet as well to add to the support. With nothing to shoot at, Yarain turned her turret so she could get a good look at the planet.

Her heart sank as she watched the proud colony claimed from the clutches of Raiders—the worst of pirates and slave traders—announce its own wounds. Pockets of orange still dotted the landscape, as did areas of gray where smoke was lifting into the air. Debris started falling with the support ships as the remains of the defenders returned to the colony they gave their lives to protect. *Maybe now Command will finally "find"* the money for a full defense system. They should have had a shield and weapon bases years ago.

Yarain's ears floated back and forth between cringe and perk as she stared at the burning city below. When she saw no other ships on her scopes nearby, she realized she couldn't do it. She couldn't sit and do nothing. She'd been doing just that for over a month, and it had yet to do anything for Sundale. It was time she took a more proactive approach with something.

"Jason," she said. "I want to join the recovery efforts."

Jason hummed in thought, which sent Yarain's ears back in worry. "I like where your heart is, Major, but I can't have an empty seat now. The enemy may not be gone."

"Lieutenant Finnley can take my place."

"Not as well."

"Jason, please. I can't sit and do nothing anymore."

"I know how you feel, but that's not enough."

Yarain thought for a moment, then found more to offer with a couple of half-ruffed words. "I can be a contact you know you can rely on down there. My nose and ears are as good as any hound, but I can **TALK**. I can make a **DIFFERENCE**."

Jason once again sighed, though this one sounded more like resignation. Yarain could only watch her station with an ear turned his way, refusing to neglect her duties while she waited for a response.

After another breath of stress, Jason tapped on his console. "Gold 1 to *Alamo*. I need someone qualified for POSN duty. Lieutenant Finnley would be my first choice, but I'll take any I can get."

"Something wrong, Colonel?" a firm voice said. "Is your POSN injured?"

"Major Yarain is going to join the search and rescue teams. They'll make better use of her natural talents than I will. But I want a full crew in case the Pols come back."

"Copy that. Stand by... Request approved. We'll get you what you need. *Alamo* out."

Jason brought the fighter to a lower orbit over the main city, set a holding auto-pilot, then looked back at Yarain. "Full tactical gear, Major. I don't want you taking any chances down there. If anything happens, I want to know, got it?"

"Understood," Yarain said.

She had unbuckled and began strapping her armor on the moment he asked for a replacement. It held the same blocky yet smooth texture of all armor, except hers covered her entire torso down to her hips and abdomen, with a thin layer covering each limb to the first joint. Her helmet covered most of her head, not counting slots for the ears, with a thin layer going out over her muzzle that stopped at the mouthline. The eyes had a thin display cover to allow for a HUD. *At least this one doesn't tickle my whiskers.* Even so, she retracted it so the protection stopped at her ears for now. More than likely, PAICCA would have all the info she needed.

"Find us some survivors, Major," Jason said.

"I'll try," she said.

Yarain snapped the strap over her sidearm on her ribs, slid a combat knife into place on her back at the hip, and deployed her pants and boots. *I'll be walking on too much rubble to chance it.* They were mostly form-fitting, though they didn't hold her entire paw shape as well as the armor during Sundale's rescue had. *I'll have to see about changing that.* She grabbed her twin-barreled plasmoid rifle and stood in the middle of the fighter.

"Miss Gilnt," Yarain said, "can you send me to one of the transports down below?"

"I can do one better, ma'am," Captain Gilnt said. "PERM already has an incident command post set up, complete with mobile transit pad. I can send you there."

"**PERFECT**. Transit when ready."

CHAPTER 2

ASHES

Yarain's body was enveloped by a sparkle for a moment, followed by a bright flash. Once it faded, she was standing on one of four large transit pads in the middle of dozens of large vehicles. Most were mobile command centers clustered in neat rows next to the transit pad. To the other side, three vehicles had merged into an infirmary with triage at one end already sorting through wounded. Personnel and materials were scattered around the command centers and the infirmary, with some wounded being carried from the red tarps onto the transit pads or toward transports sitting on what appeared to be a soccer field. A glance past the vehicles showed trees and a small scattering of simple buildings suggesting this command post had been set up inside the city park.

Yet as she cleared the transit pad and looked out at the city, Yarain couldn't help thinking how much worse things looked in person. Many high-rises were missing chunks, whole sides, or at least part of what used to be on top. Several were still burning and losing more pieces of themselves. More than the blood from the wounded, she found smoke on the wind; filling the sky over the urban district.

It all reminded her of the day her territory was attacked. She had come back from a hunt to find the land charred, half her pack dead, and her youngest cub missing. The thought of Polaris being responsible for something even worse had her hackles rising under her armor. More so because this time, she knew who was responsible, and she could do something about it.

Yarain headed for the vehicle marked "Incident Commander" to see where she could start. A short, middle-aged woman with short grey hair met her in the doorway. The woman's face held few wrinkles, and her gaze was hard and without doubt as she looked up at Yarain. Her thin body drew a line in the sand that dared anyone to question her, and her voice held more weight than a fully loaded carrier.

"You Major Yarain?" she asked, sounding winded as if having just sprinted.

"Yes," Yarain said.

The woman did not extend her hand or offer any other kind of greeting. If anything, she drew herself up a little as if she felt the need to impress someone or take charge. Yarain couldn't tell which. "Hillary King, Deputy Director of Phoenix Perch Fire. Your timing is perfect. Head back to the pads, and don't you dare crack a joke, I've had my fill."

Definitely the latter, Yarain thought as Hilary marched back to the transit pads with Yarain in tow. At the same time, several people, some of them soldiers, some emergency personnel, and some dirty civilians, were heading toward them, most carrying bags and/or equipment.

"We finally got into the residential district not ten minutes ago," Hillary said. "There's not much more you can do in the urban centers, but we've got a lot of families who were in their homes during the bombardment. I'd rather have you find us some mothers and fathers than department store cashiers. You can call me inappropriate all you like, but I'll take whole families over parts any day of the week."

Yarain was not about to argue. First, because she didn't want to risk a battle she might not win, and second, because doing so would only waste time people may not have. Could Yarain do more in the rubble of a twenty-story building versus a two-story house? Maybe, maybe not. Though with the memory of the day she thought she'd lost Sundale still strong in her mind, the idea of saving someone else from that pain had a lot of appeal.

As the group approached, many soldiers stopped to offer a salute, which Yarain returned with annoyance at the need given the situation. The only ones who didn't were a team of seven wearing thick armor and carrying large rifles that held a vertical stack of three barrels—a stunner/laser combo above, a plasmoid emitter in the middle, and a coil gun below.

The leader of this Vesper team was tall and slender with short, dark-auburn hair, and a full face that still seemed firmer than it was. He was also the first to offer a very familiar smile.

"What, you come to take my command again?" Captain John Harrison said.

Yarain gave a short series of ruffs, a holdren form of laughter, as she slung her rifle over her shoulder. "I'm here to help with the recovery efforts."

"Outstanding! Glad to have you, ma'am."

"You two know each other?" Miss King said.

"Yes, ma'am," Harrison said. "She took command of COB team for the rescue of Captain Sundale. You don't know how lucky you are to have her."

"All I care is that means there won't be any drama between you. As I was saying, Major, we have a staging area set up at Kealsy Heights, the largest of our residential areas. You'll be flashing into Griffin Park in the middle of the Heights. They should have things set up by the time you get there. Rigs and wagons shouldn't be far behind. Until then, do what you can. Coordinate with Martinez. He's already there directing things. Your armor has breathers, right?"

"**YES**," Yarain barked.

"Good. We don't have many to spare right now. The soldiers, I leave to your command. Just make sure you go through Martinez. He knows the area much better than you do. Questions?"

"Who's in charge of the civilians?" Captain Harry Fickle asked. Often called "Yoda" by the team, he stood so tall his eyes almost met Yarain's, while his hands were bigger than hers and his shoulders equally wide. His soft black hair was cut to perfect regulation, which fit a head that looked thick enough to crack through a wall.

"Martinez, unless you two work something else out," Miss King said.

"Very well. Let's **GO**," Yarain said, half-ruffing the last word.

She took her place on the transit pad along with much of the gathered group. Once as full as it could handle, Miss King gave the order to transit. A sparkle enveloped the group, followed by a flash that left them on a similar mobile transit pad in the middle of a much smaller park. It was also in much worse condition, as evidenced by the bonfire that used to be a tree grove staring them in the face. Yarain shielded her face from the heat wondering, how this could have possibly been missed.

"Don't worry, it's contained," a firm though young voice called over the roar of the flames. Yarain found its owner standing next to the transit operator.

A second glance saw the fire was indeed bouncing off force-fields which kept it from spreading any further. Another bit of thought noted that given the size of the inferno, the ambient heat was far less than normal. Yarain's mind had made her think it worse than it was, which of course made it true for a moment.

Yarain came down off the pad to face the young man.

"Next time, warn us before we transit," Yarain said, not quite raising her hackles.

"I'll try, ma'am," he said. "I assume you're Major Yarain?"

"I am."

"Juan Martinez. I'm in charge of what's left out here. If I may say, ma'am, I'm glad to see someone with more than just a wing or two on their shoulders. Getting tired of hyped-up Terrines and Caelnav lieutenants fresh from the academy. Follow me. Let's get you sorted."

While she could understand Terrines being a little too eager to help, partly because she had to keep her own desire in check, Yarain had a hard time believing it was that bad. That said, she followed without comment. Once again, the argument wasn't worth the time.

Martinez led the group to a large holo-table, sitting next to a single fire truck, this one without any fire suppression equipment. Martinez leaned on the table as members of the group gathered around it with more following from the transit pad. Most appeared to be soldiers, but many were still firefighters and civilians. Yarain and Harrison made a point to be on the inside of the gathering, though no one complained about them cutting through the crowd. The rest of "Team Cobra", the often used nickname for COB Team inspired by their three letter designation, was able to huddle within earshot of their commanders. A holographic map of the area was displayed, though it held no indicators of damage.

"The west side is a fireball," Martinez said, pointing out the areas as he went. "Not much to do but keep it from spreading. Already got several Terrines and my last field generators heading there."

"No street generators?" asked Lieutenant Maureen Hark, COB Team's demolition and equipment expert. A six-foot mountain of a woman with narrow eyes and black hair that she somehow kept in a tiny ponytail within length limits.

"We have the parts, finally. We were going to install them Tuesday."

"Why is it always Tuesday?"

"No idea. Anyway, the south was largely untouched. Assurah, I want you to take the civilians and all of the Caelors down the main streets. Start on Jackson, work your way east until you hit 9th Avenue. Check in then, see where we can use you next. There's a plot on the corner of Maple and 2nd Street you can use for triage if you need it. The rest of us, we're going to split as best we can, cover the remaining parts in grids. PAIA, change to grid view."

"Copy that," came a deeper, yet still normal-sounding voice of the Personal Artificial Intelligent Assistant. The civilian version of Interstar's PAICCA. Known to be far less adaptive, PAIA still had all the responsiveness of his military big brother. Just not as much reach as far as capability.

The map went flat, changing to slice Kealsy Heights into several grids marked by a letter and a number. Martinez tapped on his tiny console, then a few blocks, which soon painted whole sections different colors on the map.

Martinez pointed to a section marked in yellow to the northwest. "Major, I want you to take half the heavy armors and Twenty-three to this area around Shana Hanalei. The school is shielded, but the houses around it aren't – don't ask why. Not our problem right now. Search through them, check for survivors. Take 5th Street to get there."

"Do we have any equipment or vehicles?" Yarain asked.

"A couple of minivans we've appropriated for transport and anything you can carry."

"That's it?" Harrison said.

"Best we can do until the rigs get here. Take any wounded you have to Hanalei, triage there. Send the reds here for transport; yellows are your call. Once you've searched a house, leave a white X on the sidewalk in front of the address. In the top of the X, write the time you left. To the right, any hazards inside. Below, note any bodies you find. Don't worry about the left side. You have enough to remember as it is without our training. No guesses on any of it. Only mark what you saw for sure, then move on. I don't have breathers or suits to spare, so your armor will have to do."

"They'll be enough," Lieutenant Hark said.

"I hope so," Martinez said, "You'll be in command of that area, Major. I have other senior firefighters who will oversee the other search areas. Any questions?"

"What or who is twenty-three?" Yarain asked.

"*House* Twenty-three, Ma'am. Any firefighter you see with a patch from that company is going with you. They should all be waiting for you at the vans. Once I heard more were coming, I sent them ahead."

"Who's the ranking member of the house?" Lieutenant Markus Sarson asked. COB Team's technology expert, who stood only five-eight but was still well-built with hard features.

Martinez sighed with a drop of his head. When he looked up at Sarson, his eyes were pounds heavier than before. "There isn't one.

Not anymore. The survivors of the team are all lower ranks. Limited if any experience. The leaders were killed by the first volleys, but they're good men. They'll do the job; they just need someone with authority to direct them."

Yarain's mind had produced a list the second she heard that. Without a single thought, she turned to the team to check it off, though she barked and ruffed a couple of words along the way. "**COBRA**, I want you with me. Grab any heavy armors besides Cobra we're allotted, then **GET** me a count of how many I'll have. Once you do, Harrison, I want you to come back and report. The **REST** of you, start assigning search teams, no more than four per team. Captain Tai, I want you on triage. Assist any doctor in charge, run it yourself if there isn't one. Fickle, you're in charge of sorting. Hark, oversee our gear. **GET** going."

"Yes, ma'am!" COB Team said. They turned and left without any hesitation, though Harrison grabbed a couple of armored Terrines along the way.

Martinez shook his head with a breath. "God, am I glad to have you. Haven't heard confidence directed that well all day, except from Miss King."

"I do what must be done when it must be done," Yarain said.

"With respect, ma'am, you're being modest," *Not you too.* "But enough of that. I have nothing else to give you. You know everything you need, so unless you have any questions, you can link your wrist-com to PAIA here, then you can get going yourself."

"Where are the vehicles?" Yarain asked after she initiated the link.

Martinez pointed, and Yarain left without a word. She saw Lieutenant Sarson heading toward four minivans parked at the edge of the park, which was all the direction she needed. Her ears perked a little when she got a nod from Lieutenant Shillin Rad, the team's sniper. She was a thin woman with dark skin and braided hair as long as regs would allow, and a lightness in her step that made her almost silent even up close. As Yarain approached the vans, Harrison ran up to meet her.

"Twenty-one bodies, ma'am," he said. "One you, six Cobra, two FLAREs, two Terrines, ten firefighters, two of the latter do not have gear."

"Send those two with Sarson," Yarain said as she watched people, equipment, and supplies be loaded into the minivans under Lieutenant Hark's harsh direction. "What kind of extra gear do they have?"

"I think I have more in my sock, ma'am." Yarain glared at him. Hackles still, but ears straight with a soft growl all the same. "Sorry, ma'am. Each firefighter has their own cutters and breathers, aside from the two I mentioned. We have enough deep scanners for every team, but with all due respect to them, I trust your ears more than I do the units I'm looking at. I swear they're older than I am."

"Medical supplies?" Yarain said.

"Surprisingly good. Tai says he could probably save a few reds himself. They sent us an auto-surgery kit. Wouldn't trust it for brain surgery, but it can sew up an aorta as well as anyone."

"I resent that," Captain Kelly Tai said as he carried a large case past them. The man himself was tall and tan-skinned with a thin goatee as brown as his hair marking a round face that was still somehow thin.

Yarain allowed a soft, panted laugh before heading for the van Captain Fickle was motioning her and Harrison toward. "Teams assigned?"

"Almost," Harrison said. "We had the civvies and hulks assigned evenly. We'll need to tweak it with the change in numbers."

"Sorry. That's my fault."

Yarain and Harrison slid into a middle seat, then Captain Fickle got in the front passenger seat and tapped Lieutenant Hark on the shoulder.

"All aboard!" Fickle said.

The van lifted off the ground its maximum few inches, then Hark drove fast but careful around the debris in the streets.

"Think nothing of it, ma'am," Harrison said as he tapped on his wrist comm. "We both should have guessed there would be changes once you had a number. I'm sure Fickle will sort it out before we arrive. However, the deployment of COB Team is your choice."

Yarain's ears flicked back uneasily. "They're your team, Captain."

"Which as the highest-ranking officer on the field, is now under your command. And if I may, ma'am, we're outside our element here. We're used to being told who to blow up, extract, or make disappear. Going through houses looking for victims isn't our forte."

Yarain tilted her head slightly with a flick of her ear. "You're extracting targets from damaged buildings. You never trained for that?"

Harrison dropped his head. He chuckled slightly, but there was no humor there. "Guess I didn't think about it like that. Even so, we're not used to making choices on such a massive scale. We're Vespers. We're a scalpel, not a sledgehammer."

Now he's making excuses. It alarmed Yarain. More so when she remembered the moment of fear she'd sensed in him on the shuttle just before Sundale's rescue. Then, she'd thought it just a moment. It happened sometimes before a mission, even to Jason. Now she was wondering if it was something more.

Once again, though with less confidence in the choice, she decided to avoid the argument. If he wasn't going to take charge, she would. She'd sort out the fall-out later.

"I'll sort it out when we get there," she said.

"Understood, ma'am," Harrison said.

The minivans stopped at the edge of a large school complex three stories high, yet still spread out over a few acres, much of it sports facilities. The central building was modular and, despite the lighter paint, announced itself as a former warehouse or factory with straight lines and what used to be wide doors. Most of the smaller buildings around it were of similar design, though many did not have the large doors. *Probably a central point or command center once. Explains the shielding.*

As the team began to unload, Yarain and Harrison allowed a moment to scan the horizon. Their gaze didn't get beyond the block. While the west side might be a "fireball," their sector still had several fires burning, many of them vehicles still in the street. Yarain could see one small car only a few feet away, right on the edge of scorching that suddenly stopped halfway up the sidewalk. *The edge of the defense field. Must have a heck of a generator to power it.* Inside the car, despite the damage, she could see the still burning bodies of what she couldn't help guessing was a family seeking shelter. Two adults in front, three younger persons in the back, and a clean hole in the roof announcing the hit they'd taken.

Beyond them, houses, a few small stores, building after building seemed to have been damaged. Some had already fallen into a pile of rubble, while some right next door were only missing parts. A destroyed balcony here, an entire wall missing there, a house intact but on fire over there, very little of the area had escaped unharmed.

Yarain's hackles had started rising, armor or no armor, at the deed shining in her face. Torturing Sundale was one thing. At least that was against a single person and a soldier in search of intel. The scale of the destruction done to a purely civilian target was all too familiar and beyond anything she thought them capable of.

Yet her hackles fell in favor of perked ears when she saw Harrison staring at the scene in a much different way. His eyes were growing by the second, as was his breathing, yet either he wasn't seeing anything, or he was seeing too much.

"Captain?" Yarain said. "You all right? John, **SNAP** out of it."

His gaze didn't change. "Where do we begin? What do we do first?"

Yarain now recognized the gaze. A point in which the lead hunter loses his ability to process the situation, and therefore his ability to think. It seemed that what she'd thought was a single occurrence could actually be a brewing problem, and it had her worried more than ever.

Yarain shook her head with a ruff to reset her mind. She didn't have time for this. She couldn't help Harrison right now. Not directly. The best she could do was what she'd already done; be the commanding officer everyone expected her to be.

"**RAD**," Yarain barked, "take a soldier and watch the perimeter. Fickle, have you sorted the teams?"

"Not quite, ma'am," he said, stealing a glance at Harrison, "I need to know where you want the rest of Cobra."

"Form four teams, one Cobra on each, one heavy armor, two civilians. Make sure each team has something to mark the houses with."

"We're one heavy armor short for that, ma'am."

Details, Yarain. "Harrison and I will be the heavy armor for one team. When ready, send one team to that house that's burning on the corner. Clear it fast. Assign grids for the teams, then **GET** them moving. My team will wait here, link up with anyone at the school, then proceed with our searches. Maintain active links through PAIA. Questions?"

"No, ma'am!"

"Get moving."

Captain Fickle nodded and dove into the group to begin his task. Yarain turned to Harrison, who was slowly shaking his head. Progress, but she couldn't wait for a full recovery.

"Clear your head, Captain," she said, putting her hands on his shoulders. "I need you."

Harrison swallowed hard before light returned to his eyes. "Yes, ma'am. What can I do?"

"Follow and assist."

He nodded with the confidence he'd shown before. "Understood. I'm ready."

Yarain patted him on the shoulder, then led him and her team, who were already moving to join her, toward the school with Lieutenant Tai close behind.

She found an older woman with long grey hair and medium-brown skin jogging out to meet them. Behind her came three other adults, one of which was in a tan military-style uniform Yarain felt was familiar but couldn't remember why.

"Thank God you're here," the woman said. "Principal Megan Strouse. I've taken charge here since the attack."

Yarain shook the woman's hand, surprised to find it firm. "Major Yarain. We're here to help."

"I'm glad you are. What few adults we have are tied up with keeping the kids and wounded from frenzy. Survivors have been limping here since the shelling stopped. The rest have only just begun to prepare search parties."

"We'll take all the help we can get," Harrison said distantly.

Yarain allowed a concerned glance before returning her focus to Megan. "Do you have any gear?"

"Not much," Megan said. "A few fire-suits and breathers, most coming from the science lab."

"Your science lab has breathers?" Lieutenant Tai said, crates in hand.

"Our science program is pretty advanced. Still, it's nothing compared to what you have. If you share the gear, I'm sure—"

"We **CAN'T**," Yarain said, ruffing a word. Before the shock on Megan's face could turn to anger, she again remembered that humans needed details. "We don't have any to spare. More is coming, but for now, what you see is all we have, and we only have gear for ourselves."

Megan's shoulders dropped with a sigh, then she shook her head. "I guess it'll have to do. Though I'm sure you can do a lot more than anyone. Still, they want to help. Surely there's a way they can."

"Got any doctors?" Tai said.

"School nurse, maybe an EMT among the parents—that's it. Unless you count a former physical therapist for athletes."

"Better than nothing, I'll take 'em all. I need room for triage and treatment. Is your gym free?"

"We've already been using it for the wounded. Mister Brinkon, could you show him the way?"

One of the men acknowledged, then motioned for Lieutenant Tai and his chosen firefighters to follow. They did so with all the supplies they could carry or, in the case of the mobile surgery kit, push on a grav unit.

"Do you have any vehicles we can use," Yarain said.

"What do you need them to do?" Megan asked.

"Transport wounded."

The man in the military suit, a well-built fellow with almost no hair and narrow eyes, spoke first. "We can use the sports carts. Not an ambulance, but it'll get the job done."

"Got any drivers who don't mind a war zone?" Harrison asked.

The man smiled with a nod. "I know some ROTC boys who are just what you need. They'll do the job well and won't mind the fires at all."

Yarain's ears perked at the program name. Now she remembered why the uniform was familiar. Despite Interstar dressing in blue, most ROTC programs retained the early twenty-first-century style uniform. Some out of tradition, others because they didn't feel like changing, as well as a few other ridiculous reasons. The program itself, however, had continued to improve, providing Yarain with a resource she hadn't expected.

"How many and how well disciplined?" Yarain asked.

"If you'll forgive me, better than some soldiers," the man said. "Got about two dozen here, most of them have received some first-aid training. I can easily split them up as needed."

Finally, some good luck. "We have four teams. Split accordingly. Do you have communications gear that can cover the district?"

"Yes, ma'am, we do."

"Have Captain Tai, the man who just went to the gym, connect you with Captain Fickle. Send the carts to meet up with the teams. If possible, two or more vehicles per team."

"Copy that, ma'am. I'll have them out there in minutes."

Yarain ticked her ears forward in approval as the man marched off, thrilled to have so much support available no matter how young they may be.

"Principle Strouse," Yarain said, "we'll take the help with searching, but it's best to let us check the houses that are unstable."

Megan nodded with a heavy sigh. "I understand. Maybe it would be better to send our people through the streets. They can comb through the cars, bring any wounded they find here."

One of the firefighters from Yarain's team stepped forward, "Ma'am, with respect, I like her idea, but I suggest each team get at least one local. They'll know who lives where and how many may be in each house. It could save a lot of time."

"Agreed," Yarain said, "but we can't wait for them to gather."

"We'll get them to you," Megan said. "Go get started. And, Major, thank you."

"You're welcome. Make sure they get marking instructions before they leave."

"I'll do that, Major. Thank you again."

Yarain turned for the streets, pausing only to check her wrist comm. to see which area Captain Fickle had assigned her. Once she got her bearings, she led her team toward the first house on their street. The street itself was largely untouched, though debris and damaged cars still scattered the area. Smoke from the fires in the area had Yarain's lungs complaining, but she was more bothered by the many damaged houses she had to pass as not her sector. Not to mention the charred, broken, and, in some cases, scattered bodies they found on the way. While very few in number, it only took one teenager split into four pieces to get Yarain's hackles ruffling again.

Their first house was a crater surrounded by splinters. *Probably a direct hit from a torpedo or other ordnance.* They didn't bother marking it. The second wasn't much better. It looked like the walls had literally fallen outward with the floor above crumbling down.

"This one's mine," one of her team said. "No one was home. They were off-world visiting her mom's."

The man promptly stepped up to spray the X and info on the sidewalk after a glance at Yarain for permission. She ticked her ears forward, then added a drop of her muzzle. The man understood her nod as intended, and they moved on.

The next three had taken hits but were in surprisingly good condition. While each was missing chunks of the upper floor, the rest of the structures remained intact. This let them split into two teams of two, so they could search each one faster. They only found a dead dog in the first house. The second had proved a harder search because of debris, but Yarain's nose found blood that led her to a wounded couple buried beneath. When freed, they were found to be only lightly wounded, though still scared from having been just missed by a plasmoid bolt. When two small carts arrived, each carrying three young men in tan military uniforms, Yarain sent the couple back on one to be safe while moving on. She also noted Megan's street teams had begun their work, though it seemed as though almost none of the damaged cars had survivors in them.

The third house had proved an easier search but a harder find. Pictures, records, and a message left on the house computer told them they were looking for a family of three. Despite the damage, Yarain allowed the young men, who thankfully had helmets, to assist. Yet it was her that found the family huddled in a bathroom, with shards of glass and tile gutting two adults and a three-year-old girl. The shattered wall stood witness to the source.

"House clear," she said over her comms. "Three bodies, no survivors."

She allowed herself a moment to growl, even though the recipient couldn't hear her. Then she left the house. She emerged in time to see two men in dirty white dress shirts join her team as the "locals" her firefighter requested.

They had just finished marking the sidewalk when a crash sent everyone looking toward a house whose walls appeared to have fallen in one side at a time like a weird game of dominoes. A young woman was crawling out of the rubble, which was still dusting as if some of it had recently fallen. When Yarain's team rushed to her aid, the woman latched onto Yarain before they could get a word out.

"Please," she sobbed, "please, my husband's in there. He went to get the baby, and the house . . . the house . . . oh . . ."

She cried into Yarain's shoulder, driving a knife into the holdren's heart. Despite that, Yarain had to push her away so she could get the woman to focus on her. Again, she reminded herself to speak with more details.

"Breathe, ma'am," Yarain said. "Try to think. What's your husband's name? Where did you see him last? Is there anyone else?"

"Marn. Marn Garot. It's just him and our son. I think he was in the kitchen when it collapsed. It's to the . . . to the left of the . . . oh . . . of where the front door used to be. Please, you have to . . . you have to find them!"

"I intend to." Yarain looked at one of her firefighters and the two civilians to direct her orders. "Check this woman for injuries. You two stay outside, make sure Marn doesn't sneak out. The rest of you with me."

The firefighter took the woman gently by the hand while Yarain led the others up to the rubble. With careful effort, they began pulling pieces off while the firefighter called out.

"Mister Garot? I'm Peter Devilin. I'm with Firehouse Twenty-three. We're trying to get to you. Can you hear me? Mister Garot? Marn Garot."

Others joined the call while Yarain tuned her ears to see what she could hear. Between calls and moments to listen, the team peeled and slid chunks of wall off of the pile, taking great care not to disturb the balance while digging as fast as they could. It proved insufficient, as part of the debris sank into itself with a clamor. The team froze while the wife wept.

In the moment of silence that followed, Yarain heard something. A faint noise that was neither falling debris nor mechanical.

"Everyone quiet," she said. "Don't move unless you have to."

Even the woman managed to fall silent as Yarain perked her ears forward. She stepped up to the house pile and tilted her head from side to side as she tried to get a fix on the sound. As she got closer, it took form at last; a human baby crying for its mother. It wasn't where it should be, though. It sounded like it was coming from underground. Either it sat in a crater or . . .

Yarain turned to the mother, who had fallen to her knees. "Do you have a basement?"

She seemed confused at the question at first, then brightened. "Yes. Yes, it was an old hideaway used by some smuggler."

"Is there an external entrance?"

"It was on the left side of the house, hidden in the ground. But Marn sealed it years ago."

Yarain rushed to the left side, then got down on her hands with her nose working and her ears fully perked. She found only the scent of burnt grass, but the sound remained. With no visual cue, Yarain focused on her ears as she moved along the side of the house. Her head bobbed and tilted, trying to get a fix on the sound until it grew louder without apparent cause. A moment's digging in the soil found a pair of metal doors welded shut from the outside.

Yarain held her hand out. "**DEVILIN**, your cutter."

The tool landed in her hand, and she used it to undo the weld in less than a minute. She attached the tool to her belt, flung the doors open, and then proceeded under the ground with her team right behind her, except for two ROTC boys who stayed at the entrance.

The team was greeted by darkness, a lot of musk and smoke, as well as paint fumes. Yarain's eyes made the adjustment instantly, but when her team's flashlights came on, she activated the lights on her helmet since the other beams would ruin her night vision anyway.

The team moved smoothly but cautiously. They still had most of a house sitting on top of them. The basement had lost all lighting and had no windows of any kind. Several shelves of painting supplies made rows in the darkness. Others had fallen or been collapsed on, leaving the floor covered in brushes, cans, and paint; though Yarain managed to avoid stepping in any. It would have been a hard search, except the baby's cries gave them a perfect beacon. Yarain was able to follow it down a narrow pathway, through the mess, right to its owner at the base of the stairwell.

The father sat slumped against the wall, blood on the side of his head, with a broken wooden support beam beside him. In his arms, weak as he was, he still held a young child wrapped in a dirty blue blanket.

"Mister Garot?" Yarain said, kneeling beside him. "Mister Garot, can you hear me?"

He woozed around until his eyes winced in their lights. Then, at last, he found Yarain and smiled.

"Never thought I'd get to meet a holdren."

Yarain's ears perked in amusement as the others scanned him and the baby. "Can you walk?"

"Not sure. I can hardly think."

A thunk, followed by a loud moan above, announced their time was limited.

"You three get him moving," Yarain said.

"My son!" the man said. "You have to..."

"I have him."

Yarain took the baby from him, then left ahead of her comrades. The baby's cries echoed in her ears, but she didn't have time to do anything about it. She sprinted out of the basement, stopping at the door until she saw the others making their way up with Mister Garot. Yarain went to the mother, who was clinging to the last team member as if he were a lifeboat.

She forgot he existed when she saw what Yarain had. Missis Garot rushed to her the moment she got close. She took her son as the other officers carried Mister Garot out of the tunnel with the civilians close behind. Missis Garot rocked her son in her arms, humming softly and rubbing his chest. By the time Mister Garot was allowed to collapse beside them, the baby had fallen silent. A minute or two later, a loud crash announced the collapse of the house. The mother shielded her child. Yarain shielded them all, though none was needed. The rubble simply fell into the hole and settled once more.

With her baby in her arms, Missis Garot ran a hand along her husband's head while the ROTC cadets set a backboard down beside him. When Mister Garot laid his head on his wife's shoulder, she looked at Yarain with fresh tears in her eyes.

"Thank you. Thank you so much."

Yarain placed a gentle hand on hers. "I'm glad I could help. Take good care of your pack."

Mister Garot was carefully strapped to the backboard while Missis Garot found a place she could ride safely with her baby. Meanwhile,

Yarain took the spray can and marked the sidewalk with an X right above the address, happy this time to note zero bodies below. The cart drove back toward the school just as the other one was returning.

Yarain was about to head for the next house when a man came down the street running straight for her, dressed in a simple t-shirt and jeans that bore the same stains as everyone else. The fact that he was waving his hands while running suggested some new problem was headed her way.

"Please!" the man said between breaths. "We . . . we need . . . we need your . . ."

"**STOP** and breathe," Yarain said, half ruffing a word as she stepped up to the man with a motion for her team to gather.

The man did as she'd asked . . . mostly. He was taking deep breaths as if to accelerate the process. Yarain thought about advising him against it, except it did seem to be working, if only for the moment. The second he caught his breath; he used all of it as fast as he could.

"There's a crashed school shuttle on Terminus and Miles. It's full of kids and we can't get in. Please, we . . . we . . ." his breath failed him once more as he doubled over as if he might pass out.

Before he could, Yarain grabbed his arm. "School shuttle, crashed on Terminus and Miles, they need help. That it?" The man nodded between breaths. Yarain confirmed the ROTC boys knew where that was before hatching her plan. "Devilin, **STOP** him from hyperventilating, then take the rest of the team, and continue your searches. Harrison, you and I will go with the cart and ROTC cadets to the shuttle."

"Uh, ma'am," Devilin said, "with you two gone, who will lead our group?"

"You will."

Devilin lost some color in his face as his head shot up. "Ma'am, I'm a probie. I'm—"

"All this team needs." *Details, Yarain!* "I've seen you. You'll be fine. Don't think too much about the job; just **DO** the job. Trust your pack. They will help you."

Devilin took a slow look toward the others, who tried to hold their tools like weapons at the ready. It seemed to work. The color returned to Devilin's face as fast as it had drained. "Yes, ma'am. I won't let you down."

"I know you won't. I will need to keep the cutter, so . . ."

"That's okay, ma'am. We have the other one."

"Good. **CADETS**, take us to the shuttle."

Yarain and Harrison got on the cart, which then sped down the street the man had run from. They were forced to pass unsearched houses, some badly damaged, one with a body hanging out a window, but a shuttle full of children was more important. Yarain had done her best to help the houses by giving the order to continue the searches. Her focus had to remain on her current hunt.

That is until Harrison spoke up. "I envy your control."

Yarain now perked her ears at him while her head tilted very slightly in confusion. "You seem well controlled."

Harrison shook his head. "You see the surface, ma'am. When we were pinned down on the Polaris station, survival instinct alone kept me fighting. I couldn't think. It's something that's been happening to me lately."

"You're a good soldier, Captain."

"I'm a good follower. Lately, for some reason, I haven't been acting as well at the lead. I meant it when I said Yoda's saved my ass a few times. I don't know when it started, but it's been getting worse."

Yarain's mind splintered for a second in search of understanding. How could a soldier lose their nerve like that? More to the point, how could he be that out of control without her noticing? The fear she'd seen before, she could understand, if only the fear itself. As for why, she couldn't even find a possible reason. In a way, that made it worse because now she had a soldier with a flaw that could become a problem, with no cause she could find, and thus, no fix she could apply.

"Looks like we're here," one of the cadets said.

Yarain again had to bury her thoughts as she perked her eyes and ears forward. She found a small shuttle, little more than a slender passenger compartment with engines and wings, crashed head-on into what appeared to be a power company work truck. The impact had driven them both into what was left of the sandstone wall that surrounded the Heights. On the opposite side of the street were the ruins of a building so badly destroyed that Yarain couldn't recognize what it used to be despite parts of it still standing. The hull of the shuttle was dented and charred, suggesting it had taken hits from debris or weapons fire, perhaps both, before hitting the ground. The wings had been sheared off, either by the impact or weapons fire, and the shutters on the windows were closed, leaving only the doors as access.

Yarain gave orders the second the cart stopped near the shuttle. "**CHECK** the hull, see if you can find a way in. Harrison . . ."

"One moment, ma'am," he said, checking his wrist comm. Yarain held her team for a second, knowing he wouldn't tell them to stop without good cause. "Ma'am, I just got word. We have nine ambulances headed our way, as well as a full battalion of troops, some APCs, and House Nineteen, which apparently is fully intact. ETA to the school; two minutes."

Yarain perked her ears at the shuttle to listen for sounds from inside. She needed only two seconds to catch several voices, only one of them adult. "Tell Megan our situation. Request as much as they can send us, as well as any heavy cutting gear they may have. Everyone else, continue your orders."

The ROTC cadets didn't wait to scatter over the shuttle in search of any hole big enough to use. Yarain meanwhile went for the only side-door that wasn't buried under parts of the shuttle's wings. She tried the side-panel, but got no response. *No surprise.* She pulled the panel off to try the manual over-ride, but her only response was a click that told her the doors had been unlocked. *Okay, progress.* She tried forcing them open to no avail.

When the cries from inside started to get more frantic, Yarain remembered what Devilin did, as well as every other time humans were in a similar situation, and tried her best to copy it.

"I'm Major Yarain from Interstar," she called into the door. "Help is on the way. Stay calm. We'll get you out in a moment."

The cries seemed to die down a little, but she wasn't sure if that was good or bad. The best she could do was try to force the doors open again. No use. They refused to open, and her little cutter wouldn't be enough against the shuttle's thick hull. Not without taking far too long to work.

She was on the verge of doing so anyway when she noticed part of the hull above the doors was melted onto them. When she tried the doors again, Yarain found the tension suggested this as the reason they were jammed.

That's when she decided to use an even better cutter; her rifle. "Everyone away from the door. I'm going to . . ." *Let's not be honest. Humans wouldn't take it well.* "I'm going to try something."

She waited a moment, took careful aim, and fired. The plasmoid bolts sparked off the hull but accomplished her goal. Each shot shaved a tiny bit of material from the shuttle. To her surprise, the sharp claps of the rifle were met with very little reaction from those inside. She fired careful shots until she appeared to have cleared the damaged part. After slinging her rifle back over her shoulder, Yarain strained with all she had until the left side of the door slid open with a jerk.

A thin layer of smoke lifted out as the scent of fresh blood hit her. *Tell me I'm not too late.* She perked her ears while her heart stopped and waited to find out. Along the far wall, huddled together, were twenty or so crying children, not a one over fourteen. Beside them sat a single adult with a bloody arm, though he looked at Yarain with strong, attentive eyes. She went to him first while her heart got started again. She called out for the others to join her with a med-kit.

"I'm Major Yarain," she said as she examined his arm. "I'm here to help."

"It's about time," the man said, "I was beginning to think we were alone down here."

Yarain couldn't stop a pause. "I'm sorry. We came..."

The man waved her down. "I... didn't mean it like that. Honest."

Yes, you did, but it's understandable. "Any trouble breathing? Any pressure anywhere?"

He shook his head with a hand going to his arm. "It just hurts."

Yarain followed the blood up his arm to a deep gash on his shoulder. It wasn't major, but it was going to need a plug until better supplies arrived. Faced with only one med-kit to use and a lot of injured to treat, she decided to conserve them at a cost.

As the ROTC cadets arrived to help, she directed them to scatter through the shuttle while one waited outside in case anyone needed emergency loading.

She then reached for the man's shirt and prepped her claws. "Sorry about this."

"I hated the thing anyway," the man said with a huff.

Yarain's ears perked forward in Holdren approval, then she ripped the front off of his shirt. She wadded it up, placed it against the wound, and put his hand on it.

"Can you hold it there?"

He nodded. "For a while."

"That'll be enough. Are there any other adults on board?"

He nodded at the forward section where Yarain found the bodies of four or five children and two more adults. One adult stood hanging on a hunk of hull through his chest, with a young boy dead beside him as well. Yarain's ears pulled back to control the anger burning inside her as she realized what he meant.

Yarain gave the man a pat on his good shoulder before moving on to the children. She pulled up all she could remember about basic field medicine.

ABCs, she told herself.

"Air-way, breathing, circulation."

The young, muttering voice drew Yarain's attention as she left a girl with little more than a broken leg. She found the owner was a young man with short brown hair in a tan shirt and khaki pants kneeling beside a classmate. At first, she thought him an even younger ROTC cadet, until she noticed one of the patches doting his arm marked him as a member of Troop 237. This group she knew well, having been asked to speak to some of them before. Her ears turned forward in approval as she realized this young Boy Scout was performing much of the same checks she was.

"Do you know what to look for?" she asked while plugging a more serious wound with bio-gel.

The young man lifted the head of a classmate who had blood all over her collar. "Check for heavy breathing, squirting blood, and really big owies. That's how my dad always said it."

"Good enough. Let us know if you find anything serious."

"Will do," he looked into the eyes of the classmate. "Don't worry, it's not yours."

Take what help you can find, her academy instructor used to say. With Harrison no doubt playing liaison to the help they needed; this young Boy Scout was an asset Yarain felt glad to have. If nothing else, he could do what even the ROTC cadets couldn't; connect with those there to help them stay calm. Based on what she saw, he was fully capable of excelling in that role and perhaps more.

That, is until he coughed into his hand and wiped blood onto his pant leg with a stumble. Then he became Yarain's first priority.

"Sit down," she said.

He stood and faced her with more confidence than his years. "But I want to help."

"***SIT!***" she barked. He did so, though he pouted in protest. Yarain's ears went back in a Holdren apology while she checked his chest for wounds. When she found a void where two ribs should be, her ears went up in alert concern.

"Stay put, don't move," Yarain said.

"But, Major," he whined. "I want to help."

"You can help me by staying alive. I can handle things here." She turned to arrange his removal but stopped when the boy cringed. At first, she thought it was a new symptom until she saw him staring at her paw. Yarain looked down to find a model of a Scorn Fighter with Gold 1's markings on it. It was still intact despite her boot-covered claws resting on its fuselage.

Yarain picked it up and handed it to him. "Is this yours?"

He shook his head while pushing it away. "Take it. I think the *Enterprise* needs her more than I do."

"It's not mine to take, and she's already up there."

"I don't need it."

"Nor do I, now take it. There's no reason for—"

Yarain's ear flicked as Lieutenant Rad came on her helmet's comm link.

"COB Five to all units, Polaris forces within the residential district, north-west quadrant. Repeat, Polaris forces are in the residential district, north-west quadrant."

My quadrant.

Yarain forced the model into the boy's hands, then turned her ears toward the doorway as she deployed her full helmet.

A second later, Harrison's voice shattered the air. "Take cover!"

Yarain heard his rifle fire, followed by a flurry of return fire that also came inside the door. Her ears melded with her skull as she dove for cover. The children screamed while she drew her rifle with a new growl on her lips.

"***AGAINST*** the forward section!" she ordered. "Get away from the doors."

A few remained frozen as the rest crawled or limped toward the front of the shuttle. The young boy scout went to these and managed to get them moving, slowed only by more rounds of weapons fire. Spurred on by his example, the ROTC cadets did the same with anyone else not moving. Yarain noticed with some irony that he still held the fighter model in his hand as he did.

Keep it safe, she thought as she tapped her comms. "This is Major Yarain, I'm pinned down near Terminus and Miles. I need immediate assistance." She broke the connection before facing the doorway. "Harrison report! **HARRISON**!?"

"Still kicking, ma'am," he called over the fire-fight. "Our cart's shot, but we're okay for now."

That's something. "Target bearing."

"Ruins across the street. I count five soldiers. Pretty sure I'm off."

"How so?"

"Under. *Very* under."

Yarain growled again. She and Harrison had heavy armor but only two weapons between them. Three if you counted her tails. *It'll have to do.*

When the enemy fire broke for a moment, Yarain leaned around and fired a volley of her own at the enemy forces. As she leaned back behind cover, her mind caught a snapshot of the enemy. Harrison was right. There were a lot more than five, all scattered around the ruins of whatever-it-was across the street. Worse cover but far better numbers.

As she returned fire again, one of the ROTC cadets dove for the other side of the door. "Do you have a spare weapon?"

Yarain's ears went up, but before she could argue, another flurry of weapons fire made the choice for her. She held up her P-mag in one hand. "Do you know how to use it?"

"Target shooting champ last month, ma'am."

She tossed him the weapon without a second thought. "Fire between the breaks, short bursts, always from cover."

He replied by joining her in doing exactly that. While not as good as a trained soldier, she was pleasantly surprised to see his shots be on target enough to be a threat. She was also able to see Harrison and the last ROTC cadet had found sufficient cover behind the ruined wing of the shuttle.

Even so, she often had to risk firing when under fire herself. She had no choice. The one time they waited for the fire to subside, she ducked around to find two enemy soldiers advancing on them. The poor men were riddled by two rifles and the young man's P-mag before they got halfway. Yet that made it clear; if they didn't keep the enemy pinned down, they would lose distance and eventually the fire-fight. Assuming they didn't anyway because of numbers.

Yarain was contemplating a number of really bad ideas when she saw one of the enemy soldiers drop to the ground for no apparent reason. Stranger still, a second soldier did the same not three seconds later, but it wasn't until a third soldier fell that any of his comrades seemed to notice.

"Snipe—" one of them called out. He didn't even get to finish the call before falling to the coil-gun technology Interstar had continued to develop. Yarain could only guess that Lieutenant Rad was out there having target practice with her Vesper variant. More than the usual banks of coils, this version was specifically designed to be accurate, effective, and so silent, Yarain still hadn't caught even a hint of the shots.

Not only had it whittled down the enemy force, but it had created a break in their barrage that Yarain wasted no time using. She snapped around her cover so she could lay down her own barrage. This included aiming her outside tails. Both tips expelled her energy matrix through the rust-red crystal-like fur fibers in her tail tips, which turned the energy her body needed into deadly beams. She couldn't fire for more than a very few seconds lest she risk weakening herself, but those seconds still claimed an enemy and sent the rest diving for cover.

As she returned to cover, more weapons fire came. This time *at* the enemy and from the opposite side. The Polaris forces moved to defend themselves, allowing Yarain full view of them. There were indeed *a lot* more than five out there. A snap count suggested upwards of fifteen, and even that was still an under count. While some had gone to meet the new attackers, some of them were still firing at Yarain's position. To his credit, the ROTC cadet was staying safe without losing his nerve. He fired on the moving soldiers just as Yarain did, careful to expose himself as little as possible. They claimed a soldier here and there, but not enough to matter.

Soon after the second front formed, a large explosion swallowed the enemy's location. Yarain ducked behind her cover as the remaining structure was utterly splintered. Pained yells announced a direct hit, followed by a crash as the remainder of the building rained down on the intruders. Then eerie quiet, except for the whimpers of the children and a ringing in Yarain's ears from their screams.

Yarain retook her line, ready to knock down any more that remained. She saw Captain Fickle, along with the rest of COB Team minus Rad and Tai, advance on the location. Harrison joined the advance, converging on the smoking rubble that used to be an enemy fox-hole. When the combined team arrived at the location, Harrison lowered his rifle.

"Stand down," he said over the comms. "Hark's little gift pack cleaned them out good. We're secure for the moment."

Yarain huffed amusement mixed with astonishment. *I should have known.* After packing a Shoulder Mounted Torpedo launcher, or SMT, on the Polaris station, it's no surprise Lieutenant Maureen Hark had been responsible for another large blast. *That woman must be a joy to have on the Fourth of July.*

Yarain let her gut relax as Lieutenant Rad appeared in the doorway with a stare that seemed like it could somehow erase threats yet mend wounds. The scent of ozone confirmed her as their guardian sniper. The fact that she had arrived without a sound also seemed to confirm Yarain's assessment of her hunting ability.

"You all right, ma'am?" Rad asked.

Yarain shook her head as if drying off before turning back inside the shuttle. "Yes. We need med-evac."

"Already here, ma'am. Got four ambulances plus two APCs right behind them."

"Have Harrison come help clear the shuttle. I want the perimeter guarded, and I want you on top for cover."

"Yes, ma'am!"

Yarain slung her rifle over her shoulder before turning to the kids, many of whom were still cowering against the wall. "We're safe now. **COME**. Let's leave."

It took some prodding, but with the help of the ROTC cadets, they led the survivors out one by one. Each was handed off to Harrison's gathered medics as they arrived at the shuttle. Harrison himself entered with a medical scanner to check the ones they'd missed before leading them out as well.

As the shuttle emptied, Yarain went to the Boy Scout. He was curled against the wall with the model still in his hands. Seemed his courage had run out at last—not that Yarain could blame him. The last few minutes would be enough for some seasoned soldiers, never mind a ten-year-old cub.

"Come on, son," Yarain said. "It's time we got you healed."

She leaned in close, and as she grabbed his shoulder, a new scent found her nose.

Or rather, a scent was now missing.

"No."

Yarain checked his chest for breathing, then checked his neck, then perked her ears, straining to find something she knew wasn't there. They eventually fell with a cringe. Her insides quivered like an earthquake as her eyes fell on the model.

Harrison appeared at her side as Yarain held the model in her hands. "This the last one?" he asked.

She couldn't stop it. Yarain's mind went through it all. The attack on her territory, Sundale, the teenager in four pieces, the three-year-old with tile shards in her back, the family she saved, and now, this. Another cub lost. Another pack that had gone unprotected. The more her mind circled, the straighter her fur got, and the hotter her neck felt until it seemed like it might literally explode. If it weren't for her armor, every hair would have been on end like a porcupine in response to a promise coursing through her being.

This will not happen again.

"Yes," Yarain said distantly. She looked at Harrison with her ears going full forward in anger instead of pain. "The last cub I'll **EVER** lose!"

"Ma'am? I don't under . . ." He looked closer, and saw the thin blood stream out of the corner of the boy's mouth. "Oh. I see. I'm sorry, ma'am. Are you all right?"

"I will be."

Yarain carefully placed the model next to the boy's body, then turned to leave.

She was again greeted at the door by Lieutenant Rad. "Ma'am, we've got more Pols approaching the complex from the north. It looks to be a full platoon of them, maybe more."

"A platoon?" Harrison said. "Where are they coming from? A downed ship? Escape pods?"

This will not happen again.

Yarain's ears found a new maximum perk as she drew her rifle. When she spoke, a growl seemed to fill the spaces between words. "It doesn't matter where they came from. What matters is they're about to feel our fangs! **GATHER** everyone you can at the north wall. That includes any civilians we can find weapons for. Form a full defensive line. I don't want a single enemy soldier to set foot in this complex."

For the first time, Rad showed a crack in her composure.

She blinked.

"Ma'am? You want civilians on the line?"

"You heard me, Lieutenant. Find only those who have full control of themselves. **MOVE!**"

"Yes, ma'am!" Harrison and Rad said.

They left to gather the troops while Yarain took charge of those already there. The APCs were just arriving, which she directed to lay out of sight until called for. The rest she had scatter along the wall, taking cover positions where they could be found.

This will not happen again.

The vow burned within her fur so strongly that, for a moment, she swore she could shear the planet in two with one tail. She fine-tuned her defense line while waiting for the enemy to show themselves.

At last, they did. Using the zoom function in her helmet, she was able to see them dashing between rocks in the distance. Infantry only, no armored vehicles to be had. They were preparing for a charge, and Interstar was growing more ready for them. By the time they went still, Harrison had already returned along with several soldiers, a dozen ROTC cadets, and a handful of civilians, some of them first responders and police.

Yarain held them in place as the enemy suddenly broke their silence. All at once, a full platoon of enemy soldiers charged, not bothering to pick their way at all.

Their mistake. As they reached what most would consider just outside combat range, Yarain's ears pulled back, her rifle took aim, and her tail tips glowed.

"Let . . . them . . . *have it*!"

The APCs rolled out from cover as every weapon began the barrage at once.

Minutes later, nothing remained but a field of Polaris corpses.

CHAPTER 3

RETURN TO FORM

Polaris Fleet Admiral Timothy Solez stormed down the corridors of the base. He didn't even bother to tug on his dark brown uniform so the soft grey lines running up the sides of his arms, legs, and torso were smooth and straight. *Someone's head is going to roll.*

That thought kept his head boiling as he turned inside the tactical room. Everyone inside simply dropped their heads behind their stations lest even a salute draw his ire.

That only meant his ire went for them all.

"Who authorized that attack!?"

One brave soul asked, "Which one do you mean, sir?"

Admiral Solez lit the man on fire with his stare. "New Holland. What United Systems calls Phoenix Perch. I want to know who gave the order, who told them to bombard the surface, and if I don't hear the truth, you will wish you never existed."

"I did, Admiral."

The voice came from the only head that hadn't ducked. Admiral Solez braced to rip the man in half until he saw this man had a head of perfectly straight, blond hair. He had a slight belly bulge, but it was the clean black suit and blood-red tie with black lines that made his anger feel as if it had literally turned to stone.

This wasn't some admiral with his own ideas. This was the grand marshal, a man who was second only to the Polaris president. Calling him out could easily be seen as insubordination, and while Admiral Solez felt no differently about the attack as a whole, his ability to say anything about it had just ended. That left the admiral trying to chip at his frozen anger so he could be sure what feeling had taken its place.

When Admiral Solez couldn't find words, the grand marshal did.

"Let's take this somewhere private, Admiral."

Admiral Solez nodded his agreement, relieved that the order had been given without emotion. It suggested his hide would remain intact, at least for now.

The marshal led him across the room to a set of offices. They went inside one that was unclaimed and thus unadorned save for a basic desk and chairs as well as a small mirror on the back wall. The marshal took the desk seat in front of a banner with a bear outlining the full Ursa Major constellation with a star above it—the Polaris insignia. Admiral Solez took the seat offered to him on the other side of the desk.

"Now then, Admiral," the marshal said, "I gave both orders in question. Is there a problem with that? Please, speak freely."

As much as Admiral Solez wanted to do just that, he knew he needed to adjust his wording. "Sir . . . I don't understand the prolonged attack. The *Enterprise* was a worthy target, but the risk was too high, as proven by our assault force escaping with all of one badly damaged cruiser. Then to bombard the surface . . . I'm sorry, sir, but I see no point."

"Because you don't know what I do, and that's my fault, Admiral. The United Systems vice president was on the surface. I don't know what he was doing there, I only know it was the perfect chance to take him out, which as you recall, is vital to our plan."

Admiral Solez didn't like where this conversation was going. "Did we get him?"

"We did. United Systems hasn't announced it yet, but we have confirmation that we destroyed his bunker with him in it."

"Okay, but the bombardment was so broad. We're already being painted as worse than the jantans. And if I may say so, sir, I'm—"

"All a part of the plan, Admiral, though I must admit, the bombardment was a last second amendment." When Admiral Solez's face went stone still, the marshal leaned forward. "Just think of it, Admiral. What better way to ral . . . distract the populace, than for me to take the lead against such an 'evil force of murder'? To say nothing of the distraction it provides for Operation 'Second Visit.' It only helps the plan, no matter which version we need."

Admiral Solez's stomach turned at the marshal's words. *That's it? Thousands of innocent civilians killed just to strengthen your image?* Torturing Sundale had been required to get information that could help their cause, and he was an enemy soldier. Murder on such a scale . . . Surely not.

"But, sir," Solez said, "we shelled the residential district as well as the bunker. Those families—"

"Built their homes on the bones of our soldiers!" the marshal said. "Don't forget the men we lost when Interstar captured our Raider base there. They are as guilty as the soldiers that drove us off. Their blood is ample payment for their crimes."

Admiral Solez stared at his commander in utter disbelief. *Guilty as the soldiers?* Children *died down there! They did nothing to deserve . . . Oh my God.*

The last was drawn because he caught a glimpse of himself in the mirror. For half a second, he felt the age he saw. The half-grey head of hair that was half gone, a hard face that had only a few wrinkles, but it was the look of sheer horror that gave him pause. An almost perfect match to the one his own son had given him that day in the infirmary right after his son had stunned Sundale.

"Something wrong, Admiral?" the marshal said.

Admiral Solez had to pull up every ounce of discipline he could find to reset his features. He shook his head as if shaking a thought from his mind and returned his face to hopefully stoic attention.

"No, sir," he said. "I'm . . . I'm sorry I doubted you, sir."

"Forget it. You were missing chunks of information. How else could you respond? I'll try to keep you more in the loop in the future."

"Thank you, sir. If there's nothing else, Operation Second Visit *is* almost ready. I best finish the preparations."

Never one for ceremony, the marshal rose without word or salute. "Very good, Admiral. I look forward to another rousing victory from your forces. I'll be in touch."

The man left, leaving Admiral Solez alone with his thoughts and the lingering image of his own face in his mind.

All those times Simon had stared at him . . . The sick looks, the long gazes, the statue stiff attentions. Had they all been covering the same doubt he now had? It would explain a lot. Admiral Solez had played those days over his mind, wondering how he'd missed it. How he'd missed his own son plotting against him. He'd asked himself why as well.

Now, for the first time, the back of his mind began to find answers.

Compassion may be a weakness, but there are things no one should do. Such an attack felt like one of them. Perhaps Simon felt the same about Sundale's interrogation. While he never named it, Simon had left a message saying he could no longer stand by and watch wrong at work. If his heart had been unable to let go of that doubt, perhaps it drove him to betrayal.

No, this isn't the same. We have a plan in motion. One that will bring humanity together under one banner and finally put an end to the wars. We will see humans reach the destiny we are entitled to. We will bring about an age of order, of peace, of truth.

"*The* truth, or *our* truth?"

Words from his son's message. Simon had lost faith in which "truth" Polaris was really fighting for. He felt that, by his actions, he might be able to ensure *he* at least was fighting for *the* truth.

Admiral Solez looked at himself in the mirror once more. If the grand marshal was willing to go so far, how much further would he go? What else would he do to further his goals?

And what did he mean by "no matter which version"? There was only one version of one plan.

Admiral Solez's mind swirled until it felt like a tornado in his head. Then he shook his head to almost literally snap that thread. Perhaps the marshal had gone too far this one time, but they still had a job to do and an enemy to defeat. One part of the overall plan, however wrongly achieved, had been achieved. Now it was up to him to make sure he continued to salvage a broken operation that still had a chance of success.

That said, when Admiral Solez finally went to his own office to begin his work, he summoned his most trusted aide to look into other things for him.

"Keep going, Sundale. We're almost done."

Doctor Jannet Blount spoke like it was difficult, but Sundale had plenty of stamina left in him. He'd been running on the treadmill for fifteen minutes at what he would consider a medium pace. It lay somewhere between a cruising run he could hold for hours and the faster not-quite-full-speed used to keep up with running prey. While his tongue was flapping as he ran, it was more maintenance than true exertion.

More importantly to him, however, was how fluid it felt. Gone was any trace of stiffness or soreness. His injured leg, which he was once afraid to look at lest it start hurting again, now moved in perfect rhythm with his other limbs. The only thing he disliked was that he wasn't going anywhere, which was nothing more than the same minor irritant he had with most exercise equipment.

Jannet stood next to him the entire time, watching the read-outs and him with the same clinical eye she'd always had. She stood tall for human women, and she always moved with a certain confidence in her step. Yet her face was soft and smooth, with dark-blue eyes and dark-red hair that was right at regulation length. Eventually, she tapped on her clip-com, then hummed approval.

"All right," she said. "Let's see how you handle this."

She tapped the controls, and the treadmill's speed increased to the point that Sundale had to run full out to keep his place. Unlike real running, he had to think about keeping his rust red tail tips with matching bands off the "ground," but otherwise, nothing changed. He needed more speed, and his legs provided it without resistance. Nor did the blue jumpsuit he wore get in his way.

The speed was increased to a sprint, and still his body did what he asked of it. Each paw fell and moved on command, his body bounding with each step. This, he couldn't hold for as long, but he didn't have to. No more than a minute after reaching full speed, the treadmill faded to a soft walk, held speed for a short time, then slowed to a stop.

Jannet knelt to Sundale's left as he panted away the exertion. She ran a scan, then squeezed the muscles up and down the left foreleg with her hands. She lifted the leg, then forced it to move in every direction, all under Sundale's patient watch.

"Very good, Sundale," she said. "Strength appears back to normal, as does your speed. I don't feel any resistance either. How does it feel to you?"

"Normal," Sundale said. His voice had a slightly higher pitch to it without it being nasal.

"No tension? No pain? Full range of motion?"

"Everything seems fine."

Jannet motioned for him to follow while the physical therapist checked with another patient. She led him to a bench seat where they could both sit at eye level. There, she shined a light into his right eye, then unzipped his jumpsuit so she could press her hand into his flank. She sank her fingers into the sandy-gold fur on his side, back, shoulders, and all three tails. She did the same in places along his white belly fur that went up his chest and muzzle, then carefully pulled on the two-inch scar that was still a tiny bit red that ran across his right eye. Sundale gave a split-second growl of annoyance but nothing more.

"No degradation of the eye," she said. "Your wounds are nicely healed. No sign of any more seizures. Probably the only good thing to come out of your imprisonment. Fur seems soft and full. Despite it still being shorter than normal, your scars are finally hidden, as I told you they would be."

"Except the one," Sundale said distantly, though he looked at her as he said it.

Jannet slumped with a nod. They'd had several discussions about his scar before, though he'd managed to have them without ever talking about the real reason for his pain. Still, she'd come to understand why it bothered him so much. This thankfully led her to drive off a young cosman who had tried to get "the story." When a second attempter got glares from both of them the next day, it never happened again. Sundale soon after reached a point where he could sometimes forget it was there.

More than anything, that had been the beginning of his real recovery. Though the pain remained, it had begun fading into the background now that he no longer had to face it every day. His back had given a couple of twinges but never became more than a disruption in his energy matrix that sometimes popped up normally. Once or twice, that same spot in his back seemed to pulse stronger, like when he'd had seizures, though this too had been far less than before. The shudders had become less frequent as well.

As his body began to heal, so too did his heart become more willing to be near others. His time with Jannet had helped as well, for she'd softened a lot over time, allowing him to see her as a pack mate. When he let himself realize this, it paved the way for his trust to begin rebuilding itself.

Which also let him draw strength from Yarain. She was always there in the corridor, or at least her scent was. This too was helping him rebuild himself. His mother, first mother, and pack mate was staying in easy reach, ready to assist however she could. Though he could never bring himself to revisit that bond, the fact that it lay there for him every day without fail helped because the more he felt like a member, the harder it became to reject the pack he already had. Yes, he had come close to betraying them, but they were still his pack. They were a part of him.

Of course, that was also the problem. He had come that close to putting himself before them. It didn't matter why, only that he had or would have . . . *might* have. A caveat he had begun to accept. It wouldn't have been the first time what he thought he'd do didn't mesh with what he *did* do. In the early days of his training, he was convinced that eventually, he'd rip the throat out of his drill instructor. While his hackles ruffled several times a day, his fangs never tasted human blood. Well, except in a dream or two.

As for reality, he didn't know what he would have done, but the question lingered enough that he couldn't go near his pack. Not yet. Not until he stopped wondering whether or not their lives were safe with him. Or at the very least, not until he could see a Scorn Fighter without feeling caged and terrified all over again.

The former hadn't come, but the latter had, last week continuing through today. Better still was the fact that while his emotions had colored his comment a moment ago, it felt much weaker than it had just yesterday. Whether Jannet knew this or not was not evident in her response.

"Well, that's a longer process," she said. "Much as your fur will need more time to get back to full length, so too will you need time to get used to that scar. In the short term, however, sorry about this."

Sundale's head tilted in confusion as Jannet motioned for someone to join them. His ears locked onto a nurse that came from behind him without a word, causing his body to tense for trouble. The nurse stopped beside him, setting the inhibitor collar he'd worn as a POW, cuffs, a muzzle, and lengths of rope onto the bench next to Jannet. Sundale took one deep breath as the memory tried to come rushing back to him. It died before it got to the surface, but his eyes did shift to Jannet with his ears up and alert.

"What is this?" he said.

Jannet picked the collar up and moved toward him. Sundale shied away, but Jannet followed enough to ensure she was able to latch it onto his neck. Sundale's ears shifted back and forth between fear and confusion while his hackles fluffed for a second. As the collar's energy ran through him once more, neutralizing his abilities, Sundale stared at her. He found an equally stoic pose when he glanced at the nurse as he tried to understand what was going on. When Jannet put the muzzle on him, his ears and eyes settled on her, yet no growl or whimper ever formed, nor did he really resist. Though his insides were starting to shake, it was more confusion than the fear those implements had triggered before.

"What are you doing?" he said, surprised to find no shake in his voice, nor any true fear of what she would do to him.

Jannet nodded with a smile. "Confirming what I hoped was true." She instantly removed both items and zipped up his jumpsuit. As Sundale shook the disruption from his body, Janet helped the nurse pile everything back on a tray for her to take away. "You took that well. You're ready."

Sundale still felt his chest flutter like a ribbon in the wind. His ears would not let Jannet out of their focus while he silenced another odd twinge in his back. "Why did you do that to me?"

"I needed to test your emotional scars. You aren't the first one to go through something like this, Sundale. One reason I pressed you so much the last few days was so I could gauge how best to test your emotional stability. When you admitted that being helpless was the worst part of the experience, I realized the best test was to suggest the idea that you were going to be made helpless again. Your reaction, or lack thereof, proved to me that you've recovered enough to satisfy me."

"I didn't react because I trust you. If I didn't, I might have torn you apart."

"The fact that you're saying 'might have' proves my point. Trust or not, if you weren't ready for the field, you wouldn't be talking like that, and there would have been some sign of emotional distress."

Don't be so sure. "How do you know what emotional distress looks like in a holdren?"

"My father raised a lot of dogs and rescued a few foxes. Between the two, I know what to look for, none of which did I see. Uneasiness certainly, as I would expect, but no real stress. I still want you in here once a week for follow ups, but I'm making it official. You're ready."

For duty, maybe. For other things, I'm not so sure.

Sundale needed another soft shake to settle himself, but once he did, he found he had settled fully. All the concern he'd felt was gone. Washed away as if he'd run under a waterfall to cleanse his fur. This brought understanding with it. He could imagine what he'd be like if his experience had left him with more than the one scar. She had every right to be sure, and he eventually agreed that his reaction suggested he was ready to return to the field.

It was the individuals he worried about. He'd shut them out for over a month. Just because Yarain had stayed there for so long did not mean she was ready to take him back. To say nothing of Jason, who he'd not seen since Jason's comment in the corridor right after his release from sick-bay. Holdrens may not live in the past, but humans dug dens in it. Sometimes deep ones.

When Sundale's ears pulled back a moment, Janet's head recoiled while her eyes lowered. A reaction he'd seen before. It meant something he'd said or done had her concerned, curious, or both.

"Or are you?" she said. "I never did ask whether or not you *wanted* to go back."

Sundale's ears shot forward, not in anger, but in reaction to the conviction that swallowed him whole. Go back? That question had been silenced days ago. It was other things that had him hesitating.

"I do," he said, full force behind his words.

"Then what's wrong?"

I still can't trust myself. It was what he wanted to say. It was the truth. He'd decided he wanted to rejoin them. He felt he owed it to them. But now that it was time to do so, all he could think about was how close he'd come to betraying them. The question had changed from, "Do I want to?" to a more painful question: "Can I risk it?"

"I'm not sure what I had is still there," was all he could say.

Jannet stared at him a moment, then shook her head. "Gold 1 is still intact Sundale, crew and all. I confirmed long ago that your position is yours—"

"That's **NOT** what I mean," he said, half ruffing a word.

He tried to finish it. With the truth, with a lie, it didn't matter, nothing would come out. Some of it because deep down, he doubted if he meant what he thought he did. Or perhaps, if he was simply lying to himself about it.

Jannet again stared at him, but the longer she did, the smaller her eyes got. Finally, she sighed with her hand going to her temple, though her eyes never grew.

"Sundale, you told me holdrens are pack animals that draw strength from the pack, yet you've done all you can to be away from yours. Hell, you even requested permanent solo quarters. I gotta admit, I don't understand why you're avoiding them so much."

It came all at once, from some pocket deep within his chest. A single answer he didn't realize he'd been holding onto. "They want me to drop the entire thing like it never happened. I don't know how." Of course, what he left out was what "the entire thing" was.

Jannet didn't miss a beat. "Who cares what they want? What matters is what you need."

"Wild holdrens don't live in the past."

"Wild holdrens don't get tortured by crazy admirals. Though Sundale, if I may, I'm not sure I'd exactly call you 'wild.'"

"He's a scared stray." The words of Simon Solez, the young Polaris officer who had helped his rescue, echoed in Sundale's mind. Yet his ears again latched onto Jannet. Her words felt like a sharp bite straight to his heart because he feared them to be true. He'd spent years with Karol, the rest with Jason, both *human* Interstar pilots. He might have had one year of being "wild," if that. Yarain was a full-grown, experienced adult when she left their territory. The wild was ingrained in her heart and blood. For him . . . there was precious little, all of it built *after* he'd been fully grown.

Yet his blood wanted the untamed spaces, the thrill of the hunt, the closeness of the pack, even as his mind had brought him that close to going against every drop of it. Holdrens didn't live in the past, but he couldn't escape it. "My life for the pack" is one phrase that *was* ingrained in him, yet he'd almost gone against it. It all left him caught in the middle. Not wild, not tame, trustworthy, dangerous, while somehow being all at once. His ears fell as one question rose above everything running through his head.

What am I?

Shortly after his ears fell, so did Jannet. She slid onto her knees in front of him. Instinct again drove him to make room for her. When she spoke, her eyes were soft, as was her voice.

"Look, they are right that you have to move past this, but they're wrong in trying to make you do it their way. Be it the holdren way, the human way, or the ant way, you need to find your own way past this so you can get back into a Scorn. It's the only way to give that admiral the finger up his ass he deserves, but you can't do it alone. You need your pack, just as they need you. You aren't complete without each other."

My life for the pack.

The phrase churned more than his instincts. It seeped into every hair. It wasn't just a vow of sacrifice; it was a promise. A promise to infuse one's life into every pore of every pack mate. Few as they were, Sundale had felt that bond with his parents. More so during his recovery as Yarain's presence was enough to give him strength. Their lives were his, just as his was theirs. All part of the greater whole.

His mind touched on his doubt, but a snort silenced it. Jason needed him, and Yarain would never handle losing her cub a third time. Not rejoining the hunt, seeing Gold 1 with only one holdren on board, would be another victory for Admiral Solez. After everything that man had done to him, Sundale could not let him have another. Nor could he ever recover without merging his life with his pack's once more.

"Is that snort a thank you or something else?" Jannet said.

Sundale ruffed once in amusement, then tapped his nose to hers, which she flinched at in surprise.

"Thank you," he said. "I need to find my pack."

Sundale turned to leave, his mind already working on where, or rather how, to start. He made his way through the bed area into the corridor, then chose a lift to head toward. He didn't get far before he was stopped by a familiar voice coming his way.

"... lose a single one," Jason said. "Not even a civilian. I don't know what those guys were doing down there or what their plan was, but thank God Yarain was there to meet them. She definitely made the difference."

A warmth swept through Sundale as he saw Jason round the corner beside an older officer he didn't recognize. Most humans would have taken Jason's comment about God as nothing more than the general phrase. Sundale knew him well enough to know he meant it literally. The moment of instant understanding brought with it everything else Sundale knew about him. Including how worried he must be about his foxy crew mate... and dearest friend.

It was the last part of that understanding that turned the warmth into pain. While they'd never let it get in the way of their duties, the bond between them had always been strong. They knew each other better than they knew themselves most of the time, which meant Sundale knew all too well the kind of pain Jason must have been feeling these last few weeks. Knowing his best friend was hurting but didn't want him near, it had to feel like a wound all on its own. That, combined with all the guilt Sundale still carried about how close he'd come, made him wonder if maybe this whole return to duty thing wasn't such a good idea after all.

The mix of emotions kept Sundale stuck in the corridor, which allowed Jason to see him. Jason appeared to excuse himself from the officer, looked down the corridor as if confirming what he saw, and then started toward Sundale almost at a fast step. Sundale's stomach might as well have been a rock, but he forced himself to hold his place all the same. If he couldn't fight past the wounds now, he never would.

Jason stepped right up to him, warm affection touching his eyes and mouth as only a loved one would notice. "Hey, Sun. How are you feeling?"

No comments, no judgment, not even a hint of reproach. Every word held nothing but concern. Two short sentences told Sundale that Jason wasn't holding onto the past at all. It made the moment that much harder, as his heart couldn't get past all the things he'd said and thought.

Jason watched and waited for a reply, no change in his features. That meant it was up to Sundale to start, and his ears shifted back and forth as he couldn't find a thing to say. Everything he wanted to say would lead to all the things he couldn't say. After an eternity of trying, Sundale's ears and eyes fell as he wondered whether he could really do this.

This time, Jason only shook his head. "No. No, I don't want you doing that. You have no reason to cower to me."

"Don't I?" Sundale said.

"Sun, I've—"

Sundale was startled as someone else came through a door they'd been standing at. The man apologized as he'd almost run him over, but Sundale politely dismissed it since no harm was done. Sundale gave the man enough room to be on his way before turning back to Jason. Sundale found him in one of his evaluation stares but with the smallest of smiles touching his face.

"*WHAT*?" Sundale barked.

"Nothing," Jason said. "Come on. I think it's time we talked, and the corridor is hardly the place for such a conversation. Unless you plan to continue going it alone."

Sundale's insides wanted to growl, but his ears fell in submission instead. Jason had every right to that comment, and Sundale deserved the fangs he felt, even if they weren't really there.

"No," Sundale said.

"No to which part?" Jason said.

"Going it alone."

Jason nodded with another soft smile. "Then fall in, Captain."

Sundale did just that. His mind and instincts switched to follow mode as he walked behind Jason to the nearest lift. There was no room for doubt, or fear, or even pain. His first father was on the move, and he had to follow. The only distraction allowed was a check of his surroundings in case a danger was missed, and even this was mild given their location.

On the lift, Jason tapped on his wrist comm. as if checking on something. It was only then that Sundale noticed his uniform was different. While the color scheme hadn't changed, the entire suit appeared to be textured now, as if it were made of reptile scales from shoulder to ankle. Additionally, some kind of metal plating seemed to be on Jason's shoulders and in thin strips down the sides of his arms, legs, and torso. Jason's belt also seemed to be slightly thicker than Sundale remembered.

Despite the "follow first parent" mode, Sundale couldn't contain his curiosity. "They change our uniform?"

Jason looked confused, then shook his head. "Not exactly. The standard issue suit has been upgraded. Terrines have been phasing it in for weeks. The *Alamo*'s fabrication plant just finished an upgrade so Caelnav and PSC can start doing the same."

"Upgraded how?"

The doors opened, and Jason led them on. "One thing at a time, Sun. I'll tell you all about it, but first, we have other things to discuss."

Sundale's insides churned as he now worried about how badly this conversation was going to go. Still, he followed, thankful he could lose himself in the instinct so his fears didn't freeze him.

They walked right into Jason's quarters without a word between them. As a group commander, Jason got one of the best rooms available, though it was still only big enough for one couch and table facing the window seat. A tiny bench as an eating area and a desk lined one wall, while doors spoke of a separate bedroom. Still big enough to fit two holdrens and a human since the former didn't need much. *At least it used to be.*

Though Yarain's scent seeped into Sundale's fur the moment they entered. It touched his instincts in a way that brought him a sense of calm but also more curiosity.

"Where is Yarain?" he asked. Jason looked back with the human open-mouth-and-stare questioning look. "Her scent is old."

Jason shook his head, almost laughing. "You'd think I'd be used to how good your nose is by now. She's on the surface helping with recovery efforts."

"*WHAT* recovery efforts?"

"Polaris attacked Phoenix Perch. Scuttlebutt says they killed the VP. She's been helping the search and rescue teams the last few days, but enough distractions. We're here for a reason." Jason walked over to sit on the couch while Sundale sat in front of him. His ears remained half-back in fear. Here it came, and despite what he'd said, he still didn't feel ready for this.

Jason leaned forward with folded hands and looked him in the eye. "Now, as I was saying, I've been doing a lot of thinking and praying about this whole thing, and I've come to the conclusion . . . I handled it badly."

Sundale's ears came up, but so did his hackles. "That's an understatement."

"I know. I'd like to blame Yarain as well, but that's just an easy way to make myself feel better. Neither of us were listening, and we both went right on not listening until Doctor Blount put an end to it. I can think of a dozen excuses that do nothing to excuse my behavior."

The honesty flattened Sundale's fur and shamed him for all the anger he'd felt. For a moment, he was able to see it from Jason's view, which only made it worse. "You wanted to help."

Jason sighed and leaned on the arm of the couch with his hand rubbing against his temple. He then shifted to set his chin on that hand. "And a fine job I did of it too. Instead of helping you, I get into a debate with Yarain about how you should heal, completely forgetting the fact that you're right there, still in pain from the ordeal. I can't imagine what it was like, but I also know I was an idiot. I'm sorry. I shouldn't have pushed so hard."

Sundale's ears flashed back, as much to release tension as to show the pain that waved through him. Only now did he realize he'd expected another fight, maybe even wanted it. Instead, he got Jason with his paws in the air, seeking forgiveness. There was nothing to confront except Sundale's own regret and shame. Again, unable to respond, Sundale's ears and eyes fell.

Jason continued into the silence. "I thought I told you—"

"It's **NOT** that," Sundale said. He tried to say more, but the words still refused to come. Even now, with Jason surrendering, he couldn't say it. He couldn't admit what he'd been so ready to do. Why this room didn't feel like his anymore.

"Then what is it?" Jason said. "Why do you keep looking at me like I've disowned you?"

The words were coming. Sundale was forcing them forward, consequences be damned. At least they'd be out in the open. His chest felt ready to explode with the admission of all the guilt he felt he rightly deserved.

The door chime snapped his ears up. Jason looked ready to explode himself, then it switched to a frustrated rub of his face. "I'm batting a thousand. That one's my fault, Sun. Hang on. Let me take care of it."

Jason went to the door while Sundale tried to collect his innards. The words were still there, caught somewhere between his heart and the back of his mouth. *Maybe Jason would understand. He's human. The idea of self-sacrifice no matter what isn't as deeply ingrained in their . . .*

His thoughts were stopped by what Jason was given by a woman at the door. A P-mag and combat knife were there, but Sundale's eyes locked onto what they were sitting on. A small case, perhaps bigger, but very much like the one Admiral Solez carried in that one time.

The more he stared at the case, the tighter Sundale's insides got. He was there, helpless, powerless, nothing in the universe but him and those who were going to hurt him. He was caged without bars or force fields. They could do what they wanted with him. He wanted to run, to hide, but he could do neither. He couldn't even growl; they'd taken that from him, too. There was no hope of escape, no chance to fight back. Sundale sat in darkness, joined only by Admiral Solez and voices he couldn't pin down. Voices that would turn to fangs any moment . . .

It all vanished like a candle blown out. Sundale was suddenly in Jason's quarters, where he'd been the entire time, trembling as if cold. What hadn't been there was Jason. Somewhere in that time, he'd knelt in front of Sundale, put Sundale's head on his shoulder, and rested his hands on Sundale's shoulders in a firm, yet far from restricting, embrace.

There were words of comfort as well. Though Sundale's mind hadn't retained them, it had retained the emotion.

It wasn't until Sundale sighed the panic from him that Jason said something he retained. "There you go. Don't try to do anything. Just let it be."

Sundale's breathing slowed while the panic was forced out in favor of his pack. His trembling faded to nothing as he rubbed his head against Jason's. Sundale absorbed every aspect of his scent. When Sundale's breathing returned to normal, Jason pulled back so they could be face to face.

"You all right?" he asked.

Sundale huffed amusement at the idiocy of the question, only to flick an ear when he suspected it was intentional. A gentle tease to further settle his mind.

"Yes," Sundale said. "Thank you."

A warm smile confirmed his suspicions. "Don't mention it. Want to talk about it?"

"Not in detail. All you need to know is . . . the last time I saw a case like that; I lost my fur minutes later."

Jason looked over at the case on the table with a cringe. "Maybe I should quit while I'm ahead. I'm sorry, I didn't . . . of course I didn't know. How could I? Want me to—"

"*NO*," Sundale barked. "No. I need to learn how to deal with such things if I'm returning to duty."

"You sure you can? I'm sorry, but I have to ask. That didn't look like a small reaction."

Sundale had to dig around for an explanation he knew Jason would understand. "It . . . was the proverbial straw. Much like my fur, my wounds are not fully healed. The case . . . it pushed me over the edge."

Jason slid his legs sideways under him so he could sit on his rear more comfortably. "If the case was the last straw, what were the others?"

The whole truth again tried to come out. Other words came in their place. "Meeting you before I was ready. A hard conversation I just had with Jannet." His ears fell again, though nothing else did. "Trying to find what to say to you and Yarain. Fear of not being as ready as I think I am."

"In short, every emotional scar you have. No wonder it was one too many. Still, as your commanding officer, I have to be sure. If you meet Admiral Solez on the battlefield, and he has a case like that in his hands, but your orders say take him alive—"

Sundale's ears snapped forward with a ruffle of his hackles. "He'll wake up in a holding cell wondering how he got there, sir."

Jason nodded with a chuckle shaking his ribs. "Are you sure? That's a lot of straws."

"Not enough."

The conviction was born of revenge, but it was there all the same. Sundale could imagine the situation, and every time he played it in his mind, it went the same way. Admiral Solez would get all three tails, but he'd be unharmed, while Sundale would be without the slightest shudder.

Jason leaned back with folded arms, assessing Sundale with his eyes hair by hair. Sundale sat with forward ears, holding onto his newfound confidence for dear life. In this moment, fear wasn't allowed. Not even his shame could break through. He sat ready to be an extension of his first father. Something he hadn't felt since before his capture. In an odd way, there wasn't even a need to share his moment of weakness anymore. It too felt irrelevant in favor of what coursed through him right now. He was ready to return to the lines. He was ready to rejoin the hunt.

At last, Jason nodded. "All right then. In that case . . . no pun intended . . . we need to get you caught up."

Jason stood and went to the case. He slid the weapons off so he could open it to reveal a folded uniform. As Jason lifted it up, Sundale saw it was a holdren uniform, except it held the same texture as Jason's, as well as the metal plates going down the sides, though the holdren version seemed to have slightly larger plates on the sides of the main body. The tail socks were still there, though they too seemed to have metal plates, this time in a ring at the base of each tail. Any straps or belts for the weapons must have been put into the uniform itself since Sundale couldn't see any.

"Put it on," Jason said, "and I'll run through the new features with you."

Sundale shifted into his finesse form and shed his jumpsuit like a tuft of fur. Yet when Jason handed him the uniform, he hesitated with shifting ears as he looked at the silver wings with a single sun between them on his rank tab, then his name under the Interstar insignia. He'd recited that name, rank, plus serial number so many times before his will began to fade. Despite his confidence, there was still that part of him that wondered if he deserved or was strong enough to reclaim either.

"You sure you're all right, Sun?" Jason said.

Once more, the truth tried to come out. Once more, a version of it did. "There's a lot to reclaim here."

"The sooner you start, the sooner you can. That's still you, Captain. I don't care what they did to you; they failed to take you from yourself. This is how you show them that."

If you only knew.

Of course he couldn't, but then, Admiral Solez didn't either. Only Sundale knew how close he'd come. Which meant Jason was right. He could get back at Admiral Solez in one . . . very difficult, step.

Sundale huffed out his doubt before working his legs and tails into the new uniform. As he slid it up and over his arms, he was pleasantly surprised to find everything form-fitting yet far from tight. It was definitely heavier than before, but not enough to matter. Once he was zipped into it, his guess about straps was confirmed by an internal tightening of a harness built into the uniform. As he attached his sidearm and his combat knife, he felt their weight caught by these straps, keeping them in place without pulling any more than the old ones did, if not less.

After putting his wrist comm. on, Sundale rotated his arms to get a feel for it all. The uniform stretched a lot more than the old, which left him only worried about going nuts while he got used to it pressing against his fur in areas it didn't used to. As he twisted his body to further test the feel, he was surprised to find the metal plates were a lot less noticeable than expected, and in no way restrictive. Even when he shook himself, everything stayed in place, with almost no sound coming from any of it.

"Looks like a good fit," Jason said.

"It is," Sundale said. "Did they change the fabric?"

"Among other things. They tried a lot harder to make sure any extra coverage didn't restrict your mobility in either form."

"I think they succeeded."

"Well, that's good to hear. Now, let's talk about the armor system."

"What armor system?"

Jason held up a finger, then tapped on his wrist comm. three times. Sundale jumped back as, all at once, the plates slid out to cover Jason's body in a layer of metal while building around and over his knife sheath. The belt and shoulders also slid plates down to add to the layer over his torso while a solid helmet constructed itself over his entire head from the neck.

When it was done, Jason was covered in a layer of textured blue metal with a black visor over his eyes and a helmet that had lights built into the sides.

"Sorry, should have warned you better," Jason said, his voice surprisingly clear, though still slightly distorted, as one would expect.

Sundale had long settled from the surprise. "That's okay. Is that our new combat armor?"

Jason again tapped on his wrist comm., and the helmet retracted to expose his face. "Yes and no. They're calling it the Dragon Skin Armor System. Really, it's closer to a World War Two flack vest, so we'll still carry the same armor sets as before, but it's better than what we had. No more hoping you can make it to the armory in time to get armor. Thin as it is, the extra layer will give you a fighting chance."

"Why the texture of the base uniform then?"

"Because they made it stronger too. If you were to look closely, you'd see it's made of a new material that's layered like snake scales. No idea what it's made of. They'll barely admit it's an 'alloy,' though I'm sure it's still heavy on refined bug threads. I only know it now offers a very slight layer of protection."

Sundale looked at his arm to see Jason was absolutely right. He could see the "scales" laid out over his body. He rubbed his hand along his torso so he could feel the metal, yet even when he dug a claw in, he found he couldn't produce a sharp edge that might cut him. *As Jason would say, small favors.*

"How much protection?" Sundale said.

"The base layer? Not much," Jason said. "Sparks, fire, sharp rocks, maybe shrapnel if it's not moving too fast, a touch of radiation protection, that's about it. At most, it *might* deflect a sharp-angle shot or turn a lethal hit into a critical one. The deployed armor is where we get the protection, thin though it may be. New regs call for it to be deployed at condition 2 or higher. Speaking of which, you should try it out. If you look on your wrist comm., you'll see a little armor vest icon among your quick hits. Tap it three times, and the armor will fully deploy."

Sundale was a little unsure about the process, but he'd have to get used to it eventually. So as instructed, he tapped the indicated icon three times. Just like Jason's, his armor deployed over his body, covering the base uniform in a layer of protective metal, though his sidearm and knife remained on the outside of the armor. His lower legs and arms were covered in a layer of the base uniform. He felt his tails fully covered as well, followed by a thin layer of armor going the same distance. Boots also covered his paws, yet were so form-fitting, the toes and claws were fully indexed right down to tipped claws. The helmet constructed over his head, yet his ears and lower jaw remained bare.

Sundale went to a full-body mirror on the wall to get a better look at his new armor. His ears perked in surprise as he watched the armor shift to perfectly match his fur color, including the tail tips and bands. While his rank remained visible on his arms and shoulders, they were tinted to match the color of the fur beneath, though not exactly so they stood out a little. His helmet was armored like Jason's, but his eye holes looked more like black eyes instead of a visor, and there was a tiny lip of armor on the leading edge of his ears. Finally, he noticed there was a Heads Up Display more complex than before in his vision, which, as he looked around, he realized was without obstruction. He could tell there was something there at the edge of his vision, but not enough to hinder him. The best part: unlike so many times, this helmet somehow managed to not bother his whiskers at all, nor did the system feel heavy enough to slow him down.

To test that, Sundale assumed his four-legged "primal" form. The armor automatically shifted to match, including covering his front paws in the same material. He walked circles around the room, trotted some, then cut, leapt over the couch, and headed for the door only to stop, turn, and aim his tails in one fluid motion. While he felt a slight bounce from the weight, he found his range of motion in no way hindered, nor did the weight feel enough to slow him down. Even his claws felt like they were no longer removed as an option for fighting or traction.

Sundale returned to the mirror in his finesse form. "They did good work."

Jason nodded victory. "You can thank Yarain and Harmus for that."

"Harmus helped develop it?"

"I know. I couldn't believe it either. They both spent a long time letting the R&D boys get precise measurements, study how their bodies changed when they shifted forms, even allowing them to monitor changes in their energy matrix so they could program commands into the armor. We'll go over all of those later. For now, I want you getting a feel for the armor itself. The color shift you saw isn't automatic. I just had them set it so that the first time you deployed it, you could see that the option was there. Otherwise, pigment shifting is the same as it's always been."

"I like that they left my jaw open, but they covered my tails. I can't use them now."

"Actually, you can," Jason walked up and gently grabbed a tail so he could point to the tip. "The red color isn't just for show. They managed to find a crystalline structure that your natural energy beams can pass right through without doing any damage. By the way, you can retract the helmet like mine by pressing this twice."

Jason pointed to an open helmet icon above a closed version. When Sundale tapped it twice, his helmet retracted to expose his face up to his ears. It also meant he saw his scar among an almost full coat for the first time. It was a thin line, maybe just over two inches long from end to end, streaking over his right eye. His ears and tails dropped as the pain came forward again.

In most cases, a scar would be a sign of experience in a holdren. For Sundale, this one only reminded him of everything that happened. Everything he almost did. It would be there forever, and being among humans, it would be a lot harder to accept it as a part of him. Holdrens wouldn't give it a moment's thought. Humans would want to know where he got it. Even the question, however quickly refused, would take him back there. Back to the dark hole where he ...

Sundale shook his head with a growl as if shaking off an attacker. He refused to let himself go back there again. He'd been there too long already. He didn't want to give Admiral Solez the victory of always taking him back every time he thought about it.

Jason stepped beside him with heavy eyes. "You sure you're all right?"

Sundale huffed at his reflection again before looking at his friend. "**YES.**" When Jason's expression didn't change, Sundale found some details. "I still have a lot to recover from, Jason. Seeing my scar like this brought back some bad memories."

"You don't have to rush this, you know. You can take all the time you need to really heal from it. Gold 1 will still be there when you're ready."

"I've been dormant long enough. It's time I rejoined the hunt." Sundale again looked at Jason to direct his words at him. "Rejoined my pack."

Jason nodded approval while reaching up to scratch behind one of Sundale's ears, though abandoned the attempt because of the armor.

Sundale still responded with his three short barks that were only ever used for Jason.

Jason chuckled, then sighed in contentment. "I've missed you, Sundale. Gold 1 hasn't been the same without you."

"I'm sorry I've been away."

"Don't. Don't apologize for healing. I didn't listen when you told me what you needed. Hopefully I can do better."

"You already have. But I need to find Yarain so I can reconnect with her."

Jason sighed heavily this time. "Under the circumstances, I think ... there I go again. Sun, if I may ... suggest? I personally think it'd be better to wait a while. It's my understanding the worst part of the recovery is, or almost is, completed. As useful as Yarain has been, a second holdren won't change much at this point. I'll let you do what you think is best, but I think the best thing you can do is get back in a cockpit. We have relief supplies coming in the next day or two, at which point we'll be recalling all of our soldiers, including Yarain. Until then, I'm worried your presence would be too much of a distraction right now."

The fact that Jason caught himself kept Sundale from feeling anything, for there was nothing to react to. Nothing except a few valid points. If the situation was indeed close to being resolved, his talents as a holdren would be of little use. Except perhaps in finding bodies, and while he didn't think it would bother him, he saw no reason to risk being wrong. All of which left him with an easy choice: be a distraction for Yarain or get back in rhythm as Gold 1's AESO.

The choice was easy, except for one detail.

"She needs to know, Jason."

"She's still connected to PAICCA," Jason said. "Say the word, he'll tell her. Assuming scuttlebutt hasn't gotten there first. We could also send her a message ourselves. I just think having you down there will complicate things too much for her."

"I'll tell her then, if only in a message."

"Knowing her, that should be all she needs. In the meantime, we need to finish your training on the new armor system. There's still quite a bit left to cover. How to control it with your energy matrix, new features in the helmet, the shield, and my personal favorite; the muzzle blade."

Sundale's ears perked while curiosity pushed everything else out of his mind.

"Muzzle blade?"

CHAPTER 4

FROM ONE FRYING PAN TO ANOTHER

Sundale dug his teeth into his shoulder, trying to get at an itch through the light protection built in. It was one aspect he was finding hard to adjust to as he had less direct access to his body, and it was harder to properly scratch through the new material. While he'd started to find ways to do it; he was a long way from mastering it.

At least the effort gave him something to focus on. He'd been waiting in the hangar for Yarain's shuttle for what felt like decades. He still didn't know what he was going to say or do. They'd traded exactly four messages between them, with almost nothing said beyond confirmation of his status and why he was going to spend the time back behind a turret instead of joining her. As Jason predicted, she'd agreed with the decision. She'd also said she wanted to reconnect with her nose, not her ears. In other words, she wanted to smell her cub again before she could take him back.

As much as Sundale wanted that, the memory of her pained barks still rang in his mind as he switched to his hand claws to get at the itch. She'd tried several times, only to be ignored each time. In the wild, that kind of behavior would have you driven from the pack's territory, as you clearly had no intention of being a part of it. In this situation... Would she understand? Could he even explain it, in part or in full? Did he even deserve to be accepted back?

The fears swirled as Sundale managed to silence the itch. The only thing giving him hope was how quickly Jason had taken him back despite Sundale insisting he retain his own quarters. Except Jason was human. Holdrens do things a lot differently.

It only got worse when the shuttle finally appeared at the end of the hangar. As the lights guided it to a pad, Sundale found himself unable to move. He didn't know what he'd say or how he should feel, so his body stayed still while his heart bounced around in his chest. A dozen times a second, he almost left, but he couldn't seem to run away either. The only thing he could settle on was one thought: as first mother, it was up to her whether or not he got to come back.

His ears stayed forward, waiting to find out which it was as the shuttle touched down. A moment later, Yarain walked out ahead of six other soldiers with a model of some kind in her hand. They all wore the new uniform, though the other soldiers had larger weapons or other additional gear that Yarain did not.

Sundale almost recognized the first man behind her, his voice as familiar as if he were remembering a dream. "It's not that simple, ma'am," the man said. "Nor would it be that easy, even for you."

"I'm aware of that, Harrison. I'm also aware... that..."

She trailed off as her eyes and ears locked onto him. The others followed her gaze to him, at which point many smiled or nodded, save for one woman who barely moved at all. When Yarain did nothing beyond perking her ears, Sundale forced his ears to go forward as he softly barked the same call she'd given him weeks ago. In holdren terms, he was saying, "I am here."

That proved to be enough. She ran toward him without a word. Sundale held his place, allowing his first mother to dictate the encounter. When she got to him, she didn't slow for the slightest sniff. Yarain started licking his head and muzzle, her ears soft and affectionate whines coming non-stop. With their hands on each other's shoulders, Sundale did the same, matching her affection as they reforged the bond. At times, Yarain would pulse her energy matrix, sending an invisible wave out to feel her cub. Sundale returned it every time, with great care to ensure it matched his first mother's frequency. There was no room for thought here. It was two pack mates remembering who the other was after being apart for so long. Anything else was ignored.

As the licking faded, Yarain rubbed her muzzle against the side of Sundale's neck and head. She tried to tap her cheek gland to his, though he managed to avoid letting it happen without her noticing since it would betray the turmoil within. When she spoke, she used the Holdren animal sounds humans couldn't hear. *"It's about time you came back to me."*

No snarls, no raised fur, not a single fang. Just like Jason, all she seemed to care about was that he was there. Sundale had nothing to hide behind now, nor did he have a reason to fear.

"I had to heal my way," he said.

"You've returned to the pack. How you got here is irrelevant."

What matters is the present. She'd said that right after his rescue, and it had caused much of his pain at the time. Now it was the source of his joy. She didn't care about what happened before. She only cared about the now. In the now, they were together, ready to rejoin the hunt. Somewhere, a part of him wondered if she would have chased him out had they been in the wild. Her words and emotions kept it silent. Who cares if she would have? She wasn't now, and that's all he cared about. That said, he still didn't let their cheek glands meet. It would let her read him in a deeper way, and she might find the truth he was still hiding from her. Thankfully, she didn't seem to notice as they traded rubs and licks.

Yarain broke the affection. She took a step back to look at him, and he at her. Only then did he notice a second star between the falcon wings on her shoulders.

"You got promoted?" he said.

Yarain's ears flashed back in a holdren blush. *"Jason did it, so I could better lead your rescue."* One ear turned toward the soldiers who were standing near, but at a respectful distance, until Yarain motioned for them to come closer. "This is COB Team. Otherwise known as the Cobras. They're the team that rescued you."

The captain she'd called Harrison chuckled with a shake of his head. "We hardly did it alone, ma'am."

"If you call me modest one more time, I *will* bite you."

The team laughed, and Sundale panted one of his own. *That sounds like her.* He offered a hand, which Harrison stepped forward to give a firm shake. Their proximity gave Sundale a chance to catch his scent. Memories popped in through a fog. Not enough to react to, but enough to know this man was there beside his mother in his defense.

"I'm glad to actually meet you," Sundale said.

"The pleasure's all mine, sir," Harrison said. "I'm glad to see you're well."

That's a bit of a stretch. "I'm ... better."

"I'll take that. You had a lot to recover from. To see you standing tall once more proves we did our job."

Sundale looked at Yarain even as pained memories forced his ears back. "I had help, too."

Yarain's ears again showed blush while the team nodded. "Don't you start," Yarain said.

Another round of laughs went through the gathered group.

Sundale dropped his ears and eyes in apology, playful though it may be. Though when he did, he saw the model in her hand. Now able to see it, he saw it was a Scorn fighter with Gold 1's markings, as well as what appeared to be light fire damage.

"What's that?" he asked.

Yarain looked at it, then held it to her chest with falling ears. The entire team folded their hands with a soft bow of their heads in a similar display of mourning. With no words to offer, Sundale could only let his ears shift in confusion.

"It's ... a reminder," Yarain finally said.

"A reminder? But holdrens don't—"

PAICCA cut him off. "Gold 1 report to F-Con One immediately. Repeat, Gold 1 report to F-Con One immediately."

Yarain gave a soft growl before going to her wrist comm. "Yarain and Sundale acknowledge. I'll explain later."

Sundale's ears turned back in a moment of submission. In holdren terms, he'd agreed to drop the conversation, though his confusion remained beneath. Yarain handed the model to Captain Harrison. "Put that in my quarters, then get your team some rest. They earned it."

Harrison accepted it with a half-hearted salute. "Yes, ma'am. Captain, be seeing you I hope."

"So do I," Sundale said.

Yarain and Sundale left first for the nearest lift. After Yarain ordered it to deck 16, her ears turned to her cub.

"There was more meaning in your reply to Harrison," she said.

Sundale's ears fell again, this time more in pain than anything else. *"Part of me is questioning whether I should return."*

"I thought your wounds were healed."

Not all of them. *"It's . . . the emotional that has me doubting."*

Yarain leaned over to rub her head against his. *"Whatever you decide, the pack will endure."*

To a human, it might have sounded callous. To Sundale, it was anything but. The phrase didn't mean the pack would go on without him. It meant the pack would still be there to assist him. In other words, stay or resign—she wasn't going to reject him. It lifted more weight from his back as she had yet to show any sign of reprimand or judgment of his actions. If she felt anything about it, it had been left behind in the past. She was just glad to have him back, even if he were to resign. Something that seemed less likely with each passing second.

When the doors opened to deck 16, Sundale felt that chance had been reduced to zero as he followed his superior officer toward the core of the carrier's hull. They didn't say another word as the walls took on a thicker, blocky look to go with the increased armor that protected the command center of the *I.C.V. Alamo*. Each corridor intersection around the command block was covered by two small-scale turrets with long, mounted rifles that ended in miniature Gatling barrels. These Personal Mini Guns, or PMGs, were manned by soldiers in the fully deployed, new standard-issue armor. Each set of doors beyond was flanked by two more guards in the same with standard plasmoid rifles. A small downgrade from the days of old when Interstar had a harder time keeping out Marcallan boarding parties. Back then, there would have been soldiers in full combat armor or with said combat armor in a place to be donned within no more than fifteen seconds. Much to the delight of said guards, Interstar got better, and thus security could be laxed a little.

This meant Sundale and Yarain, being well known and summoned, could pass by without any kind of verification. They moved on past the Flag Ready Room and Security and headed into the room marked "Flag Conference Room One." The room wasn't any different than any other conference room—round table, controls all around, and displays in the middle and on the wall. The only difference was that it was reserved for flag operations, meaning whatever they had been summoned for was guaranteed to be classified and/or incredibly important.

Jason was already there, as was Admiral Redding; an Asian man who stood as tall as Jason did, but with lighter skin, large body and cheek bones, and slick hair that still remained clean looking. However, his features currently had more weight than the entire ship. "*This can't be good*," Sundale and Yarain said to each other as they saluted.

Admiral Redding's arm seemed as heavy as his face in his salute. "At ease. I'm glad to have Gold 1 back at full strength, especially now."

"Well, that's ominous," Jason said. "With all due respect, sir, what's wrong? Why do you look like someone died?"

"Might be worse, Colonel. A few minutes ago, we intercepted a priority message from Polaris leadership to one of their field commanders.

It contained orders to secure a recently confirmed target of great strategic importance. We don't have confirmation, we don't know for sure it's real, it could all be nothing,"

Yarain didn't even blink. "We wouldn't be here if you believed that, sir."

Admiral Redding leaned on a chair and drummed his fingers in thought. Yarain and Sundale perked their ears while Sundale fought the urge to growl, wave his tails, or both. *Just spit it out already.*

Redding sighed two or three times before facing Sundale and Yarain directly. "Polaris may be sending a fleet to secure your homeworld."

For a moment, not a hair moved on either holdren save for their ears shooting forward. Shock of the words had to burrow past Sundale's frozen skin, then search for a neuron that would accept the message. Even then, his mind couldn't, wouldn't, shouldn't accept it. After so many years of searching, could it be possible? The idea that the answer might be "yes" kept his mind from thinking about any other part of it.

Jason had gone nearly as stiff and no less wide-eyed. "Come again, sir?"

"If the message is confirmed, and we're checking that now, Polaris has found the holdren homeworld, and they want to 'secure' it. More than that wasn't in the message."

Sundale had started breathing again, which meant he was able to touch on the idea of Admiral Solez gaining control of his homeworld. The thought turned his stomach into a pretzel, flattened it, and set it on fire, a dozen times a second. The only good part was he was so busy being sick there wasn't room for any shudders or darkness.

That said, there was still room for a growl he had to keep from forming. "What are we doing about it?"

"First thing we're doing is getting confirmation," Admiral Redding said. "For all we know, this is either a trap, or a ploy to pull us away from their real targets. We're talking about a point of space we've never seen before that's unnervingly close to Polaris space and is two and a half days away at group maximum. Less if we left half our escorts behind, which I think we all agree would be a bad idea."

"We ***CAN'T*** let them gain control of our homeworld!"

"And we won't," Jason said with no emotion at all, "assuming we can be sure it's really in danger. Much as I hate waiting, Admiral Redding is right. Polaris is absolutely capable of putting together a trap or hoax with this kind of bait. We need to be sure they really found it before we can take you home."

The word "home" left an almost audible echo in Sundale's ears. His insides tightened into a knotted ball as, much like before, his mind took him somewhere. Except this time, the sensation was much different. While he didn't for a second lose reality, a moment flooded through his mind that was coherent, exact, and most importantly, crystal clear.

My ears fell as far as they would go. I knew what was coming. Not exactly, perhaps, but the general idea was enough to send my insides shaking like an earthquake. Instinct drew a growl from me as my body tried to defend itself from a fate I knew I couldn't prevent. Each breath I took shook my gut as I prepared to face that fate. My only hope was Simon. The turmoil was still there in his eyes as he watched everything unfold. My eyes locked onto him, asking, begging him to do something. Even if that something was to kill me, at least it would be over.

"I won't doom my pack by helping you," I said.

Admiral Solez's tone lost all semblance of benevolence. "By being in Interstar, you already have. Face it, Captain. You've doomed your entire race by siding with them." Admiral Solez recoiled as if someone had punched him in the gut. There was a sharp change in his scent, too, as if he were suddenly terrified of something. Whatever it was, it lasted but a second. The breath he took came back out in a sigh. "I could stop that. I could even let you go home. All you have to do is give me what I want!"

The change in him, mixed with the joke that he'd actually let me go, filled me with enough fire and confidence to send my ears up and my throat into a full snarl in his direction. Had I not been restrained; I would have torn him in half with one bite. "As you humans say, over my **DEAD BODY!**"

"As you wish."

The memory hit so hard; Sundale could almost feel it. Yet, at the same time, it remained in the past the entire time. In fact, it passed so quickly, by the time Jason's eyes darkened with concern, Sundale's ears were already perking in response to his certainty.

"It's real," Sundale said.

"What makes you say so?" Jason said, curious but in no way doubting him.

Sundale hesitated so he could fight past the memory to collect the details humans would need. "When Admiral Solez . . . interrogated me, at one point, he talked about how I had 'doomed my entire race' by siding with Interstar. The moment he said it, I could smell fear on him, and he seemed to have to recollect himself. After that, he said he . . ." A soft shudder and a growl shook him as Sundale fought to keep the fear of that time from taking over. He had to shake his head once to win the battle so he could continue. "He said he could stop it and let me go home if I gave him what he wanted."

Admiral Redding folded his arms while his lips vanished into a thin line. "He could have been messing with you. Men like him will say anything if they think it will break their . . . God, I wish I had a good word there."

"Prisoners," Jason and Sundale said.

Admiral Redding's lips lifted into a soft smile. "Right. Anyway, there's no way to know. I still need more."

Yarain's hackles started rising, yet the scent Sundale got was fear, not anger.

"We **CAN'T** sit by and do **NOTHING**," she said, half ruffing some words.

"We're hardly doing nothing, Major. Intel next door has their boards white hot trying to . . ."

He trailed off as the inner doors opened, and a young man with clean, clear, chiseled face lines and dark black hair walked in with a clip-com.

"Admiral, we just got—" Simon Solez stopped cold. He managed to gasp despite being mid-sentence. His eyes locked onto Sundale with all they had, which let Sundale see the turmoil was long gone. It had been replaced with the same certainty that had let him trust an unknown human many years ago.

Though Simon was not that human, he wasn't the same as he'd been when Sundale last saw him either. More than the change in his eyes, Simon's face was somehow smoother. Cleaner shaven, maybe? He definitely stood straighter as if he were claiming the spot he stood on. More visible to all was that he was wearing an Interstar uniform with two falcon wings on his shoulders and a tiny ship icon below it that marked him as a Lieutenant Junior Grade in Caelnav, the main fleet branch of Interstar. More surprising to Sundale was the intelligence tab on his chest. *How did he earn that so fast?*

Simon was about to take a step forward when Admiral Redding turned to face him. "You were saying, Lieutenant?"

Simon shook his head, offered Sundale a nod, then pulled himself up into something close to attention. "I'm sorry, sir. We just got word from your scouts on the line. A Polaris fleet is definitely being gathered. There's also this, sir." Simon handed Admiral Redding the clip-com while shooting Sundale another smile. "I used the last of the codes I took with me to catch this. It's direct orders from someone within the Polaris leadership to secure a world scouted during Operation Digs fourteen years ago. It appears to confirm everything we've heard so far, sir."

Admiral Redding looked over the report while the members of Gold 1 waited, two of them with shifting ears. Even they knew that right now, Admiral Redding needed to be left alone.

"Just who is this 1-18-7?" he finally said. "And how is this proof?"

"I can only guess blindly, sir, but if you read on, there are communication protocols, order protocols, and reports from that old mission that frankly can't be faked, sir. Not in this kind of detail."

While Admiral Redding read on, Sundale turned an ear toward Jason, whose head had snapped up at the mention of "1-18-7". It had been among the code names in the info the Marcallan Prefect gave them. Sundale could see Jason's eyes begin to almost vibrate, a small tick most humans would miss, which suggested Jason's mind was hard at work about something. Sundale racked his own brain a moment and found only one reference to the name: a code name on secret communications between members of some jantan/human conspiracy. This made zero sense, considering Prefect Colark had been certain that "1-18-7" was someone from within the United Systems Republic. The idea that he could be wrong, or worse, could be right, had Sundale's ears perking toward Jason as he formed a question.

The question was shot-down with a subtle wave of Jason's hand. When Sundale turned his head at him, Jason repeated the gesture to make the order clear. "Say nothing." While Sundale didn't understand why, he yielded to his first father in this matter, even as he prayed to any god listening that it wasn't a mistake.

Sundale had just ticked his ears forward in understanding when PAICCA chimed in. "Admiral, that message you were expecting? It's here. Details on console one."

Admiral Redding tucked the clip-com under his arm while stepping up to the table. Yet the moment he did, Yarain stepped forward, "Excuse me, sir. May I see that report?"

"Looking for something, Major?" Admiral Redding said.

"Confirmation of a theory, sir."

Admiral Redding shrugged and handed it over. He then tapped at the console to bring something up on a smaller screen next to it. Sundale watched his shoulders rise and fall and hoped they were orders settling the matter.

When Admiral Redding looked up, Sundale could almost see the man's hackles rising.

"Command wants us to confirm and defend," Admiral Redding said.

Sundale couldn't help a breath that felt like he'd just cut his weight in half. "Then let's get moving."

"Not so fast, Captain. We're down two cruisers that are too damaged to make Hyper Light. The Rhine Carrier group is a day behind us. I, for one, would much rather wait for them to be sure we can handle anything we run into."

You can't be serious. "We don't have time for that. If Polaris gets there first . . ."

Sundale felt the darkness closing in, so much so that he had to cringe and focus to keep it from swallowing him whole. As it was, he still heard the voices, and he felt the panic send every hair on fire as he looked for exits he knew weren't there. Or at least, that's what it felt like for the moment it took.

Yarain's hand on his shoulder ended it. Her eyes bored into him as if they could find—and cure—the injury causing his pain. Jason, meanwhile, had gone stiff as a board with eyes like lava.

"Sundale's right, sir," Jason said. "We let Polaris beat us there, they'll be entrenched, and a lot can happen in a day."

"Which is exactly what I'm afraid of, Colonel," Admiral Redding said. "We go it alone; we'll be on *our* own for that day. Their reinforcements will be closer than ours. It's not worth the risk. After all, they aren't our civilians. That should keep them safe for a while."

Now it was Yarain and Sundale whose hackles started rising. Their ears went straight as well, with a growl forming in both of their throats. Yarain opened her mouth to speak, but Jason had raised a hand without skipping a beat. It stopped both her sentence and both of their growls.

"Easy, you two," he said. "With respect, sir, that makes them all the more vulnerable. With Phoenix Perch, they had to worry about our response. With the holdrens, in their minds, they don't have to, because they don't know that we know about it. They were brutal with one holdren, sir. Just think what they'd do if they had thousands."

Admiral Redding took a breath like he was about to yell. Then it stopped and came out simply angry. "Captain Sundale was an enemy combatant with information they wanted. These holdrens are pure civilians. There's no reason to mistreat them."

Again, Yarain tried to speak. Again, she was stopped, this time by Simon stepping forward with a deliberate stomp of his foot. "*Sir*, with all due respect, look at Phoenix Perch, look at Sundale's eye, and try that thought again."

While no one knows if Admiral Redding thought of Phoenix Perch, he did take a moment to stare at Sundale's scar. When he noticed the stare, Sundale turned his head so the admiral could see nothing else of his face. *Maybe this scar does have its uses*, Sundale thought when he saw the admiral swallow as if trying to keep his lunch down. Seeing it was working; Sundale opened his uniform so he could work with his belly fur. He managed to part it just enough to show a small portion of the long gash that would be forever buried under his fur.

"There were more that healed," Sundale said.

Yarain pounced before she could be stopped again. "There's more, sir. If I read this right, it was Polaris, not Raiders, that bombarded my homeworld all those years ago."

"Probably both in a way," Simon said. "Operation Digs was to find a new base for our 'non-ships' after we lost New Holland. What you now call Phoenix Perch."

The ears on both holdrens shot up in shock. Jason's face made up for the lack of ears that could do the same. "Wait," Jason said, "are you saying the Raiders are actually Polaris?"

"Yes, sir. There are a lot of people out there who are true and honest pirates, but a great many were actually our ships. It was . . . seen as a way to steal resources without anyone knowing it was us. Later, it became a way to do the same without anyone knowing we survived."

Now Jason turned to stare at the admiral. "Well, that explains a lot. More to the point, back then, they didn't know a thing about holdrens. Just imagine what they'll do now."

Admiral Redding again swallowed, sighed, then nodded with heavier eyes. "All right. You've made your point. Fall in."

Sundale rezipped his uniform as the gathered group followed Admiral Redding through the inner doors onto the Flag Bridge, otherwise called the Combat Information Center. From here, Admiral Redding had direct command over the carrier group, and any extension beyond that wasn't allocated to someone else. One wall was covered in displays, while the room itself was filled with several stations. In the center of the room was a ring of stations surrounding an area with a large holo-map and two smaller ones capable of displaying a three-dimensional grid of a battle, details of a fleet, or anything the admiral wanted.

Admiral Redding led the group toward the holo-table. Once there, he turned to one of the stations around him.

"Get on the horn to the *Yamamoto*. We need to borrow two cruisers, a battleship, and any other ships they can spare for our mission. They'll have ample reinforcements in a few hours, and our two wounded birds can still fight if they need to. If they can spare Scorns to cover ours that are lost or damaged, I want them too."

"Already on it, sir," the officer said. "Command sent word we may need them with the orders. Though if I may, sir, they didn't say anything about additional ships."

"I'm not charging into an unknown situation without some extra beef. Get me the ships, Petty Officer. As many as you can. Don't take no for an answer, and don't be afraid to tell them why we need them."

"Aye, sir."

Admiral Redding turned from him to a different station without so much as a huff. "Once the Scorns are aboard and all ships are transferred to our command, have the group assume cloak and proceed at group maximum to the coordinates listed in the message. It's time we got these foxes home."

CHAPTER 5

SECOND CONTACT

Sundale lay on the window seat, watching the stars through the window while trying to get his heart to settle down, or at least make up its mind.

"Home." An odd twinge had been running up and down his spine ever since Admiral Redding used the word; and not the kind that was still touching his energy matrix from time to time. It felt so strange, like something that didn't apply to him. While he'd felt more than comfortable, no place he'd been had ever felt like "home." Now that he might finally be going to the place of his birth, it too failed to offer any kind of extra emotion. He might as well have been going to Jason's mother's house. Yet, at the same time, a part of him was in that excited-and-afraid type of anxious. Even if there wasn't any emotion to it, he was finally going to find his homeworld. That meant something, or it was supposed to.

The problem is, every time he thought about it, his mind latched onto other words.

"Scared stray."

They rang in Sundale's mind. Though, unlike previous times, this was simply a thought that wouldn't go away. The scared part was discarded, for even as he had stood defiant at the time, he had been afraid of what was going to happen to him. *And with good reason*, he thought, taking a breath to stop a shudder before it started. It was the "stray" part that bothered him.

A stray has no home, no place to run to in search of safety, no family to protect them. He'd always had that. First with Karol, the Interstar officer who raised him, then with Jason and Sundale's parents. Later, the circle of protection grew to include parts of the Gold Group and others. Now he was going home. He'd been wishing for years he could find it, and now he had. In danger or not, he was going home.

So why do I still feel like a stray?

Sundale didn't know where the feeling came from, only that he couldn't hide from it. A part of him said he only had himself to blame. Though he'd upgraded from the basic room now that he was back on duty, he had still chosen to stay in his own quarters alone. As part of a lead fighter, he got one of the few rooms with a dedicated separate bedroom and bathroom, a cut-out desk workspace on one wall and a comfortable, if tiny, love seat and table with a window seat for eating or relaxing. Yarain and Jason had expressed surprise but otherwise didn't push him on it. As much as they had welcomed him back, the idea of living with them still threatened to trigger his wounds.

Perhaps it was his own choice and his own fault, but try as he might, that didn't feel like enough of a reason for how he felt right now. Jason, Yarain, and the Gold Group had all welcomed him back with open arms, literally in Carter's case. He'd even felt cherished and cared for again.

Yet he could almost see himself sitting in front of a door, rain soaking his fur, wishing he lived on the other side in warmth and safety. Despite all the reasons to feel otherwise, Sundale still felt like he was trapped on the outside of that door.

Nothing he remembered seemed to help either. Not the hunts he'd shared with his parents, not the days spent absorbing the wild, not even the fond memories of his time with Karol and Jason respectively. Memories he neither regretted nor wished to change, in spite of everything else that came with them. Still, there was always that door he wanted to enter but never could. And he couldn't understand why it was even there.

Unfortunately, he had little else to do besides ask the questions. The fleet had prepared as best they could, but they were still over a day away when they ran out of ways to do so. Jason and Admiral Redding had laid out the plan, with Yarain offering insight on how best to make contact should they arrive first. Sundale could only listen, having too few memories of "home" to offer enough help. Though he did have to remind Jason not to take on the risks alone, so perhaps his presence wasn't a total waste. Even so, Sundale felt out of place there, which only kept the "stray" feeling that much fresher in his mind.

More so when he realized he doubted he could offer much in the way of insight or help. He'd interacted with his parents, sure, but there were other elements to the wild Holdren life that he didn't know. How does one greet another pack? How are you supposed to respond to someone you know? What do you do if they reject you? Or worse, try to kill you? Yarain knew all this by heart. Sundale barely had any idea. *Scared stray indeed.* Sadly, all he could do was lie next to the window, his thoughts light-years away and not all in the same direction.

It was Jason that found him that night. Sundale had barely responded to the door chime other than to grant entry, but it was a sigh from Jason that announced the conversation before it began. "I see it runs in the family."

Sundale turned with perked ears, oddly not frustrated by the intrusion. A tilt of his head asked for clarification.

"Window-moping," Jason said. "When we thought you were dead, Yarain spent all of her free time on the window seat. I thought you were foxes, not cats."

Sundale gave a gentle growl, but he knew Jason was teasing. "We're holdrens. We do what we do."

Jason leaned on the arm of the couch with crossed arms. "And what are you doing? Yarain seems to think you're just worried about going home again. Maybe because she's uneasy about it herself. Doctor Blount is of the mind you're still processing your scars. So, what is it?"

All of the above, and a thousand things more. "I have a lot on my mind."

"That's not an answer, Sun."

Sundale glared at him with a soft growl and an even smaller rise in his hackles. "You can't help with this, Jason."

"Says who? Look, Sun, I can't imagine what you're going through, but you can't face it alone."

Sundale perked his ears further. "That's ironic coming from you."

This time, Jason's smile held no joy at all. "You're definitely feeling better. I'm trying to get you to let us help you, Captain."

"I **WILL** . . . when I know how you can."

Sundale tried to add the rest in his glare. He couldn't form the words, but these were things no human could fully understand. Not even Jason. After all, Sundale couldn't figure it out himself. Until that changed, he needed to sort it out on his own terms. Anything else would only get in the way.

Jason sighed, nearly growling himself, but he was nodding. "All right. I won't make the same mistake again. But don't you dare leave me or Yarain out of it. We care too much to let you fight your battles alone. Can you do that much for me?"

Depends. Can you start doing the same? "**YES**," Sundale barked the word, but it only made Jason smile. He rubbed Sundale between the ears and respected his request to leave it be.

And leave it be they did. The topic never came up again the rest of the way. Instead, they spent the time getting Sundale more acquainted with the new uniform. He'd gotten qualified to use it, but Sundale still wanted to get as seamless as possible with it. To say nothing of getting used to the fact that it shifted as he moved more than the old one. Then again, by the time they arrived, he'd already stopped thinking about it.

The fleet stopped near the sun of a nearby system, then a probe was sent to check for Polaris ships. When they found none at all, Gold 1 was given clearance to proceed.

Admiral Redding met them by the fighter as they prepared to leave. "Be safe, you three. First Squad will stay in high orbit to watch your back. I've got the rest of the Gold Group and the Three-Piece squad on alert-standby. Say the word, they'll be at your side in fifteen minutes or less."

"Thank you, sir," Jason said. "Sun, Yarain, let's get moving."

Jason turned to enter, but Admiral Redding grabbed his arm in the doorway. "Remember your orders, Colonel. Don't throw your life away if you don't have to. You have assistance. Use it."

Jason shook his arm free. "Everyone seems so worried about me going it alone. I'm not alone, sir. I have Yarain and Sundale with me."

"For now," Sundale said. "You've tried to leave us out before."

Jason raised his hands in surrender. "All right, all right. If things turn ugly, I promise I'll call for help. Is that sufficient, sir? Sun?"

Admiral Redding nodded with a tilt of his head. "I think so. So long as you honor it. Good hunting, Gold 1."

They traded salutes, then Admiral Redding left.

Gold 1 lifted off without a word between them beyond the preflight. Sundale still had a full mind, and he suspected Jason was still a little hot from the pre-launch conversation. Not that he'd ever admit it of course.

Just as well. The closer they got to the planet, the tighter Sundale's insides got. The anxiousness was, of course, part of it, but those words—*scared stray*—were still echoing in his mind. More so because he still wasn't sure what to do once they got there. Jason would be relying on him for help he couldn't offer. The only thing that helped was that as second seat, one of his jobs was making sure their emissions didn't overpower their cloak while still allowing sensor bursts for Yarain's scopes. That balancing act gave him something to focus on besides his constant ping-pong of emotions.

First Squad dropped out of hyperlight well short of their target. Almost immediately, Sundale's console woke up as expected.

"There's the radiation alert," Sundale said. "I have a better idea why. The sun's magnetic field is highly irregular and is creating a larger than normal radiation field throughout the system."

"The probe told us we'd have some bad weather," Jason said. "Anything else I need to know?"

"Sensor stability down eight percent. Communications will need adjusting."

"PAICCA will have that done shortly," Yarain added.

"Roger that," Jason said. "Scopes?"

"Clear," Yarain said.

"Copy. First Squad, hold position while we check the planet."

The rest of the squad hung back while Jason flew closer, still under cloak. It wasn't long before a small sphere grew into a larger one with blue oceans and land masses that held only brown, white, orange, and yellow on their surfaces. Beyond that and different continent shapes, the planet didn't seem that different than Earth. Twin moons lay on the far side in an impossible yet undeniable orbit of their own. Even in the short time it took Gold 1 to reach the planet, it seemed as though the moons spun around each other like a bolo yet maintained their position to each other and the planet. Meanwhile, just as Jason came to a halt in orbit, the planet itself had something else for Sundale's panel to comment on.

But Yarain spoke first. "It's real."

Sundale couldn't help turning to look at her, as did Jason. "What do you mean 'it's real'?" Jason asked.

"We found our home, Jason."

"How can you be sure?"

"It looks just as it did the last time I left it."

Home. Yarain used the word yet for Sundale, it felt hollow, empty, as if it was only her word. He checked his targeting screen so he could get a better look at the planet below. He stared at it and felt nothing. It was someone else's homeworld. Someone else's door.

Jason, meanwhile, had returned to facing forward. "Hard to argue with that, I guess. Still; Sun? Any chance of confirmation?"

Sundale remembered his sensor screen that was showing the result of the latest sweep. His voice was heavy as he looked over the data. "I'm showing holdren life signs . . . millions of them."

"That settles it. If it ain't home, it's one really big colony. Have First Squad join us in orbit. Sun? Anything I need to know before we go down?"

Sundale's voice was nowhere in the galaxy. "I'm not the one to ask."

Jason's voice came back hard enough to drag an ear up, yet still attentive. "Hey, don't you fall apart on me now, Captain. You're still my AESO. With the sun going nuts, I need you to tell me what the risks are or if there are any other surprises to be aware of."

That I can do, Sundale thought, remembering the first thing his sensors had noticed. "Aye, sir. The planet's magnetic field is also irregular. It's stronger than anything on record."

"Is that going to cause any problems?"

"No."

"What about the radiation? Do they cancel out?"

"No, but our energy matrix will cover the difference. As for you, you won't need treatment unless you're down there for more than five days straight."

"All right then. How do we proceed from here?"

Sundale again fought to keep his ears up while Yarain took her turn to answer. "I'm scanning for a good LZ now. Try to keep our descent as slow as possible and drop the cloak. Let them see us."

"You want us in the open?" Jason asked. "And for that matter, won't an unknown flying . . . *thing* scare them?"

"No more than a meteor. It's **BETTER** to be where they can get a good look at us without exposing themselves."

"Okay. Once we're down, what then?"

"We wait a while before we emerge. Then we walk out, slow, calm, and as relaxed as possible. Sundale and I should be naked."

"But not me?" It was almost a request rather than a question. One Sundale understood. Humans didn't like being naked. He never did understand why, aside from the very real need for shoes, but humans did a lot he didn't understand.

Yarain didn't miss a beat. "It won't matter. Might as well have you in uniform to prepare for that conversation."

"I guess I can see that. Anything else?"

"If I tell you to do something, don't ask, don't look at me, just **DO** it. When we're outside, don't speak at all until Sundale or I tell you it's safe. Leave your weapons in the fighter."

"Not happening. If things turn south—"

"You'll be **DEAD** before you know what hit you. Going without will keep you from entering an aggressive posture, which *will* get us killed."

Jason's sigh weighed a ton. "Copy that. And I thought combat was dangerous."

"They're wild animals, Jason," Sundale said.

"That's what I'm afraid of. Intentional or not, you missed when we first met. From what Yarain just said, it sounds like these holdrens won't. I'm worried about triggering their instincts by accident. Even a sneeze could set them off."

"Listen to me, and we'll be fine," Yarain said, a smile in her voice.

"I hope you're right. Got a landing zone for us?"

"**YES**, sir. Sending coordinates."

Jason waited for the rest of First Squad to arrive, then clicked off the cloak just before the nav-shields flared at entry. Sundale's view was obscured by the flames for a moment, then they faded to allow a better look at the territory below. The forest appeared to be a lush carpet of yellow and orange that stretched for miles around, broken only by mountains, streams, and smaller clearings. Against one of the mountains were two large lakes, one appearing to feed the other in a waterfall big enough for the mist to be seen from high above. Their descent was slow, as requested, but also silent. Jason no doubt focused on the task at hand, Yarain possibly pondering her return.

As for Sundale, he continued to feel nothing. As the carpet slowly became individual trees and patches of grassy meadows, there was no emotional connection to it. He was about to land on his homeworld, yet he still felt nothing. Well, almost. He was nervous about the conversation they were going to have with these holdrens, assuming they were able to manage it at all. With that came the concern about keeping themselves safe. One thing he *did* know was that holdrens were fiercely territorial. If this pack felt threatened, they would not hesitate to kill to defend it. Even if they did make contact, there was still so much that could go wrong.

Oddly enough, Sundale's scar proved to be a calming force. To holdrens, it would be a sign of strife survived. Add the fact that his eye was clearly intact, and the pack would see it as a sign that he was strong enough to recover from such a wound. That strength, combined with Yarain's intact instincts, might be enough to keep the interaction from turning lethal.

Yarain's course took them toward a forest that seemed to be in spring, with a large clearing in the middle of it. Jason dove straight for the clearing so he didn't fly over the trees. Sundale ran a quick scan to confirm there was at least one pack in the area nearby.

As the clearing came into view, Sundale could see a meadow of low grass with a scattering of wildflowers covering the area in their usual array of colors. It gave way to thick trees all around, most of which had branches that ended in medium-to-thick bushes of leaves, much like the cottonwood trees from Jason's hometown. Others were a thick bush at the top, or smaller bushes at the end of branches, while still others were more like thin oak trees.

As they approached for a landing, Jason said, "Incredible. From this angle, it's like the entire forest is on fire. Certainly explains your fur color. A still holdren would vanish in that."

"And we often do," Yarain said.

"Bet that makes hunts easy. Prey could walk right by without seeing you."

"So do predators."

"You say that like you have to worry about any."

"We do."

"Hold that thought." Jason landed the fighter so gently there was hardly any thud to it. He shut down the engines, then stood and faced Yarain. "What do you mean you do? Pack animal, large size, *sentience*, your tails, what's out there that keeps you from being apex predators?"

Yarain and Sundale had already begun removing their gear and uniforms. Sundale kept his eyes on his sensors while Yarain answered Jason's questions.

"Among them? Large cats with venom that can kill us. Flocks of birds that have their ways to outmaneuver groups. And there's the jesween, which is immune to our tails and far too large for a pack to fight safely."

"Immune?! Great. Even if we do survive first contact, something else may get us."

"I wouldn't worry, Jason. The jesween prefers desert climates. The rest have a hard time hunting large groups."

"*We* are not a large group."

"The pack is," Sundale said. "If we make contact, we'll become part of their group."

Yarain added, "We'll be fine, Jason. Just stay alert."

"Yarain, between your homeworld and the Polaris fleet that is who knows how far behind us, I don't think I could get any more alert."

Yarain ruffed once in amusement as she and Sundale draped the last of their gear on their chairs. Yarain checked her screens while Sundale joined Jason in looking out the window. For the first time, things felt familiar for Sundale. Something in the trees, in the birds that were in the air, pulled on an instinct he couldn't place. It was only a sense that he'd been here before. Whether or not that meant he'd been *here* before, he couldn't tell.

Though it was soon soured by the same feeling he'd been facing the entire trip. More than ever, it felt like someone else's door. Worse, it was Yarain's door but not his. She grew up out there, led a pack, hunted for so long, she knew trails by instinct. He'd been taken away long before his first hunt. His instincts even now tried to tell him things, but they were distant whispers that meant little to him.

With no sign of the pack, Sundale checked his sensor screen to confirm that not only were they out there, but they were approaching their position. He then took his primal form and waited for Yarain to give the word to exit.

Jason held his vigil, though he did watch Sundale land on his paws. "This is your show, Major. How long should we wait?"

Yarain checked Sundale's sensor screen before replying. "We go now."

Yarain didn't wait to ask. She punched the console to open the door, then she too took her four-legged form. Jason hesitantly left his knife and P-mag on his seat, then followed Yarain as she led him and Sundale out into the meadow.

Sundale got a taste the moment the door opened, but it wasn't until his paws found dirt that things came alive inside him. It was actually his energy matrix that reacted first. He could instantly feel the planet's magnetic field in a way he'd never felt before. It was like a wind he could tap into and almost see if he focused. Direction became instinctive, as if he could find his way blind were it not for terrain or other hazards.

Then came the smells. A wave of sweetness that only healthy grass has. The flowers, still varied and vibrant like Earth, offered their own arrays of smells on the wind. A breeze brought more sweet, sour, and heavy scents that tried to tell him things he should know. Some were trees, some were creatures, some were merely damp bark and soil that suggested rain had fallen not that long ago. Warmth filled the air, but only just enough to help the forest dry out. All things considered, with his fur still not back to full thickness, he wouldn't even need to pant unless he exerted himself.

The grass was shorter than he thought, but still tall enough to just brush his under-belly, which provided a soft contact that woke more of the wild than anything ever had. Once he felt the warmth of the sun, and a soft breeze brush his fur, a wave of emotion crashed through him that forced his eyes to close as it took all thought and feeling away.

When his eyes opened again, he had no rank, no title, no serial number. He was just a holdren, standing in the wild with his pack. There wasn't a door anymore. There was a forest that, granted, was not his, but it was where he belonged. His instincts knew what to do and where to go here. It wasn't quite home, but for the first time, he saw a chance of that changing.

The moment was broken when Yarain started barking. It was a series of short barks given in quick succession, much like his call of affection for Jason. Her call, however, went on for several barks, was much louder, and carried a very different message that Sundale was surprised he fully understood.

Jason turned to Sundale, then visibly swallowed the question. Yarain turned an ear his way, offered a quick glance, then said, *"You can tell him what I'm doing. Remember, he needs details."*

Sundale ticked his ears forward, then turned to Jason. "She's announcing our presence to the owner of the territory. It's like ringing a doorbell. At worst, we'll be warned to leave. At best—"

A single, yelling bark came from the forest. Sundale and Yarain turned their ears toward the call, which was soon repeated. Whoever it was, the holdren was laying claim to the territory. Sundale and Yarain responded with a higher-pitched series of barks like the one before. In their terms, they were asking to speak with the pack's first parent. A long moment of silence, then the voice came back with a long, whistle-like howl that was soon answered from deeper in the forest. The holdren was calling for their pack to gather, and they were responding to say they were coming. Luckily, the howl held no malice or urgency, which was a very good sign.

Sundale looked at Yarain, who turned her ears back. *"We're being watched now. We shouldn't speak anything but Holdren."*

Sundale ticked his ears forward to show his understanding. All he could do was stare at Jason, who was staring at the forest with growing breath. Sundale kept his ears forward and his fur flat, though he needed a soft growl to get Jason's attention. Once he had it, they locked eyes, and Jason instantly calmed with an appreciative nod. Sundale had no idea how much Jason was able to infer, but there was nothing more he could do to help him. The rest was up to Yarain and the ever-awakening instincts in Sundale.

The trio watched the forest for eternal seconds. Then, at last, they saw movement in the trees. Just shadows at first, then yellow figures, then the first members of the pack. Three scouts had their ears up, and though their tails were waving, they weren't stiff or curved over. Another good sign. Soon after, more of the pack broke the full cover of the forest. Sundale could now see their markings varied heavily; some with only a few bits of orange, others with more white, some with less, some that only had markings on their legs and tails. He even saw one that was colored just like he was, save for a very minor variation on how the white touched the muzzle. The only consistent marking was the red tail tips for all, with matching bands for the males.

The scouts led the way with the pack close behind, yet they moved together as if all were a part of a greater whole. Every ear was up, every tail was waving, but there were no other signs of aggression or threat. Once the pack was out in full, Sundale counted fifteen members, though he doubted this was the entire pack. He and Yarain lowered themselves, pulled their ears back, and tucked their tails. One went between their legs, the others on either side of their bodies. They made a point to aim the tips down to complete the submissive display. Jason slowly dropped to one knee and further lowered his torso to make himself appear less threatening.

The moment he did, the pack halted, and one member lifted his head and tails, though the tips never curled over. His nose twitched up, testing the wind.

The first father, Sundale thought. *This could be good or bad.*

The pack, and their first father, watched them for a minute that felt like years. Then he turned and ruffed at one of the pack. It was a name and a command, but because of the distance, Sundale couldn't catch either. A young female emerged from the group alone, slow as the sun and cautious as a mouse. She made her way toward the trio, stopping several times to watch and test the wind. Sundale and Yarain held their pose, as did Jason, only changing their view to respect this emissary coming to investigate them.

The female stopped several feet away, well out of leaping distance. Her tails fell still, and her ears perked forward. It was then that Yarain gave the same ruff the other first parent had given. *"Go meet her, Sundale."*

Sundale couldn't keep his ears from falling for half a heartbeat. Here it was. An interaction that he had no understanding of yet could mean the difference between life and death for all three of them. That said, his mother, first mother, *and* superior officer had given him a command. So, however uncomfortable he felt, Sundale moved forward to follow it.

He let his tails sneak out behind him, but they, and he, remained low. His ears were back to further the submissive display while his eyes remained locked on the female. The gold of her fur was slightly deeper than his own, and she had no white anywhere on her body. Orange ran down her back from the red of her tail tips all the way to her forehead. At her neck, the same color formed a natural collar as if it were a necklace instead of fur.

She watched him with stilling tails that signified she did not see him as a threat. That said, her ears were up and her whiskers fully forward, which also made it clear she was watching him. Sundale walked up to her, slow and steady, careful not to show any aggression or claim. He let his instincts guide him, which took him all the way until they were two feet from touching noses.

There, his ears finally came up. Not as perked at hers, but then, this was her territory. They looked at each other, noses hard at work, trying to find what they could of each other. Soon, the female took a careful step forward, bringing her nose to his right cheek. She kept going, sniffing at the scent gland at the base of his jaw. He, in turn, sniffed at the same on her. For a holdren, this was the proverbial handshake. The scent conveyed not only identity but also the individual's mood.

Even with his limited experience, Sundale found nothing to fear from her scent. Caution of course, a touch of fear, though that could easily be uneasiness at the fighter and Jason, but otherwise, he found no sharp scent of deceit, aggression, or malice. Things that could only be found in this close examination of the gland.

A softer scent mixed into her smell, something Sundale took as curiosity or confusion, possibly even concern, but more the kind one feels for a wounded pack mate. Something he never expected to find. When they retreated enough to look at each other again, he saw much the same in her eyes, and in the curious perk of her ears. He didn't know how to respond, so he waited for someone to help him out.

Thankfully, she did. *"Why are you lost?"*

The question sent Sundale's ears up and his head tilting in confusion. Of all the questions he expected, that was nowhere close to any of them. *"I don't understand."*

"You smell unsure, like you don't know where you are. Why is that?"

"I don't know." It was possibly the most honest answer Sundale had ever given.

The female stared at Jason a moment, then came back to Sundale. *"Is it him? Is he keeping you from your pack?"*

"He is my pack," Sundale said.

"He can't hear us. We can free you."

"We're not captives! We run and hunt as one. He is worthy of trust."

The female again stared at Jason. This time, Sundale looked back to check on him. Jason was still low on one knee, but his eyes had come up to match the female. He swallowed once with a breath, showing a degree of worry Sundale shared. While the interaction wasn't going bad, it wasn't exactly going well either.

It got more complicated when the female stepped toward Jason in the same slow, analyzing manner as before. Even Yarain had twitching ears, unsure how to handle this. The female ignored her. She went straight for Jason, neither of them losing sight of the other. The fact that she never tensed or waved her tails kept the concern limited, but no less there. If she went for him, they were dead. Yarain and Sundale would try to defend him, but the pack would defend their envoy. The best they could do was wait and hope.

The female kept going until she was inches from Jason's face. There, she stopped, and Jason took slow, terrified breaths. He knew what holdrens were more than anyone. He knew he was staring into the eyes of a wild animal. He also knew there was thought behind that animal, which was probably the only thing keeping them alive. What he didn't know was how to respond, and neither Sundale nor Yarain dared speak now. The shock could be disastrous.

At least they thought so until the female said, "Who are you?"

Yarain and Sundale both recoiled while their ears shot up. *They speak English?!* While Sundale didn't remember much, he knew for a fact that holdrens didn't "speak." Yet here was this female doing just that.

Jason's recoil was softer, but the jolt in his body said he was just as startled by it as the others. "My name is Jason," he said after a moment. "What is yours?"

"Reneca. Do you own these holdrens?"

Jason couldn't stop a laugh. "No, ma'am. No one ever could. I've seen what happens to those who try. No, they are my friends and comrades. They are my pack mates."

"They are not of your blood."

"Doesn't matter. We stand together. Each of us would give our lives for the rest. Blood or not, we are a pack. Feared by our rivals, respected by our friends."

Drop the dramatic, Jason. Still, the fact that Reneca was talking was a good sign. She didn't even sound angry, though there was a touch of reprimand hidden in her tone. Otherwise, her English voice was firm, and brimming with confidence as if her words were her will unchallenged, or unchallengeable. Yet, at the same time, there was a smoothness to it. Much like Marcy when she was being hard, but caring at the same time.

How Reneca felt about Jason's attempt at the dramatic was undetectable in her reply. "Why are you here?"

Jason didn't miss a beat. "I must warn your alp . . . first parents. A . . . large pack is coming that poses great danger to *all* holdrens. I have friends who can help, but we need to warn as many packs as we can so they can be ready to face or avoid this danger."

"Why would this pack come here?"

"That is . . . a very long and difficult answer. One I would rather give once. Please, I must speak with your first parents. There is little time before the threat arrives."

Reneca stared a moment longer, then looked at Yarain, who did nothing more than perk her ears and level her tails. This more than anything had Reneca's ears perking in surprise. *"You would fight for him?"*

"I would die for him," Yarain said, not quite snarling.

Reneca's ears stayed straight in shock. She turned to Sundale and found him raising his head and ears for the first time. He was conveying the idea that, much like Yarain, he was ready to die for Jason. Reneca bounced between all of them for a moment, then approached Sundale.

She stepped right up, once again checking his cheek gland. Sundale did not return the favor this time. He merely let himself be examined for whatever it was she was looking for.

Once she was done, Reneca stood back with straight ears. Sundale could only guess at her thoughts, but before he decided on one, Reneca gave a soft, barked howl, summoning her pack. Sundale instantly felt lighter, for her call was nothing more than a request that they join her. There was another twinge in his back as well, but a soft ripple of his energy matrix kept that from turning into more. *Now would* not *be a good time for that to come back!*

Reneca's pack began a careful trot toward them while Jason's eyes darted back and forth. Reneca herself stood before him without raising a single hair.

"Karfen is my first father. He will speak with you," she said.

Jason now breathed his own sigh of relief. "Thank you, Reneca. I thank you for welcoming us into—"

"You have not been welcomed. You have convinced me you pose no threat to us. Anything **MORE** rests with Karfen."

Jason dropped his head. He would have dropped his ears too if he could. "I apologize. I didn't mean to overstep my boundaries. Can he speak my language as well?"

"We all can."

Yarain and Sundale both perked their ears in shock, but it was Yarain that spoke first. "**WHAT?** We never used English before. Why would we now?"

Reneca opened her mouth to reply, then seemed to literally swallow it. "I'll let Karfen explain that."

That doesn't sound good. It took a lot of focus for Sundale to keep his tails from waving. Holdrens didn't usually keep secrets unless the first parents had a darn good reason. The idea that these holdrens might have a secret that clearly had Reneca uneasy made Sundale feel much the same about the coming encounter.

The pack held their pace, stopping only a few feet away. Then a single male stepped forward, his tails raised higher, though still at a soft angle rather than straight up. *That's gotta be Karfen.* He appeared slightly larger than many of the pack, while his fur had orange on his muzzle, cheeks, and forehead. His legs were socked in the same color just past his ankles, and it went down the back of his head to the base of the neck, stopped there, then reappeared along his tails. His underside was white but did not infringe on the orange of his muzzle. Otherwise, the gold of his fur was the same shade as Sundale's.

Karfen briefly sniffed at each of Yarain's and Sundale's cheek glands, then stepped up to Jason. Jason slowly shifted onto both knees, never losing eye contact with Karfen, who sniffed at him from a distance. Karfen advanced so he could sniff at Jason's ear, which Jason couldn't help shying away from slightly at first. Karfen followed, showing no sign of any emotion at the retreat. He soon stepped back with relaxing tails, which relaxed Sundale twice as much.

"You are their first father?" Karfen said in a hard yet non-threatening tone. Even without it, his voice, much like Harmus, was that not-quite deep tone that would make him sound gruff even when he wasn't.

Jason nodded. "I'm Lieutenant Colonel Jason Harlem. I am their first father by title only. I consider them closer than that."

"There is nothing closer than the pack. The young male looks at you as he would one of his own. What is he to you?"

"My comrade. My friend. My loyal pack mate."

Karfen's head tilted ever so slightly. "**DO** you know the meaning of that term?"

"He does," Yarain said. "I can say from experience that he leads our hunts with wisdom and concern. He protects us as I did for mine before."

Karfen perked his ears toward Yarain. "You were once a first mother?"

Yarain's ears flicked back for a second of pain. "For a time."

"And yet you speak out of turn."

"Not out of turn," Jason said. "I've learned long ago we don't think the same. Yarain understands the difference. She is here to bridge the gap so we may better understand one another."

Karfen began to speak, but an older male holdren with orange socks and shoulders spoke first. "Did you say, Yarain?"

Karfen snapped toward the male with a growl, though only a slight ruffle in his hackles spoke of any real anger. *"This is not your conversation."*

The older male flattened his ears in submission. *"Forgive me, Karfen, but I may know her. If I may?"*

Karfen's growl faded, followed by a turn in his ears that gave permission. The male stepped forward, one ear on his first father, the other on Yarain. She watched him with perked ears and a slight tilt that spoke of deep thought within. They traded sniffs at the cheek, and then the male recoiled with erect ears.

"It *is* you," he said.

Yarain gave the older holdren a confused tilt. "I'm sorry. Your scent is familiar, but I can't remember you."

"We only hunted together for twelve meltings."

Yarain tilted her head the other way a second. Another second saw her eyes brighten. Without warning, she and the older male began rubbing and licking like old friends. Sundale watched Karfen but found only an amused perk in the first father's ears.

"Milsol," Yarain said. "I'm sorry. It's been so long. I've missed you."

"And I you," Milsol said. "When you didn't come back, I feared something terrible had happened."

Yarain ears again flashed pain as the rubbing ended. "I was held captive for three yea . . . meltings. He and others rescued me, but an accident turned me back into an orgigon. Airless sky is very different when you can't feel the ebb and flow of the environment. I couldn't find my way back."

Jason leaned close to Sundale. "Meltings? Orgigon?"

"Solid holdren, like me," Sundale said. "A pure energy holdren is known as an energon. The melting of snow, or a 'melting,' is how holdrens mark years."

"And airless sky?"

"*SPACE*."

"Of course. Should have figured."

Karfen ruffed a soft chuckle as Milsol and Yarain traded another quick rub.

"It's good to see you again," Milsol said. "Did you find Sundale?"

"Yes."

Yarain looked at her cub. Milsol followed her gaze, then perked his ears in excitement while his tails completely relaxed. Sundale's ears shifted up and down as Milsol began to walk around him, examining him like a father. Sundale looked to Jason for support, only to find Karfen's stern glare telling Jason to let Sundale and Milsol be for the moment.

Milsol stood in front of Sundale after he'd finished his circle. His ears were erect in pride. Sundale's were back in nerves.

"You seem to have grown strong," Milsol said. "Your fur looks a little thin, though. Did something happen when you hurt your eye?" Sundale's ears flattened as he prepared for a shudder that never came.

Milsol tilted his head while glancing at Yarain. "Why does that question hurt you?"

Sundale shook his head to try and unlock his ears. They only came up a little. "It's a long story I'm not ready to relive right now."

"Then we won't. You're alive, and well. What happened before no longer matters."

"Not quite," Yarain said. "I would like to know what happened to our surviving cubs."

Milsol got Karfen's permission before leading Yarain to a pair of females close to Sundale's age. Sundale thought he remembered playing with them, but it was so long ago he only knew that if they were of his pack, they were born to another pair. Something holdren packs allowed more often than "wild animals," yet was still uncommon.

Meanwhile, Karfen watched them with softening ears and tails that had relaxed completely. "She was a good first mother."

"You have no idea," Jason said. "May I assume this means we are allowed to stay?"

Karfen's tails stiffened again. "For now, Colonel. How long that lasts depends on why you are here."

"I'm here with a warning. A large pack of dangerous hunters is coming. They want to make you their servants, kill you, or worse, and believe me, there *is* worse with them. Not just your pack either, but *all* holdrens."

Karfen's ears perked forward. "Tell me about these hunters, Colonel. Who and what are they?"

Sundale watched the calming state of Karfen's tails as Jason tried to put the Polaris Confederacy into terms Karfen could understand. Karfen prodded with questions in an even tone that held only curiosity and, at most, concern for his pack. Not once did his fur ruffle, which meant he was taking the conversation pretty well.

Sundale thought about joining Yarain, except she was inspecting a young Holdren the same way Milsol had done with him. Another the same age stood nearby, her low ears suggesting she was next, with a third seemingly eager to get her turn. This was a tender moment between former first mother and pack that he did not want to intrude on. As for the pack, they watched their first father with upright ears showing great attention and twitching tail tips showing equal concern. *Jason is choosing his words well.*

Unfortunately, that left Sundale feeling like he was outside that door again. He couldn't rejoin his mother, and Jason was doing so well without him that the conversation faded into the background in favor of a weight inside Sundale's chest.

Some homecoming. A pack of holdrens not four feet from him, yet he still felt alone. A "stray." Yarain apparently knew some of them, but aside from that third female touching something in him he couldn't quite grasp, *he* didn't. Even Milsol was unfamiliar. None of the pack cared about him either. They only had eyes for their first parents. Current in the case of Karfen and Jason, former in the case of Yarain.

Sundale's head fell onto his paws as he began another visual search for anyone he might have once known. He was about to try and rekindle any relationship he'd had with the young females when Reneca approached him again. She slowly got close enough to check his cheek again with nothing but a curious perk in her ears.

"Can I help you?" Sundale said.

"Not yet," Reneca said.

When she tried to continue sniffing, Sundale growled softly to push her back. "I'm not here to be examined."

"I thought you were here to greet us."

"Greet. Not become a spectacle."

"This *is* greeting. You know that." When Sundale only glared at her, Reneca's ears perked in surprise. "You *don't* know that, do you?"

Sundale's ears fell, embarrassed at the admission. "Not well."

"How can that be?"

With the floodgates cracked, the rest was impossible to stop. "I was raised by humans. Jason's race. It wasn't until my fourth... melting that I reconnected with another holdren."

Reneca stood still with straight ears for a moment. "Then you've never learned how to be a proper holdren."

Sundale couldn't stop his growl. It was short and soft but no less reprimanding. Yet the word "stray" began to echo in his head to the point that he could almost feel it in his ears. This more than anything sent his ears and hackles up. He wasn't just angry at Reneca; he was trying to chase away the feeling.

He rose to his paws, not caring that some were starting to take notice. "I am no **LESS** of a holdren than you are!"

Reneca's ears flattened in full apology. "I didn't mean that. I meant you were denied the experience of being a wild holdren."

Sundale's fur started to fall, as did the attention of many of the eyes that had been on him. "I've **BEEN** wild."

"Have you? Where are you most comfortable? Is it under the sun following a trail, or is it inside that fighter?"

A dozen answers rolled around in Sundale's mind. He'd spent most of his time in one fighter or another, but he'd had moments of the wild, too. There were hunts with his parents, days spent miles from any technology, weeks on end where he only felt sun on his fur and dirt beneath his paws. Yet, he had to admit, even the best of days still didn't feel... *wait a minute... fighter?*

That was a term wild holdrens shouldn't know. Not in that context. Yet Reneca had clearly meant Gold 1. Her eyes had fallen on the ship as she asked the question. Now Sundale stared at her with ears and whiskers forward. His tails gave a single wave in response to a similar wave that went through his energy matrix.

Sundale had a question in his throat, but it was stopped by the wave becoming an odd ripple that streaked up his back. He tried to realign it, except the moment he did, his body flinched in response to most or all of his matrix rushing to his back in one sudden pulse. When it happened a second time, it felt like his body was trying to compress into a ball, drawing a sharp yip of pain despite not feeling any.

Every ear turned his way, but Sundale found his focus turning inward. His energy matrix felt like it was being set ablaze. There was also a pressure that was pressing out and in all at the same time. His back was throbbing like someone had slammed a fist into it, and it was growing stronger by the second. His breathing became erratic as the pain, pressure, throb, and a touch of panic tried to freeze his lungs. There were voices, but Sundale couldn't hear them through the firestorm in his back. He couldn't tell anymore if it was physical, just his matrix, something else, or all of it combined.

Whines started coming with the breaths, but they did nothing to settle him. His body was locked in place, though his paws tried to dig into the ground as if clamping down could help. Jason knelt in front of him. His hands gently touched the side of Sundale's head. The contact allowed Sundale to see and hear him.

He then wished he couldn't, for the panic he felt was two-fold in his friend's eyes. "Talk to me, Sun. What's going on? Another seizure? Something else?"

Sundale couldn't form a reply. He could barely breathe and when he did get a breath, only whines came from it. The only thing he heard was Yarain's voice, and a hard ruff from Karfen to silence the pack. It almost worked for Sundale, too, but his back was only getting started. His matrix pulsed like nothing he had ever felt. For a moment, he felt like a reactor about to go critical.

Then, in one burst, his back took the next step. Pain gushed from his back and shoulders as if someone had pulled a zipper to let it out. His own cries of pain echoed in his ears even more than his torture as a POW. His eyes closed as he lost all feeling in the rest of his body. He couldn't see or hear anymore. He couldn't feel anything except his back erupting like a volcano of agony. A fitting description, considering his back and shoulders felt hot enough to be one. As the eruption continued, Sundale's breath began to fail him. He couldn't even whine anymore. There was nothing in his world beyond whatever was going on with his back.

Then, nothing.

Everything was gone. No pain, no sound, no feeling. As quickly as it had started, it seemed to end.

Sundale wasn't sure if he'd blacked out or if his mind had just turned itself off for a moment. He only knew that he went from being unable to exist outside of the pain to laying on the ground out of breath like he'd been running for days. A sharp pain still resonated from his back and shoulders. He had started panting at some point, though each breath shook his ribs, which did his back no favors. Some part of his mind remembered where he was, but there was still so much pain one could hardly call it consciousness.

A pinprick in his back sent Sundale flinching. He expected things to start up again, but instead, the pain began to ease. His panting faded into heavy exertion, and though things still hurt, it quickly fell to a point where he could begin to think again. His eyes were still sealed shut with pain, but at least he could feel his body enough to know that.

It was Jason's voice that broke through first.

"Easy Sun. Just . . . just take it easy. Try to . . . uhm . . . just relax for a bit. Don't try to move . . . anything."

No argument this time.

Sundale panted out the pain and exhaustion while he waited for things to recover. His back and shoulders still felt warm with an odd tingle among the pain, like when things "fall asleep," as the humans put it. He couldn't get his eyes open, though most of that was not wanting to let the sunlight in until he was sure it wouldn't make his head explode. Even so, he could feel the attention of the pack, though not a word was being said among them. He thought he heard a brief conversation between Karfen and Yarain, but he was in no condition to try and catch any part of it.

Feeling returned in slow steps that took years. First came dirt under his paws. Then, a breeze through his fur. Then he began to get complaints from his legs, most of them about stiffness. His shoulders were still screaming, though they too were starting to quiet down, while his back had fallen silent at last. Only the warmth remained for now.

With his breathing down to a low pant, Sundale decided it was time to risk opening his eyes. Jason was kneeling in front of him while Karfen sat at Jason's side with perfectly erect ears. Reneca and Yarain were both standing nearby in finesse form, Yarain with an injector in her hand, Reneca with Gold 1's med-kit at her paws. They too were staring at him with straight ears. *This can't be good.*

As his nose came back to life, Sundale found a lot of tension in the air. Though, as usual, Jason's scent spoke of the most calm. It seemed to grow calmer when Sundale was able to look straight at him. Jason's shoulders rose and fell with each breath, yet his gaze was the same watchful, absorbing look Sundale had seen a thousand times after his switch flips.

Jason offered a soft smile when their eyes met. "Hey there, Sun. Nice to see you again. You feeling all right ... uh ... considering?"

Jason's hand seemed to gesture to Sundale's back for some reason. Sundale dismissed it in favor of shifting so he could get into a more comfortable laying position.

That's when Sundale felt a strange new weight on his back that silenced his reply. At first, he thought it was a bandage. He rocked his shoulders to see if he could silence the feeling, only to find they felt like they had something more attached to them just above the shoulder blades. He didn't smell any blood, nor did it really hurt, so he couldn't understand why they would have needed any serious treatment.

Then, true feeling came. Sundale could feel the grass under him where his body wasn't. It was as if he'd grown new legs that were laid out to his sides. Curiosity forced him to brave the pain and look back in search of what was going on back there.

Sundale forgot his pain in favor of straightening ears. He'd grown something all right, but it wasn't new legs. Instead, attached to his shoulders, he found a pair of large, feathered wings. They appeared to be the same color as his fur, though the leading edge seemed to be a tiny bit darker. They also had a striped pattern, a lot like the hawks he'd seen flying around Jason's home on Earth. Stranger still, there seemed to be some sort of ghost-like veil covering the primary feathers. As far as he could tell, this veil matched the color of the feathers it was attached to, yet slid over each feather individually like some sort of sheath over every one. Sundale tried to lift the wings, and though they barely moved, he could feel them respond to his command.

He looked at Jason with a wavering voice. "Jason? Where did those come from?"

Jason stammered a second before he could form a coherent thought. "Uhhhh, they ... grew. In just a few seconds, they emerged like a butterfly coming out of a cocoon."

"How?"

"We're not sure. The scanner can't make sense of anything. The only idea we have ... uhhh ... is ... pretty out there."

"Jason? I just sprouted wings. **TRY ME!**"

Sundale more barked the last words, but Jason seemed to understand anyway. He looked at Yarain, and motioned for her to proceed.

"When a holdren turned into an energon," she said, "they would grow a set of pure energy wings that could never be turned physical. When you began that change years ago, it started in your back because the wings always came first."

Sundale's ears shifted in thought as he tried to make sense of it all. "But the change was stopped by the same accident that turned you into an orgigon."

"Apparently not," Jason said. "Our best guess is for some reason, your body decided it wanted the wings it never got. We think Marcy's treatment for your seizures, and the ... collar you wore as a POW, might have paused the process and might have even prevented it had either been left on long enough. Once both were out of the picture, the process resumed, soooo... congratulations, Sun. You have wings now."

"But I'm still an orgigon... aren't I?"

"*YES*," Yarain said.

Jason added, "As to whether or not you're going to stay one... good question. It's not the only one we have, either. For one thing..."

Jason was cut off by a sharp ruff from Karfen. "We can ask those questions later. Sundale, how *are* you feeling?"

No wonder he's their first father. His tone remained soft, like a father comforting his cub. There was an almost visible aura about him as well, as if he were creating a place where no harm could come to anyone. The two features quickly eroded Sundale's fear and helped ease his pain as well.

"I think I'll be all right," Sundale said. "Things still hurt."

"That's good," Reneca said with some true relief.

Sundale perked a curious ear at her, but before he could think at all, Jason's wrist-com chimed to life. The entire pack turned their ears up, though a few, like Reneca, seemed more focused than others.

Meanwhile, Jason sighed at it. "Now what? Go for Colonel Harlem."

The voice of Gold 8's third seat came over the comms. "Proximity alert. Unknown fighter entering the area. On course for planet-fall."

"A Polaris scout?"

"Not sure. The markings are different, and the design is unfamiliar. Do we engage?"

"Negative. Monitor and shadow, but stay out of the atmo. Advise if you see—"

"Hold on, Colonel," Karfen said. "Is there an insignia on that ship?"

Jason stared at him but went to his wrist-com after only a moment. "Gold 8, can you get a look at an insignia?"

"Stand by, Gold 1." There was a tense silence as everyone waited for the reply. "Affirmative. Looks like some kind of green snake or lizard curved into a C. Looks like a brown line runs through the body of the snake. I think I can see a trail of some kind coming off the back of the snake's body. Might be a chain, or a ribbon, can't quite tell."

"You can stand down, Colonel," Karfen said. "She serves the same fleet that contacted you."

Jason's eyes narrowed, but more in searching than suspicion. "What? Gold 8, have you received word of any contacts in nearby systems?"

"Negative sir," Gold 8 said. "Scopes at ten lics, all remain clear."

Many ears and eyes locked onto Jason, but Reneca spoke first. "There should be an entire task force only a system away. They didn't contact you when you came in?"

"I doubt they saw us," Jason said. "We entered the system under cloak. Gold 8 and the rest of my squad still are. As for other ships, we haven't seen a one within ten light-years."

"That answers a few things."

"Orders, sir?" Gold 8 asked.

"Maintain overwatch," Jason said. "Watch for additional contacts. Stand by for further orders. And have the *Alamo* double-check their sensors. Sounds like we missed a base in the A-O."

Sundale could see a military stiffness take over Reneca's body. He'd felt it too many times to miss it. It showed itself further as she snap-turned her head and shoulders to Karfen. "Something must have happened."

"Agreed," Karfen said. "But you and Gold 8 can relax, Colonel. That fighter is no threat to you or us."

Jason couldn't keep the accusation out of his tone. "Really? And how long were you going to wait to tell me you knew all about starships and fighters?"

Karfen didn't even blink. "Not until I knew who you really were."

Jason tried to hold his glare, but even Sundale could see the wisdom in Karfen's perspective. Jason must have as well, for he soon nodded. "Fair enough. I suppose if I were in your position, I'd hold any advantage I had, too. I apologize."

"No need. I understand."

Definitely a good first father.

Karfen was holding his ground yet was willing to see Jason's point of view as well. While the wild life often saw conflict resolved with tooth and claw, being able to be diplomatic would help keep the pack together and might prevent a few clashes from turning violent.

However, Sundale had an issue even Karfen couldn't help him with. With an unknown fighter coming in, friend or foe being irrelevant, being caught on the ground with spread wings did not seem wise. He'd have a lot of learning ahead of him, but for the time being, he just needed to fold them.

While Jason adjusted his orders to Gold 8, Sundale got his paws under him, then flexed the wings in search of the muscles. They twitched at first, then only moved a little as he found the various bends in them. Whenever the wings were extended, the veil over the feathers seemed to move out as if extending as well. He could almost feel them combing the feathers, and he thought he was starting to feel the veil itself.

Reneca had since retaken her primal form. She now sniffed at one wing with Yarain watching a few steps away.

"I wonder if you can fly," Reneca said.

"I need to learn how to move them first," Sundale said. "Better step back."

Reneca did so, and Sundale tried to lift his wings again. He expected them to be weak like before, so he tried to put a lot of effort into it. They instead responded to the full force of his lift, which sent them snapping straight up above him with a soft *thwap*. The entire pack flinched, many of them yipping or ruffing in surprise. A couple of tails curved over, but dropped once they realized there was no danger.

"Impressive," Reneca muttered.

Sundale, meanwhile, could feel his legs bracing from the force of the flap. More than just the movement, there had been a definite power stroke there. The idea of flight felt more likely than ever, considering that was just one flap.

He held his wings there and examined them again to see if he'd missed a bend. He noticed that the underside of the wings was still textured like the top side, yet it was also a lighter, paler sandy-gold than the rest of his pelt. He also noticed that the veil over the feathers had indeed extended; creating a sort of ghost image of the wings that was maybe as long as the feathers they were attached to. More to the point, he could now say for sure that he could feel this veil and that it was somehow connected to his energy matrix. Yet, at the same time, these energy feathers were somewhat solid, creating a surface that he could feel catching the air with the slightest movement.

Sundale pushed those thoughts to the back for the moment as he worked with his wings in an attempt to fold them. Bit by bit, he managed to retract the energy feathers, then tuck the end feathers in, then find the bends enough to bring them into his body. Trial and error were his only guides, yet it proved to be enough. In a relatively short time, Sundale had managed to fold them together, though they were still more or less straight up on his back.

He gave a soft growl at the position. Too much risk of injury, and it felt rather awkward. Since they looked so much like them, Sundale thought back on the hawks he'd watched around Jason's home. He made some adjustments to the fold, and eventually managed tuck them comfortably at his sides. They now covered his flanks and shoulder joints, though when he looked back, he saw the physical wing stopped right at his tails. *Good, I won't break any feathers when I sit.*

"Looks like you figured it out," Reneca said.

"For the moment," Sundale said. "Using them is going to take much more time."

Jason only shook his head. "I'm now working with a winged fox. Just when I think I've seen it all . . . Is that your friend, Karfen?"

Sundale and many others followed Jason's finger to a small craft just appearing in the sky. Karfen looked for a moment, then ruffed an affirmative.

Jason went to his wrist-com, but Karfen's voice stopped him. "No need for that, Colonel. She's here for us. You'll get to meet her soon."

"Except she doesn't know *me* or my ship. How will she respond to *us*?"

"She won't see you as a threat because you're clearly with me."

"Let's hope not."

Sundale watched the speck of a ship grow into a pointed, triangular fighter a little smaller than Gold 1. The leading edge appeared jagged all the way down her sides, and she was painted a lavender shade with what appeared to be a darker underside of the same color.

Definitely a combat fighter. Though most might miss them, Sundale was able to find her weapons built within the hull on the outside edges.

As she passed over them, he noticed a pod between the two engine pods, which he felt sure held some kind of ordnance. The only question was bombs, missiles, or something else? The engines sounded more like a throb than the soft hum he was used to, yet he still felt an energy backwash just like with Interstar ships. *She must use some kind of ion engine as well.*

The fighter landed in the clearing just outside of the gathered pack. Some moved to approach with an excited perk in their ears, but Karfen barked them still. It would appear the pack did indeed know the pilot, and Karfen didn't want them smothering her. Or it had something to do with the presence of Gold 1.

The cockpit opened, and parts of the hull folded to create steps. The figure that emerged was humanoid, dressed in lavender pants and a shirt with large, dark-red patches covering the shoulders and a thick helmet on her head. Her arms had a small patch with a pattern that looked like four lines crisscrossing over each other as if weaving. On her chest was the same insignia painted on her ship. Now, with a closer look, Sundale could see that the trail coming off the snake's body was indeed some kind of decorative chain.

As the pilot stepped away from her ship, the breeze brought a familiar scent to Sundale's nose. His ears came forward as it stirred memories of home, of love . . .

Of abandonment.

"It can't be."

Sundale stepped forward, testing the air to confirm it. The pilot removed her helmet to reveal a human he had to pick apart to be sure it was real. She still had a hard yet smooth face; with short, blonde hair flowing behind it. Her build remained medium while still smooth and lithe, like a runner who could walk a tightrope. She tucked the helmet under her arm while Sundale felt his heart stop.

"Karol?" Sundale said. "Is that really you?"

The woman dropped her helmet when she saw him, and her chest heaved with pained breath. "Sundale?"

Sundale's breathing started to fail him again, but not from pain . . . exactly. "Yes."

"But . . . but how did . . . but I . . . and who is . . . and what is . . . and when did . . . I . . . you're alive!"

"I could say the same about you. Last time I saw you, you were leaving me behind with half the Marcallan fleet on your tail."

"It's a long story, Sundale."

What pain there was turned to anger, which made him glare at her with stiff tails. "As is mine. I wonder whose is more painful."

Karol cringed with a hard swallow. *Maybe I did strike a little deep. Then again, so did she.*

Jason, meanwhile, glanced back and forth between them. "Care to clue me in here, Captain?"

Sundale had to swallow a moon in his throat before he could reply. More so because as much as he was angry with her, the love he felt for her was still there.

"Jason, this is Karol. She's the woman who raised me."

CHAPTER 6

THE MORE THINGS CHANGE...

J ason had to fight the urge to throw his hands up in the air. *Of course she is. Why wouldn't we run into Sundale's adoptive mother? It's only the most improbable addition to an already impossible day. Tell me God doesn't have a sense of humor.*

He had a hard time seeing that humor through Karol's cringe. When she came out of it, even he could see tears being held back.

"I'm surprised you described me so well," she said. "Sundale, I tried. I was shot down. It took me days to lose the jantans, days more to make enough repairs. I went back for you. I scanned every inch of that planet three times. All I found was old blood on the edge of a gator-infested river. What was I supposed to think?"

Boy, do I know that feeling.

Sundale's hackles ruffled though his breath spoke more of pain than anger. "You **PROMISED** I'd never be alone. I nearly *died* alone because you left me behind. What was I supposed to *feel*?"

Tears escaped Karol's control as she nodded. "And now? After all this time? What do you feel now?"

Sundale's hackles went still despite his best effort to keep them up. His ears fell soon after, and then he gave a cringe of his own.

"Confused."

"That's good enough for me."

They both ran to meet each other. Karol knelt in time for Sundale's head to fall against her chest. He rubbed against her while she hugged him with all she had.

Tears continued to stream from her eyes. "Sundale. I've missed you."

"And I you."

They held their embrace for several minutes. Jason watched and waited with folded arms. *I know that feeling, too.*

A different feeling, one of uncertainty, took over when Karfen stepped next to him. "Didn't expect that during your mission briefing, did you?"

"Karfen," Jason said, "after eleven years around him, I've learned to expect nothing. Even the unexpected has a way of being unexpected."

"Isn't that the same thing?"

"No, it's not. Never mind. It'd take too long to explain."

Or, more correctly, I don't understand what I said either.

Karol finally pushed Sundale back so she could look at him. She rubbed over his ears, pausing at his scar. "My little Sundale. You've changed so much since I last saw you. And I don't mean the wings. You look good inside, solid. I see strength in your eyes. You've matured so much."

Sundale's ears flicked, though Jason couldn't tell why. "I've become a soldier. Interstar was my best hope of finding home... of finding you."

Karol lowered her head in another cringe. Jason took the opportunity to step in before they got too deep in old wounds.

Jason extended his hand to Karol. "Ma'am? I'm Lieutenant Colonel Jason Harlem. I'm Sundale's CO."

She took his hand and gave it a firm shake. "Major Karol Torzon."

Jason froze his shake when he realized who this pilot was. "Torzon? The lead pilot of Interstar's first Gold Group?"

She nodded without reaction. "That's me. I've heard of you, too. Praise from your instructors, you defended President Sharp, a few of the brass had their eyes on you. I see their attention was not misplaced. It seems our coin-flip rookie turned out to be a heads."

Jason huffed while fighting a laugh. *If only she knew.* "Actually, I was a tails until I met Sundale. He... he gave me something to fight for. Speaking of which, I'm curious; How did you find Sundale? And what are you still doing out here? Our history books say you're dead."

Captain Torzon chuckled. "Hardly, colonel. I found Sundale a long time ago when I followed some Raiders to this place. They bombarded the surface so they could land without fear of the locals. I drove them off before they could hatch their plans. I found Sundale soon after. He was just a cub, legs broken, fur charred, his parents dead beside him. He would have never survived alone, or so I thought at the time. I took him with me in the hopes of giving him a full life. I raised him through his early years."

"So why did you disappear?"

Karol knelt down and began stroking Sundale, who leaned into her with no sign of his previous anger. He didn't stop when her hand brushed across a wing, either.

"When he got older, he started speaking English he'd learned listening to me. That's when I learned for sure he was sentient. I began to give him formal lessons in reading, writing, and speaking too. I wanted him to be ready for the day he was discovered. Instead, I learned about the terrible mistake I'd made. He learned enough to tell me about the way holdrens live—in packs. His was larger than the body count I'd seen, meaning he would have been cared for. I was about to take him home, to make things right, when Marcalla began their offensive on the Golian outposts."

Jason nodded with a stinger in his own heart. "I remember. I was there for it. I watched over half my group get wiped out trying to defend the research facility. I also watched Sir Scorn . . . well, let's just say the jantans didn't get an easy prize."

Karol only hummed. "I barely got Sundale out before the base was hit. The CO ordered everyone to scram, head for better-defended lines. I had several fighters chasing me the whole way. I couldn't lead them here, nor could I allow Sundale to die with me. I left him on an M-class planet so he at least would live. I managed to lose the jants, but not before taking critical damage. Took me forever to get hyper–light back online. I went back for Sundale, but all I could find was his blood. On the day I accepted his fate, I vowed that no other holdren would die alone like he . . . like I *thought* he had. I took it upon myself to guard this world from any who would threaten it." She looked up at Jason with narrow eyes. "*That*, Colonel, is why I 'disappeared.'"

Jason cringed with a touch of guilt. Without meaning to, he had come off as accusing instead of curious. It was nice to learn about Sundale's adoptive mother, though. He'd never really talked about her, and now Jason had some idea why. There seemed to be a number of old wounds connected to her. Something Sundale seemed to have a hard time talking about.

Yarain stepped forward before he could think of a response. Her tentative steps left him certain of the topic before she took her first breath.

"Major Torzon," she began carefully. "My name is Yarain. I am his mother. Harmus, his father, is living on Earth at the moment."

Karol leaned forward from stroking Sundale. "What? But the pair I saw near him . . . the male and female. Who were they?"

"Members of our pack."

Karol's hand went to her chest. "Yarain, if I had known . . . if I'd had any idea . . . can you ever forgive me?"

"I can and have. Your heart was in a good place, and Sundale landed in a good place as well."

Major Torzon could barely squeeze out a soft "thank you."

Jason stood by with an odd lump in his throat. *If only we had more time.* In a matter of minutes, Yarain had found members of her old pack, and Sundale had found his foster mother. The latter had his tails more relaxed than they'd been since his rescue. As both of his mothers rubbed an ear, Sundale released so much tension it was as if he had begun to shrink. It was far from a full repair, but Jason could see the emotional scars receding.

Unfortunately, they still had a mission to complete. Jason tried to drum up the will to break things up when PAICCA chimed in from his wrist com.

"Set condition 2! Gold 1, condition 2 in effect. Intel inbound."

I thought I told him to stay quiet.

Ears shot up everywhere. Even Karol started staring at him. "That doesn't sound good," she said.

"I can promise you it isn't," Jason said. He tapped his wrist com. "Talk to me PAICCA."

A different voice responded. "Admiral Redding here, Colonel. Command just sent word. We've got trouble."

"Polaris?"

"Worse. Polaris with a jantan friend or two. They're reading two full carrier groups inbound."

Naturally. "ETA, sir?"

"Four hours at last ping. Tell me you made contact."

"Yes, sir, we did, and we can confirm the target *is* the holdren homeworld. But . . ." he trailed off as he looked at Sundale, then at Karol, and failed to find anything close to the right words. "Things are rather complicated, sir. I recommend you bring the fleet into the system. I should have more for you by the time you arrive."

"Work fast, Colonel. *Alamo* out."

Jason dropped his arm like it was a lead weight. His mind tried to pick where to start, but between Sundale's wings, Karol, and a task force that should have been there but wasn't, he had a hard time choosing.

Thankfully, Karol broke the silence. "Polaris? As in the Confederacy? I thought they were wiped out. What are they doing in bed with Marcalla?"

"It's a long, long story, Major," Jason said. "Right now, we need to talk about defending this planet."

Karfen's fur had risen, though Jason didn't think it was in anger. "Are you certain you need to? It sounds as if this Polaris is *your* enemy."

"They're here because Sundale and Yarain serve with me. Polaris came here specifically to find their homeworld. To them, you are at best a liability. At worst, a definite threat. That scar on Sundale's eye? Let's just say that's the best of what they did to him. If they get their hands on thousands of you, they will do far worse."

Karfen's fur and ears fell, though the latter only for a moment. "Karol, call for reinforcements."

Karol's shoulders dropped. "I already did when I picked up Harlem's fighter. But they're hours away."

"How many hours?" Jason asked.

"Best case? Six, maybe five."

"Worst case?"

"Nine or more."

Jason almost pinched his nose into paper. "We'll never hold out that long. We don't have the ships to fend off two carrier groups."

"So don't."

Karfen's ears were among the many that went straight toward Karol. Sundale broke the silence. "We can't let them gain a foothold."

Karol's lips twisted into a devious smile. "We won't be. This planet, Holdre 4, is a member of Kapon, a federation that comprises three different races: the haaj'kar, the unatilin, who I doubt even know how to argue much less fight, and as of about nine years ago, the Holdrens. Many of whom are active-duty soldiers. We can fight them here on our terms."

So, I wasn't imagining it. Jason stared at Reneca, noting how, even now, there was the same military stiffness his own crew could exude. "So what rank are you, ma'am?"

"Commander, sir," she said with equal soldier precision.

"Same system as ours?"

"Not quite," Karol said. "Kapon combined the officer ranks so each rank has its own title, then rearranged them a bit. There's no 'lieutenant commander,' for example, just 'commander.' It alternates between the two sets of ranks, starting with ensign as the first officer rank, then ending with colonel being the last one before you start getting stars. Reneca is a commander in the Kapon rank system, which would be the equivalent of a captain in the PSC system, while I'm still a major in both. God knows why they like it better, but they do. Though do yourself a favor; don't try to translate or understand what they did with the enlisted ranks without a cheat sheet. I still struggle with it. And don't get me started on the stars.

"The good news, sir, is we can have a couple hundred soldiers who know the land and that Polaris doesn't know about on the ground and waiting to make their lives miserable."

Hope forced a tense smile out of Jason, but one thought soon silenced it. "Troops won't mean a thing against capital ships. And that's assuming..."

Jason trailed off as the thought took an unexpected turn. Soon after, a devious smile of his own began to form. Polaris had shown an ability to detect cloaks, but not all the time, and only near bases or when certain ships were in the area. With the local star messing with sensors even a little... *it might be enough.*

"What's the plan?" Sundale said with a smile in his voice.

Jason chuckled. *He knows me so well.* "Dangerous. And not just for us. Karfen, despite my warnings, it's up to you. There's no guarantee we can hold until reinforcements arrive, and the battle could claim a lot of lives and territory. If we do nothing, there's a chance we can evade until help arrives, but Polaris will have time to dig in. I don't have time to find your representative, so I ask you; do we fight, or evade?"

Karfen didn't hesitate. "Defend my world, Lieutenant Colonel."

Karol came in on his tails. "There's a mountain range to the south that has some caves and ridge lines. Would serve as a good defensive position and marshaling point for escape pods."

"I'll contact other packs so their soldiers can meet you there. Those of you that are soldiers, remain with Karol. The rest, follow."

Karfen led his pack into the forest, leaving Reneca and seven members behind. Jason watched them go with a shake of his head. *Now that's what I call a first father.* The way Karfen commanded explained a lot of the interactions he'd seen between Sundale and his parents. Sundale was the subordinate, but there was always something more to it than that. Karfen barked orders like a Marshal, yet the tone was even, soft, like a father. Jason had no doubt the pack saw him as one, and he pitied any being that dared threaten them.

Then his switch flipped, and a list appeared in his mind.

"All right," he said, "we've got work to do. Major Torzon, get on the horn to that task force of yours. Tell them to pedal faster."

"Already done," Major Torzon said. "Once I heard we had incoming, I triggered a burst distress signal. Should go undetected. If they can speed things up, they will."

Yarain spoke up before Jason could check his next item. "I'll take charge down here." When Jason stared at her in doubt, she shocked him by perking her ears further. "You need a Holdren who knows Interstar, and two members of my former pack are here. That combination is too valuable to ignore."

I was hoping Sundale could do that so we didn't need to dance around his wings. However, much as he wanted to have to leave only one Holdren behind, he couldn't find a counter to her point. To say nothing of the fact that, unlike Sundale, she was a first mother once. That, more than anything, made it easy. Even if it meant he might have to go without both of them, depending on what the armorers could do with his uniform to fit his wings.

"Very well," he said. "Take the troops here to the mountain range, but I'm going to need someone to come with me to the *Alamo*. When that fleet arrives, we're going to need a voice in a well-protected position to identify our ships as friendlies."

"I can do that," Karol said.

Reneca ruffed a word too badly to be caught, then flattened her ears in submission when Karol glared at her anyway. "With all due respect, ma'am, Colonel Harlem's fleet will need you in your fighter. I respectfully suggest I serve as liaison."

"Why you?" Jason asked.

"I'm trained in combat comms, sir, and I'll be more useful to you on the ship than the ground."

Jason had his doubts about that, but the other points were good ones. Karol would be more useful in the fight, and he knew Reneca slightly more than any of the others. *That's not saying much.*

With that decided, there was only one tiny detail left. "Do any of you Holdrens know the mountain range Major Torzon is talking about?" Three Holdrens indicated they did. "Good. Major Yarain will be your contact unless she says otherwise. Get going. I'll send troops and armor ASAP."

The gathered soldiers left without a word. Yarain had already retrieved and donned her gear at some point. Jason hummed approval, then turned to Karol and Reneca. "Major, follow me up. Commander, with me. You can hitch a ride on Gold 1."

Reneca's head tilted. "*SIR?*"

"We'll take you in our fighter," Sundale said.

"Understood, sir."

The two crews dashed for their ships. Jason slid into his seat and powered her up before he even started with his buckles.

"Sun, you may need to help her with the buckles."

"No need, sir," Reneca said.

The next second, he heard the click of the restraints from both sides. Reneca's side was only a half beat behind Sundale's, which triggered an amused huff from Jason. "You sure you've never seen a Scorn before, Commander?"

"*POSITIVE*, sir," came the simple, half-ruffed reply.

Jason looked back as the engines reached power and noticed her hands went for the controls, only to stop with falling ears and a soft growl.

"Problem, Commander?" Jason said.

"*NO, SIR*," Reneca barked.

"Why the growl then?"

Reneca's ears again shifted back, almost as if she expected a corrective nip. "The controls are similar to what I'm used to, sir. I know I would master them quickly, but my training says I shouldn't try."

Jason *so* wanted to follow that rabbit hole, but he'd wasted too much time already. Though as he lifted Gold 1 into the sky, he did skirt around the edge.

"Best to bury that pride, commander. It will do you and your world no good in the coming hours."

Jason heard a low ruff from Sundale first. After that, nothing. He had no doubt something had been said, though he could only guess what it was.

CHAPTER 7

ONE IF BY LAND, TWO IF BY SEA

Dim alert lights blinked in the cockpit. Part of Jason worried it would give them away, even as he knew the cloak would cover the slight emission. Even so, considering the crazy plan about to be hatched, his nerves would not be satisfied.

Who could blame them? Even Carter, the pilot of Gold 2 and Jason's second in group command, seemed close to fainting when Jason had laid out the plan. Major Torzon had turned to stone in much the same way. If it weren't for Admiral Redding brightening once the explanation was complete, Jason might have doubted himself. He still did, yet no one had offered a better idea while all had agreed; Holdre 4 *had* to be defended.

Which is how Jason found himself with his heart in his head and palms sweating like a pig on the roast. This was the plan. If it worked, it would give them a chance. If not, he'd live just long enough to curse.

He was actually glad to have Lieutenant Harkson Finnley, once again filling in for Yarain, shatter his thoughts. "Fighters in position. Marker beams are functional."

Let's hope they stay that way. The plan depended on the almost-undetectable beams working despite the very same radiation they were counting on to ensure "almost" became "totally." If either part of that interaction failed, they were dead before they started.

"How are your wings, Sun?" Jason asked.

"Annoyed," Sundale said.

I'll bet. The techs had barely managed to come up with a cover for his wings before it was time to launch. It was little more than cloth bags made of the same material as the uniform, but at least his suit would keep him safe in a vacuum. Now all they could do was wait.

Which they didn't have to do for long before the Polaris fleet warped into the system. Finnley was seconds behind with the tactical report.

"Two carriers, ten battleships; two of them Marcallan, twenty-four frigates, eighteen cruisers; four appear to be battle weight, twenty corvettes, three troop transports."

"No destroyers?" Jason asked.

"None on *passive* scopes."

"Small favors. All right, move in."

Jason guided his fighter toward the enemy task force while minute changes in the marker beams gave orders to the other ships. As he drifted forward, he managed to get close looks at the enemy fleet. Most of the ships he'd seen already. As reported, there didn't seem to be any "hedgehogs" among them. Though some of the corvettes, nicknamed "wasps" by Interstar, did pique his attention for a moment. All of them had a short, relatively thin main body with curved back wings like a swallow, but the back quarter of the ship varied wildly depending on the pods attached. Some were almost like an extra set of wings, some were a smooth bulge with lots of weapons crammed onto them, and some looked like a small hangar. This style dominated the current flotilla, which made Jason wonder if they were brought along as additional support rather than combat.

His eyes then shifted to the three ships that resembled large, somewhat flat beetles. The limited weapons and large deployment doors made it clear these were really only made for landing troops rather than ship combat. He marked them as non-targets for the coming strike. If the plan worked to perfection, they could deal with the ground troops with ease. If it failed or didn't work as well as hoped, it wouldn't matter how many troops Polaris landed.

Jason had to swallow his heart back down when he got a clear view of two large vessels he knew all too well. They were built like elongated triangles with rounded corners and spheres built into the frame going down the middle and across the back of the ship. Their hull was painted dark-purple which would have made them almost invisible if not for the sun's light.

He'd seen these "bubble boomers," as the fleet called them, before. First when he saw his group wiped out near a research station. Then many, many times in the hundreds of engagements that followed over the years. These Marcallan battleships were mean and hard to take down, but they were also sluggish compared to Interstar's *London* class battleships, and they never carried drones. They were marked as priority targets since, even Polaris couldn't match them in terms of raw firepower.

The fleet had arrived in standard defense formation—carriers in the middle, then a sphere of ships from biggest to smallest going out from there. But as the Gold Group drifted among them, the fleet began to spread out. The space between ships grew all the way to the point that Interstar's heavy cruisers could have flown between them with room to spare. In minutes, it was more of a stretched-out parade version of the formation, which almost completely negated the tactical advantage.

Overconfidence leads to defeat. The words of Jason's flight instructor echoed in his head. The Polaris fleet thought they were alone and had grown complacent. Considering they weren't conducting any heavy scans; it seemed they didn't even think there was a chance they would be engaged. *Small favors.*

It bred an excitement he had to squeeze out into his controls to avoid losing composure. He checked his speed, finding it to be below ten meters a second. He might as well be drifting at that speed, but he needed to keep it slow to avoid detection.

So, Gold 1 drifted, everything powered as low as they could afford, through the enemy formation with Jason sweating bullets as he got ever closer. Weak beams, more like primitive laser pointers, signaled the location of the other fighters and relayed target data. The lattice bouncing around the group was risky, yet required to be sure their first strike was as effective as possible. Time moved slower than they did as they waited for everyone to reach their points.

At last, Jason stared down the rim of a Polaris carrier launch tube. He could see the closed doors maybe ten meters into the tube. Seemed incredible now that such a short rim of protection had proven so effective at protecting the carrier's hangar bays. Of course, the turrets above and below helped, but when you are close enough to spit through them, it can seem rather silly that they would work at all.

"Positions at 70 percent," Finnley reported.

"No change in enemy posture," Sundale added.

Big, big favors.

Jason took deep breath after deep breath. Any moment now, they'd get their chance. They needed every advantage they could get if this was going to work. Yet, with each passing second, his eyes darted at the troop transports. If those things started moving at the wrong time, they'd have to take their chances. Or if the scatter field over their fortified position flickered for a second, shields would snap on everywhere and do more damage to their chances than anything.

Just when he started to consider risking a full scan, the doors in front of Jason opened. He could see soldiers walking around the hangar in no particular hurry. Rows of fighters and transports filled the bay. Some were still being loaded.

The timer had started. They wouldn't have long to take advantage of this opening. As such, Jason ordered a low-level pulse scan. Just enough to check conditions.

"60 percent bay opening," Sundale said.

"We could wait," Finnley offered. "They may open more."

Jason thought about it, but when he saw many of the transports closing their doors, he knew the timer had already run out.

"No," Jason said. "It's now or never. Finnley? Send the signal."

"Sending signal, aye," Lieutenant Finnley said. "Timer will be set for fourteen thirty-three."

Jason flipped the cover off of his fire button and waited. Seconds later, Gold 1 emitted a soft radiation pulse. It triggered an automatic timer in all the fighters in the area. Cloaks would be dropped on the nearest full minute to ensure a synchronized attack. While they could have fired while cloaked, full combat power was more valuable once the attack began, and no cloak in the galaxy could hide that. If Polaris detected it at all, they'd have ten seconds to determine if they'd actually seen it and then try to decide what it was. Only the most alert or paranoid fleet would have acted so fast, and this fleet had given all the signs of being neither.

At fourteen thirty-three on the dot, three groups of Scorn fighters decloaked among the enemy fleet. A soldier in the hangar pointed toward Gold 1. Any free-standing comrades froze when they followed his finger. Jason's finger was already on the heavy weapon trigger. The second there was sufficient power, torpedoes left the racks between Gold 1's cockpit and engine nacelles two at a time. They were joined by several additional torpedoes fired from the other Scorns. Many were headed inside the open hangars. Others went for targets like the shield generator, engines, and main weapon batteries. Still others made strikes on critical points on the other ships scattered all throughout the enemy fleet.

The space between ships erupted in a bright flash as dozens of torpedoes impacted the enemy fleet like a thousand fireworks in the night sky. The burst of energy fire followed by the shaped charge that earned them the nickname "shells" cut through enemy armor, sending streams of expanding hot metal cutting through key components, while any charges that went off inside created more than enough air pressure to do additional damage. The hangar Jason had been staring at became littered with scattered and ravaged craft and bodies.

Seconds after the first shell was fired, the rest of their weapons received power, and the bombardment intensified across the enemy fleet. Cannon fire, turret fire, lasers, and exactly three salvos of missiles each ripped into the various enemy ships. Jason could see his fire tearing into the unarmored inner walls, dealing untold amounts of damage to the systems behind the primary hangars.

The barrage continued for fifteen seconds before the Scorns withdrew in unison. The enemy had yet to offer a response, allowing Jason to check the carnage. A smile crept onto his face, though his stomach did its usual turn when he did.

Both enemy carriers were little more than smoldering ship hulls with hangars attached. Their cruisers ranged from lightly damaged to useless, and the Polaris-built battleships showed signs of respectable damage. Only the corvettes and Marcallan battleships appeared largely or completely untouched.

"Sit rep," Jason said. "How did we do?"

Sundale's reply was delayed by the first volleys of the enemy's reply, weak though it was given their range. "**BOTH** carriers are disabled. Four battleships down, three more heavily damaged. Three cruisers down. Five frigates down. Two corvettes down. Light or moderate damage to all other ships."

"What about the bubble boomers?"

"Light damage only."

"Probably the only part of the fleet that was awake and paranoid."

"We do have that effect on jantans," Finnley added.

"True enough," Jason said. "Hold onto your teeth. This battle's only begun."

Jason pulled the fighter around to prepare for the second phase of the battle. The Polaris fleet had begun to reorganize into a layered formation designed to protect the corvettes and battleships that were now gravitating toward the center of the formation. Their remaining ships came together to form a fierce crossfire while, to Jason's utter shock, several enemy fighters were launching from the burning hulks that used to be their carriers. The corvettes didn't matter much, but the battleships had to be taken out if they were to have a chance of defending Holdre 4. Getting to them would be difficult, but Jason had a plan already hatching.

Apparently, so did Admiral Redding.

"New orders," Finnley said. "All groups are to gather, then charge. Gold Group is to take point. We'll begin the charge, and on your order, odd ships will go right, even ships go left. All fighters are to kite the enemy, not fully engage. Our goal is to pull their fleet apart, make an opening in their formation."

Great minds think alike. Though he wasn't sure he'd tell Admiral Redding, this was precisely the plan Jason had in mind.

He banked Gold 1 toward the area where the groups were collecting. It didn't matter that the enemy could see them. Only that the formation was too busy defending themselves to worry about the surface. *Let's hope it stays that way.*

Once the fighters had assembled, Jason gave the order and led the charge forward. Three groups of Scorns flew straight toward the enemy fleet, their formation loose and undefined. It appeared to be a standard bull rush tactic, which the enemy fleet was adjusting to match. Cruisers and corvettes shifted to barrage their ranks the moment they were in range, with fighters ready to go after those that split off.

So far, so good.

Jason glared at the enemy fleet, his chest growing tighter by the second. He knew when to split, he just didn't know what would come next. No one ever did.

Then, right at the edge of Polaris Point Defense Fire turret range, he gave the order.

"Break!"

One stream of fighters became two that split off around the sides of the enemy formation. The first round of enemy fire went where they had been, then chased after them. All Scorns stayed at maximum PDF range. Hits were few and far between, with damage being absorbed by flaring shields. The various defenders went with the fighters, moving like offensive linemen trying to peel off a blitzer. As the Scorns gained more distance from the enemy fleet, the defenders tried to follow, leaving the center barely guarded.

Finnley then sounded with new orders. "All fighters, turn and engage. Allied fleet inbound."

Right on cue, Interstar's fleet dropped their cloak. The splitting Scorns turned and charged head-first toward the outside defenders. Most of the enemy ships turned to plug the hole, only to leave a major gap in the side defenses. The Scorns had no problem flying past the now scattered side defenses. Once in range of the Marcallan battleships, they twisted and danced like hummingbirds, pounding the enemy shields with their weapons while avoiding most of the point defense fire. *Typical Jant PDF.* Parts of the Polaris fleet turned to engage the now very real threat to their heavies.

"Turn and run," Jason ordered. "Everybody out!"

Every Scorn flipped on their back and left the way they came. Turrets alone peppered the battleships, then turned to face the few fighters seeking to retaliate. The Scorns weaved around each other, using well-practiced maneuvers to ensure no ship took more than a few shots at once. Polaris ships gave chase but, in so doing, had forgotten Interstar's fleet.

The *Alamo* and her escorts unleashed fierce barrages of plasmoid fire onto the Marcallan battleships. Data from the Scorns allowed them to land precise hits at long range, yet none of the shots were able to do more than hull damage or take out weapon batteries. Interstar corvettes, six-sided boxes with pointed bows covered in large Gatling cannons and a single twin-barreled heavy-cannon battery top and bottom, moved through the enemy fleet. They darted and turned like leaves twisting in the wind. A battlecruiser was their target, and with squads of Scorn fighters from the *Alamo* helping, she didn't last long.

When the chasing fire ceased, Jason again adjusted their tactics. "Turn back in. Dip and dive, skirt around the back, take out those bubble boomers. Odds on one ship, evens on the other. Sundale—"

"Ready on targeting scanners," Sundale said.

"Link stable," Finnley said. "Ready to transmit."

Once again, all three groups reversed course. With the Polaris fleet now desperately trying to defend their heavy hitters, the fighters had no trouble getting to the backside of the formation. Once there, the Marcallan battleships felt the full force of Interstar. Scorns on one side fired their cannons. Data from them allowed battleships and destroyers to pummel them from the other side while hovering at the far end of target range. For a moment, both ships were nothing more than large shield flares until the combined fire proved far too much for their generators. Holes were open in seconds, through which lasers, torpedoes, missiles, Gatling cannons, capital ship batteries, and even some rarely used kinetic rounds from battleships tore into their armor. Seconds later, all shields fell, and the ships were quite literally carved to pieces by the combined fire.

"All ships out," Finnley called. "No more dives. We are to hold the enemy at arm's length and pray reinforcements get here in time."

Pray indeed.

Polaris still had more support ships, and enough fighters to prevent even the combined groups from doing as they pleased. Polaris drones were growing into thickening clouds as well. Jason himself had to turn and face Polaris fighters before a chase could form. A turn that still claimed Gold 8, though not her escape pod. *Small favors.*

Worse still, a leading voice seemed to have risen among the Polaris ranks. The ships were gathering into a very effective layered defense, which had already claimed an Interstar cruiser that didn't run in time. Polaris fighters darted among the ships, picking off drones that tried to get in. More Scorn began to fall. Interstar had given themselves a chance, but they still needed reinforcements to win this one.

A fact made all too clear by the flashes of light on the surface below. The troop transports had been allowed through. A ground battle was beginning. There wasn't enough strength to stop them, and neither fleet dared break their side of the tug-of-war to provide support. The only saving grace was the fact that the surprise attack seemed to have driven them to right where Interstar wanted them.

Get it done, Major, Jason silently ordered. *Make me proud.*

CHAPTER 8

HOMEFIELD ADVANTAGE

Yarain perked her ears in pride. Her small force, not more than fifty Holdrens, was watching and waiting like the seasoned troops she suspected many of them were. Every ear and eye was watching the sky or forest, checking to be sure they were secure while watching for the Polaris landers. The *Alamo* had managed to equip them all with the old-style vest and helmet that covered the muzzle she once used, and no one complained. Nor had they needed any real instruction in operating the SMTs and PMGs they now carried. Yarain herself wore heavy, tight-fitting armor specially fit for her. The protection thinned out over her limbs and was so form-fitting, her claws remained fully indexed. Even her tails had a thin layer on them, though they'd fixed the problem from before of her helmet tickling her whiskers too much. It left her feeling like the others were under-protected, but the *Alamo's* fabricators could only do so much in the time they had. It would have to do.

The team didn't have to wait long before the first of the Polaris landers made their approach through the atmosphere. A long fireball like a comet suggested they weren't being slow about it either. Two more fireballs indicated the others weren't far behind.

"*Trajectory?*" Yarain asked in the Holdren language.

A Holdren named Thon, who had orange all over his back, neck, and upper joints, checked his scanner. "*Grid 14-A.*"

Right where we landed. It was hoped they would take the biggest clearing they could find as well, and they had. Who wouldn't? Under normal circumstances, the space from the forest would provide enough safety to avoid guerilla tactics. They were likely expecting the local Holdrens to be, at most, "wildlife" to contain, if not potentially allies to recruit. They weren't expecting trained Holdren soldiers, who could easily strike unseen from the distant cover.

That said, Polaris had created a different problem. "*How far behind are the other two ships?*"

"*Two minutes,*" Thon said.

Too little. The plan had called for their ambush to fully disable and disarm one of the ships, hopefully with most or all of the embarked troops rendered inoperable. But with supporting ships that close behind, she would have to settle for the next best thing.

"*Prep your weapons,*" she said. "*Aim for the engines and be ready to drop and run on my order.*"

The group gave a unanimous, "*Yes, ma'am.*"

"*Thon, can you get us a good angle?*"

Thon again checked his scanner as the landers grew in size above them. "*Yes.*"

"*Lead.*"

Thon wasted no time turning through the forest. The group followed on his tails, not worrying about sound, yet staying to cover all the same. As the first lander approached the clouds, the assault force was already lifting their weapons.

"On my mark," Yarain said. *"PMG's first, count three, then SMT's."*

All ears were pulled back. Not in fear but in warning. When about to fire from their tails, Holdrens would often tuck their ears back to reduce the risk of hitting them and as a final warning. It was habit, and instinct, and there was no one around to see it anyway.

Yarain did the same, but her eyes were trained on the transport. The second it broke through the clouds; she gave a harsh bark. Ten PMGs lit the lander up like a Christmas tree. Three seconds later, another ten SMTs streaked from the forest toward the same target. Both salvos were precisely on target. The PMG fire weakened the lander's shields, which the SMTs quickly finished. Despite their limited experience, the Holdrens were still able to reload and fire the SMTs with tremendous speed. Three salvos were in the air before the first had even hit. Four had hit before the lander even tried to evade, but damage had already been done. The same turn meant to evade became a death spin as their damaged engines couldn't maintain control. More salvos did additional damage, sending her spinning to the surface.

"Drop and run," Yarain barked.

Heavy weapons were discarded as the entire force went on all fours to sprint the way they'd come. Seconds after they did, weapons fire from the other landers pounded the forest surrounding their former position. Their abandoned munitions were detonated in the blast, but the assault force itself had left the area hit before the first shots fell.

The sprint was slowed to a run as Yarain checked back on their work. The first lander pounded into the ground with a thud she could feel despite the distance. The ship was on fire, badly damaged, and had no chance of ever taking off again. *One down.*

Unfortunately, the other two ships were thus far untouched. One was already beginning to land, while the other flew over the forest with random shots splintering the trees. *Good. The scatter field is still working.*

Yarain paused the retreat long enough to speak English into her comms. "COB Zero to COB One. Fire at that lander with a PMG or two."

Captain Harrison's voice came back confused. "Ma'am? At that range all we'd do is . . . oh . . . never mind. We're on it."

Streams of PMG fire erupted from the same mountains Yarain's group was heading for. The lander did just what she expected them to do; turn toward them to eliminate them. Except once it approached the mountains, the four starship-grade heavy cannons hidden on the highest ridge opened up. The lander's shields flared heavily as she tried to bank away, but all that did was slow her down. Between the PMG fire and the heavy cannons, her shields were unable to keep up. Her armor felt the sting of SMT's adding to the barrage, and she soon hit the ground hard enough to test Yarain's stance. The cloud of dirt kicked up was almost as big as the ship, got sent twice as high, and was laced with flames. *Two down.*

"Continue on to the mountains," Yarain told her group. *"I'll meet you there."*

"You shouldn't hunt alone, ma'am," Thon said.

"I'm not hunting. Go. I'll be safe."

"Yes, ma'am."

The group continued on their way while Yarain hugged cover to inspect the situation. The first ship had put out the fires, and men seemed to be working on the loading ramps. Meanwhile, the third ship was landing nearby, still untouched.

Yarain again hit her comms. "Milsol, are you in position?"

"Yes," came the reply. "About to strike now."

"Disable only. There's nothing . . ." Yarain trailed off as she saw the first ship's loading ramps drop. "**NEGATIVE! ABORT** strike. Zone is too hot."

"That lander can't be allowed to support their advance."

Yarain's ears shot up as her heart sank. Tanks were rolling out of the first ship without any signs of damage. "I said abort! Tanks on the field. Repeat, tanks on the field."

"My life for the pack. We will not fail."

Yarain's ears fell. She knew they wouldn't fail. She knew they wouldn't get out. She knew she couldn't stop them. For a Holdren, the idea of giving their life to protect the pack wasn't just some battle cry. It was their blood. By invoking the phrase, Milsol had made it clear; he felt he had to give his life, and that of his team, to protect his pack.

Which made them the most dangerous force currently on the surface.

That did not keep Yarain's heart from burning and shaking as she saw the fire from Milsol's team. Just like hers; it came fast, hard, and accurate. Being landed, the ship was easily disabled, but it still took a moment for the shields to be stripped and then for the SMTs to crack through the armor enough to reach the critical systems beneath.

In that moment, the newly deployed tanks were able to turn and aim.

"**DROP** and run!" Yarain ordered.

The streams ended, but it was too late. No more than a second passed before Polaris tanks opened fire. The forest erupted in bursts of fire, dirt, and leaves. Though she couldn't hear any cries, Yarain did see bodies fly. One even flew into the clearing, still burning.

She cringed in pain, then turned for the mountains herself. She could do nothing for Milsol's team now. She could only do her best for the rest of the planet.

She ran on her hands and paws toward a mountain range that looked shallower than it was. The trees mostly ended at its base, though some hold-outs pocketed the surface, as did the occasional bush. The ground beneath her paws was compact and firm, with few rocks or patches of dirt to slow her. As she scaled the sides, she could see the ridges and rock formations that already held Interstar's tanks behind them. Infantry moved behind the ridges, laying down SMT rounds and preparing sniper positions to help defend their fortifications. Up at the summit of the mountains, four large, twin-barreled cannons sat, waiting for Polaris to come into range again.

Yarain crossed one of the ridge lines, then headed for a cave while retracting her helmet. No one bothered to stop their preparations to salute, nor did anyone pause to look. Soldiers and tanks continued to perfect their positions while Yarain turned inside an old lava tunnel that had become their command post.

Several mobile terminals and other similar equipment lit up the cave like it was daylight inside. Guards at the mouth watched just in case any Polaris troops got lucky and to serve as runners should the need arise. Yarain marched past them all toward Harrison, who was looking over a sensor display of the mountains and clearing below.

He turned to face her, but also skipped the salute. "Good to see you in one piece."

Yarain's ears shifted back again in another cringe. "We weren't all as lucky."

"I know. I know he was part of your pack, though, with respect to you and him; five minutes after I met him, I knew he was more stubborn than you are. You couldn't have stopped him."

Harrison did not know how right he was. Though that fact did little to ease the ache in Yarain's heart. "Where do we stand?"

"See for yourself."

Harrison indicated a display that showed the mountain range, as well as where the many tanks and defensive positions were. Yarain could see the lines were well-defined, with multiple points of fire scattered among the rocks and ridges, as well as a few sniper teams hidden away from the main clusters. Other dots and lines signified charges laid beneath the ground one or two hundred yards from their lines. The clearing below was largely populated via visual scanning, though vibration sensors had been hidden throughout the forest to create a sort of sensor net unhindered by their own jammers.

As she looked it over, Harrison pointed to two points in the middle of their lines. "We finally got the other two cannons set up. We'll be putting them here."

Yarain looked over the topography and felt a day's worth of thoughts become clear in a second. "**NEGATIVE.** Split the cannons on the flanks. Move the others there as well, and realign as many tanks as possible along those lines."

Even the tech looked back in confusion. "Ma'am?" the man said. "That will leave our forward defense pretty thin."

"They're smart enough not to charge into the antlers. They'll try a pincer, force us to divide our troops."

"What if they shift to our front?" Harrison asked.

"By the time they realize it's weak, they'll have to fight through our flanks to get there."

"And if they do 'go for the antlers'?"

"Then we'll close on them like a set of jaws."

Harrison's face turned into a devious smile. "Understood, ma'am. See to it, Sergeant."

"Aye, sir," the tech replied.

Yarain gave the mouth of the cave a long look, then sighed. "Let me know when the enemy moves."

She barely heard the confirmation as she left the command cave. Her force was well trained. There was little for her to do until things started happening. So instead of watching screens that would tell her nothing more, she stood on the edge of the ridge, looking out into the forest below.

The Polaris army was like an ant hill below, watched over by two giant beetles. Troops and equipment continued to fill the clearing with a ring of armor protecting the area from any further attacks. The more it grew, the more it became clear that Polaris still had the larger army. Though Interstar had position and prep time, it would be a hard task holding long enough for the Kapon fleet to arrive.

As tanks moved around the mountain to adapt to her orders, Yarain saw a group of Holdrens make their way through the lines. She rushed toward them when she saw Milsol alive and well among them. Though her elation was tempered when she saw other members of his team being carried, holding an arm, or sporting burns in their fur.

Despite the pain, they met with traded licks on the cheeks. "*I'm glad you made it,*" Yarain said.

"*So am I,*" Milsol said.

"How many didn't?"

"Fifteen. Another twelve are too wounded to fight." Yarain's ears fell in a soft cringe. *"Don't. They gave their lives for their packs."*

Yarain stared into his eyes with pain behind hers. *"Doesn't keep it from hurting."*

"No, it doesn't."

They traded a brief rub before Yarain insisted he get checked out before rejoining the lines.

Yarain returned to her vigil. She watched the wounded be taken into another cave, then watched the troops scatter around to their new positions. Small teams were being sent behind the mountain to meet the escape pods that were beginning to land. She tried to think of something she should be doing, but she again concluded there was nothing to do but wait. Unfortunately, that also gave her a moment to feel the weight on her shoulders and for her thoughts to wander a bit.

These men, women, and foxes were all depending on her to lead them well. It helped that the division commander was the first to support the idea of her having so much input. He'd seen her in action during her "stunt" on Phoenix Perch, and the Holdrens responded to her better than they would have ever responded to him. Jason had said she'd make a good unit commander, and now here she was, leading the defense of her home. The next few hours would tell if he was right or not.

Those thoughts felt strange to her, too. "Her home." She wasn't sure if this was her territory or not, but some things about the area did seem familiar. Particularly the lakes in the distance. Her instincts said this was home, though she couldn't tell if it really was, or if they were responding to being on the planet again, or if it was just a reaction to the current situation. Either way, she was a first mother again. She was the spear of the pack. Their lives were hers to protect . . . or accept should the need arise. Fifteen had already given that sacrifice. Be it human or Holdren, that number would soon rise.

Her ears shifted back a moment at that thought, but her fur rose as well. This was her home . . . *their* home. They would see it defended to the last for if they failed, there would be no one left to defend the other packs on the planet. And that outcome was simply not allowed here.

"Been a while since . . ."

Harrison's voice caught Yarain so off guard she jerked like the startled animal she was. Though she faced him with open jaws, they closed just as fast once her mind caught up with her body.

Harrison remained well composed, though his hands had come up a little. "Sorry, ma'am. I didn't mean to startle you."

Yarain's ears shifted out, the Holdren version of a dismissal. "No harm done. What were you saying?"

"I . . . it's nothing, forget it."

"Captain. Let's have it."

Harrison sighed, fiddled with his hands, then gave a sheepish smile. "It's been a while since I've seen . . . well . . . you ma'am. The solid leader that provides a spark to the troops."

Yarain's ears fell again. "I think you're imagining things, Harrison."

"I doubt it. I've heard similar things from the other soldiers, human and Holdren. Anytime someone expresses fear or doubt, another reminds them that you're here, and that doubt seems to vanish. Like it or not, ma'am, the troops seem to trust you. I haven't seen that anywhere for a long time . . . including the mirror."

Yarain's ears shot forward, and her hand went to his shoulder. "Then you need to look harder."

Harrison seemed ready to protest, but he never managed a sound. All he could do was stare at her ears, lips, and whiskers all forward, with her eyes burning into him. Yarain had seen the potential in him. She'd seen all the reasons why he'd been given his Vesper team in the first place. What she couldn't see was why he doubted himself so much. So, in that moment, she was refusing to let him go there. With no idea how to do it for a human, she only knew the Holdren way.

The first mother's way.

That thought brought a softness to her ears. How quickly she'd fallen into those instincts—and how right it felt. With Holdrens, a first parent would prevent destructive thoughts assertively, preventing the member from allowing them to linger. In that way, she was not allowing any room for Harrison's doubts. Her gaze and the physical contact would force a Holdren mind to focus entirely on her, which would leave no room in their minds to spare for negative thoughts.

Despite him being human, it seemed to work. The cloud of uncertainty faded from Harrison's eyes. He then put his hand on hers with a nod.

"I'll do that," he said.

Yarain dropped her hand and returned her focus to the ground below. Harrison stood beside her in silence until they saw the Polaris troops begin to collect and move into the trees. *Here we go.*

Yarain turned back for the cave with Harrison close behind. She went straight for the sensor display to confirm what she suspected. The enemy was moving out. While the main sensors were basically useless, the vibration sensors had no trouble seeing heavy armor versus light.

At first, it seemed to be two split lines of APCs and tanks. Then Yarain asked for a wider sensor reading. She saw a second group behind both primaries comprised entirely of heavy armor.

The division commander, a man by the name of Colonel Turik Tanner, joined her at the display. He was a tall, bald man, built like a linebacker, and had skin as black as humans got.

"Interesting tactic," Tanner said.

"But smart," Yarain said.

"How do you figure?" the sensor tech asked.

"The weaker force will scout our defenses, then the heavy armor will be able to target them."

Tanner shifted so he could get a better look at the defensive positions. "We can fend them off for a while, but I don't know for how long. Got any ideas, Major?"

Yarain's ears perked more in confusion than surprise. "It's your division, sir."

"We've been over this. This is your world, your people, and right now, I trust your instincts better than mine."

Yarain's ears now shifted back unsure, but she watched the display anyway. When the enemy lines didn't change, she went with her first thought. "Small arms only until they commit their armor. Once their heavies show, then we open up. If possible, try to create a roadblock with their own carcasses. If we can force their tanks into choke points, we'll be able to hold a lot longer. We should also hold our charges until their advance takes ground."

"Why do that?" Tanner asked.

"It will break their lines for a moment, trap a group of their tanks between hulks, and give us a chance to add to that line of dead tanks to buy us more time."

Tanner gave her a laugh that caused his teeth to contrast against his skin. "See what I mean? You have a devious, cunning mind. I like it!"

Harrison said, "Still going to be hell holding them back. I figure they have two full divisions, maybe more, and it looks like it's all armor. At best we have one total to match, and not all of it is tanks."

"Don't go soiling your trunks yet, Captain. I know you PSC boys can be a little soft, but I've put my men through hell in training for a reason. When this one hits, it'll be another day at the office."

That's Terrines for you. "We also have the Holdrens. We should send everyone we have out wide along their flanks. Careful guerilla tactics should limit their losses and hopefully slow the advance."

"Won't they be more use with us on the lines?" Tanner asked.

"They're hunters, sir. Let them hunt."

Tanner nodded with another deep chuckle. "Roger that, Major. All that's left now is get the flanks covered."

"I'll command the left."

Several eyes turned Yarain's way, most confused, except for Tanner whose were pure question. "I thought you were going to help me command this battle. You can't do that from one flank."

"Holdrens don't lead from the den, sir," Yarain said. When Tanner glared like he wasn't going to accept that, she continued with other arguments. "I can't lead a battle I can't see, and with all due respect, sir, do these displays tell you everything about a battle as it unfolds? And if I'm honest, sir, once the battle starts, I won't have much to offer anyway."

Tanner's lips slowly curled into a knowing smile. "The more I learn about you, the more I agree with Colonel Harlem. You have all the makings of a fine commander."

"Don't you start ... erm ... with resp ..."

Tanner waved her down before she could finish. "At ease, Major. I know exactly what you mean. I felt the same way when I was where you are in your career. The left flank is yours. Captain Solov will be your second. She's already there, and by now, she probably has the entire flank tuned to one channel. You won't be fighting anyone else for orders. Harrison!"

"Sir!" Harrison said.

"Take Major Barely. You two will command the right flank. I'll monitor the battle from here."

Harrison's eyes started to grow. "S-sir? I don't see how—"

"**LOOK** harder," Yarain said.

She was giving him that same glare. Only Tanner seemed to notice. When he saw the glare, he gave Harrison a sideways look of his own. "Problem Captain?"

Harrison's eyes had already begun to return to normal. When Tanner questioned him, he snapped into perfect attention. "No, sir!"

"Good. I think we're set, then. See you all in the mess hall afterwards. Drinks are on me." Tanner turned so he faced the center of the cave. "Any of you need to pray, now's the time. I got no tolerance for calls to God, spirits, or dead great-grandmothers in my foxholes, understood?"

The cave echoed with a unanimous, "Understood, sir!"

"Good! Now then, let's blow stuff up."

As he walked toward another of the terminals, Yarain couldn't help casting a glance at Harrison. "Isn't that Hark's line?"

Harrison had to stifle a laugh. "No, ma'am. Her's is, 'No boom today? There's always boom tomorrow.' You stay safe out there, ma'am."

"You as well, Captain." She turned to leave, paused, and put a hand on his shoulder again. "Remember: *I* believe in you. Don't you dare make me wrong."

Harrison nodded his thanks, then she continued on her way.

CHAPTER 9

BUNKER HILL

Yarain grabbed a rifle from the rack at the entrance, then made her way to the highest ridge of the left flank. Soldiers hurried to their positions while the remaining able-bodied Holdrens left down the sides to prepare for their harassment. Her ears ticked forward in approval when she saw Milsol leading the left flank group. The only wound she saw was a slight patch of black fur on his far-right tail, and she doubted it was more than fur deep.

Yarain found a small group of soldiers gathered on a perch that gave her easy sight of the mountainside without exposing herself too much. She recognized one of them as the indicated Captain Solov. The others seemed to be support staff, some of them huddled around even smaller portable displays than the command cave. Yarain took a moment to check her perch. From there, she could see every position, every tank, every soldier . . . every life that now lay in her hands. She let that thought simmer in her mind a moment, then blew it out a sharp exhale.

"Status," she called.

Captain Ishka Solov, a tall woman with scars on her forehead, black hair, and tan skin, stepped up beside her. "We're ready for them, ma'am. All units on this side of the lines are keyed to channel twenty-one-oh-four. Any orders given or received beyond that will go through these men. If it helps, think of them doing the same job you do on a Scorn."

That actually does help. "What about our defenses? Did you receive details about our change of focus?"

"Yes, ma'am, and the men have been apprised of the change in strategy. We've got all three cannons covering the approach. SMT and Stiletto caches have been distributed among the troops, and I have the detonator for the charges. We have the approach pre-sighted, though we can't use mortars any more than they can with the canopy up."

"What's the redeploy time on the canopy?"

"Five minutes, ma'am. No sooner."

Too long. As had been discussed before, the same invisible shield that was keeping them safe from artillery, and orbital fire for that matter, was more important than being able to use their own. Five minutes would be more than enough time for the enemy to wipe them from the surface at too long a range. They would have to survive this battle without it, somehow.

Yarain again reminded herself that she was dealing with humans, then tapped her comms to address her side of the battle. "All units, listen up! **DO** not fire until ordered. I don't care if you can reach out and kiss them. Hold fire until my mark, not before. Listen for orders, don't wait for explanations, and above all, remember what we're fighting for. You all know what they did to one Holdren. Just think what they'd do with thousands more. We are all that stands between them and that fate. **PROTECT** and serve!"

Her half of the mountain erupted with the reply, "Honor and uphold!"

No matter the cost.

It was the lesser-quoted third part of Interstar's motto, but everyone knew it all the same. In part because the three comets in the logo represented those three "tails" of their guiding principle. Though the third tail was more rarely recited, everyone knew it was there. Especially when all three were about to be put into action.

Yarain held her vigil over the coming battlefield. Trees shook in the distance, chasing the birds into fearful retreat. Polaris apparently didn't care about being subtle, or their remaining leaders weren't as bright as she thought. Whatever the reason, it seemed easy to track the enemy as they moved. Even so, Yarain deployed her full helmet and waited with perked ears.

The rustle in the distance grew closer, but the treads of the Polaris armor sounded much closer. Too close to match the disturbance. They technically could have started firing already, but she wanted to minimize damage to the forest if at all possible, and the trees would have blocked a lot of their fire anyway. Better to lure them close, then hopefully rattle them further with the first salvos.

"Load and target!" she ordered.

SMTs got their first loads, rifles were fitted with twelve-inch-long Stiletto micro missiles, and PMGs came to bear, all in less than five seconds. A soft clatter drew Yarain's ear next to her. She looked down and saw Lieutenant Shillin Rad already lying down, sniper rifle to her eye, like she'd been there the entire time.

"What are you doing here?" Yarain asked.

"Keeping you safe, ma'am," Rad said.

She said it like it was obvious, which brought an amused ruff from Yarain. *Guess I made an impact after all.*

She didn't have time to explore that thought. The rumble was very close now and unmistakable. The leading edge of the attack was there, just among the trees. Some metal hulls and barrels could be seen despite the thick cover, though not quite enough to get a good look at any particular vehicle.

Yarain slid behind her cover. "Stand ready. On my mark, small arms only. Tanks and cannons, hold fire."

An eerie silence fell over the mountain. Even Yarain's ears found nothing.

"Any second now," Rad muttered.

Any second turned out to be three seconds later.

The mountainside was peppered with a barrage of weapons fire, sending dirt and small debris scattering everywhere. Smaller boulders were turned to rocky splinters, while others lost chips from their sides. Just after the first volley, short, stubby APCs rolling on omni-wheels emerged from the forest. Most carried turrets of varying firepower on their tops, with a few having additional small arms turrets on the sides. Every weapon was screaming as the force charged forward.

Wait for it, Yarain ordered silently. *Hold . . . hold . . .* "Engage!"

The mountain returned fire with streams of PMG and rifle fire, picking at the limited shielding of the APCs. Only when the flaring stopped did SMTs and Stiletto rounds tear at their armor. Some APCs were splintered into bits of debris, while others ground to a halt as burning wrecks. Some veered into their comrades and knocked them onto their sides to become easy prey themselves. Those that survived were bombarded by PMG fire that acted almost like laser beams burning away at their targets.

The first wave of Polaris tanks emerged soon after. They were low-sitting blocks of smooth armor with a heavy turret in the center and additional small arms turrets on each corner. Treads beneath them rumbled as they advanced in and around the burning APCs to deliver their own rounds of fire. They, too, felt the sting of the mountain's defenses, but their heavier shielding allowed them to advance farther before going down.

The defenders chose their targets carefully. Any tank that seemed about to veer away from the remains of an APC often became a burning heap of slag themselves soon after getting around their fallen comrade. PMGs continued to carve holes in their shields and often went right on carving all the way into the crew compartment, assuming the hole wasn't blown apart by an SMT or Stiletto. These token attackers quickly fell back from the barrage, though they had managed to gain a fair amount of ground before doing so.

"Shift positions," Yarain said. "Clear any soft cover you just fired from. Try to stay hidden."

The troops did as instructed without delay. Infantry moved their hard points. Some positions simply got distance from the cover they had just been hiding behind. Only a token few chased the enemy into the woods and out of sight. Then they, too, moved from where they were.

"Well, that was too easy," Lieutenant Solov said.

"That's just the probe," Yarain said. "The real attack—"

The real attack cut her off as it blasted at the mountainside. Empty cover positions were obliterated, while some points that were still manned took hits. SMT teams and other groups died on hit. Very few managed to cry out. The Polaris tanks advanced in columns out of the forest. Their cannons continued to pepper the mountain with fire, searching for the defenders.

Yarain hit her comms. "Yarain to Milsol, begin your raids. All units, weapons free. Repeat, weapons free. Remember the plan."

The mountain returned fire with fierce revenge. Three heavy cannons on the plateau claimed tanks on their own in just a few shots. Interstar tanks built more like the bottom of a human dress fired their twin-barreled heavy cannons from cover and camouflaged positions, adding extra damage with their smaller auto-cannons that were very similar to the Scorn's turrets. The first column of Polaris tanks went up like a Roman candle before they knew what hit them. The second tried to avoid the remains of their comrades, only to add to an already thickening line of burning remains. Some tanks tried to use the carcasses as cover but were focused on by the cannons.

Explosions in the forest announced the beginnings of Milsol's raids. Whether it was Milsol's team or the tanks returning fire, or both, could not be determined. Yarain could spare no time to figure it out, though. This battle had only just begun.

When infantry tried to weave through the carnage to reach defensive points, Yarain fired her rifle from cover, using a Stiletto round whenever she saw exposed armor. Other times, she tried to pepper a tank's shields to drain them even a little more. Between bursts, she directed troops like an air traffic control tower.

"Squad four, move right."

"Focus fire on the lower column."

"Check left flank. First platoon, fill the gap."

"Battalion going high—cut them off!"

On it went for what felt like two lifetimes. Orders given were put into action without delay. Polaris forces trying to be sneaky were obliterated on command as if Yarain could trigger their demise at will.

The line of dead tanks continued to build, forcing Polaris to file through narrow lanes, only to be bombarded if they got through. Still others tried to use the remains of their comrades as cover, but Interstar made sure they added to the wall soon after.

However, Interstar's losses were starting to mount as well. Several positions were burning hulks themselves, and more than a few cover positions were now piles of pebbles with blood, bodies, and body parts scattered among them. The explosions in the forest had stopped, suggesting Milsol's team, for one reason or another, could no longer maintain their raids.

When Polaris managed to form a line and push forward with it, Yarain decided the time was now for their surprise. "***HIT*** the charges!"

Her order hadn't even faded before a row of burst fire plasmoid emitters at the base of the mountain ripped into the undersides of the enemy, followed by a fierce explosion as they detonated. A column of tanks that had been on it became a column of popped crew compartments. Small bits of rock tinked off of Yarain's helmet as they rained on the area for a moment. As expected, an entire separate column was trapped between lines of dead tanks.

"Focus fire. Finish those trapped tanks!"

The remaining defenders reduced the trapped units to burning wrecks, but not before they managed a few potshots at the highest ridges. Yarain saw a tank take aim. She dropped her rifle, jumped on top of Lieutenant Rad, and literally rolled them both to safety. Following her lead, Solov and the others made similar mad dashes with the comms equipment in tow. No sooner had they left their position than it was erased from the lines. Dust and pebbles fell around them, but otherwise, all had escaped harm.

Rad and Yarain looked at the crater where they once were, then Rad tilted her head at Yarain. "I owe you one."

"No, you don't," Yarain said.

Yarain found her rifle astonishingly intact but had to duck behind the remaining cover again as another volley hit the plateau. More positions fell, though thankfully, many saw it coming just as she had. The heavy cannons, however, weren't so easy to move. Their size made such maneuvers rather slow, and rather slow wasn't fast enough. One cannon was destroyed outright from a focused barrage, while a second took hits just below it. It seemed undamaged until the ground gave way beneath it. The operators managed to jump free just as the cannon slid and tumbled down the mountainside.

Even Yarain couldn't keep her heart from sinking. With only one cannon left, their lines were now in dire straits.

"Flankers, make your run now. Small arms, maintain pressure on forward tanks. Armor units, focus on their back-line. Let Colonel Tanner know we lost two of our cannons."

A battalion of Interstar tanks rolled from the far side of the mountain, guns blazing. The omni-directional treads underneath their armor allowed them to jab and dodge at impossible angles, at times literally making a ninety-degree change in course. It was a reserve tactic meant to lessen pressure for a moment, but the many dead Polaris tanks made it hard for their living comrades to maneuver. The remaining heavy cannon picked off a great many, and the flanking Interstar tanks claimed many more in their assault.

The combined assault inflicted severe losses on the Polaris army. The flankers, meant to lessen pressure, were remaining largely untouched several minutes after they were expected to have fallen. The remaining cannon seemed invincible and able to only land kill shots. With Polaris tanks falling en masse, a retreat became a rout as more positions joined the barrage. Interstar tanks that had been dead turned their turrets and added to the mountain's defense. All across the lines, it was as if the dead were coming back to life, so they could hold the line that much longer.

The Polaris tanks once again slid into cover. Yarain ordered a halt to the pursuit, and the mountain fell silent. While ears stopped ringing for the time being, the troops once again rearranged themselves without so much as a look from Yarain.

"Your voice carries," Lieutenant Rad said.

Yarain turned an ear toward her. "What do you mean?"

"Just noting how the men respond to you, ma'am."

"I agree," Solov said. "I've been on the front lines before. I can count on one hand the number of times I've heard such calm in the middle of chaos. It bleeds into the troops. Not a one is leaning on their rifle or bending over to breathe. The only ones not standing at the ready are those who physically can't."

Yarain sighed near a growl. "I'm getting tired of people trying to push me into a command."

"Only because you won't open your eyes, ma'am," Rad said.

Yarain again sighed, but at the same time, she couldn't help looking out over her lines. She wanted to see the state of their defenses. Instead, she saw what they saw.

Engineers were working on the few tanks they thought could be kicked – in one case literally – into moving or fighting again. PMG hard points were set and manned on boulders not yet touched by weapons fire. Injured were taken to the medical cave, soldiers gestured at each other to perfect their new positions, and through narrow paths in the mountains, Milsol's Holdrens were making off with crates of SMT and Stiletto rounds.

Not a one seemed to even take a second to breathe.

If anything, she saw pockets of what looked like laughter pop up in some places. Several PSC Cosmen, Caelnav Caelors, and Terrines teased each other as surviving crew from orbit were integrated into the defense. She even saw a five-way battle for a PMG be won by rock-paper-scissors. It was like seeing her old pack just before a hunt. The one she'd failed by leaving them to spend time in space, then failed again by getting caught in her attempt to retrieve Sundale. Though a part of her chest felt pierced by that memory, other parts were filled with energy the more she looked. She saw no fear of the danger or concern over failure. Only the joy of the pack and the excitement of the coming hunt. The thought broke into Yarain's soul, touching a part of herself she hadn't realized she'd lost.

"My pack," Yarain breathed.

Two heads nodded beside her.

"I suppose that's one way to see them," Solov said.

Yarain continued to scan the troops. She made eye contact with one group, who gave her a nod, a soft salute, then continued setting up their new hard point. That one act left her warm like she was laying by a fire, and lungs full of enough air to last for days.

They trusted her.

Outmanned, outgunned, desperate to hold the line, a battle on the other side going who knows how well, yet they trusted her. Nothing else could bring that kind of calm in such a situation. They looked at her with the same certainty her old pack used to. As if they knew without a doubt that she would do right by them.

She still questioned if she had, but in the moment, Yarain felt as if bits of her being were splitting out to touch the members of the current pack.

Those bits would then return, carrying with them a connection only a first parent would truly understand. They were part of her, and she was part of them. She may lead, but they remained one being fighting for survival. A human might have seen it as a burden or weight on her shoulders. For her, it was empowering. It rushed through her veins, focusing her thoughts and feelings on the moment for the sake of the pack.

When her ears caught the rumble of the Polaris tanks preparing their next advance, Yarain understood what Jason meant about a "switch," for one of her own flipped. Her ears perked forward, her lips vanished, and if it weren't for her armor, her fur would have been on end. In that instant, she knew exactly what she wanted to do, how she wanted to do it, and nowhere in her being was there a fraction of doubt or hesitation about her choices. *This will not happen again.*

She turned to Solov. "Set any charges we have left on the current perimeter. Try to put them on paths the enemy tanks will try to use. Move the cannon to the secondary position. Prepare all units to do the same on my mark. I want the remaining flanker tanks to set up at the secondary position now as well. Set any immobilized tanks to auto-fire and abandon them. Leave them dormant until ten seconds after the charges are detonated. Yarain to Milsol, hold your raids until I call a retreat. When I do, focus on the middle of their advancing forces. Once we're set, return to our lines. Solov, we'll need any ammunition they can send to left flank position two ASAP."

Her orders were acknowledged and put into action almost the second they were given. The only delay was the time it took to relay them across the lines. The remaining flanker tanks moved down pre-sighted paths to get them through the lines as quickly as possible. The terrain made it slow going, but the pre-planning kept things moving.

Lieutenant Rad, meanwhile, hadn't moved a muscle. "Planning another warpath?"

"Something like that," Yarain said.

"Can't wait to see this one."

Yarain ignored the comment in favor of watching the shifts. The flanker tanks were largely behind the line now, and the main cannon was making its slow trek to the secondary defensive position. Several soldiers were rigging what explosives and fire-burst charges remained along the line, in some cases placing them mere feet from a hard point. Meanwhile, tanks that were too badly damaged to move had their crews evacuated. While auto-fire wasn't as efficient without a mind behind it, in the coming scenario, it would be more than enough.

The rumble in the forest continued to shift around itself until it all at once fell silent.

"***HUNKER*** down!" Yarain said. "Here they come."

Any preparations not finished were abandoned. Troops flooded the lines, weapons at the ready. The air once again fell still. Yarain knew better than to doubt her ears. It was only a matter of time.

Polaris didn't bother with anything special. Their tanks roared forward in one massive charge. The mountain once again erupted in fire to fend them off. Polaris began paying a hefty price for their advance, but their numbers were large enough to absorb it. Carcasses were pushed aside or used as battering rams to push into the fray. While the many dead tanks did slow the advance, Polaris continued to gain ground, inch by blood-bought inch. At the same time, they sent a barrage of their own. Rocks were chipped into splinters, and hard points were erased once exposed. Infantry again tried to filter through, though small arms cut them down before they could claim any positions.

After what felt like another lifetime of assault, Yarain had to give the order.

"***SMOKE*** their lines. All units, fall back to second position. ***MOVE, MOVE, MOVE!***"

Those that could picked up their gear and ran. Others carried the wounded while tanks fought with the terrain to retreat as well. At the same time, two rows of smoke were sent out to blind the enemy, if only a tiny bit through modern technology. Though they continued to fire at the ridges, most of their targets were long gone. Only a few wounded hard points or damaged tanks remained to cover the retreat. Soon after, the middle of the enemy columns felt the sting of Milsol's raiding party. The Polaris tanks slowed to deal with the new threat, greatly reducing the pressure on the retreating defenders.

Yarain waited until the bulk of the force was on the move before leaving herself. Her command staff and Shillin Rad were right on her tails. The entire defense force picked their way through the ridge lines. The tanks at times had to go single file to make it through the paths, but the movement remained steady. Some took up positions to cover the rest while the defenders rushed for their secondary line.

The ridges here were much lower, with fewer rocks and boulders to provide natural cover. However, expecting an initial retreat would come sooner or later, Interstar had erected defensive walls, complete with a thin layer of particle shields, to fill as many gaps as possible. While the primary line would have taken considerable effort to put in even a minor improvement, this secondary position offered far more open, or mostly open, ground to build on. As such, since the start of the battle, additional hardpoints had been set up. These held mounted cannons better than a PMG, though still less than anything an armored unit would carry. Their remaining heavy cannon was just arriving on the ridge while tanks and infantry took position behind their new cover.

As Yarain again found a covered place on the high ground, she noted a second heavy cannon was approaching to join their one.

"Where did that come from?"

"The right flank," Solov said. "Tanner managed to sneak out some human teams to compliment the Holdren harassments. From what I hear, they've been supremely effective. The right flank is holding strong."

Idiot. I should have thought of that. Yarain made a note to mention it the next time someone talked command around her. Then brushed it aside in favor of the battle at hand.

She set her rifle down so she could check the state of their first line through binoculars. Polaris had been slow and wary about approaching the line. Given the events of the last hour or two, Yarain couldn't blame them. Little did they know how valid those fears were.

The Polaris tanks finally committed to advancing up the mountainside. Infantry filtered through, checking positions and in some cases throwing grenades into empty ones before checking. *Every round wasted helps.* They eventually reformed their lines once past the former defensive positions, and began a slow march up unknown terrain toward the secondary position.

Yarain went to her comms one more time. "All units, this is our final position. We hold or fall here. Stand ready to engage."

Silence again fell, save for the rumble of the Polaris tanks. Then, just as they reached maximum range, Yarain gave the order. The mountain once again pummeled the Polaris tanks with even more fire than before. Shields or not, entire squads went down at once. Their comrades behind them returned fire, mostly catching the reinforced walls for now.

"*HIT* the charges!"

The Polaris back lines were again rocked with a blast that took out clusters of armor and left a great many of their comrades trapped between dead friends. Before the dust could settle, over a dozen Interstar tanks believed to be dead came to life and began firing on the nearest Polaris tank. The trapped tanks were obliterated before they could decide where to return fire.

A moment of calm covered the field as the Polaris columns behind the carnage caught up with their fallen comrades. The only action for the moment was Polaris ensuring every Interstar tank was well and truly dead, which also meant wasting time on tanks that had never fired a shot. *Every second is more time bought.*

During the lull, Milsol's team scurried and limped through other narrow paths to join the lines. Yarain's heart sank an inch when she noted it seemed even thinner than when it first left.

When Milsol joined her on the lines, she couldn't stop the question. *"How many left?"*

"Fifteen," Milsol said. *"Eight that can still fight."*

"And you?"

"Well enough to fight."

It was still a hefty toll of their own. The weight on her shoulders felt like a tank when she reached for another Stiletto round and found the crate had only five remaining. When she looked up to ask, Solov shook her head.

"That's all we have left."

"SMTs?" Yarain asked. "Clips?"

"All running low. The right flank is still holding, but they're getting even lower than we are."

Yarain's heart sank further until she turned back to Milsol. Her old pack mate wasn't even looking at her. Much like the rest, he was too busy checking his weapon in preparation for the next assault. A glance down the lines saw more of the same across the board. Be it trust, commitment, or a lack of other options, all remained focused and steadfast. Yarain's chest filled with pride, even as it also ached at how many more would soon fall.

Impacts on the walls announced the arrival of the next assault. The lines returned fire as best they could, though the missile barrages were starting to thin. The heavy cannons were holding strong, though one had already taken a few glancing shots.

Still, the lines fought on. Even as tanks were destroyed or hard points were hit, there was always someone there to take their place. Troops were chucking grenades in place of their missiles and doing a fair bit of damage in the process. The battle was a yo-yo of gains and losses, but Polaris continued to gain inches each time they pressed forward.

About the time Yarain considered dropping the canopy to allow for mortar fire, something else broke into her comms.

"*Alamo* to ground forces, drop the canopy. Repeat, drop the canopy. Reinforcements en route, but they can't land with that shield up."

As far as Yarain's heart had sunk a moment before, it now rose twice as far. "You heard them. Drop the shield. All units, reinforcements are en route. Repeat, help is coming. *Hold. This. Line!*"

The fire intensified as a soft glow came and went over their heads. The shield was now down. How long it took Polaris to notice was anyone's guess.

Before they could however, fireballs dotted the sky like a field of stars. Some soon cleared into fighters much like Karol's, but others appeared to be some kind of tear-drop shaped charge. Some coming way too close to their lines.

Solov beat Yarain to the call. "Incoming fire! Danger close!"

"**NEGATIVE**," Milsol barked. "Those are drop pods, not weapons fire."

"Are you sure?" Yarain asked.

"**YES**."

Yarain gave Solov a straight-eared look, then turned her ears out to brush it off. "All units, disregard. Apparently, those are drop pods, not ordnance. Maintain fire."

The drop pods moved far faster than the fighters. They barraged the surface behind the Polaris lines. Instead of exploding, each one hit with a soft, mechanical thump. Soon after, smooth-hulled, slender tanks that seemed to be hovering off the ground began assaulting the Polaris tanks from the rear. Interstar's artillery positions had opened up as well to pepper the Polaris tanks with long-range fire. Alien fighters that matched the one Major Torzon flew joined the barrage. Entire columns were erased in a single run. It was like a human firework display as half a division ceased to exist in a matter of seconds.

It only took two runs before the Polaris tanks held their advance and fire. Seconds later, another call came over the comms.

"Tanner to all units, hold fire, hold fire. Repeat, hold your fire. Polaris has surrendered. I say again, Polaris has surrendered."

Cheers erupted from the mountainside. Hands and rifles raised in the air to celebrate victory as the Polaris survivors crawled out of their tanks, and infantry threw down their weapons.

Yarain, however, had to put her hand on the rock in front of her to keep from falling over. The strain of battle left so fast it left her dizzy.

She panted like she'd been sprinting for hours. She looked out on the expanded battlefield, watching with sinking lungs as Polaris troops were disarmed and wounded from both sides were tended to.

They'd done it. Though the cost was high, they'd held the line long enough. Somewhere in her mind, Yarain knew she should be thrilled. Perhaps in that same spot she was. But all she could see were the bodies and the fires alien craft were putting out. From there, her mind refused any further thought. There was nothing but exhaustion. An empty void where the weight had been, even as her body felt three times as heavy as it was. Even when she again scanned her battle lines, she couldn't find a thought or even a feeling. It was as if her mind suddenly couldn't process any idea other than, *I'm tired*.

"Best not to try," Solov said. Yarain perked her ears toward her. "I know what you're going through, ma'am. I've been there several times. Colonel Tanner calls it 'combat hangover.' It fits. The common response is to search for something to fill it. In my experience, it's best you don't. Just let your mind do what it will. It'll find something soon enough."

"Thank you," was all Yarain could manage.

Somewhere, she thought to retract her helmet. A soft breeze brushed her fur and took much of the new weight with it. She could almost feel her blood slowing now. Her mind was still a void, but only because it no longer needed to process things instead of being unable to. Yarain looked back at Milsol, who was just standing there, waiting for her to lead. Somehow, that cleared everything. Though her body still felt like a boulder, it also had enough strength to make it stand somewhat straight.

"We need to check the troops," Yarain said. "Make sure everyone is cared for. Also, check the lines for survivors—theirs and ours. And can someone tell me if Gold 1 survived?"

Solov's smile grew with each order. "Yes, ma'am. I think . . . Hello. What's this?"

Solov pointed to a group of aliens who were talking with some of the troops. When a soldier pointed at Yarain's position, the group marched her way without much comment.

Yarain's hand tensed on her rifle as she took stock of these aliens. All but one wore thick armor over a body that appeared to be reptilian. A glance down the lines found many more of the same assisting with taking the Polaris forces into custody, as well as a few similarly clad Holdrens. Yarain noted with some interest that while the reptilian legs were digitigrade like the Holdrens, they all wore some kind of boot that seemed to go just past the ankle joint. All had long, thick tails, as well as heads resembling snakes and lizards, some familiar, some not, some more like dragons from human fiction. Many had the same neck frills as Earth lizards and scale colors ranging from dark to light brown. Markings on their heads and tails varied along reptile lines as well, though little else could be seen through their clothes and armor. As for the one without armor, aside from the boots, Yarain couldn't discern much beyond him wearing the same lavender uniform as Captain Corzon.

She indicated the approaching group of aliens to Milsol. *"Do you know these beings?"*

"Yes," he said.

"Tell me what you know."

"They're called haaj'kar. The man in the middle is General Orel Manster. He's a supreme leader in the Kapon military. As a whole, they're very exact about protocol. Respect is more important to them than it is to a first parent."

We'll see about that. Yarain thought with a ruff. "*Stay with me.*" She turned to Solov. "Let Tanner know the Kapon commander is here and coming to speak with me."

"Roger that," Solov said. "Should I have him come here as well?"

"Not yet."

As the group got closer, Lieutenant Rad made a point of taking position next to Yarain. Yarain turned an ear her way, then perked her ears forward to show approval. *Nice to have someone standing with me as protector.* Solov and the others stood behind, though Milsol took a queue from Shillin and stood with Yarain as well.

Shortly before conversation range, Yarain managed to get a better look at General Manster. Unlike Captain Torzon, his shoulder patches were blue instead of red and were full of pins and other markings, along with four blue stars on his shoulders. His arms held a small insignia of six lavender lines crossing over each other like Corzon's four but again had four blue stars going up the middle of the pattern. His scales seemed to be a dark-brown–dark-grey mix, and his head was large and broad, much like a crocodile, though no longer than a Holdren's. He was unarmed aside from a pistol of some kind on his belt, though the soldiers with him stared at every rock as if any one of them might be a threat.

Once the group arrived, General Manster addressed Yarain in a firm, deep tone that held a slight accent close to, but not quite, a thin British one.

"Are you Major Yarain?"

Yarain ticked her ears forward while giving a soft salute. "I am."

Manster returned the salute without so much as a blink, though Yarain's ears perked curiously when it was the same one she had given. "At ease, Major. You've been tense long en . . ." He seemed to stare at

Yarain until she realized he was staring at her armor. Or, more correctly, at her name on her chest. "You're not a Kapon soldier?"

"No, sir," Yarain said.

"Explain yourself, Major! Who are you? How did a Holdren end up serving with these aliens?"

Yarain couldn't stop a glare or keep her hackles from rising. *Fresh from a grueling battle, and he wants to grill me?* "You have my name. The rest is a long story."

"Start talking! Two attacks by alien aggressors is too much for my taste. I want answers and in short order."

A growl rushed up Yarain's throat. *We give everything to protect this world, and this is the thanks we get?* She almost wished he were a Holdren so she could pin him for his attitude. Instead, she glared and growled, to which he replied with a stern stare of his own.

"Careful, Major," he said. "I won't stand—"

As the humans say, that was the last straw. "You are **NOT** my superior! If you want answers, you will have to—"

Yarain stopped when Milsol took a hard step beside her. His breathing was erratic, and his eyes didn't seem to be focusing. Yarain recognized the signs, but Rad was even faster. She was in place and ready just in time for Milsol to collapse into her arms. He was still conscious, but his eyes were closed, and he had to be helped to the ground so he could lay on his back in a daze.

"*MEDIC*!" Yarain barked. Her ears ticked up when she realized General Manster had made the same call. She then forgot he existed in favor of her soldier and pack mate.

Yarain gave a soft growl when she noticed Milsol had additional burns in his fur, some of which were through his armor.

"Stubborn fool," she said. *"You were in no condition to fight."*

"I learned from you," Milsol said.

Yarain sighed, more so because of how right he was. They'd have had to sedate her, then cage her, then fly her off in an escape pod to have a chance of keeping her from the lines. For Milsol, not even Jason's god could have stopped him.

An Interstar medic was making their way up, but a haaj'kar soldier in armor light enough to show some of her white shoulder patches arrived first. A Holdren came with her, who quickly assured Yarain to let the lizard work. That said, Yarain refused to leave Milsol's side, though she did dismiss her own medic. No sense having two medics when so many others needed help.

The haaj'kar medic made quick scans, then asked, "What happened?"

"I'm not sure," Milsol said. "All of sudden, I felt dizzy and weak."

"Could it be the wounds?" Shillin asked.

"He said he was fine," Solov said.

"He wasn't," the medic said, her E sounds running longer than normal. "Whatever hit him, it disrupted his energy matrix. The strain of the battle did him no good either."

"Is he all right?" General Manster said, not sounding angry for the first time.

"He will be. He just needs rest."

Milsol opened his eyes at last. It was slow, but they were able to focus on Yarain again. Confident he was in good hands, she rubbed her hand on his shoulder, then rose to face General Manster.

Her ears were still forward, but she kept her growl silent. "With respect, sir, now is not the time for this. I have hundreds of dead and wounded soldiers to care for, and I am not the one you should be talking to anyway."

General Manster nodded with a sigh. "Of course, Major. I apologize. My tone was inappropriate. My answers can wait while you recover from the battle. With your fleet so badly damaged, I'd like to offer my ships for your troops. They're at your disposal for medical care or a soft bed to faint into. It's the least I can do to repay them for their sacrifice."

That's more like it.

Yarain breathed relief that maybe they wouldn't end up trying to kill each other after all. "Thank you, General. I will ensure you stay informed of our status."

"I appreciate that, Major. Men! Let's go pay our respects to the invaders."

A snicker from his guards suggested he had some rather unpleasant things in mind. Yarain didn't bother thinking about what they may be. She still had an army to care for, and a cub to check on later. Then there was certainly to be a debriefing, probably more dealing with the haaj'kar, then maybe she might get a chance to rest before she was too tired to remember she had a name, much less what it was.

PART 2:
AS THE STARS MOVE ABOVE, STILL I SHALL HOLD MY PLACE AMONG THEM, WHEREVER IT MAY BE.

CHAPTER 10

WILD HOLDRENS

Sundale lay on the floor with all four paws twitching to match his lips. At times, a soft grumble would escape, but otherwise, it seemed as if he were fighting with something for control of his body. Yet his eyes remained shut the entire time.

That is, until a soft, wet something touched his paw. The twitching instantly turned into a mad spit and snarl as he snapped to his paws. Every hair was on end, his ears were flat, his wings partially spread, and his fangs dared the wet something to try that again. Then, as quickly as he'd reacted, the snarl faded into heavy breathing, though his heart continued to race as if he'd been sprinting for hours.

Sundale's eyes soon began to register the world around him, but his mind was still sorting reality from fantasy. It drove him to check his tails to be sure they were still there, then to look around a moment for the bars. He instead found his quarters on the *Alamo*, his discarded uniform hanging on a chair, and a very real Reneca standing on four paws in front of him. Her eyes watched him like she would a predator. Her ears were back in submission, but her tails had begun to curve over just in case.

A shudder shook his shoulders as remnants of his nightmares finally began to fade. Though it took a swallow, Sundale managed to accept that *this* was reality. One in which he was safe and unharmed. His breathing quickly slowed, as did his heart at last.

"Are you well?" Reneca asked.

Her use of the wild language touched Sundale's instincts, helping to ease his nerves even further. That said, he had to check his tails again before he accepted they were truly there. Seeing his wings brought him all the way back into the present. He folded them back against his sides, then half-collapsed into a laying position where he'd been standing. "Just a dream. Just a dream."

Sundale couldn't be sure if he was talking to her, himself, or both.

Reneca responded anyway. "Are you well? At one point, you appeared to be running for your life."

I probably was. "I'd rather not talk about it."

The shudder returned, and grew until it shook his entire body. All around him he could still hear voices, noises, threats. He couldn't move, because that power was held by someone else. Whoever it was, they had him, and he knew he could do nothing about it. Walls he couldn't see were going up, containing him in his space. He had to get away, but he couldn't.

Sundale flinched when he felt fur brush his side. His ears shot up to check it, and he found Reneca lying there beside him. She was close enough for their fur to touch, yet far enough that nothing else did. She was giving him a sideways stare, no emotion at all in her eyes, ears, or fur. She wasn't offering a single word of comment anywhere in her body. She was just there, her body beside his, her gaze rooting his mind in the present.

Unsure what he was supposed to do, Sundale stared back. The longer he did, the more everything settled. The shudder was gone. The voices were fading fast. He couldn't even remember where the walls had been, much less where they went. Very soon, there was nothing left but him, her, and the room. The only other thing was fatigue, and that was something he didn't mind at the moment.

"Thank you," he finally said.

Reneca gave him her full attention. "Are you sure you don't want to talk about it?"

Sundale's ears pulled back, but the shudder couldn't push past Reneca's aura. "Yes."

"Why?"

Sundale rose and shook himself loose. "It's something I have to deal with alone."

Reneca recoiled while her ears went erect. "Since when does a Holdren say such a thing?"

It's a long story. "I'm not a normal Holdren."

"Wings don't change what you are."

"That's not what I mean. I . . . I was raised by humans . . . I think differently."

Sundale made his way to the window seat, where he stretched out in an attempt to make his body relax. Below, he saw the yellow and blue planet that was Holdre 4, one half covered in darkness, the other bathed in light from the sun that was just peeking over the northern pole. The window tinted over the glare to prevent eye damage, though it was still a bright light in Sundale's view.

Yet his eyes were on the planet itself. He didn't even know why, really. He and Yarain would often lounge on the window seat in Jason's quarters after a battle and gaze out at whatever they could see. They rarely looked for anything specific. It was just a distraction. A way to reset their minds after the strain of combat.

Except this time felt different, and not only because he wasn't in that room anymore. This felt more like an exile getting as close as he could to the home he couldn't reach. As if he were trying to absorb the planet into his fur so he could take some part of it with him. It started to feel as if he really could until the glare suddenly faded. Sundale's ears and eyes snapped to where it had been to see why. He found the *Kraskit*, the Kapon warmaster that had come to their rescue, blocking the sun's glare.

She was huge. Bigger even than the *Alamo* or the *Berlin*, though not by much. She had a spine-like design running the length of her fuselage and pointed pods like huge wings whose tips were curved forward. These "wings" were stacked flat now, though Sundale could easily recall the awesome sight of them deployed like a lizard's mane when the ship arrived. The pods had spewed fire and fighters seconds after arrival. The combined sight might have tainted Sundale's dreams if he weren't dealing with enough of them already.

It didn't help that he'd spent over an hour on board the *Kraskit* being scanned and prodded by haaj'kar doctors. If it hadn't been for Janet's insistence on being present and her subsequent sharp words while there, the doctors' enthusiasm would have gotten them bitten or shot. As it was, Sundale couldn't have left their medical bay fast enough once they were done. Jannet had been first to the door, and the doctors' reactions to her stare after she told them they were done still roused an ember of amusement in Sundale's chest.

Even so, seeing the *Kraskit* was too much for him at the moment. Sundale leapt down from the bench, then froze when he realized he had no clue what to do with himself.

Jason had been wounded—not that he'd let that stop him, of course—and would need some time for proper treatment. Yarain was ear-deep in diplomacy and debriefings that could easily keep her busy for days. Sundale's wings were getting stronger every time he moved them, but he still wasn't ready to even think about flying. The Gold group had been taken care of. All of which left Sundale with nothing to do and nowhere to go while he waited for several sides to determine his fate and future all without any input *from* him or options given *to* him.

He could feel another shudder forming, but Reneca's voice stopped it cold. "Why does that disturb you?"

Sundale tilted his head, confused. "What do you mean?"

"It's clear the *Kraskit* disturbed you. Why?"

"They were not gentle when they examined me."

Reneca's ears pulled back a moment in a soft cringe. "They can be energetic sometimes, but they just wanted to be sure the wings are the end instead of the beginning."

"I hope it's the former. The wings were painful enough. Almost worse than when I . . ." Sundale's ears fell and eyes closed as he fought off another shudder. Between the moment and his time on the *Kraskit*, his time in captivity was closer to the surface than ever. "Never mind," he finally said.

"I don't understand you," Reneca said. "I heard from Interstar soldiers what happened to you, but I don't understand why it haunts you so much."

"You can't know what it was like for me."

"But it's the past. It's done. Yet you seem as if you're still locked in that time."

Another cringe closed Sundale's eyes as he fought back the pain. *If she only knew.* "It's . . . not that simple. I can't . . . I can't forget what happened. Not when I wear a reminder I can feel with every blink."

"You can't live in the past, Sundale. You have to leave it behind if you're ever to recover."

"Jason said the same thing."

"Then it's time you listened to us both. Come with me. Run with my pack. Be the wild Holdren you never got to be."

Sundale ears again fell. He stared at the window, trying to catch some part of the planet in his sight. He was born there, but it might as well be an alien world. He knew nothing of it. Its prey, its predators, even the Holdrens were a mystery. He'd misunderstood a simple greeting gesture before. What else did he not know that could potentially endanger him or others? Yet when he finally saw the northern pole, he felt its call. His moment on the surface had been enough to awaken instincts he never knew were dormant. He wanted more of it. He wanted to revive those instincts in full.

But he also feared them.

"I don't know, Reneca," Sundale said. "I may still be recovering."

"The haaj'kar say you're well enough to hunt."

"Even grounded, I have duties to perform."

Reneca stared him down with a slight ruffle in her hackles. "No, you don't. Yarain asked me to tell you that General Carson has granted both of you special shore leave. You're absolved of all duties until the fleet is ordered elsewhere or you've been here for a week. Whichever comes last. He wants you to have a chance to spend time on your homeworld, by order, if necessary."

"What about Admiral Redding?"

"Total agreement."

I'm not sure if I want to thank him or kill him. General Carson had stolen the last of Sundale's excuses. At least excuses Reneca wouldn't pin him for. He'd have to face a world he didn't know. As well as a fear he didn't want to admit.

Reneca's steady glare told Sundale she wasn't going to take no for an answer. When he didn't move, she nuzzled him to confirm his attention. "Come Sundale. It's time you came home."

Home. The word again vibrated through Sundale's mind. Followed closely by Simon's words. "Scared stray," he'd called him. Now more than ever, Sundale actually felt like one. He had no home to run to, and going anywhere had him so terrified his ears went as low as they could go. Which allowed one last excuse to emerge.

"Home," Sundale echoed. "I'm not sure that is home. I don't know anything about it. What to hunt. What to avoid. I don't even know how to interact with my own kind. I'd be a cub in an adult body . . . a liability."

Sundale desperately wanted to walk away. He could feel his legs tensing to move, except he still had nowhere to go.

Much as she had before, Reneca exuded an aura about her. Though nothing was actually happening, it was as if she were extending her energy matrix to prevent any harm from entering the zone. Yet as she did, her fur relaxed, her ears were back as if being cautious, even her tails hung low. When she spoke again, though still in Holdren sounds, her voice carried an air like she was pleading.

"Holdrens care for those of the pack who need help, no matter what kind of help they need."

"*I* am not *your* pack."

"You will be today. I will be there beside you to keep you safe, and to teach you what you need to know. Please Sundale. For *your* sake, leave this cell you've put yourself in, and join me."

"I'd hardly call it a cell I put myself in."

"You're isolated, cut off, and I understand it's all *your* choice. It's time to make a new choice."

Sundale shook for a moment while his terror at the thought ran through him. Reneca's aura and her pleading stare kept it from lasting. During that same moment, he found himself getting lost in her. Almost as if he could feel her essence. There was power there. Strength he'd only ever felt in Yarain and Jason. The thing that finally settled his insides was the confidence behind it. This wasn't arrogance; this was experience. Reneca had been there before—wherever "there" was —and had conquered it. So long as she was there with him, he'd be safe there as well, which left him nothing else to hide behind.

Sundale gave a half sigh, half ruff before ticking his ears forward. "All right."

He headed for where he kept a communications collar for such situations.

"You won't need it," Reneca said.

Sundale's ears perked her way. "I need to stay in contact."

"Sundale, you can't be a wild Holdren wearing a collar."

"No choice. When the fleet is ready to leave—"

"The haaj'kar will know how to find us."

Sundale actually had to stop himself so he could think about why he even cared. He'd gone into the wild without contact before. Why did this time feel different?

Then it hit him. It *was* different. He was going "home." He'd never spent time among other Holdrens before nor gone to a place he didn't have some understanding of. More than that, the idea of doing so had never scared him so much. Being able to call for help . . . to call for Jason, would have helped alleviate that. But as Reneca said, it would also keep him from being the wild Holdren she wanted him to be. That *he* wanted to be.

Though it was but a few seconds, it felt like days, and Reneca stood patiently while he sorted it out. While her aura remained, she wasn't pressing him any more than she already had. That freedom allowed him to take the time he needed to understand the truth, adjust to it, and then reject it. If he was going to be a wild Holdren, he would have to go wearing nothing more than he was born with . . . erm . . . wings notwithstanding.

Sundale finally ticked his ears forward again. "Okay. How are we getting down?"

"We'll use your transporter," Reneca said.

"Is there a transponder down there?"

"There is now."

They sure didn't waste any time.

Sundale led the way to a transporter room, and in no time at all, they were flashing into the same clearing that so many fleets had used recently. Most of the grass had been flattened by Polaris tanks, Gold 1, Karol's fighter, and even the Kapon troops when they landed. The mountain in the distance that had been Interstar's bunker still showed signs of charring from the battle, as well as sections of the forest around them the battle had touched.

Yet Sundale soon forgot all of that when a gentle breeze brushed his fur in welcome. In the same breath, sweet sap and grass pollen filled his nostrils, as did so many others he had no name for. The sun warmed his upper coat and wings while his paws found the damp soil beneath the grass. The feeling only grew when something within had him lift and slightly spread his wings so the sun could warm all his feathers directly. He had no idea how much he missed it all until he felt it washing over him. Without any kind of mission or objective to worry about, he was allowed to just be, and he was being with a deep breath, closed eyes, and wings slightly extended for the moment.

"The untouched wild feels good, doesn't it?" Reneca said.

Sundale couldn't stop an amused ruff as he tucked his wings. "Tank treads notwithstanding. So, where do we go now?"

Reneca simply cantered into the forest with Sundale at her tails. Grass gave way to bare ear—soil, covered only in twigs, leaves, and occasional shrubs. The moist scent of the forest floor took over, though Sundale still found plenty of pine, citrus, and tree sap among the scents he didn't know. Some of it was plain forest dirt, but that somehow made it all the better.

Reneca led him through the forest with occasional glances back to be sure he was still there. At times, she seemed to intentionally weave around trees, almost as if she were testing his agility. Sundale stayed right with her, a happy pant forming as she increased her speed with a yip.

They only ran for a minute or two before she slowed at the edge of a break in the tree cover. There, Sundale's ears perked when his eyes found a sight he didn't know what to do with.

He saw the pack that had come to meet him, and more scattered across a very small clearing. They were all lying or sitting in the sun, many of them sleeping or just panting away the day. A few younger Holdrens were play-fighting off to the side. Another pair chased a stick around like it was trying to run away. He found several cubs against a small hillside on the other side of the clearing. Some were so young they must have just emerged from the den, while others were almost full grown, though tails with little or no red showed their age. Most of them played and wrestled and chewed on sticks under the steady gaze of adults on the hill.

Playful barks and growls echoed off the trees. A cry was heard only when a game got a little out of hand. Cackles and growls spoke of a difference of opinion or two. But otherwise, it was calm, quiet, and more peaceful than anything he'd ever seen.

It also wasn't Sundale's territory. A pack just over twenty strong lived here, and unless you counted Milsol or Reneca – which Sundale didn't – he didn't know any of them. His ears somehow stayed up, though he could feel panic trying to steal his breath.

"You sure I'm allowed to be here?" he said.

"Yes," said a firm bark from above.

Sundale cowered while Reneca looked up with a curious tilt. From a low branch, Karfen leapt down and stepped up to them very lightly. Reneca rubbed against him with a soft whine that was instantly returned. Sundale meanwhile followed the first instinct he found. He hugged the ground with his ears back, and his tails laid alongside him.

Karfen looked him over a moment, then ruffed amusement. "You have good instincts, but you may relax. You are a guest today." Sundale rose, though his ears refused to. Karfen watched him a moment more, then his tails gave a single wave. "That's progress, at least. I admit I cannot remember your name."

Sundale had to swallow his fear before he could remember himself. "My name is Sundale."

"I greet you, Sundale. Where is Yarain?"

"Trapped in civilization," Reneca said with a growl. A tilt of Karfen's head asked for clarification. "She's stuck doing debriefings and reports. She'll join us once she's finished."

Karfen's ears turned back a second. A passive cringe, much like a human shaking their head in dismay. "That poor Holdren fights so hard only to have to fight again. Well, until she arrives, please make yourself comfortable, Sundale. I would like to talk with both of you when I get back."

Sundale's nerves had settled enough for his ears to perk forward. "Where are you going?"

Karfen looked over as most of the pack was gathering three older cubs nearby. The cubs weren't all that much smaller than the adults, though their tails had no more than a tiny hint of red, marking them as being only one melting old.

"I'm overseeing a first hunt for some of our larger cubs," Karfen said.

Sundale had started watching the cubs the moment Karfen looked their way. Some part of him vaguely remembered watching his pack's older litter go on their first hunt and how excited he was at the thought of someday going on his own. Milsol then had to tell him a few times to be patient. "You're not big enough yet," he had said. Despite his age at the time, Sundale had been willing to accept this wisdom. Didn't keep him from dreaming of his own hunt, though he couldn't remember what his young mind had inserted for the prey at the time. Nor could he remember if the other cubs had been siblings or if that other female Yarain had inspected earlier had been there somewhere.

Reneca's voice brought him back to the present. "Perhaps you should join them. It would be a perfect opportunity for you to reconnect with the wilds here."

While Sundale's ears were up in surprise, his lips and whiskers were already pulling back. His ears didn't take long to follow. "No."

"Why not?"

"I... I don't know enough about the terrain, the skills, and especially the prey. The cubs probably know more than I do."

Karfen's ears perked his way. "A convincing argument. I think Reneca has an excellent idea. You could learn with the cubs."

"Oh, that would be fun. An adult learning the basics alongside cubs without any color in their tail tips. Thanks, but I've been humiliated enough this year."

Karfen's ears perked forward as his gaze became hard. A short growl sent Sundale to the ground again. "You won't be humiliated! You will be respected as an adult, you know that."

"No, he doesn't," Reneca said. When Karfen's ears snapped her way, she explained. "Karol raised him before she met us. She didn't know what he was then. He was taken before his first melting."

Karfen now stared at Sundale a moment, then cringed as if he had gotten a headache. Sundale continued to hug the ground, unsure if this change was good or bad. With few other choices, he waited to see what Karfen did next or for something to react to. Whichever came first.

When Karfen spoke again, every hair and sound was calm, even a touch apologetic in his ears. "You never got to know your own kind, did you?"

The question held a sorrow Reneca's hadn't. One that allowed Sundale's ears to rise. At least until the truth of his past caught up with him. Then they fell once more in pain alone.

"I . . . No, I guess not," Sundale said.

"How? Didn't you learn from your parents?"

Sundale tried to stop words that felt like a betrayal of Jason's efforts over the years. Yet even as they slipped out, he couldn't deny their truth. "I found them after I had been grown for some time. Even after, we . . . we never got to live a truly wild life."

"That's why you're so nervous," Karfen said. "You've spent so much time in a starship, you don't know anything else. You really should come with us. It's the only way you can be what you were born to be, and I promise, you *will not* be humiliated."

"Nor should you fear it," Reneca added. "I'll keep you safe if that's what you're worried about. The rest you will learn alongside the cubs, or beside me if it would make you more comfortable. However you do it, you should take this chance to experience the pack."

Sundale's ears perked in surprise. They were almost begging him to join the hunt. Their concern hurt in its own way. Yet, at the same time, his tails had swept out behind him, and he could feel his legs relaxing from their cower. Reneca pleaded with her eyes while Karfen stared him down with the same glare Reneca had given him on the *Alamo*. Sundale tried to resist, to find another excuse. Instead, he found a longing to accept. He'd been called a scared stray, and over the last few days, he'd even begun to see why. Now, he had a chance to cure both. How could he possibly refuse?

Sundale focused on Karfen as he rose once more. "All right. But only with Reneca beside me. She's the only one here I feel comfortable with right now."

"A good reason," Karfen said. "I am happy to have her as well. Follow."

Reneca and Sundale did so as Karfen walked to where the others were gathering. The cubs started barking and spinning around once they saw Karfen heading their way. Their excitement created a warmth in Sundale's chest he hadn't expected. He didn't know why, nor was he about to ask. He only knew something about it had him relaxing more and more by the second. *Maybe this won't be so bad after all.*

Karfen stepped up to the three cubs, flicked an ear, then gave a short, low growl to silence them. They all sat, though their tails refused to stop swishing along the ground. Karfen's ears shifted in satisfaction before he addressed them. Sundale couldn't help perking his own ears, more in curiosity than anything else.

"This is your first hunt," Karfen said, "so I expect you to watch and listen. Play is very different than a real hunt. Mind your ears, keep the wind in your nose, and stay near the group. There is danger out there. Follow."

Karfen turned toward the forest at a slow trot that would swallow distance with little strain. The group stayed close behind as it started to spread out, though all three of the cubs still wiggled with excitement at times. Even so, they never tested the boundaries of the group. The cubs remained in the center of the hunting party, an eye or an ear always checking to be sure they weren't straying too far from their protection within the group.

It was yet another sign of how good a first father Karfen was. There was a well instilled discipline there. The adults held their place around the cubs, and the cubs knew not to stray beyond their boundaries. Though he knew little of Holdren pack life, Sundale knew the pack reflected the first parents. Only the best of first parents would have a pack this well maintained.

In an odd way, it left Sundale relaxing all the more. It helped that Milsol, despite still having singed fur from the battle, was part of the group. Sundale thought he remembered Milsol being told to rest. Then again, Jason had told Sundale the same thing after his first seizure. First thing Sundale did after a nap was hunt. *I wonder if the haaj'kar understand any more than humans do why, for a Holdren, this* is *rest.* Whether they did or not, having someone there who knew him as a cub provided a connection he could trust. With Reneca staying close to him the entire way, the meeting area had barely fallen out of view before Sundale's nerves had faded away.

This allowed his senses to awaken in a way they hadn't done since Jason first found him. There was always that part of him that was thinking about civilization. Down here, among forests untouched by so much as a stone tool – not counting the recent battle – there was no need for that. The wild fox got to come out in full, and it had a lot of catching up to do.

First was damp soil stirred by the movement of the hunting party, as well as the light musk of the other members. It only took a few minutes of trotting together for him to recognize and internalize their individual scents. Yet, at the same time, all their scents held a similar velvet feel to it. At first, he thought it might be something he never noticed among Holdrens until he realized that neither he nor his parents held that element in theirs. If anything, his scent was hard and heavy, almost like rock, whereas Karfen's pack was more like rose petals in full bloom.

Still not quite comfortable enough to ask about it, Sundale ignored his confusion in favor of the territory around him. The forest was coming alive more and more with each sight and scent he found. Many of the trees carried sweet scents, yet they still held traces that reminded him of Earth pine, oak, and even barley at times. One scent on the wind even managed to combine all three, though Sundale couldn't figure out how that could be. There was an acrid smell in there as well. Something soft, something... whimsical, and so incredibly familiar. He wasn't sure what the source was, yet his instincts found comfort in it like no other scent he'd ever found.

Every leaf and needle was the same yellow of Earth's fall, with only small portions holding bits of orange and dull red of the same kind. The soft breeze created a rolling rustle in the thicker trees and brushed along Sundale's fur like an old friend. Birds similar to Earth, and some that seemed impossibly long and slender, fluttered and sang about the trees. A few of the songs were similar tones, if not patterns, though others somehow managed to find a tone that seemed dead middle between mockingbird and great horned owl.

At one point, Sundale flinched when something that sounded like a hummingbird buzzed by his ear. Much to his relief, no one said a word, though a few panted a laugh that spoke more of 'I've been there' than anything mocking, which allowed the moment to fall away as unimportant while also putting him at ease. When the sun snuck through the trees, or they went through a thinner patch of trees, the warmth soaked into his fur and body as if he could feed off it. For all he knew, he could, for it relaxed his body better than the longest nap and made the constant trot so easy he felt he could maintain it in his sleep.

There was also a hum, for lack of a better term, running through his energy matrix that created a similar sensation. Unlike the EM fields that were frequent among human buildings and ships, this was something his energy matrix did not try to fight. If anything, it made his matrix feel smoother, more stable than he could ever remember. He could feel different currents in the field, and he was sure they held a wealth of information for someone accustomed to feeling them.

Someone other than me.

The thought was poorly timed, for Karfen slowed the group so he could examine a scent at just that moment. Sundale's instincts were waking up to a world they were born into, but he still knew as much as, if not less than, the three cubs. Which meant the scent being examined was as alien to him as, well, the entire world really.

Sundale couldn't keep his ears from falling, which is what drew Reneca's attention.

"What's wrong?" she asked.

Sundale knew better than to try anything other than the truth. "My body says there is so much here, yet I don't even know how to read the trees."

"So don't try. Read what you know, listen for what you don't."

"It's still hard when I'm the only adult who can't read that scent."

"I know. But you only need to read it once, assuming you need to at all. Karfen will call the cubs if it's a trail of interest. You needn't worry about anything else."

I wish I could be so sure.

Sundale's ears were up, but his insides were still tight. Karfen said there were dangers out here, and Sundale wouldn't know any of them until they bit him. By then, it might be too late.

Reneca's stare didn't let him stay there long. He ticked his ears forward to reassure her he was okay. He then turned those same ears back to Karfen, who was promptly marking the same tree he'd been examining.

Before Sundale could guess why, the shadows in the dirt caught his eye. Part of it seemed to be moving, and not in the rolling way leaves in the wind do. Curious, he looked up in search of a twisted branch that looked like the shadow, for that was where the odd movement seemed to be. He soon found it, and just above it, in the sunlight, he saw something large, brown, and moving. He thought he saw a head, but at best, he was only guessing. Though he felt sure that whatever it was, it was moving toward the trunk of the tree.

More curious than anything else, Sundale gave a sound that was somewhere between a whine and a ruff. A sign of curious attention that was asking for others to join him in it.

"Reneca," he said, "look there."

He stared at the moving brown thing as several ears turned his way. A few adults stepped closer to the cubs as well. Reneca followed his gaze into the trees with careful attention. A moment later, her head leaned forward. Then, in a smooth motion that was elegant yet resembled a robot changing modes, Reneca's ears pulled back, her head ducked down, and her tails curved over her head. She then fired from all three tails at the brown thing.

Ears shot up everywhere, and each cub suddenly found at least one adult standing beside them with their ears back, their tails curved, and their tips glowing. Much as a skunk stomps its feet before spraying, this was a final warning to anyone in the area to watch their step very carefully.

"Reneca?" Karfen said. "What did you f—"

He was cut off as the head of a snake slightly bigger than his own fell from the tree in front of him. He and many others jumped away, then watched as the snake's body flowed onto the same spot like a massive spaghetti noodle. Whatever this snake was, it was roughly eighteen feet long, and it had specks of yellow in its scales along with the dominant brown. More than enough to bind and swallow a Holdren and probably a few things even bigger.

Karfen was the first to sniff the dead snake, though many in the group were checking the trees and surrounding areas for more dangers. Every Holdren that investigated the snake did so with shifting ears and curved over tails. Most retreated at seemingly random times during their investigation. A lingering instinct to be wary of something they had never seen before.

After eternal seconds, Karfen looked up at Reneca. "How did you know it was there?"

"Sundale pointed it out," Reneca said.

When Karfen shifted his gaze to him, Sundale had to take a breath to keep his ears up. "I saw a change in the shadows," Sundale said. "I looked up to find the source and saw that moving along the branches."

"Why did you kill it, Reneca?"

"It's a danger to our pack," Reneca said.

One of the younger adults who was sniffing the body looked up with perking ears. "How can one snake threaten a pack?"

Karfen growled at him. "We are not invincible, Ahrum. However, Reneca, explain."

"It's called a shole," she said. "They can snap their tail around the throat of their victim—usually the last member of a pack—before they can make a sound. The same squeeze renders the victim unconscious very quickly. They are then lifted into the trees, choked to death, and swallowed before the pack even knows they're missing."

"Wouldn't the pack hear something?" Sundale said. "Even the victim collapsing would make a sound."

"The victim is often held in the air once struck. The hold is too tight to allow any sound at all."

"And our tails?" Karfen asked.

"Can save us, but the time to react is very small. You have to understand what has you, find it, and hit it before you start to weaken."

Karfen ticked his ears forward in approval. "You once asked why curiosity is so important, Ahrum? Sundale's curiosity may have saved one of our lives. All of you, remember, learn, and be a better Holdren."

Sundale's ears pulled back a little in a Holdren blush. "I didn't do anything special."

"You did enough."

With tails finally falling, the cubs were allowed to examine the shole's body. Sundale would take his turn along with any adults who thus far hadn't, but he first had to get his ears out from a Holdren blush. He never did like being the center of attention, and now he was being used as an example. The whole thing made him want to turn and run, except Reneca standing beside him pretty much negated that option. She might just pin him if he were to try. That left him fighting to get his ears up, and he noted with some curiosity that the leading edge of his wings were holding tighter to his body in much the same way. It wasn't conscious, yet it was there all the same.

This gave his mind the distraction it needed to come out of it at last. He, too, absorbed the scent of this shole, remembering it as a danger should he find it on the wind again. He noticed it held an air similar to damp moss as if it had slithered across a riverbank on its way there, yet dry soil and wet scale were the primary scents to be found.

With a careful ear turned to Karfen, he risked asking Reneca, "Why are you the only one that knows of this shole?"

Karfen merely perked his ears to hear the reply, which Reneca gave without emotion. "Other Holdrens told me of it. They aren't native to forests this far north."

"How did it get here then?"

"Any number of reasons," Karfen said. "None of which matter to us. We now know of it should we encounter it again, though that may never be. Anything more is unimportant."

Sundale's military training screamed in protest, but his instincts understood completely. Worrying about things out of one's control only breeds stress and fear to no good effect. If the snake is not native to the area, it may never be seen again. If that were to change, the pack will be alert for it. No further effort was needed.

Which left Sundale with a very different question. "We have a kill. Do we continue the hunt?"

Though some adults turned an ear as if surprised by the question, Karfen didn't move so much as a hair. "We do. Wost, you, Jilton, and Furahna take the shole back to the pack. Tell them what Reneca told you. All others, follow."

The three members shifted into their finesse form to better carry the large carcass while the pack gathered and continued on in a different direction. Karfen kept the pace slower than before, which allowed the adults to check the wind and grass for a trail. All except Sundale, of course. His nose was still sorting one scent from another, to say nothing of that one that would not stop touching his instincts. He wouldn't know prey until he ran into it, so he hung back, trusting the pack to find it for him. Only Reneca's presence kept him from feeling utterly out of place.

Though it didn't stay perfect. At one point, Karfen stopped to examine a bush under a tree. When he called the cubs over to have them do the same, Reneca was quick to literally nudge Sundale forward so he could as well. Sundale resisted until she glared at him with a ruffle in her hackles. He then surrendered, knowing by now that it was futile to fight her on this. Though it helped that no one even turned a curious ear at it. If anything, he noticed a few were perking their ears toward Karfen as if they also wanted to learn. It kept the shudder from forming, but it did not keep his wings from pulling tighter again.

Karfen gave his presence with the cubs no special attention at all. "Take in this scent," Karfen said.

The cubs began to sniff at the bush one by one. Sundale took his turn, all-be-it somewhat hesitantly. While he still didn't like admitting he knew nothing of the area despite his age, if he was going to be anything other than a burden, this was the only way to do it. So, he found a way to literally swallow his frustration and join in on the lesson. As promised, the pack continued to show him the same respect. Ahrum was the only one to even begin to comment, and he didn't get to finish a word before Karfen's glare silenced him.

Seeing his status defended, Sundale's wings finally relaxed, allowing him to actually process what he was smelling. It was mostly earthy, damp sweat, much like Earth horse, though it seemed heavy, almost as if the scent itself weighed more than usual. There was a sweetness among it, though, as well as a soft, semi-sweet metallic scent that Sundale knew all too well.

We have our target, he thought.

Before he could take that thought further, Karfen spoke. "Now, what is it?"

"Bilark," One cub yipped.

"And?"

"Fresh blood," another said. "And something that smells like puss."

"What does that mean?"

"It's injured, and the wound is infected."

"Correct. You have been listening. Can you tell me anything else?"

When none of the cubs spoke up, Karfen perked his ears at Sundale. In an odd way, it wasn't questioning but confidence. Like he knew that Sundale knew and was helping Sundale realize that.

It worked because Sundale felt nothing as he said, "The scent is strong. It's close by. It's a prime target."

The approval in Karfen's ears felt like it washed a layer of doubt from Sundale's chest. "Exactly right. Young ones, follow well, watch carefully, and be silent."

All three cubs ticked their ears forward. All nine tails swished their excitement.

Unlike dogs, Holdrens had to get quite hyper or be playing for their tails to move that much. Even Sundale noticed the 'oh, great' hidden deep behind Karfen's eyes. The pack's first father repeated the order to follow well and stay silent, then continued on. Sundale could only pity the first cub to make a mistake. *Which should only take about five minutes . . . or less.*

The pack moved together more carefully, though still at a brisk pace. The trail of blood and puss was sporadic but still in a more or less straight line. Moreover, it was not alone. The longer they went, the more Sundale found multiple variations of the same scent among the trees and grasses.

As the scent grew stronger, so did Sundale's heartbeat. He'd felt the thrill of the hunt before, but this was different. He had a full pack with him this time. He could feel himself among the group like a round in a magazine, waiting for its turn to be fired. Further, this would be a complicated hunt. One that would require him to play his part and everyone else to play theirs. This was the bond in his blood that had never been touched before. There was no room for nerves. Only the hunt.

The pack followed the trail for some time before they began hearing deep calls that sounded like they came from a dove the size of a hippo. When Karfen led the pack into a trot towards the sound, Sundale guessed these were the sounds of the bilark or some other prey just as viable. Karfen led the pack toward a large meadow with only a few thin trees dotting a field of grass almost as tall as they were.

In the middle of the meadow was a herd some thirty to fifty strong of large, deer-like animals. They had a head and antlers like a reindeer, but their main body resembled a camel without its hump, and their fur was mostly orange with some white and black mixed in. Sundale couldn't help flicking an ear at the odd mixture. While it might be common prey to the pack, to him, it was something he'd expect to see coming out of a genetic engineering lab. Yet his attention never wavered from them or Karfen. The first father watched the herd carefully as they chewed on the grass and tree leaves. The rest of the pack waited in the shadows, still, silent, alert for instructions. Wisdom and experience granted each one of them patience for the right moment.

At least the adults were. All three cubs couldn't hold it together. When they weren't rocking on their haunches, they were looking around like they were afraid they'd miss the call to attack. It was growing worse, which Sundale knew could give them away.

With the risk reaching a breaking point, Sundale eased close to a cub and nipped at him to get his attention. With a simple, low growl followed by a softer ruff, he told the cub to settle down and to pass the warning on to the others. The cub's ears flattened in submission, though a sign of understanding came with it. With the cubs passing and heeding his directive, Sundale returned his focus to the hunt at hand. He found Karfen looking back at him with perked ears. Sundale first perked his own to catch any comment, then when none came, flicked an ear in a Holdren shrug. Karfen ticked his ears forward in approval, then turned back to the herd.

Karfen crouched down against the ground while moving forward with pin-point paw steps. The pack followed close behind, their bodies vanishing under the grass. Still not entirely certain of his hunting skills, Sundale kept close to the cubs. At least he could make sure they stayed controlled. As the pack advanced, a single red tail tip appeared just above the grass. Karfen's tail tip. A beacon for the pack to follow as he inched them toward their prey.

Though his focus was split between the tail tip and the cubs, Sundale's heart thundered all the same. His paws moved so lightly, even he didn't hear them fall. The advance was so slow and careful the grass barely moved around his body. He, like those he could see, kept his head still, independent of his body. His eyes were locked onto his prey and his first father. His ears kept watch over the cubs, though at last, they too had settled into the hunt.

They skulked through the grass like specters in the daylight. The bilark chewed on the same shrubs, yet none knew of the Holdrens' presence. The same heavy, dirty, wet horse smell lifted on the winds among the soft sap from the grass. *I wonder if they taste like wet horse, too.*

Sundale's thoughts froze with his body as the bilark rose their heads all at once. Ears and eyes scanned the grass, and Sundale cast a glare at the cubs to be sure they remained still. When he turned back, he could swear one of the bilark was staring right at him. Perhaps he was. Sundale could only hold his pose, careful not to so much as flick an ear.

Time itself seemed to freeze. Pack and prey might as well have become a museum piece for all the movement either group showed.

Then, Karfen's tail slid below the grass. A moment later, his snarl shattered the silence.

Maybe it was the few hunts with his parents, or it was a latent instinct. Whatever the source, Sundale knew exactly what that meant. He was right with the pack as it erupted out of the grass like a dozen alligators from a lake. The bilark sprinted away at the same moment, and the chase was on!

Sundale's legs moved with mechanical precision as they tore through brush and over small rocks after the herd. The cubs ran beside him, their pants more giddy than the serious exertion every other adult held. Meanwhile, the thunder of the bilark's hooves pounded ahead of them as hard as Sundale's heart.

No one said a word. The pack spread out to drive the herd forward while Karfen led two others in a sprint ahead of them. The pack had formed a spread-out, curved line that gave the appearance of trying to corral the bilark, which made the herd crash into itself when Karfen charged directly toward them. The few that stood their ground were ignored.

Karfen ruffed and turned on a sharp angle toward a smaller group of bilark that were separated from the herd. The pack followed close behind while tightening their ranks. The small group tried to run, but they had slowed too much, thinking their fellows and the calves within were the target. By the time they reached full speed, their group already had Holdrens among it. Jaws snapped at legs and hindquarters. Some landed, though none managed a hold. It didn't matter. Even Sundale could see the plan working.

The more they were attacked, the more the bilark scattered to get away. Very soon, the pack had driven a single member away from the group. The pack fanned back out to keep the herd from coming to its aid while the lone bilark began to stumble as the pack closed around it. Two stumbles only slowed it down. One more saw it hit the ground. Karfen caught a leg mid-stride, and the beast crumpled.

Though it bellowed a challenge, it was as hollow as an empty bone. The rest of the pack rushed in, planting jaws on the hips, shoulders, and neck. The bilark rolled onto its side as its throat was sealed shut or ripped open by Holdren jaws. Sundale tried for a hold high on the back of its neck to keep the antlers honest, though that meant he was the only Holdren along the bilark's back as it struggled.

His fangs had just touched flesh when Reneca's bark stopped him.

"Sundale, evade!"

Too late.

Sundale turned in time to see another bilark charging in, antlers low, eyes locked on him as its target. He didn't have time to run. His wings were too alien to use. He was exactly one second from being split in two by antlers he'd never seen before today.

It took a fraction of that second for his combat training to kick in. Much like a pilot avoiding incoming fire, Sundale rolled along the ground out of the bilark's path. It tore streaks in the soil where he had been half a second ago. It charged past, and Sundale's hunter saw an opportunity. In an act of pure instinct, he continued his roll until he landed on his paws, leapt around, and latched his jaws onto the bilark's hind leg. Bone cracked beneath his fangs. His claws dug into the ground to stop him and it. Oddly enough, his wings spread out as well, the veil extending further beyond the physical feathers, though no flaps ever came. Sundale felt another crack as the beast's momentum ripped its leg from its socket. The beast bellowed in pain, then pounded into the ground so hard it rattled ribs.

Sundale released his hold on impact. Before the vibrations had subsided, he had leapt onto the bilark's back with one awkward flap of his wings to try to help him make the jump. From there, he clamped his jaws on the back of its neck. His fangs sank as deep as they could go. Blood seeped from the bite, as well as where his claws scratched at the bilark's side. He even gave weak flaps of his wings to help keep him steady in his perch. The bilark tried to toss him off. It only widened the wound.

Bone cracked. Blood turned Sundale's chest, neck, and muzzle red. He refused to let go. Sundale felt its heart slow, its breathing weaken. Soon, the struggles stopped, the beast slumped onto the ground, and then, at last, it fell silent beneath him. He held his hold a moment more to be sure before releasing. Sundale slid onto the ground in a heavy pant as he folded his wings. A pack of erect ears greeted him, including Karfen's as he stood over the other kill.

When no one said a word or moved, Sundale couldn't help it. "What?"

"I have never seen a Holdren move like that," Karfen said. "I hope you were all watching. What you just saw was what we talk about when we say 'controlled instinct can create a powerful hunter.'"

I'm really glad Holdrens can't blush. Though his retreating ears showed the same, it helped that he couldn't turn bright red like humans could. Even so, Sundale shrank into himself from embarrassment. When a pained whine escaped, Karfen ruffed as much to call attention as to try to reassure him.

"A fine pair of kills," Karfen said. "But remember, young ones, this was an easy hunt. They are often much harder. Colain, you must learn patience. You almost ruined the hunt. A hunter who cannot control his emotions will not feed his pack. Understand?" They all said yes. Pulled-back ears showed real attention this time. "Good."

Without another word or ear flick, Karfen dug into the first bilark. His example started a controlled frenzy as the pack began to eat their fill. Most of the pack attacked the first kill, with Karfen claiming the liver as was his right. Those that couldn't fit on the first joined Sundale on the second. There, he had to scare off some of the cubs as they went for the better parts of the kill. It was one of the few things he had no doubt about. They were full hunters now; they would have to get used to the general muscle and meat. The better parts were reserved for the mothers and the youngest cubs back at the dens.

Sundale stopped his eating when he realized just how much reverence the young ones were giving him. Just a few snarls had been enough to force them to other parts of the kill. He looked around and found the other adults didn't seem to care that it was him doing the chasing. If anything, some seem to show approval of his actions. Even more surprising, not a one was challenging him for his portion, even as others got into minor disagreements that sometimes erupted around a kill. Karfen's promise was continuing to ring true. He was being respected as a full adult. Perhaps more, given the lack of challenge. He returned to his meal, though the meat paled in comparison to the warmth he felt brewing within.

Karfen eventually nudged his way in beside him. Sundale happily moved aside to let him have full reign of the kill. He'd eaten his fill by then anyway. Anything more would have been additional stores he didn't need right now.

Much of the rest of the pack was already taking their finesse forms. Though not the preferred form for most Holdrens, it would allow them to carry more of the kills with them. Sundale remained close to the cubs while portions were removed for those still at the meeting area. A soft ruff of amusement escaped him as the cubs started nipping at each other, playing with the fresh blood on their muzzles.

The ruffs ended when Karfen approached him. Sundale's ears perked toward him, ready for whatever he had for him. Sundale's eyes joined his ears as Karfen laid the second liver down in front of him.

"That's yours," Karfen said.

Sundale went still as stone. "Excuse me?"

"You earned it."

"Karfen, I'm not a first father. I'm not even a member of your pack."

Karfen looked over at the cubs, at Sundale's kill, nudged the liver closer to him, and then stared at him. "That's yours."

Sundale lay between Reneca and Milsol near the dens, admittedly thankful to have his fur clear of blood. He'd shed enough of his own recently to make it unnerving. It didn't help that he had more on his mind than the emotional scars he still carried.

Though they were still confused by it, neither Milsol nor Reneca had lost patience as he continued to ponder the events of the hunt.

"I don't understand it," Sundale said. "Surely he has a mate here. Why give me prime meat? I'm not even a member of his pack."

"I don't think he sees it that way anymore," Reneca said.

"He hasn't claimed me."

"Not yet. He may be waiting for something. Only he would know."

Milsol panted a soft laugh. "He does sometimes have odd timing, but I've never seen it be wrong. As for me, I've never had a liver before. How did it taste?"

Sundale couldn't keep a slight, joyful perk out of his ears. "It was the best. But I don't know what him insisting I take it means."

"It means you earned his respect," Reneca said.

"Simple respect doesn't earn prime meat."

"I'd hardly call it simple," Milsol said. "You handled the cubs and the hunt *exceptionally* well. And the way you took down that bilark . . . none of us could have done that—not even Karfen."

"But what does it mean?"

Reneca growled with a ripple in her hackles that lasted only a second. "Sundale, you're looking for something that isn't there." Sundale's ears fell as his search for answers seemed to be futile. Yet the moment they did, Reneca's nose tapped his cheek to get his attention. "Holdrens don't do things that have deeper meaning. Karfen insisted you have prime meat because you proved yourself an asset to the pack. Such members get the best when it can be spared. If there is any 'meaning' to what he did, it is nothing more than his belief that you are a Holdren who can be vital to helping preserve and protect the pack."

Then he places trust where it doesn't belong. Sundale couldn't deny that he'd done good things on the hunt. Keeping watch over the cubs had given him a sense of purpose he didn't expect to be possible. And yet, his scar wouldn't let him forget how close he'd come to putting himself before his pack.

"I don't deserve it," Sundale said.

Both Milsol and Reneca recoiled with straightening ears.

"What madness is that?" Milsol said.

Reneca added, "Did you see and hear nothing today?"

Did you see and hear anything a month ago? "You can't understand."

"Don't you dare say 'never mind' again. I may not be as kind as I was before."

Sundale growled but with pulled-back ears to match his pain. Those ears shot up when he heard a bark not far away. When he heard it again, warmth drew him forward toward Yarain's voice. *It's about time they let her escape.* Milsol was right on his tails, with Reneca close behind. Sundale slowed to let her catch up in full and was surprised to see a joyful swish in her tails instead of a rise in her hackles.

It didn't take long to find Yarain rubbing cheeks with Karfen near the main clearing. Her middle tail was between her legs, and her outside tails were just as close on either side. They traded whines barely audible to human ears. More from Yarain, but they shared a common sense of the pack. Sundale's ears perked in surprise when he realized that Yarain was being claimed. He remembered doing the same when they'd been reunited for the first time all those years ago. The question of why Karfen would take in a first mother, who already had a mate no less, had Sundale's mind swimming.

Milsol, on the other hand, merely turned his ears forward in approval. "That didn't take long."

Sundale directed his surprise at him. "You expected this?"

"Not specifically this, but I figured Yarain would find a territory for herself."

"I wouldn't expect Karfen would risk the competition."

While Yarain and Karfen exchanged friendly rubs and licks on their muzzles, Reneca flicked a thoughtful ear. "He wouldn't, which tells me there isn't any."

"A first mother isn't competition?" Sundale said.

"Not if she convinces him there isn't any. A pack this large might even benefit from her experience."

"What about her mate?"

"He'll be claimed when he gets here. Karfen would never separate a mated pair."

What about a family? Sundale's chest began to swirl with too many feelings to track. He was more of a stray than ever. No pack to call his own. Even his parents had a home without him. As impossible as it sounded, he suddenly had fewer places to go than he had a little while ago.

His nose pointed at the ground, but he didn't see a thing. His insides felt like they'd turned to a soup being stirred in a bowl of ice. When he spoke, his words were for no one in particular. "Where does that leave me?"

Karfen's voice snapped his attention forward. "Here, if you want it."

Through the mixed emotions, Sundale had missed Karfen approaching. The first father now stood before him, ears forward, tails raised. Normally a show of authority much like a human father's folded arms, this was instead closer to what Reneca had done on the *Alamo*. Karfen was claiming the space he stood on, but he wasn't taking it *from* Sundale; he was keeping it safe *for* him. He was creating a space where Sundale would be provided for, protected, cherished . . . safe.

Sundale stared with straight ears for what felt like hours. Karfen only watched and waited. Then Sundale's paws moved forward. He dropped his ears and tucked his tails just as Yarain had done. The two of them first sniffed at each other's cheek glands. Sundale found the same smooth scent as before and more. There was a warmth there. The closest comparison he could think of was hot chocolate, yet stiffer, bold, and musky. The scent seemed to seep into his entire body, relaxing him as if injected with a sedative. For a moment, he swore it was actively healing wounds he didn't know he had.

When Karfen didn't move, Sundale did. He gave Karfen a single, gentle rub along the side of his head. Karfen dropped his tails and began rubbing his head on Sundale's in deep affection. Sundale could feel Karfen's energy matrix along his fur, but it struck into his own any time their cheek glands met. Sundale forced his matrix to drop its guard and let the strikes streak down his body lest he be expelled as an intruder. It went further and deeper every time and filled Sundale with a warmth he'd only felt with Jason and his parents. They began to trade whines of the same affection, though unlike Yarain, the amount was almost equal.

The only difference was that Sundale soon sought out the strikes. He could feel his energy matrix shifting slightly, but all he cared about was that, for this single moment, there was absolutely nothing. No scars, no shame, no memories, no soil, no fur. There was only the bond of the pack. While this one had to be forged instead of rekindled like with his parents, that only made it easier for it to seep into his soul. Karfen had accepted him as family. Not a single other thing mattered. The only one that survived was a distant thought that noted the strikes were touching the veil over Sundale's feathers, which suggested they were indeed a part of his energy matrix.

Karfen offered a few seconds of grooming, added a playful nip below Sundale's ear, then trotted away ruffing a chuckle. When a female darted across his path, he soon vanished after her in a playful chase.

Sundale watched them go with his ears up and his tails floating behind him. When he noticed Yarain trotting toward him, Sundale straightened his body—as much to ground himself as to reset his mind—and gave a sharp sigh that was close to a snort. As he went to greet her, he felt like a lot more than air had been expelled in the process.

Every drop of fear, every doubt, was gone. His energy matrix still tingled with the memory of the bond now forged. He felt light enough to fly without his wings and at ease as if he'd just tossed off a field pack he'd been carrying for several days. For a moment, he forgot about everything that wasn't this world and this pack. He could feel their presence in a way he never had before. Like blips on a sensor screen, he knew they were there to support him. Here, in this place, he was not alone. Not even close.

More so when he and Yarain traded sniffs, rubs, and licks of their own. Sundale noticed Yarain's hard and heavy scent had been replaced by the velvety one Karfen's pack seemed to carry. He still had no trouble finding his mother, so the curiosity was forgotten as quickly as it had come. Instead, he caught her cheek gland and noticed it held a level of calm he hadn't found . . . *Come to think of it, ever!*

With the greeting done, Sundale pulled away so he could ask, "Have you talked with Harmus?"

Yarain's ears ticked forward. "It's one of the reasons I was delayed. Marshal Garmon was waiting for confirmation Holdre 4 was actually here and secure. By now, he's already on his way home aboard the fastest cruiser we've got."

Home. For the first time, that word only made Sundale feel lighter. In the span of a day, he'd proven himself an asset to the pack and been claimed by its first father. He'd been reunited with a former pack-mate, and now his mother was there with him in that same pack, out in the wild where they belonged.

When Sundale thought about how that word had made him feel before, his ears ticked back slightly, more remembering the pain than actually feeling it.

That was all Reneca needed. "Are you well?"

Sundale's ears perked at her. She'd asked that a few hours ago, right after the mother of all nightmares. He'd rather effectively dodged around the question then. Now, he had an actual answer to offer.

As well as a devious plan he just couldn't pass up.

"Yes," he said. "It's just that . . . well . . . never mind."

Reneca's hackles started bristling again until she noticed that Sundale's tails were starting to sway.

The moment her play growl started, Sundale was off and running. She chased him from one end of the meeting area to the other, a happy pant on both of their faces. Milsol and Yarain were close behind, though he couldn't tell what their plans were.

Not that he cared. Once Sundale reached the edge of the pack's protection, he stopped and faced Reneca with his head low and his tails swishing. Reneca made a big display of growling at him while moving forward as if preparing to attack.

When Milsol and Yarain caught up, Yarain stood beside Sundale while Milsol stood beside Reneca.

"You two must learn your place," Reneca said, though her swishing tails confirmed she was still playing.

As was Yarain. "I was a first mother five minutes ago. There's a reason for that."

Yarain gave the same play glare she'd given in Jason's quarters all those months ago. Instead of cowering, Reneca made the first move. She lunged forward and got into a harmless snapping match with Yarain.

Milsol did the same with Sundale, but Sundale danced around him, then tackled him like he was 'going for the kill,' though every growl and cackle was pure play.

Soon after their 'battle,' the four of them spent much of the day relaxing with each other and other members of the pack. Other periods of play would erupt, followed by the soundest naps ever recorded. As Sundale fell asleep, everything outside of his fur was thousands of light-years away. There was only his pack. His territory.

His *home*.

CHAPTER 11

ENEMY OF MY ENEMY

Birds that were in formation scattered as Sundale flew over them. They no doubt thought his outstretched paw was reaching for them. He thought about it, but he'd already eaten, and today was reserved for more general practice. That extended paw was merely an adjustment as he tipped his wings to curve around. The turn was so crisp and fluid he might as well have been a Scorn.

No. Better. Scorns, even at their best, still resisted. Still had to fight to get where they wanted to go. Sundale's wings held none of that. Not anymore.

Gone were the shakes, the tenderness, the hap-hazard flutters to avoid a plummet to his doom. Sundale didn't need to think anymore. He chose his path, his paws led the way on a turn, and his tails followed tight together behind to steady his flight. Wind rushed through his fur and feathers with every wingbeat and beyond. This helped to keep him cool through the exertion, though any time that wasn't enough, all he had to do was open his mouth and let his own airstream do the rest.

Despite being energy, the phantom feathers were solid enough to catch the wind. They extended down the shafts of the physical feathers like a ghostly echo to almost double the wing's surface area, which gave Sundale the extra lift he needed despite Holdrens being a little lighter than their size would suggest. Yet, the energy feathers remained opaque enough to match the dull sandy gold with a hawk-like striped pattern of the physical feather they were attached to. His legs were kept tight against his body except when he turned, and even then, only the corresponding front leg extended a small amount. Soft flaps kept him moving and airborne with growing ease each time he flew. Thermals above the forest made some periods even easier. When he found the right ones, all he had to do was hold his wings steady and let the rising hot air carry him wherever he wanted to go.

Sundale rode them often so he could enjoy the view. He could see the forest for miles from up here. A never-ending carpet of yellows and oranges; broken only by mountains, large clearings, and a few scars from the battle. He approached the clouds and saw the shimmering blue waters of the twin lakes he'd swam in the day before in the distance. Territory still unclaimed for reasons no one could remember. They only knew it allowed any pack to enjoy the waters without fear of reprisal. *Reason enough to leave it unclaimed.*

Sundale could also get a clear view of his audience. Reneca, Yarain, and Milsol stood below in a smaller clearing with their tails brushing their own excitement. Theirs could only pale in comparison to his own, however. With confidence came a rush of joy. Much as running wild on the soil had done, flying free in the air had left all of Sundale's stress and fear behind. When he rode the thermals, it was as if he were floating on nothing. Only the rush of his feathers, physical and energy, reminded him of what kept him airborne. *Let Reneca try to chase me now. She'd never catch me.*

Joy brewed a desire for something more. Sundale had been comfortable for a couple of days now. Turns, ascending, descending, it was all as easy as walking. It was time to test his limits.

With more than enough altitude to work with, Sundale chose a bushy tree below for his first test. He angled himself around, then his wings swept back, his body curved down, and he found himself in a rush like nothing he'd ever felt before. His ears tucked back for comfort as wind whipped across his body. His fur and feathers fluttered as the tree charged at him. He tucked his legs as tight as he could, and his speed increased. The thrill of the hunt filled his lungs. Joyful exuberance filled every muscle, even as they held his body in as tight a spear as possible. This was more than any final sprint. This was ecstasy in motion!

All except for Reneca and Yarain. They started walking toward the tree in spurts as if trying to figure out where to catch him. Milsol kept close watch with tails devoid of any excitement.

Sundale understood their concern, but he didn't share it. He could feel his wings catching the wind like wheels guiding him on his path. He could have changed that path at will without effort or fear. Minute changes in his wings and tails were already keeping him on target. It would have been easy to turn from that tree to another or toward prey, or toward the others had he wanted to.

Instead, he chose to alleviate the concerns of his audience. Sundale leveled off well short of the tree, slowing his descent to a slow glide. He let his momentum slow as he passed over the trees, though he did angle so he could glide right over Reneca and Yarain. Reneca ducked despite how far above her he was. She then barked in protest as Sundale regained altitude. While he wasn't sure what she took exception to, the bark didn't sound serious, so it could have been simple teasing.

Sundale wasn't done testing himself, however. He'd proved to his pack that he had control. Now, he wanted to really see what he could do. His wings worked hard to get him as high as he could, only to dip down into another dive. This time, instead of a soft level, he pulled up hard. In the same motion, his wings flapped to push him skyward with his bleeding speed. His legs kicked out as if he were swimming to help absorb the hard strain the wings were now asked to carry. It worked to perfection, for there was hardly any strain at all. Sundale again glided in a soft circle right after to prove to the others that he remained in control of himself.

The dive was repeated again, and again, and again. Each time, Sundale took himself closer to the top of the tree while gaining a growing understanding of what his body did when he did this or that. His timing was getting better, allowing him to choose the path he took and exactly when he pulled up.

Sundale tried for his closest run yet. He aimed to just graze the top of the branches. With any luck, he might even manage to bite off a small twig along the way. *Just as I might now be hunting birds.* The wind rushed; his fur bristled—he had it! The tree came at him. He pulled up . . . too late.

Sundale abandoned his bite, but he was committed. His legs kicked out as before and caught the upper branches. The tree swallowed him whole. He could only yip as he tumbled through the twigs. Sundale's paws shot out. They hit enough branches to push him out of the tree at an awkward angle. He managed to fold his wings just before he rolled along the ground. When he came to a stop, Sundale stayed on his side, still whining as he tried to find the difference between pain and damage.

The patter of paws announced the others arriving to check on him. Yarain sniffed at his shoulders while Reneca came to his head.

"Are you well, Sundale?" Reneca asked.

A whine was his first reply. "That hurt. That hurt a lot."

Sundale rolled onto his paws; certain more than a few spots would bruise soon.

Milsol tested Sundale's shoulders with his nose and tongue. He got no response. "I don't see any blood. Anything feel broken?"

Another whine came as Sundale settled into a more comfortable lying position. Yarain continued to search for injury with nose, tongue, and muzzle. She rubbed against Sundale's bones in search of any breaks. She found spots that didn't like being pushed on, but nothing more.

Sundale tensed his wings since they hurt the most. They moved without resistance, though they weren't exactly happy about it. "I think the worst I suffered is damaged pride."

Reneca ruffed a quick laugh. "Then I'd call your condition serious."

Sundale growled at her, to which she panted more laughter.

Yarain gave an amused ruff of her own while still inspecting his hips. "I'm not finding anything either. Even so, perhaps you should stay on the ground for a while just to be sure."

Sundale rose slowly so the pain didn't hit too hard. He found only the same sore spots repeating their complaint. "No argument here. Next time, I may test myself on something else."

"How about a cloud?" Reneca said with another pant.

Sundale glared, then nipped at her. She jumped away, trilling more tease. She got low on her forelegs with more barks of false challenge.

This time, Sundale gave her a real, though very soft, growl. "I want to recover first."

Reneca rubbed her muzzle against his in an apology he found unnecessary. She couldn't know how he felt.

Milsol flicked an ear, then looked to the forest behind them. "Now what's this?"

Sundale followed his gaze to the edge of the clearing where Jason and General Manster were being led toward them by another Holdren. A part of Sundale suddenly grew heavy with guilt. He'd barely given Jason any thought. Yarain had confirmed he'd make a full recovery, and since then, all thought had been on the pack and the wild.

As it should be, Sundale's instincts said. Didn't keep him from feeling like he might have abandoned his friend and first father... well, former first father. Though somehow, Jason still retained the position in Sundale's heart. It did help that Jason was in full uniform, weapons and all, with no signs of ongoing treatment remaining.

Reneca stayed close beside Sundale as the group trotted up to meet the approaching soldiers. The other Holdren vanished into the forest toward the pack's meeting area while Jason nodded with a hum Sundale didn't understand. For one thing, he couldn't tell if Jason was humming at him, Yarain, the Holdren that just left, or something else.

However, the forced smile on Jason's face was all too familiar. *Uh-oh.*

Reneca spoke first, switching to English.

"**GOOD** to see you well, Colonel. Your wound had me worried."

Jason nodded while a hand went to his left shoulder. "Had me worried too. Hit a little close to home."

I'll say. If it weren't for the new armor, you'd have added to that scar.

"What do you mean?" Reneca said.

Jason shook his head as if to clear it. "Never mind. It's a long story I'll have to tell you at another time."

She growled at Jason, then at Sundale. "So that's where you get it."

"Huh?" Jason looked to Sundale for answers.

Sundale could only offer an amused ruff. "I'll tell you later. I can see we have more important issues at hand."

Jason folded his arms. "How do you always know—"

"Eleven years, one near-death experience, several thousand engagements; need I go on?"

Jason glared, though not without humor. All but Reneca panted a soft laugh.

General Manster shook his head. "You have quite an officer, Colonel. He's lucky he's in your military instead of mine. He'd have my fingers in his scruff and be whining an apology if it were up to me."

Jason looked as appalled as Sundale felt. *Kapon allows that?*

"For what?" Jason said. "Reminding me how well he knows me? I knew haaj'kar were strict with protocol, but with all due respect, General, that's a bit much."

"Protocol keeps a unit sharp, Colonel. The Holdrens understand that. They never let a subordinate get out of line."

Yarain stepped forward with her tails stiff and level. "As any good parent would. What you're talking about is a hierarchy, which is **NOT** how a pack operates. We call the head of a pack 'first parent' for a reason."

"Yet, you still use your fangs to get their attention."

"Only when necessary. And even **THAT** is done in the **BOND** of a pack. Protocol helps, but without that trust, even a military will be weak."

General Manster stared her down while his hand tensed again and again. It seemed as if he wanted to make good on his threat of fingers in the scruff. That, and the glare, had Sundale's hackles rising. This was becoming a direct challenge to his pack. One thing his time had done was teach him just what that meant. To say nothing of the instincts that had been revived and refined in so very little time.

Before anyone could make a move or say a word, Reneca stepped between them with a growl meant for them all. "With respect, we're getting sidetracked. I assume you had something important to tell us, sirs?"

General Manster breathed out his fury but did let his shoulders sink. Yarain's tails and Sundale's hackles relaxed as well.

Jason gave his own sigh of relief before breaking the silence. "President Priolozi was right. The enemy of my enemy can still become an enemy if we're not careful. Something for us both to remember as we move forward, General."

General Manster nodded his agreement, though not without another annoyed sigh.

Jason's statement was replayed a few times in Sundale's head before he caught what it meant. When he did, his ears perked toward his commander and friend. "Jason, what did we miss?"

Jason smiled—almost laughed, actually. "Quite a bit. We've all been hip-deep in negotiations between the Federation of Kapon and the United Systems Republic. Gotta be the longest two weeks of my life, but I think in the end, it was worth it."

Two weeks? Has it been that long?

No wonder his time had felt like an eternity. Two weeks, no thoughts of Jason – *sorry Jason* – no politics, no war, no details, no civilization of any kind. Just him, his pack, his fur, flight training, and the wilds he was born into. For all he knew, quite literally given how many scents seemed familiar in recent days. He'd even managed to track some smaller prey without having to be told it was prey. Best of all, not a single shudder or nightmare. Not even a hint of one.

The thought that he'd had that long left Sundale almost giddy. Though it soon soured when he realized it was about to end.

Meanwhile, Yarain asked the question Sundale had been too busy reflecting to ask. "So, they were a success?"

"After some growing pains," Jason said. "But, we did manage to come together in the end. So much so that, as of yesterday, the Federation of Kapon and the United Systems Republic have forged an alliance against Polaris."

Four sets of ears perked.

"How full?" Milsol asked.

"Complete," General Manster said. "In fact, orders just came in this morning, Earth time. The *I.C.V. Alamo* will be supported by two Kapon cruisers, as well as the *Kraskit*. They'll be replacing some of the ships we couldn't salvage, as well as bolstering the group's strength."

Reneca and Milsol's ears went perfectly erect.

"The *Kraskit* was assigned to their group?" Reneca said. "With respect, General, that speaks of a lot more than an alliance."

"They assaulted two of our worlds, Commander. The first, a diversion meant to blame Interstar for piracy."

"And draw off the rapid response fleet for the area," Jason added. "Kapon feels an immediate show of unified force is required. The next time the *Alamo* sees action, she'll be flanked by the *Kraskit*, while the Gold Group will see Kapon fighters among their cover on bombing runs."

Reneca sighed with a glance at Sundale. "Then may I assume, sir, that you came to tell us leave is canceled?"

General Manster nodded. A slight growl came from the other Holdrens.

Sundale felt the same way, but not for the same reason. A ruffle through the energy part of his wings, which was nothing more than a common disruption automatically corrected, reminded him how much had changed. *I suppose it's not all bad. At least I'll get to spend more time at home.*

Sundale didn't bother offering that lie to the others.

"Take it to them, Commander," he said. "Make us proud to call you a friend."

Reneca tilted her head at him, but Yarain beat her to the question: "You talk like you won't be there."

Sundale looked back at his still sore wings. "No doctor would clear me for duty after these. If the battle hadn't been so urgent, I wouldn't have been allowed to fight it."

"On the contrary, Captain." General Manster said. "Our doctors have given you . . . how did your admiral put it? A clean bill of health?"

Sundale's ears perked with hope, but he had to work hard to keep the sarcasm out of his voice. "With respect, sir, I just sprouted wings."

"And have yet to have another symptom since. We asked Jilton, another member of your pack, to watch for any signs of trouble. He's confirmed what our doctors found from your scans and tests. The wings are the final stage of a, shall we say, disrupted transformation."

Sundale just about turned his head upside down in confusion. Jason couldn't help a stifled laugh when Sundale moved an equally confused stare onto him.

"You should have changed into an energon eleven years ago, Sun," Jason said.

A perfect answer from King Obvious. "The accident on Mars stopped that."

"No. The accident on Mars *changed* it. You were almost fully grown when the process started, which is apparently about when it happens. Roughly your . . ." He turned to Yarain. "*Second* spring or summer?"

"*THIRD*," Yarain ruffed.

"That's right. Second is when you get the red in your tails and start shooting things. Anyway, the final stages of energon growth mean turning into pure energy and growing a set of wings that let you fly through space. That process had to finish, but the accident made it impossible for it to take its intended course. Earlier this year, it found its way to finish the job. Being a purely physical change . . ." Sundale could almost feel his eyes glazing over. *Why do humans insist on so much detail?* Jason must have noticed, for he smiled with a knowing nod. "I guess the details don't matter. While we don't know why it took so long, all you need to worry about, is it's over. No more seizures, no more problems, no collar for treatment. They're confident you can return to duty."

Sundale's ears turned while his tails gave a similar, thoughtful wave. *Surely, it's not that simple.* "And Command accepted their judgment?"

Jason tossed his head side to side. "Enough to let you serve again. They want the haaj'kar to conduct a check-up every day for a while, just in case they missed something. And before you ask, Doctor Blount is going to be there every time. I feel for those doctors. Otherwise, you're cleared for duty."

Sundale's sides ached at the memory of the last time he was examined by the haaj'kar. The thought of enduring that every day was enough to make him refuse. After the "tender care" Admiral Solez had given him, the idea of anything similar threatened to trigger another of his shudders.

The thought of letting Yarain and Jason fight without him and his mother staring and waiting for confirmation silenced both. He may have a new blood pack, but his combat pack, as apparently were the terms among Kapon Holdrens, still needed him. Yarain would never be the same without him, and Jason was still a first father, though how

Sundale could have two was enough to give him a headache. As such, he didn't try to understand the feeling. He only accepted that he'd have some things to endure for the good of the pack.

Not that it helped him keep his ears up. "I guess I can live with that."

Jason nodded with a deep breath. "Good. Things haven't been the same without my favorite foxes."

"We've only been gone two weeks," Yarain said.

"Still too long. Come on. Let's get you two up to the *Alamo*. We have some things to cover, and we need to get you in your new armor."

Sundale's head again tilted. "*New* armor? Again?"

"You grew wings, remember? The suit bag idea was a stop-gap. They spent every minute after the battle working on a long-term replacement. They think they have it, and for once, I tend to agree."

More techs poking and scanning and tugging to "make sure it fits." I can hardly wait. "Lead on."

Jason turned to lead his crew back the way they came. Reneca barked to stop them. She faced General Manster when Jason paused to listen.

"Sir, I'd like to request a reassignment."

General Manster tilted his head in a very Holdren way. "You're asking me now? Here?"

"Because the request involves **BOTH** parties. I'd like to be posted to their carrier, sir, as a liaison between our forces."

General Manster traded glances with Jason. Then the General said, "Can you give me a reason that will fly with the senate, Commander?"

Reneca looked at Sundale with an amused ruff. "I've developed a good rapport with Sundale and Yarain. I can use that bond to help bridge the gap between our forces. Perhaps prevent arguments like the one we just had."

Jason rolled his eyes in thought, then shrugged. "Makes sense to me. During the battle, the *Alamo* took a beating. She slipped right into a turret station without batting an eyelash and acquitted herself quite well in the process until we could get a trained replacement through the damage. She's seen how we operate, she knows my crew, and she seems able to interact with our forces without too much friction."

"What about Major Torzon?" General Manster asked. "She knows Holdrens as well as you do, but she's human."

"She's far more useful in her fighter. More than that, if our fleets are going to work together, having two perspectives from two places will help us iron out the kinks. That's worth a lot in my book. I'm sure General Carson will go for it, and I think Admiral Redding will see the appeal. The rest is in your court." General Manster tilted his head again. "It's your choice, sir."

General Manster hummed. Almost sounded annoyed again.

Sundale kept silent while the general drummed his folded fingers on his hands. Sundale sat and listened, hoping for an answer in the affirmative.

Though he found himself wondering why. True, Reneca was part of his blood pack, and she'd made him feel more comfortable as he got reacclimated to Holdre 4's wild, but what was that other part? The one that suddenly hoped very strongly for the chance to evaluate her further. This wasn't anything like a crew evaluation or the explorations he'd done before when possibly adding a new friend. This was something different. Something instinctive, similar to curiosity, yet so much stronger, too. His mind could only compare it to a scientist wanting to dig into her DNA. It felt oddly accurate, even if he couldn't understand why.

It didn't help that he didn't need to see her tails twitch or her breath grow stronger to see she, too, was nervous. He could sense the change in energy and smell the change in her scent even from a few feet away. She definitely wanted more than to play mediator between their forces. The question was what that "more" was, and for that matter, what it was *he* wanted out of *her*.

General Manster finally stopped his drumming. He stared at Sundale and Reneca both, and they stared back. He hummed again, then bounced his folded hands.

"Very well. Come with me. We'll discuss how this exchange of officers will be handled."

Reneca swallowed a breath before it could escape. "Thank you, sir. You won't regret it."

General Manster hummed again. The more of those Sundale heard, the more he was beginning to decipher them. This one sounded reactive, like he was thinking about her tone. Even Sundale could tell she wasn't being reassuring; she was being confident, as if she knew she were right. Whether or not she was remained to be seen, but Sundale was still glad she would be within reach.

Milsol flicked an ear before stepping forward. "I'll pass the word to the other packs, sir. We should have everyone ready for transport in a few hours."

General Manster waved his hand. "No need, Lieutenant. Runners are already being sent. Ships are on their way to pick up soldiers as we speak."

"Then I may as well come with you, sir. I was recently posted to the *Kraskit*."

"I agree. Lieutenant Colonel?"

"Go ahead," Jason said. "We'll use our transponder to flash to the *Alamo*."

General Manster bowed, then led Reneca and Milsol into the forest, no doubt toward their ship.

Once they were gone, Jason turned to Sundale without so much as a sliver of a smile. "Major, I need to talk with Sundale about something in private. I'll meet you at the transponder."

The use of her rank made it clear to Yarain that this was a professional topic and not up for debate. As such, her ears fell a moment before ticking forward. "Understood, sir. May I ask—"

"You may not . . . but I can say it isn't something you should worry about."

He knows her too well.

Jason wasn't going to be deterred, even as he tried his best to reassure the mother that would always be there. She gave another forward ear tick before trotting off toward the larger clearing.

Despite the reassurance, Sundale's own ears were falling fast. He half expected a scolding and did not expect anything good.

"There's no need for that," Jason said. The ears didn't move. "As you wish. At least I know I have your attention." He paused, then knelt in front of Sundale. Sundale's ears finally came forward, all-be-it still somewhat low. "Sun, I may not know Holdrens as well as I like to think, but even I can tell there's the potential for something more between you and Reneca. It may just be the bond of the pack, I know how strong that can be, but I'm not so sure. Regardless, given the state of things, I have little choice. I need to ask you something I never thought I'd have to ask."

"Which is?" Sundale said carefully.

Jason hesitated with a cringe as well. "Will Reneca's presence affect you, your duties, or your judgment? Don't just answer. Think hard.

Can you stay focused should she get hit or, God forbid, killed? Do you even know yet?"

Sundale never thought that protocol would come into play for him. He and Jason had been together for so long, he never considered serving with someone he cared about enough for it to come up.

Assuming that's what it was. Holdrens didn't do "love" like humans did. He was intensely curious about her, but that wasn't the same as wanting to mate. Then again, he didn't really understand what it was he was feeling, which made it that much harder for him to find an answer.

The best he could do was try as hard as he could to imagine it. Sundale tried to make the scene real to himself as he played it over and over in his mind.

He and Reneca are on the field during a firefight. They're both picking their way through cover, returning fire as best they can. The enemy continues to fire their own bursts, pinning them at times. At one point, Reneca leans around to fire. Rounds spark across her chest and shoulder. She yips and falls. No movement, no sound. By all accounts, she's dead. *Now, what do I do? What do I do?*

If he can, Sundale checks on her, unless a medic beats him to it. If not, or if she is indeed dead, he continues on. There's nothing to be done for her now. He keeps his mind on his mission and his ears tuned for Jason's orders.

I'm in control. I worry, I may even hurt, but I'm in control.

Sundale prayed he was right as he looked into the real Jason's eyes in front of him. "I'll be fine," he said. "Reneca's presence won't affect me . . . anymore than my presence affects you."

An amused smile formed on Jason's face. He nodded with a rub on Sundale's shoulders. "Any other officer, I'd ask for more. From you? I'm willing to accept it. Come on. We still have bears to fight. Gotta make them pay for that scar."

He was teasing, but Sundale had to fight another shudder as Jason turned to lead the way. Jason couldn't understand. He didn't know why the ordeal still hurt as much as it did. Or why the mere mention of anything close to Admiral Solez's actions sent ripples down Sundale's spine.

Jason didn't know. No one did. And if Sundale had his way, they'd never find out.

Kor'Agel Giller Colark, or "prefect" for the humans, rubbed the side of his head to try and alleviate the sharp pain growing there. The layer of antennae on his head, shorter and thinner than normal for jantans, gave a ruffle over his head where humans would normally have hair. He closed his eyes and took a breath, trying to relax the features on his long, oval, grey face. His lower body was coiled under him and resembled an Earth millipede, complete with tiny legs and a carapace-like skin for his entire body, under the soft purple clothes with silver highlights he now wore.

When none of his efforts helped, all he could do was let out a sigh. "I wish I could say they weren't ours, but ... Well, you know why I can't. Are you *sure* they were our ships?"

Colonel Harlem nodded on the video screen. "As sure as we can be. We're examining what wreckage we can, but you know how thoroughly Marcallan ships are scuttled. There's not much left."

"I do indeed. I can't offer much, Colonel Harlem. I don't know how or why our ships would be flying with Polaris. Even knowing what we know about certain forces. But I can assure you, those ships were there without our permission. Though perhaps I need to officially—"

"No need for that. We have our hands full with Polaris. Command won't want to stir up a new war if they don't have to. Oh, it'll come up next time our sides meet for talks, but the most you'll get is more official questions from our diplomatic corps. That said, it's a disturbing development we can't ignore."

"I agree. I will tell you what I learn when I learn it. I can't promise more."

"As will I, prefect. For now, keep your ears sharp. Secret talks are one thing. Flying side by side . . . I'm trying really hard not to think about what that could mean."

The prefect sighed and rubbed his head again. "I know what you mean. Galla be with you, Colonel. I hope to have more for you soon."

"As do I. Harlem out."

The screen flickered off, leaving Kor'Agel Colark alone in his tiny office for a moment. He stared at nothing while his mind tried to put things together, not that the well-insulated comms office had anything to stare at besides bare walls and a desk with a computer.

Marcallan ships, fighting alongside Polaris . . . He couldn't imagine a worse indication of things. More than proof of a conspiracy, this was proof of a full-blown alliance between forces he felt quite sure *did not* have Marcalla's interests in mind. They might claim to, but Marcalla had heard such calls before.

Vultoo, a Kor'Agel from many years before, had claimed the same thing. He had sworn that jantans were the rightful rulers of the galaxy, and they had every right to claim it. He had left Marcalla with a high body count and stolen freedoms. He had to be violently removed from office, but once that was done, all usual honors for him had been stripped and burned.

Now the current prefect had to face the possibility of someone else acting behind the scenes in the worst way possible. The idea of them allying with an old enemy only made his head hurt more.

After another rough sigh, Colark pressed a button on the console. "Jals, Forin, come to my office at once."

Both officers acknowledged. Prefect Colark sat coiled and staring at the door with all four of his arms folded. He already knew how much he would tell them, but he also knew it was time to risk poking the cancer to see if answers would emerge. He was tired of waiting for the enemy to come to him. It was time to go on the hunt for a change.

Forin arrived first, wearing a simple dark purple uniform that covered his entire body except for green sleeves and legs and several markers of awards on his lower arms. Considered a general "at work" uniform, it didn't have much else, not even armor or a weapon belt. The man himself had a lighter complexion, a very narrow face, and thinner arms, even for a jantan.

The Hilishan—what humans would call a "five-star admiral"—cupped his left hands so that one sat above his heart while the other sat below in the Marcallan salute. Colark accepted by covering his heart with both left hands, then told him to stand and wait. They didn't wait long before Jals scuttered in the door and stood with his own salute. He wore the same uniform Forin did, though his face was a little shorter and rounder than Forin's. The vertical slits of his eyes remained tighter than usual as if he were always studying what he was looking at, even at his most relaxed.

Colark again accepted the salute, then folded his arms once more. "Two of our battleships were seen engaged in battle against Interstar alongside a Polaris task force. Who has an explanation?"

Both soldiers flattened their antennae as Jals worked his mouth as if chewing while Forin swallowed hard. Kor'Agel Colark stared them down with a ruffle in his own antennae.

Forin eventually huffed as if annoyed, though his tone was pure respect. "On my honor, I swear to you, no Marcallan ships were engaged."

When Prefect Colark turned to Jals, the Auro—or human four-star admiral—swallowed nervously. "I know of no missions, Kor'Agel. I can't explain it."

"You just 'lost track' of another ship."

Jals glared and rattled his antennae. "Or *you* began an operation without orders again."

Colark vibrated his own antennae. "*Stop!* Bicker on your own time. If you two didn't know about this, then I suggest you find out who did. Today. Do not stop until you have an answer."

Jals snapped into a perfect, smooth curve. "Yes, my lord!"

Forin stood in the same way, though not as tight. "Yes, my lord! Though, if I may ask, how did you hear about this battle?"

Prefect Colark managed to remain perfectly still while his mind debated what to say. In an hour-long internal conversation that took a second, he made a series of decisions he prayed he would not regret. "I'm afraid you are not allowed to know."

"Kor'Agel, with respect, as a Hilashan and a close friend..."

The prefect held his hand to his own neck, signifying Forin should stop vibrating his vocal cords. Forin trailed off with another sigh. "Do not push me on this," Colark said. "Find answers before this starts another war. Forin, dismissed. Jals, remain. I have other business with you."

Forin repeated the salute, then left with another quiet huff. Prefect Colark waited for the door to close, then settled into a looser coil with another rub of his head.

Jals stepped forward and spoke gently. "Can I get you anything, my lord?"

Colark smiled at him, shook his head, then chuckled again when he remembered reading humans had the same gesture. *So many things we share and do not realize.* "No, my friend. There is nothing to do but let it pass."

"As you say, sir. What more do you need of me?"

Colark gave the Auro a long look, then sighed again. "I need my friend, Olon, not my Auro, Jals."

Jals recoiled at first, no doubt surprised to hear his first name during such a formal conversation. He then nodded. "Of course. Anything I can do . . . Giller."

Colark chuckled to hear his friend struggle to drop the rank. They had known each other years ago before either began their current paths. Both were architects with big dreams and bigger ambitions, but the calls to serve were too loud for either to ignore. While Olon had joined the defense forces, Giller had gotten into politics. The day Giller had earned the title of Kor'Agel was a happy one, though soured by the understanding that many of those dreams would never come to be. Or, perhaps more correctly, they had been replaced by very different, wider-ranging dreams.

Giller motioned for his friend to coil beside him, which Olan did with soft attention. "Forin overestimates how close we are, but you, on the other hand, I cannot keep earless; I am in contact with the crew of Gold 1. They were at that battle. Colonel Harlem himself reported it."

Olan stared at Giller with straight antennae. "What? Are we sure we can trust him as a source?"

Giller looked straight at him. "Yes!"

Olan breathed for a moment, then nodded. "Then something is indeed going on."

"Yes. Far more than you know. And perhaps I waited too long to tell you all of it."

"You always knew when to keep things to yourself. You don't need to stab yourself for doing so again."

Giller again chuckled while patting his friend's coil. "Even so, there is much I think you should know. In part because it would be nice to have an ally against the dangers that may come my way."

"Dangers? What do you mean?"

"I'll get to that. But there is a conspiracy working behind the scenes that may be a threat to our nation."

"What about the Festival of Robes? Anyone can give the anniversary address that starts it. If you are in danger, will you give it to someone else?"

This time, Giller shook his head solemnly. Part of him wanted to, but he had already had that debate with himself several times. He didn't need to do it again.

"The Kor'Agel has begun the festival since before we could reach another planet. I will not break tradition. Besides, old friend, the danger cares far more about Interstar than me right now."

Olan nodded with a smile of his own. "I was going to suggest you go through with it, but I had to ask first. However, confiding in Colonel Harlem . . . seems dangerous to me."

"He is a man of honor, Olan. I trust him in that regard. He wants peace as much as I do."

"He would kill you if he thought it would bring peace."

I somehow doubt that. "As you would kill him for the same reason. But you let me worry about Gold 1. For now, let me explain what I know. Then I want you to find out what our ships were doing at that battle. And from the mouth of Gala, do not relent until you find answers."

"Even if the answers mean war?"

"If they do, I want to know all the more."

CHAPTER 12

FINAL MISSION

For Colonel Harlem, the only thing worse than not flying was not flying during an active battle. His group was out there risking their lives alongside Kapon fighters they'd spent the last month learning to fight with. Where was he? On a landing pad inside the *Alamo*, waiting for assault weapons to be mounted and tuned according to specific parameters outside of the norm. A process that was taking a lot longer than usual for some reason.

Jason could hear them working on the hull. Clunks echoing along the walls at least confirmed he wasn't trapped in the hangar doing nothing. Nor was he alone. His own status screen showed the presence of first and third squads in the same waiting game.

That almost made it worse. Carter had just over half the group out there while the rest of them prepared for a final assault. One that he had yet to be clued into. In some ways, he almost missed Holdre 4. There, the battle had been frantic, costly, and direct. More to the point, he'd had more control over his group's actions. Then again, that had come with more of the weight for any mistakes. At least now he only had to worry about fighting, staying alive, and following his orders. *Assuming we ever get any.*

When the sounds of work ended, every muscle tensed. He could almost feel his ear turning back to listen for Sundale's call of a completed installation. Each second saw his insides turn into a tighter ball of rubber. *What is taking so long?*

An odd whine from Yarain drew his attention. Jason looked back, more curious than worried since it sounded cut off. He found nothing more than her shaking her head after the end of a yawn. *I should have recognized the sound.* He'd heard it enough the last few weeks when she came back half asleep from who knows what.

"You all right?" Jason asked.

Her head snapped toward him, ears straight up. Something else he'd seen a lot of lately. Now, like then, she relaxed without so much as an ear twitch.

"I'm just a little worn," she said.

I've heard that before, too. "A little worn from what, Major? This has been going on for a while. I also know you've been spending time in the *Appalachian's* sim room."

"It's nothing you need to worry about now."

"Not good enough, Major."

That got a growl from her. "Mid-combat is **NOT** the time for this. For now, try to trust me when I say I'm fine. This will be the last time I ask that of you."

That, he *hadn't* heard before. In and of itself, it didn't mean much. But the levity of her last sentence had Jason a little worried and a lot curious.

"What does that mean? Yarain, is there something—"

"Installation complete," Sundale said. *He can have the worst timing.* "Assault weapons loaded and ready."

Yarain returned her full focus to her console. "Both squads report the same. We're good to go."

Jason knew avoidance when he saw it, but he had no time to fight through it. The battle called. He'd have to deal with Yarain later.

Jason tapped his systems to combat status while noting the torpedoes listed on his ordnance screen. "Do we have clearance for launch?"

"Not yet," Yarain said. "Another fighter is landing ahead of us on priority."

"Damaged?"

"It doesn't say."

Jason looked out his window in time to catch the wing of a Kapon Vindinsa class fighter float by. She didn't look damaged, but she sure landed in a hurry.

"That's Karol's fighter," Sundale said. "Why would she be landing on priority without battle damage?"

"A good question," Jason said.

Beeps from behind silenced the matter.

"We're clear, sir," Yarain said. "Standby for launch. We're ordered to engage enemy fighters until given further orders. Our shells are to remain unarmed for now."

"That sounds ominous," Sundale said.

"Agreed," Colonel Harlem said. "But it's not our call anymore. Lock and load you two. Yarain, be sure the group is ready to follow me out, then check that sensor data. Sundale, I'll need targets by priority the moment we're out."

"Yes, sir!" they said. A month of hearing that unity had been much more welcome.

The rubber ball in Jason's chest became a ball of lightning, as it often did. He waited only a moment before lifting the fighter into a hover above his pad and into the flight lane. He knew Yarain would have the group floating as well. The flight crew hugged the wall while Jason watched the lights above the hangar doors. Much like the beginning of a race, red became a flashing yellow, and then the bay was flooded with green. Jason and his group followed the running lights out into the stars, maintaining formation while taking a direct line toward the battle.

Jason could already tell little had changed. The battle was still being fought by the fighters. Polaris ships held position over a planet that looked more like a sandy marble. Swirls of orange that filled the surrounding space reminded everyone of the unique charged material in this system that kept foe and friend alike from using their HLS drives. Would be a favor, except Interstar's capital ships were hanging back to avoid leaving their strike craft stranded without support in Polaris-occupied territory. Polaris didn't want to risk their ships, and Interstar had their own plans, which Jason had yet to hear a word of. Both fleets were at the edge of where target data could be used to land reliable hits, but with neither side able to get any fighters close to the other, no one could maintain reliable targeting for long enough to matter.

Thus, the fire and light show going on between the fleets. Dots grew into fighters as the newly armed squads rejoined the battle. Long, slender hexagons that were the Interstar corvettes provided a line of defense, while red Scorns flashed beside lavender Vindinsa class fighters in the melee. Jason had grown to admire the Kapon ships, and a previous skirmish, while minor, had shown Captain Torzon could use one just as well as the old Phantoms the Scorn replaced. *Too bad she refused a Scorn. She'd probably put me to shame.*

"Glad to see you back out here, Jason."

Captain Carter Gomez reminded Jason of the situation before his own attention did. A Polaris fighter flew past chasing a Scorn. Gold 1 was on his tail with a Vindinsa on her wing before he'd gotten far.

Jason fired quick bursts, then let Yarain and Sundale take their shots while he kept on their prey. "Good to be back, Captain. How we doing?"

"Bombers aren't a problem. Their fighters have been. I think they upgraded their shields. Still have 'em on the run, but it hasn't been easy."

Jason's target tried to turn back and face him. He instead got a face full of missiles from Gold 1 and the Vindinsa beside her. The debris continued to spin while they split off to find other targets.

"Time to change that," Jason said. "Get on my wing. It's time we—"

"Bulldogs!" Sundale called. "Port beam, they have lock!"

Shit!

Jason threw the throttle open with a hard spin 'down.' Flashes through the windows told just how close he'd cut it. Shudders through the hull said he hadn't lost them.

He didn't expect to. Sleek and thin with razored points at the fuselage and twin nacelles, these Viper class interceptors, or "Bulldogs" as Interstar called them, had proven near-impossible to shake. They were glass cannons, really, but only if you could catch them or your turrets got a lucky few seconds to wear their shields down. Normal training said to turn into an attack, but that only worked one-on-one, and rarely without damage yourself unless you could get the right angle. Two turned it into a long shot. Jason had *four* on his tail, all with an active target lock. At that point, even he could only do two things.

Evade and pray—*hard.*

Jason spun, slid, and wove around anything to keep them from getting a solid lock. Any time he managed to flip on his back or twist around a piece of debris to take a shot, the Bulldogs split off like roaches and restarted the chase from a better angle. The only thing such tactics did was keep them from concentrating their fire long enough to wear down his shields. He could hear Yarain calling for help about as hard as he was trying to make sure they lasted long enough to save. On one turn, he noticed one Polaris fighter get into the line of his ally to take a far worse shot. *Never thought being such a target would be a good thing.* It seemed they all wanted the kill so much they were preventing the kill from happening at all. Though even that wouldn't save him forever.

Jason pulled around the remains of a Vindinsa fighter. The Vipers blasted right through it. He expected alarms to sound any minute. Instead, he watched the Bulldogs' blips vanish from his screen one by one. The fourth peeled off to run. Jason flipped Gold 1 on her back in time to watch a pair of Vindinsas tear the last Viper apart.

"Sorry for the delay," A haaj'kar voice, one with their long E accent. "Couldn't get a safe target."

And some say Scorns are still the better interceptor. After their joint training to merge their forces, Jason no longer agreed. "Forgiven, pilot," he said. "Nice flying. If you don't mind, what say we—"

"*NEW* orders, Jason." Yarain barked.

Sheesh. I can't finish one of my own today. He followed another squad of Vipers with his saviors in tow. "Talk, Major."

"Enemy ships escorting heavy transports. We're ordered to break through the shields of one with our torpedoes. Do not destroy or disable.

REPEAT, *do not* destroy or disable. No details will be given. Kapon forces will be flying escort."

The last Bulldog broke up before Polaris Comets could save him. They, in turn, became Gold 1's next target. They were gone like fireworks before they realized their mistake.

"We load up for that?" Sundale said. "What's Redding planning?"

"No details, Sundale," Yarain said. "Just a note to ensure Captain Torzon survives. She'll be following us in."

"That doesn't help much."

"Not our problem," Jason said. "We have our orders. Gold 1 to group, assume bomber formation. Those without shells assume outer positions. Kapon will cover our butts. Let's get this done!"

Constant practice made the operation like walking. The two squads of Scorns with heavy weapons condensed into a tight formation, some belly to belly. Gold 1's main weapons were taken offline to fortify her shields and increase the turrets' rate of fire, though both would need to be watched lest they overheat too much.

Jason's main screen changed to show a readout of targets with possible lanes to them. The *Alamo*'s CIC already had a transport highlighted, as well as the best route to it.

Jason followed that path while taking in the real view. The Polaris fleet was indeed moving out of the nebula with three heavy transports tucked within them. Allied heavy hitters were engaging the escorts, creating a deadly crossfire of light between them.

And his route had him flying right by it.

Unlike standard bombers that Interstar had mostly abandoned, Gold 1 had a strong edge; at their core, Scorns would always be fighters. The group charged at high speed, weaving around debris with agility only smaller craft could achieve.

"Enemy fighters inbound," Sundale said.

"Bulldogs?" Jason asked.

"None as yet."

Small favors. "Prioritize and target. Concentrate fire, don't consolidate. Let the Kapon fighters do the chasing. Yarain, remind the group to hold course no matter what."

"Yes, sir," she said.

The fighter shuddered at each hit they took. It lasted but a few seconds as a dozen turrets tore the offending fighter apart. More charged head-on. Jason stared them down as if he could bluff them into veering off.

Carter took care of that. He led a charge of Interstar and Kapon fighters right at them. Their formation splintered, and a hole opened.

Some hole. Polaris battleships were above and below, trading shots with Interstar warships. These things were two very large, very long fuselages stacked on top of each other that were flat and blocky, except at the ends where they came to abrupt points where their specialized spinal cannons resided. Between the bulks laid a short wing structure built like a rounded pyramid sticking out each side that ran the middle third of the ship and was several decks high at the center. These wings held many of the weapons that barely managed firing arcs over each other as the wings tapered down to the ends, while the main bodies bristled with Point Defense Fire turrets. The only thing that made the narrow space between them a "hole" was the sorry state of their armor. They were being turned into flaming hulks by the chunk-load. They weren't going to be a threat for long, not that it made Jason feel any better.

He gunned the engines anyway. This was their chance. Their escorts led the way. Plasmoid bolts paved a path for them.

And Jason began a rare ritual.

"As I lay me down to sleep, I pray the Lord my soul to keep."

Their escorts peeled off. The Gold Group flew between the enemy ships unchallenged.

"If I should die before I wake, I pray the Lord my soul to take."

Nothing between them. A few fighters. Not enough to matter. They had lock. Gold Group fighters without heavy weapons provided an additional screen. Sundale confirmed weapons armed, tuned to each other to control their combined blast yield.

"Amen!"

Tap-tap-tap. Heavy torpedoes left the racks two at a time. They were joined by others from the group. Their thrusters glowed like a dozen stars as they headed for their target. The total amount was carefully calculated by the *Alamo* and Sundale to achieve their unclear objective with little room to spare.

Jason pulled away, still in formation. The Polaris battleships were ablaze. Interstar forces weren't even firing at them anymore. Then, all at once, they were lit up by a bright flash from behind. The torpedoes had hit home.

"**PERFECT** detonation," Sundale ruffed. "Forty percent got through. Her shields are down; heavy damage to her armor. She is still underway."

A Vindinsa fighter blew past with others on her wing. Jason didn't need Yarain to tell him who it was.

"I still don't get the plan here," Sundale said.

"Nor I, Sun," Jason said. "I'm sure Admiral Redding will tell us when it's prudent."

"In other words, he never will."

"At least we know what to expect."

Amused ruffs sounded from the foxes. Jason chuckled right with them. They'd gotten to know their FCO pretty well over the last few months. Not all of it had been pleasant.

Jason stopped that train before it left the station. He couldn't afford a trip down frustrated thoughts. He still had a job to do.

"Yarain," he said, "any updates for us?"

A small alarm went off in Jason's head when his screen nearly cleared of targets all at once. This time, however, it was unwarranted.

"Field clear," Yarain said. "All targets that could, have fled the area. The rest have been mopped up or are surrendering. Fleet status changing to condition 2. Stand by . . . Admiral Redding wants us in CIC ASAP."

"Did he say why?" Jason asked.

"Marshal Garmon wants to talk with us. There's also a warning: Councilor Goodheart will be there."

Jason looked back toward Yarain, too confused to be angry. "Goodheart? What's he doing on the *Alamo*?"

"He never left. Too dangerous to transport him off ship."

"And standing on the deck of a carrier in the middle of a battle isn't? I must read the rule book again. Well, the sooner begun, the sooner it ends. Get me a landing vector."

"Already done."

Jason almost wished for an ambush. It would be a nice excuse to stay away. Councilman Goodheart, who scuttlebutt said had already been chosen as the new Vice President, had somehow maneuvered himself onto the *Alamo* so he could get more acquainted with the military, both Interstar's and Kapon's. That meant a lot of red carpet, a lot of protocols, and a lot of headaches for all on board. More so when the *Alamo* was called to pounce on the enemy fleet, and no other task force of sufficient strength and/or equipment was close enough. Even an hour would have been too long. So here they were, in the thick of it, with a member of United Systems' executive branch they had to babysit and cater to. Worse than that, he was a civilian councilor who normally wouldn't have anything to do with the military at all. No one understood how he still managed to get on board at all, much less anywhere near the lines. They only knew that it happened, and the fleet had to deal with it.

Wonder if they would thank me if I shot him. The thought was nowhere close to serious. Just a quiet vent Jason could channel his frustration into and then toss it aside.

With a sigh doing exactly that, Jason sat Gold 1 down on the hangar deck with the rest of his group. At least those that had made it. As they exited their fighter, a small number of empty pads marked the fallen, though many may yet be found in escape pods. Jason paused and let the weight sit where it fell. He never liked losing members, even as he'd learned to accept it as part of the job. Now, like always, his mind whirled around, wondering what he could have done better to keep them safe.

Sundale shaking behind him snapped him out of it. The fox chewed at his shoulder before ruffling his feathers.

"You okay, Sun?" Jason said.

"***FINE***," he yipped. "Not sure I'll ever get used to sitting on my wings."

"So says he who swore he'd never get used to the uniform." Sundale gave a soft growl, to which Jason shrugged. "Just saying, Sun."

Sundale nipped at him, though nowhere near in range to land it. Jason flinched away, pretending to dodge it. Sundale panted. Jason laughed. *Only my crew.*

The joy vanished when he noticed Yarain watching them intently. A joyful swish in her tails couldn't hide a look he'd seen before. A heavy decision had been made, and it was weighing on her.

"What's wrong, Yarain?" he asked.

"I'm going to miss this," she said.

Even Sundale had his ears perked, but Jason spoke first. "Miss it? What are you talking about? Why would you—"

Reneca's voice cut him off. "Colonel Harlem?"

One sentence. Can I finish one important sentence today, please?

Jason rubbed between his eyes, trying very hard not to punch Reneca in the muzzle. She'd approached through the hangar carrying a clip-com in her hands. Her uniform was much like Karol's lavender shirt and pants, except Reneca's was sleeveless, stopped at her knees, and was tight against her body, just like Sundale and Yarain's. Her shoulder patches were also bright red, which he'd learned marked her as ship crew as opposed to Karol's strike craft dark red. She had the same style of rank patch on her arm as all Kapon officers, though she only had three lines weaving over each other.

"Yes, Commander?" Jason said.

Reneca's ears shifted nervously. "I'm sorry, Colonel, if I—"

"Don't . . . don't worry about it." *Revenge!* That cooled him off a bit. "What do you need?"

"Colonel, I need to talk to you and your leaders. Kapon intelligence finally cracked data from the Marcallan ships at Holdre 4. It's a bit unnerving."

"Why come to me with it?"

"Kapon's senate has another matter they want to put forward. They wanted me to include one of you in it."

Garmon, Goodheart, now Reneca. At this rate, I'm going to need a secretary.

"On my six, Commander. We're headed to meet with Marshal Garmon now."

She stepped aside so Jason could take the lead. He heard a soft whine and checked back to see Sundale sneaking a rub against Reneca's muzzle. He shook his head at them as they left the hangar.

The pack never ends, though I wonder if those two are on the road to something more. Jason had seen similar interactions between Sundale and Yarain before and, in fact, saw it happen again with her and Reneca. But it had not been as frequent. Almost every time Sundale and Reneca met, there was some kind of greeting between them. Though he had noticed that most of the time it was Sundale making the first move. It could be that they were a full pack instead of just parents and cub. Still, the curiosity was there, and the chance at there actually being something more created a happy warmth in Jason's chest.

The four of them made their way to CIC where most of the stations were still active and operating. The displays on the walls showed fleet status, sensor data, and a few casualty lists. The central holo-hub was only showing graphics for the fleet, the planet, and a few dots for the fighters running mop-up patrols.

Marshal Garmon, Admiral Redding, and General Manster stood by the center table talking about something with a fourth figure that had a head of blond hair, a small beer belly, and a black suit with a blood-red tie with black lines on it. Their conversation ended as all three soldiers looked up at the approaching group while Councilman Goodheart folded his arms with contempt. *Good thing only the president and Marshals can give orders to the military. I'd hate to take orders from him.* Jason and his crew stepped up to the other side of the table and snapped to attention with a salute. Reneca echoed the same only a half step behind.

"Gold 1 reporting as ordered, ma'am," Jason said.

Marshal Garmon returned the salute too smoothly for his liking. Last time Jason saw weight like that, she was about to tell him they'd found Sundale. He didn't want to consider what she had in store for him this time.

"In the command room, Mister Harlem. This is for you and your crew alone."

This can't be good. I'll wait my turn for now.

"With respect, ma'am," Jason said, "is this an urgent matter?"

"You were given an order, Colonel," Goodheart said. "Just follow it."

Garmon held a hand up to silence him. "I can speak for myself, Councilor. Colonel? Explanation?"

Goodheart seethed, and Jason couldn't help enjoying it. Not that he was about to let him know that. "Commander Reneca is here with data from Kapon intelligence. If our matter is not urgent, I think we should hear what she has for us first."

General Manster cocked his head at Reneca. "When did this come, Commander? And why did you get it instead of me?"

Reneca didn't flick anything. "Just before the battle, sir, and I don't know. I only know you all *need* to see it."

Marshal Garmon gave Reneca a long, hard look. Reneca countered with a glare of her own. Jason tried to make a low ruff sound. Sounded more like a cough, but it worked. She glanced at him before letting her ears soften.

Marshal Garmon nodded. "Better. What do you have for us, Commander?"

Reneca took a breath as if to settle herself. "We finally managed to extract and decode data fragments from the Marcallan ships at Holdre 4. We didn't recover much."

I'm not surprised. When jantans scuttle a ship, they really scuttle it. We didn't even find bodies in the debris. "But you said you found something unnerving," he said aloud.

"Yes. Classified itineraries for your entire Command Council, as well as the Marcallan prefect. Message fragments that seem to come from both Polaris and Marcalla. One set of deployment orders that appear to be directed *at* the ship *from* Polaris. Supply orders written in English. Control protocols written in English. In fact, every line of code has been in human characters."

Okay, that does count as unnerving. Jason couldn't even find a crazy reason for a Marcallan ship to be without a single line of jantan code. Even if they gave Polaris a pair of ships, replacing the code wouldn't do much. Any way he looked at it, this spoke of an alliance growing tighter by the day.

Goodheart, however, just huffed it away. "You call that 'need to see'? I admit it's a mystery, but it's hardly a problem."

Reneca's hackles fluffed, but she kept it out of her voice. "That's not all there is, sir. We've been able to analyze some of the debris. The alloys are a perfect match to Polaris designs and show none of the markers for Marcalla."

"What are you saying, Commander?" General Manster said.

"I'm saying the same shipyard built those ships and several other Polaris ships."

General Manster gave a growl of his own, then glared at Marshal Garmon. "And yet their Prefect still insists he had nothing to do with the attack. How much more do we need?"

"Quite a bit," Jason said. "With all due respect, General, Kapon is about to get a rude awakening when it comes to intergalactic relations. I know the Marcallan prefect personally. If he says he had nothing to do with it, you can take him at his word."

"And this only confuses things further," Admiral Redding added. "I've faced Bubble Boomers before, General. Those things went down way easier than they usually do. We've also yet to find a single drop of jantan blood on any debris. What if they weren't true Marcallan ships?"

Well, there's a fun thought. Interstar had often toyed with copying the same frames Marcalla used but abandoned it since the frame was pointless without the matching tech. If Polaris had found a way to make it workable or simply decided the trade-off was worth it, things could get very complicated very quickly. Especially since the sensor signature had been identical. Everything about the ships had appeared to be vintage Marcalla, except their performance, as Admiral Redding had noted.

General Manster folded his arms, but Reneca spoke first. "There's one more thing intelligence sent. If I may, ma'am?"

She indicated the holo-table. Marshal Garmon motioned her permission to use it. Reneca set her clip-com on a port, then had one of the smaller tables show a map of allied territories and the surrounding space. Each known government held its own color, with dark red showing what little territory Polaris had taken thus far. Several blips appeared on the map, some in bright red, some in yellow.

"Each of these red marks is an attack by Polaris. Each yellow mark is a better strategic target they ignored. Many of them were targets they had every reason to know about. As you can see, most of the strikes are along the Sagittarius arm. Phoenix Perch was the first major attack on the Crux arm. Further, several of these bases were completely overrun with minimal Polaris losses. They could have pushed on to other strategic targets without any relevant resistance."

"But at what cost?" Sundale said.

A lot of these also happened before we rescued Sundale. That may have rattled them. Jason stopped the words before they left his throat. Sundale didn't need the reminder, and he wanted to hear more of this data.

Plus, he was evaluating Reneca for command presence and ability to take comments. She was doing better, though unlike Sundale or Yarain, she seemed to be having no trouble giving expanded details. *May want to borrow some notes from the Kapon training regimen.*

"Not enough to negate the damage done to your infrastructure," Reneca said. "Further, time after time, they passed on the chance to destroy or capture vital points that could have helped their war effort far better, and they still focused on the Sagittarius arm. Their attacks have stayed on the border of both nations, though never where your border meets with Marcalla."

Goodheart continued to seethe. Jason would have been enjoying it if he weren't losing faith in the report.

"No offense, Commander," Jason said, "but as important as this all is, I've yet to hear 'you need to see this.' We're not ignoring our border with Marcalla, especially not after seeing their ships at Holdre 4. Beyond that, I don't see how this affects the war effort. We haven't lost territory for over a month now, and we've already begun to reclaim some of it. Their plan seems to have failed."

"***HAS*** it?" Reneca said. "What is their plan, sir?"

"I agree with the Colonel," General Manster said. "This doesn't hold the weight you claimed it would."

Reneca couldn't stop a growl. All three military leaders cast reprimanding glares across the table. That didn't stop her. "We need to keep looking at this. We can't let overconfidence—"

"Cut it, Commander!" Jason said, his hand sweeping in front of her as if he were doing it for her. "You've made your report, and believe me, we'll be looking into it. There's nothing more you need to do here."

"Sir, with respect..."

Sundale put a hand on her shoulder. Jason was certain Sundale said something, but he had neither the eyes nor ears to hear it. Reneca's ears pulled back as she sighed again. She removed the clip-com, the screen went blank, and she set it aside.

"All our data is on there. Please don't ignore it."

"We won't," General Manster said. "Dismissed, Commander."

"Sir, there's—"

"*Dismissed*, Commander."

She left without a word or salute.

Marshal Garmon watched her go with a shake of her head. She waited until the doors closed behind Reneca to speak again.

"I jolly well hope she's the exception rather than the rule. So far, Mister Harlem, your crew has been far more dignified."

Yarain beat him to the comment. "If you mean are all Holdrens like that, your answer is no, ma'am. I may have to talk with her about it."

"Not if I do it first, Major," General Manster said. "She's one of mine. Perhaps it's time we did this our way."

Jason tried not to think about what that would mean for Reneca. He'd heard Manster talk about their way. He didn't care for it.

Perhaps neither did Marshal Garmon. "A decision for another time, General. For the moment, I have a discussion with Gold 1 that cannot wait any longer. Gold 1, if you will?"

I'd rather not.

Jason followed her into an adjacent office with his crew in tow. Felt more like a funeral march. A part of him feared that's exactly what she had in store for them.

Marshal Garmon stood to the side of a small holo-table close to one wall. A couple of long tables with a few chairs lined the edges of the room. One wall was all display board, currently blank. Jason had seen a room like this only once before. Not long after, he saw most of his group mates killed and was himself captured by the jantans.

For a moment, Jason returned to the nervous lieutenant he was back then. He had no idea what he was about to face, then or now. The memory didn't make his insides any looser about the immediate future.

"Something wrong, Jason?" Sundale asked.

Jason shook himself out of the past to face the present. "Just old memories, Sun. Like when I brought that case into our quarters."

The backward turn in Sundale's ears said he understood what Jason meant.

"Please, Gold 1, take a seat," Garmon said. They all chose their seats on the opposite side of the main table. Yarain and Sundale were pure business. Jason was a rock pile of nerves between them. General Garmon took her seat, then bounced her folded hands on the table.

She soon shifted her gaze to Yarain. "Perhaps you should start, Major."

I didn't know my brain had shields. Jason sure felt them raise as he stared at Yarain whose ears were falling with a cringe.

"Yarain?" he said. Jason bounced between her and Garmon. "Start what? What's going on, ma'am?"

General Garmon took a breath deep enough to swallow the table. "I'm afraid you'll be getting a new POSN."

"What? Why? Yarain's record continues to be exemplary."

"Which is precisely why we're here, Mister Harlem. Major Yarain has put in a request to join the Vespers, and it's been accepted. She'll begin training immediately."

It took Jason a moment to decide if he was relieved or not. Hardly the bombshell he was expecting, but a bombshell nonetheless. One that had Jason's chest fluttering between tighter than a bow string and bloating like a burp that needed to come out already.

Meanwhile, Yarain's ears had gone just as straight. "*WHAT*? I only put in the request last night."

"Which Captain Harrison made me aware of. I was in the process of approving it when this battle came up. The *Alamo* will be returning to base to prepare for her next operation. You'll go straight from there to Laney PSC base to begin your training. I have to say, if you continue to perform like you have, you may be one of the rare ones to come out leading a team."

Those internal shields went back up. *How nice of her to talk to me about it.* Sundale sat like he'd turned to stone, leaving Jason alone to deal with the shock. It didn't stay shock for long.

"A transfer," Jason said. "You applied for a transfer. And you were going to tell me . . . when?"

Jason just about killed himself the second the words escaped. What a thing to say after forcing her to lead the mission to recover Sundale. Never mind all the times he'd tried to convince her she deserved a command of her own. While this wasn't such a command yet, he had a feeling it wouldn't be long before she got one.

Yarain's ears and tails fell. "I was going to tell you this morning. Then the mission happened, and I thought it best to wait."

"Okay, not wrong *there*. But why not tell us days ago?"

"I didn't decide until yesterday."

"And what? You didn't want advice?"

"No one could have helped me with this, and it was a maybe until yesterday. It wouldn't affect the unit until my choice was made. Until then, it would only serve as a distraction."

"And your time on the *Appalachian*?"

"Harrison wanted to run me through a few simulations with the team to be sure I knew what I was getting into."

"I take it you did well."

Garmon chuckled. "According to the report I saw, she did a lot better than that. In fact, I have letters from every member of COB team begging for her to take command if she passes. Lieutenant Rad was particularly insistent, while Harrison said, and I quote, 'she will make our unit whole in a way I didn't know it needed. Trust me, you want her in command of my unit like you want Lieutenant Colonel Harlem in command of Scorns.'"

Talk about a ringing endorsement. The more Yarain spoke, the more Jason's anger melted. Lack of expression or not, he could hear a ruffle of emotion hidden so deep, Yarain may not yet realize it was there herself. He couldn't think of anything to say in the face of it.

Plus, he would have struggled to find enough breath. His insides were a bubbling soup of prickling pain and steaming pride. Gold 1 would never be the same. It had been nice having his crew fully intact again. Now, mostly of his own doing, really, it would never be so again. Part of him regretted saying a word. The rest was too busy getting ready to beam that pride back at her. *A Vesper, huh? Not what I had in mind, but perhaps it's even better.*

Before he could think of a reply, Sundale started growling as he stood. It didn't entirely leave his voice when he spoke, though Jason was more worried that it seemed a shudder had just ended.

"This entire time . . . you were planning to leave us. And you never **ONCE** consulted us?"

Yarain's hackles rose, though her ears didn't, and Jason suddenly wished he had a different seat. "It was my decision to make."

"And **THEN** what? Were you going to drop this on us without warning?"

"I thought I'd have more time."

"You **DID** have more time!"

Marshal Garmon slapped her hand on the table. "Enough, Captain!"

Sundale snapped to attention. His growl was silent, but even Jason could see the flames of anger pushing on his lungs. Jason himself felt just as tight as he worried how much damage Sundale had just done to his own career.

Thankfully, though Garmon's stare remained hard, her tone was more apologetic. "I understand this is a shock to you, Sundale, but she doesn't answer to you. In rank *or* pack, if I understand things correctly. If the pile of recommendations is to be believed, this is the best thing for her. It's time she got to spread her wings . . . erm, so to speak."

Sundale's body shook through one breath, then his ears came up. "Then it is decided. With respect, ma'am, I see no reason for me to remain. I ask to be dismissed."

Garmon nodded, and Sundale charged out. Jason called after him, but Sundale didn't even slow down. Jason rubbed his hand across his face, trying to figure out what just happened. Or rather, what he needed to do about it. The whole situation was a mess. Sundale acting... well, hardly like a Holdren, didn't make it any better.

"First Reneca, now Sundale," Garmon said. "You sure it's not typical, Yarain?"

Well, there's item one on my list.

"Permission to speak freely, ma'am?" Jason said. Marshal Garmon nodded. "Think back. There had to be a time when a friend or comrade out of the blue said they were leaving. I don't care who you are, that can rattle you."

"Enough to forget discipline, Mister Harlem?"

"In a setting like this? Yes, ma'am. There's no combat to distract him." Jason shifted to Yarain so he was sure she understood as well. "Right now, he's hurt. This is a bit of a shock for both of us, and you too by the sound of it. In hindsight, you really should have told us about this sooner."

Yarain again cringed. "I didn't want the uncertainty to distract him or you."

Marshal Garmon huffed. "I'd say your fears were justified."

Jason had to swallow a growl of his own on that one. "If you mean within the regs, ma'am, I disagree. I know him. If we were under fire, he wouldn't let this stop him."

"How can you be sure? He's never acted like this before."

Never thought I'd see you grasping at straws. "Just proves he's sentient, ma'am. Holdrens, in many ways, are even more creatures of habit than we are. A sudden separation like this is quite a blow for him."

"Please," Yarain said with a hand up. "You're only making it worse. Sundale's emotional state, whatever it is, is my fault."

Jason nodded with a sigh. *Almost glad I'm not a parent for once.* He waited for Marshal Garmon this time. When she didn't speak, he went with what he had.

"As they say, hindsight is twenty-twenty. What's done is done. We can't change the past. We can only adapt to the now."

Yarain looked up at Garmon. "Or I can change my mind."

Over my dead body. "Oh no you don't. I'm not letting you pass this up. Not after everything you did to earn those recommendations. Uh-uh. You're going to Vesper training, you're going to ace it, and you're going to come out in command of COB team. I won't accept anything less."

"Jason . . ."

"Major, no. You worked too hard to get this. This is your time. You can't protect Sundale forever. He's been an adult for a long time now. He has to learn to hunt on his own."

"He's my cub, Jason."

"And as your cub, you have to let him lick his own wounds. Otherwise, he'll never learn to survive on his own. His hunts will fail, and he will starve."

Yarain looked and breathed like a cornered animal. Marshal Garmon meanwhile flopped into her chair with her hand going to her forehead.

"Mister Harlem, I don't know how you do it, but you always find a way to give me a headache while making sense at the same time."

Jason tried not to smile too much. "Natural born talent, ma'am. Just ask General Carson."

She shook her head, then folded her hands on the desk. "Are you certain Captain Sundale is still fit to serve?"

"Yes, ma'am. It was too much too fast with nothing to distract him. Once he licks his wounds, he'll be fine. I'll stake my career on it."

"Your career is not my concern, Colonel. Your life, and his, are."

"No need for that, ma'am. He's still the best I've ever seen. I can assure you that—"

"Marshal Garmon to CIC immediately. Repeat, Marshal Garmon to CIC immediately."

You gotta be kidding me. Jason fell into his chair, barely controlling a laugh. He was doing so well, too. A long conversation without interruption, only to have today's curse hit him again. *Either God has it in for me, or He's messing with me again.*

"Colonel?" General Garmon said. "Are you all right?"

Jason had to swallow the worst of the laugh before he could reply. "Yes, ma'am. Just hasn't been my day for finishing sentences."

"I see. I assume you have nothing further to add then?"

"No, ma'am, nothing further."

"Then I'll see what they want of me," She walked out but stopped at the doors. "Get your fox patched up, Colonel. You already have one officer to replace. I'd rather you not have to replace them both. In the meantime, we'll reach port in a little over thirty-six hours. You have until then to choose a new POSN before we choose for you."

"Understood, ma'am. Thank you."

The doors closed behind her. Jason returned to a much more controlled Yarain. Her breathing still spoke of emotional pain, but he felt certain the perk in her ears was one of thanks.

"Seems that god of yours listens to me too. If Sundale had lost his position—"

"Yarain," Jason said. "Enough. Sundale is my problem now. Yours is becoming the best Vesper Interstar has ever seen."

Yarain's hackles rose, though not for long. "I can't not care, Jason."

"I'm not asking you to. I'm asking you to let him go. He's an adult now. He has to hunt his own prey. Don't worry. I've got his back."

"Tails and all?"

"Well . . . two of 'em anyway."

Jason took her panted laugh as his victory.

CHAPTER 13

YOUR SHOE, MY SIZE THREE PAW

Sundale still couldn't figure out how he ended up in the mess hall. He remembered the trip, just not the reason. His mother had just told him she was leaving the fighter. Leaving his pack, for all he felt. It was all too much in the moment. Too much pain, too much shock, too tired from combat—it was too much to stay. So, he left the command room, CIC, even left the deck. Anything to get away.

Next thing he knew, Sundale had something on his plate that might be raw steak or some kind of meatloaf. With humans, you never could be sure. *At least they left off the barbecue sauce.* The scent was bad enough. Having to taste it would have been torture.

Sundale had faced enough of that already. There were other soldiers not two seats away, yet the room might as well have been empty to him. The echo of voices and silverware ringing in his ears did nothing to penetrate his own little world. Sundale didn't mind feeling alone for once. It let him face the knife he still had in his chest.

That is until a familiar voice broke in. "Usually, one eats their food instead of staring at it."

Sundale only kept his hackles down because it was Reneca and not some random soldier tempting fate. She sat beside him with a leg of something he didn't recognize on her plate and small vegetables soaked in too much butter. *That won't go down well.* Two weeks in the wild was enough to teach Sundale the futility of trying to drive her away. So, he tried utterly ignoring her instead.

He should have known better.

"So, what is it?"

"Steak," Sundale said.

"I meant what's on your mind."

"I'm losing Yarain."

Reneca just about dropped her fork with attached carrot while her ears turned his way. "***WHAT***? Did something happen after I left?"

You could say that. "She's training to become a Vesper. Without a word to either of us, she's transferring elsewhere. I thought she cared about me."

"What makes you think she doesn't?" Reneca bit into her carrot, only to hack it up a second later. *Saw that coming.* He saw a chance to avoid the conversation.

"Never get carrots from Chef Miles," Sundale said.

Reneca ruffed at her plate as if said carrots might bite her. "Guess that's what I get for risking human cooking."

If that's your first venture after all this time, you have a lot of learning ahead of you.

Sundale kept his thoughts silent while biting into his own meal. *Thank goodness. It's actually steak.* A small step upward in his long day of stresses.

"You didn't answer my question," Reneca said.

The hunk of meat he had to swallow took his growl with it. *She won't let it go. Probably wouldn't let me go if I tried either. So much for a peaceful meal.*

"She's been thinking about it since Holdre 4," Sundale said. "Yet she never said a word about it. She obviously didn't care enough to talk to me about it."

Reneca looked up from her careful inspection of her meat. "I doubt that. She had to have a reason."

"Not a good one," She stared him down. She cracked into her leg of meat without looking away. Sundale became very interested in his own food in the hope it might work, even as he knew it wouldn't. *Stubborn female.* Her stare bore through Sundale's fur until he surrendered. "She didn't want me thinking about a maybe. Like that's worse than a bombshell all at once."

Reneca's ears turned in thought, then flicked. "Could have been. Perhaps you should let it finish exploding before you decide much of anything."

Now Sundale's hackles rose. The only thing still was his tails, and that was not a good thing. "Then what? Just go back to Gold 1 like nothing happened? We've been serving together on Gold 1 for almost five years now. I deserve more than to be treated like some lieutenant fresh from the academy."

Reneca didn't even pull an ear back. "And she deserves more than hate born of pain. I think I know her well enough to know she did what she did because she *did* care. Is there really a reason to think she wasn't trying to protect you?"

Sundale tried to find one. He went through a dozen thoughts and excuses. It was easier than facing the pain of the shock. But as each one got rejected, his hackles fell in favor of a growing tightness in his chest that seemed to steal feeling from his limbs.

"No," he finally growled. "She still should have told me."

Reneca's ears gave that thoughtful turn again. "Possibly. Then again, not knowing if she would or wouldn't be leaving could have been harder on you. You can't know how you'd feel."

"I know how I feel now," Sundale rubbed his scar, cringing at a pulsing sensation within it. "I don't like it."

Reneca brushed his hand away, then licked his cheek. It caught him more than a little off guard since, aside from some quick rubs, they'd shown very little blood pack affection since leaving Holdre 4. Greetings, yes, but nothing intimate. More than that, the odd curiosity rushed to the surface. Not that he'd gotten any closer to understanding what it meant.

"Pain never feels good," Reneca said. "Yarain may or may not have done you wrong, but you can't hate her for it."

Those feelings didn't last long. A short growl was all Sundale could manage at first. His tails were still twitching as if reacting to his scattered thoughts.

"I don't know what else to do. We were just getting back into the way things were. Now . . . I feel like I'm losing her. This time with no hope of getting her back. I'm sorry, but Holdren or not, I can't just brush that off."

"Of **COURSE** not. But we *are* Holdrens. We lick our wounds and learn from them. They don't define us."

Sundale's hand went to his scar again. He had to fight to keep a rush of swirling voices and sensations from triggering another shudder. As it was, his breathing grew deeper.

"Don't be so sure," he said.

This time, Reneca just growled at him. "Sundale, let it go. Let *him* go. Fear not the future, for it does not exist. Fear not that past, for it has no hold. There is only the now."

Sundale tried to growl. At her or at the shudder, he wasn't sure. Instead, he wound up cringing with his ears pulling back. "The now hurts too."

Her hand went to his muzzle. Gently, not a full grab, but enough to turn his head so he had to look at her. His ears were up, but only partly because she had his attention. The rest was closer to surprise, which somehow pushed everything aside.

"It doesn't have to," she said. Another flick of her ear had Sundale nervous again. "And I think I know a way I can help. There's still a matter Kapon's senate wants me to discuss with Marshal Garmon and a member of Gold 1. You might be the best choice."

Sundale shook his muzzle free, then ruffed amusement. "Or I could get court-martialed. I'm not in the best of emotional states right now."

Reneca perked her ears, almost playful. "You're not growling or ducking for the nearest den. You'll be fine. Come. I really think it'll help."

It didn't take long for a sigh to become an ear turn in the affirmative. They tossed their half-eaten meals in the disposal before she led him to Marshal Garmon's office just down the hall from CIC.

When Sundale heard her idea first hand, he knew that had she told him first, he would have gone looking for that den at record speed. Or driven her away as insane. Instead, he found himself in a position to gain something more valuable than he knew.

A chance to understand why he was so curious about her.

Jason sat in his quarters and flipped the clip-com in his hands, trying to decide if this was the one. The pile of candidates was small, given they could only pull from the carrier group and dry-dock. Small did not mean weak, however. Any one of them would serve well in Gold 1. One already had in Yarain's absence.

Sitting beside him on the couch while watching with a soft smile was Carter Gomez. His old friend and, as pilot of Gold 2, his second in group command. His tan skin was smooth and hardy, like he lived in the outdoors, and he was slightly taller than Jason. He was fairly well built, too, though that didn't show as well through the standard uniform. Jason had called him in as a sounding board who also knew the group well. It helped that he wasn't quite as close with Yarain, which limited the blow for him.

"You have experience together," Carter said. "That means a lot."

Jason only nodded. "But some of these others have incredible marks on their record. This isn't simply replacing a fallen soldier. This is a command fighter. They have big shoes to fill."

"Well, not really. Yarain doesn't wear shoes."

Jason chuckled but also rose. He wandered over to the window and sighed.

It was hitting again. Yarain was gone. She had hitched an early ride on a frigate bound for Laney PSC base. What very few items that could be called hers had gone with her. That was only a day ago, yet Jason's heart turned to a hunk of metal like she'd been gone for years.

The stars just didn't look the same without her on the window sill. The quarters felt a touch empty without her there, like somehow a part of him had gone with her. It didn't help that Sundale was still insisting on his own quarters.

Worse yet was he didn't have all that much time. The *Alamo* was on her way to a small base to repair ships as needed, resupply, try to convince Goodheart to leave the ship . . . replace the fallen. But the entire area was basically under EMCON Bravo. All communications were heavily restricted. Even Goodheart couldn't get a message out. *Guess he's getting a bigger taste of the military than he bargained for.* Though little had been said officially, it seemed to validate the scuttlebutt that said the carrier group was slated for a highly classified and risky operation.

Even without Garmon's deadline, Jason needed to fill his third seat soon so the group could get used to the new dynamic before their next operation. As good as Yarain became, her first days were far from smooth. Jason wished he could have more time to make his choice, though he knew he wouldn't have gotten it even in times of peace. Assuming he had any at all, which rarely happened.

Carter had since leaned forward so his head could rest on his folded hands. "Moping isn't going to do you or the group any good, Jason."

Where's my switch when I need it? "No, but I can't seem to stop. You'd think she was dead for all I felt."

"Why not? You two have been through a lot together. Two crazy foxes fighting with an equally crazy human. That's a lot of history that won't be walking through the door anymore."

"You're not trying to moonlight as a councilor now, are you?"

Carter drew himself up while pretending to hold the folds of a button-up shirt in front of him. He tried to copy a German accent, but it came out bad, with a touch of Irish or Scottish sneaking in. "But of course. Doctor Gomez, shrink M.D. Please, Mister Harlem, lay yourself on ze couch, rest your feet, and we shall talk about your childhood." When Jason only laughed with a shake of his head, the persona melted away. "I'm gonna miss her too, Toro. It won't be the same hearing orders from someone else."

A lot won't be the same. "I just hope Sundale can get over it. He didn't take it very well."

"Give him time. He's been through a lot the last few months. Captured, tortured, recovered, found his home world, grew wings, gained a pack, got back in the groove, and now his mother is leaving the group. Holdren or not, that's a lot to process."

That it is.

And perhaps that was why the Gold Group had been given the extra downtime. The lead fighter needed a replacement, and the rest of her crew was still in a state of shock. They'd need time to deal with all of that. For all her talk, Marshal Garmon seemed to understand that and was giving them as much time as she could to work past it.

In that time, Jason had actually seen very little of Sundale. He might have worried; except he suspected Sundale was spending much of his time with Reneca. *So he should.* They were of the same blood pack. With his combat pack in turmoil, the stability to be found there was the best thing for him. Plus, Jason continued to wonder if something more might not be brewing between them. At any rate, it gave Jason an excuse not to remind him of the change they had thrust into their laps.

That didn't make it easy. Jason stared at the clip-com for close to an hour. Thinking. Praying. Not quite making himself admit he had his woman. Finnley had filled the seat before during Sundale's rescue,

Holdre 4, and Phoenix Perch. Efforts that had recently earned her a promotion to captain. She'd requested a permanent position, with a fair amount of heat backed by Captain Gilnt—or so rumor said. Perhaps this was her time to get it. Carter merely let him think or joined him in prayer. He knew too well that sometimes Jason just needed to know he wasn't alone.

Jason finally fought through himself to make the call. He got as far as the couch before Reneca and Sundale walked in. Both in finesse form. Full uniform. Reneca with a pair of clip-coms in her hands. Not so much as a flick in any of their tails.

"Uh-oh," both humans said.

Reneca turned to Sundale as if concerned, but Sundale only perked his ears at her.

Not helping. "I take it this isn't a social visit," Jason said.

Reneca's ears perked again, though Jason wasn't sure what this one meant. "No, sir."

She handed Jason a clip-com, then folded her hands over the other one. Still. Silent. Patient. If Jason had tails, they'd have been waving.

He tried to ignore it while setting the personnel file down so he could scan the new clip-com. It was mostly blah-blah "in accordance with this after careful consideration of that" stuff. He had to read it a second time when he got to the actual info.

"An exchange?" Jason said slowly.

Reneca's ears ticked forward again. This time, Jason recognized it as a signal in the affirmative. The replacement for a human nodding.

"Exchange?" Carter said. "What kind of exchange?"

Jason read aloud for his second in command. "*Blah-blah*, officers from both fleets will be trained and will serve with the other, *blah-*

blah, will be treated and will act as if full members of the other fleets, *blah-blah* . . . oh boy . . . Year-end report to evaluate possibility of the Federation of Kapon joining the United Systems Republic."

Carter's eyes nearly doubled in size. Jason would have been right there with him if he hadn't been reading. Captain Torzon said the haaj'Kar move fast, but this? Barely a month, and they're talking sign-on? Jason silently read a little more to see what else they had in mind. Most of it was the usual officer exchange program that had been done before on Earth before humanity unified. Interstar had tried with the Coylins a few times, but it never got anywhere.

Jason soon found a personal note from Marshal Garmon. One area she wanted among the exchange: fighter crews. He looked up from the clip-com at the two Holdrens standing in front of him. He suddenly remembered his seventeen-year-old self asking a church camp director, "You ever wonder what a sign from God looks like?" He didn't remember the response, but he could almost see the director standing there, gesturing at the foxes.

"Now what?" Carter asked.

"Oh, nothing," Jason said. "Just a very subtle addendum here from Marshal Garmon saying that among the areas she wants included is fighter crews."

Carter first hummed, then leaned on the back of the couch. "I think I know where this is going."

To their credit, neither Holdren flinched.

"I want to serve on Gold 1," Reneca said.

Of course she does. Jason's body hit the couch. *He* ended up on the *Alamo's* keel. He motioned for both Holdrens to stand on the other side of the table. "Look, Captain, you did well during the battle of Holdre 4, but third seat on a Scorn, the lead ship no less, is completely different. Now that pile of candidates there have all proven themselves capable of handling the position, and from them, I have chosen the one to fill the position. She has high marks in turret control, not to mention practical experience with us. I'm sorry. I don't see how I could possibly allow you to take that position."

"Read this, sir."

Jason sighed as she handed him the second clip-com. This one contained Reneca's performance read-out from a series of tests in the sim-room. Her marks were good. Very good for someone who says she's never handled a fighter turret before. She'd also acquitted herself rather well in terms of performing POSN duties, even in the lead fighter position.

Carter had watched and waited as long as he could. "Well, Toro? What is it?"

Jason looked over the clip-com at Reneca while he considered the idea. He didn't like the way he had to be about it.

"Simulation reviews. Apparently, Reneca has been busy."

Carter folded his arms much in the way that Jason felt. "Really? How did she do?"

"Not bad. I'm impressed." Jason flopped the clip-coms on the table in front of him. "It's not enough."

Reneca's hackles rose ever so slightly. "My marks are better than most lieutenants. I showed you what I can do at Holdre 4. What more do you need?"

Wondered how long she could hide herself. Jason rose, calm and smooth. He wished like crazy he had his own hair he could raise. Despite her being taller than him, Reneca seemed to get the hint anyway. Her ears fell, as did her fur.

Jason nodded approval. "More of that would be a good start. If you plan to work with Interstar, you're going to need to bury your pride."

Her ears went further. She definitely got the message now.

Sundale put a hand on her shoulder that perked them back up. "I still haven't heard a no, Jason."

Great. Tag-teamed by my best friend. He had a point, though. And for the life of him, Jason couldn't find the will to say no.

That said, "yes" wasn't on his tongue either.

"Give me a counter then, Sun. Give *me* some reasons. You know Captain Finnley. She can do the job. Reneca did well in simulations, but she's also demonstrated some traits that concern me. Simulations aren't like the real thing, and you know it."

"She did outscore Interstar officers. And she did well on the *Alamo* when a turret station lost its gunner."

"True. But that was an emergency situation, it was brief, and it did not come with the additional responsibilities. This is a calculated decision. I can't ignore my concerns. Plus, how the hell do I explain this to the group, or Captain Finnley?"

"Politics," Carter said. "This wouldn't be the first time it reared its ugly head, even in wartime. They may not be happy, but it will still be your group, and you can tell them that you're just as unhappy about it as they are."

"And that animosity could threaten the group. If they don't accept her authority, it could cost lives."

"Come now, Colonel. You've trained them too well to let that happen."

Et tu, Brute? Jason started counting on his fingers. "All right, how about this? As Gold 1's POSN, it will be her job to: oversee the training and qualifications of the rest of the group, prepare briefings, gather intel and information on upcoming missions, plot courses in and out of combat, convey information to the group and the fleet while in combat, and relay orders to said group. She will be in a position of authority without the experience to own it."

Carter blew a sigh through his lips as he leaned back. "He's got a point. Third seat on the lead ship has a lot of responsibilities. If they aren't done well, the group could be at risk."

Sundale's ears perked in a way Jason felt certain replaced a devious smile. "Then the group better do their job."

Jason gave a very Holdren head tilt. "I sense something behind that comment. Do share, and don't skimp on the details."

"Marshal Garmon and Yarain herself suggested that the training could be done by the group. Several members are under review for higher postings, and by teaching Reneca how to do *her* job, they will, in turn, be teaching themselves and the group."

"And I take it while doing this, they'll be evaluated for these higher postings."

"Correct, sir."

"And you talked to Yarain without me, why?"

"Marshal Garmon called her in before she left. We . . . we didn't want to risk the thin ice we were standing on."

Jason cringed because he knew exactly what Sundale meant. Marshal Garmon hadn't seen the best side of Holdrens recently. Had they insisted they loop Jason in, it might have been the proverbial straw. In the same position, he'd have done the same thing. Being unable to be mad at them for it meant he could only feel the sting of her absence again.

He could feel himself losing this battle, mostly because the more they talked, the more it felt like the right call. However, he did have one last salvo to throw at them.

"Why my ship? Why Gold 1 instead of Gold 12 or 20? Don't tell me there isn't a reason. I know her better than that."

"You know Holdrens," Sundale said.

"So does Carter. So do a lot of the Gold Group."

"Not like you do. We're also of the same blood pack. She wants to see how that bond operates in *our* fleet."

Carter hummed again. "Never mind the fact that you two are doing the dance."

Both Holdrens tilted their heads at him. "***DANCE***?" Sundale yipped.

"Oh, come on, Sundale. Everyone has seen the moments of affection between you two. The only thing missing is a tone-deaf waiter and a plate of spaghetti."

"That is nothing more than the bonds of a blood pack, sir," Reneca said.

"Is it? Are you sure about that?"

"***YES***."

I think her nose is growing. Well, actually, Jason wasn't so sure she didn't fully believe that. It was Sundale who had an ear turned toward her, yet slightly back. There were a lot of gestures Jason missed, but he'd seen that one before. Something about the comment had gotten Sundale's attention enough to make him thoughtful, though that was all he could be sure of. Finding out exactly how or why would require pressing, and there was a Jupiter-sized stop sign every time his mind considered trying.

So instead, Jason sat on the arm of the couch, feeling like his fighter had landed on his back. He had a lot staring at him, literally in Reneca's case, though she managed to keep it from appearing threatening or challenging. Sundale clearly wanted this for more reasons than just politics, though that could be as simple as having a member of his blood pack on the ship. Jason couldn't be sure there. Reneca was determined, and even Carter had started looking at him, waiting for a decision or the next salvo.

Jason looked over Reneca's evaluation again. It didn't cover everything, but in a couple of areas, she actually scored higher than Captain Finnley did, though Reneca was also beaten in others by wide margins. It was this that had Jason looking for something more. Something he couldn't quite put his finger on.

"I don't know," he said. "There's a lot of concern here."

"Such as?" Reneca said. Nice and respectful for once.

"Beyond that animosity I mentioned? How are your ground combat skills?"

"Moderate at hand-to-hand with our weapons."

"Side arms, tails, and rifles?"

"Above average on all points."

"What about—"

"**JASON**," Sundale ruffed, "You can read Holdrens better than anyone. If our fleets are to merge, we'll need a bridge. The three of us can be that bridge. Reneca and I know each other much like you and I do. Combined, we'll know everything about each other long before anyone else."

"Assuming we survive to learn it," Carter said. "You've made some good points, but her lack of skill could get her, her fighter, or any number of the group killed. In my world, that matters a lot more than politics."

"Then I'll get **BETTER**," Reneca said. "Give me a chance, and I will show you what a well-trained Holdren can do."

Jason didn't miss a beat. "We already know. You're standing next to one."

Reneca paused with shifting ears while glancing at Sundale. Her ears then fell a little, though her tails didn't move. "I meant no disrespect, sir. I joined to defend my world. This is the best way to do that. Please let me, and I will more than prove my **OWN** worth."

Not exactly a rousing speech. While he didn't actually think she meant any slight toward Sundale and Yarain, it didn't silence his concerns about her. Then again, her plea seemed to be the whatever-it-was that he had been looking for. He could hear Reneca's commitment in her voice. Unlike so many, her confidence sounded like it was practiced, like she'd done this before. Jason still worried about respect issues, though he hadn't seen her disobey an order yet. In the end, he had enough reasons to take the risk despite the many that said not to.

Jason eventually blew out his stress, tossed aside the clip-coms, and prayed he wasn't being too emotional.

"Armory," he said, "deck fifteen, section 41, room 4-A. Get fitted for Interstar armor and uniform. Start thinking about where you want to carry your blade and sidearm. Once you do, hit the range and then the gym. I want you rated on marksmanship and hand-to-hand combat by the end of the day. Sundale can show you where to go and can probably facilitate your evaluations. Let me be clear; if you're going to serve on my fighter, you're going to use our uniform, our armor, and our protocols. You answer to our chain of command first, last, and everything in between. Meaning the buck starts with me, ends with me, then my superiors, then theirs, and so on. You *will* be leaving Kapon at the airlock. *Do* I make myself *clear*, Commander?"

"*PERFECTLY* clear, sir," Reneca said with a ruffed word. "Thank you."

"Dismissed."

They left, and Jason fell through the hull again. His body thankfully stopped at the couch, but his eyes still closed tight in stress. "Oh God, please tell me I didn't just make a horrible mistake."

"You did not make a horrible mistake."

Carter's voice was deep enough that for an eighth of a second, Jason's mind did a double take. It was long enough for his eyes to pop open in the direction of the sound. When Jason pouted at him, Carter laughed.

"Fear not, Toro. I don't think you did. It may not seem like it at first, but this feels right somehow. And not just because you'll be keeping two Holdrens behind you."

"Maybe," Jason said. "I guess we'll see. In the meantime, what in God's great galaxy am I going to tell the group? Lieuten . . . *Captain* Finnley, has been pretty vocal about wanting a permanent position, and frankly, with good reason. So has Captain Gilnt, for that matter. The two of them are starting to make some real noise. I need a good explanation to offer them *and* the group."

"I told you, politics. If you feel the need, pull the Marshal card."

Jason smiled with a shake of his head. *If only it were that easy.* "Right. I'm sure that'll smooth it right over. Especially after I heard them both talking about missing open posts because they hoped to get one with us. Of course — you could help me talk to the group about it."

Carter pretended to check his wrist-com. "Gosh, I'd love to, but I have a very important meeting with this red-headed chick. She's fast, she's tough, but she is quite the catch, I must say."

"Yes. Too bad I saw her in the hangar, necking your POSN."

"You didn't!"

"I did. Sorry, old friend. You helped talk me into this, now you get to help me break the news."

"But señor, I no speaka—"

"Vamanos, Señor Gomez!"

They didn't actually go anywhere for some time. They joked, they laughed, and then they talked seriously about how to handle everything. The 'Marshal card' really was the best one to play, not that Jason felt much better about it. He felt for Captain Finnley, too, who really did deserve a more permanent posting, and not just rank and file.

Truth be told, the entire decision scared him to death. Yet the more he thought about it, the more he agreed with Carter. Something about it felt right. Just like the time he helped a strange fox with sandy-gold fur all those years ago. First thing that fox did was shoot at him. Second thing he did was trust him. The rest, as they say, is history.

CHAPTER 14

...THE MORE THEY STAY THE SAME

Admiral Solez looked up from his clip-com, trying to unhear what he'd just heard. The poor aide stood on the other side of his desk, swallowing again and again to avoid collapsing on the spot. The stare he was getting didn't help, but Admiral Solez couldn't help it. His own mind was stuck between bewilderment, anger, and outright panic.

"What do you mean you lost him?" the Admiral said. "How do you lose the Grand Marshal?"

The aide swallowed again. "We... we can't reach him, sir. He's not responding, his security isn't responding, in fact, none of our assets are responding."

"I'm not surprised. After the last purge..." Admiral Solez felt another stinger hit his heart. Interstar had conducted a sweep for assets after Red

7 got caught trying to stop phase one. But after Simon's defection, they'd been able to do another, more effective purge of Polaris assets. What few remained had gotten gun-shy or made a run for it. Many of the latter got caught trying, putting those left behind at further risk. Only the Grand Marshal and his security team had managed to avoid suspicion. Even so, Admiral Solez had seen his deep, detailed network reduced to a scattered shell that was too scared to operate. His son's betrayal was the wound that kept on bleeding... and not just because of its damage to the war effort.

Admiral Solez had to swallow himself in order to fight down the lump that had been getting bigger each time he thought of Simon. "The marshal said something about laying the groundwork for his final plan and using all of his clout trying to find out more about a pending Interstar operation."

"Yes, sir," the aide said. "But ever since that transmission, we have heard nothing from him. You... you don't think..."

"We'd have heard. One way or another, there would be no missing him being killed or captured."

"So, what now?"

Solez sighed, then rose to his feet. He looked at the desk, the smooth floor, the wall of his small office that held only the Polaris flag and a shelf of pictures, and finally, out the full-length window at the city beyond the base. So many lives. The people and their descendants who were saved. Ever since the spectacular failure of Operation Second Visit, their future was growing ever more in jeopardy. Most of the plan was still in play, but parts were moving faster than expected; some were cracked like glass ready to shatter, and their conductor was out of touch.

"Go to Operations and tell them to stand by," Admiral Solez said. "I'll be there with new orders within an hour."

"Aye, sir!" The aide saluted and left.

Admiral Solez went into his own files to check the version of the plans he had. The Grand Marshal might be arrogant, but he'd left instructions should such a situation arise. Besides, Admiral Solez had been involved in planning almost everything. There wasn't much he didn't know about.

He had found the information he needed when another soldier came in. "Sir? Lieutenant Tua told me this had to get to you immediately."

The day keeps getting better. Lieutenant Tua had been one of five people he'd trusted with his own operation. One that could get him executed if anyone realized what he was doing. But ever since the attack on New Holland, Admiral Solez had felt a burning need to be sure of things before they got out of control, assuming they weren't already.

"Leave it there," he said. "I'll take care of it in a minute."

The soldier set the clip-com on the desk, saluted, and then left.

The Admiral finished internalizing what he needed to about the next operation before looking over the new clip-com. Most of it was routine orders the grand marshal had signed off on. Munitions, parts, general supplies, trivial things that only graced the marshal's desk because it involved one of their most secret staging bases, and the upcoming Operation Dove Hunt.

However, Admiral Solez stopped cold on one section. Among the items listed to be transferred were medical and scientific equipment, followed by an order to transfer captured enemy soldiers to the base. The key part that sent his stomach into a pretzel was that it said *additional* enemy soldiers, suggesting this wasn't the first group to be sent there.

The more he thought about it, the tighter his stomach got. Soon, his lungs were too busy trying to understand what was going on to do their job properly. When he found a set of orders attached, he tossed the clip-com onto his desk like it was too hot to hold, then held his hands in the air as if he could will his stomach to stay in place.

Surely he wouldn't. Surely this isn't happening. Torturing Captain Sundale at least had a specific goal in mind. The captain had information Polaris needed that could have shortened the war, maybe even ended it outright. Admiral Solez still heard the whines in his sleep sometimes, but it could have done so much to protect Polaris . . . and his son.

The orders on the screen were nothing of the sort. There was no goal in mind, no purpose, no possible tactical advantage that would have been worth it. Just like New Holland, it seemed to be nothing more than an act of revenge. Assuming it wasn't that other reason that his mind didn't want to even touch. The one that again asked what other secret "versions" the grand marshal had of the plan.

Admiral Solez stared at the clip-com like he could make it cease to exist. Of the many things suddenly swirling in his head, Simon's letter rang the loudest.

I'm sorry father, but I can no longer carry on like this. We say we are soldiers of order, peace, and truth; but I have begun to question this. I am no longer certain if Polaris is fighting for the *truth, or* our *truth. I can only do what I feel is right. If I am wrong, then I will face the consequences, but I believe this is the only way I can be sure I am fighting for* the *truth. The* real *truth. Soldiers of order and peace would not do the things I have seen. I hope you can forgive me for what I must do. And I hope, one day, you can understand why I felt the need to act.*

For the first time, Admiral Solez did, and as he looked out again at the city, a similar question began to ring in his own mind.

"What truth is the grand marshal fighting for?"

Reneca pulled at her uniform. The pieces of her deployable armor felt like they were pressing on her shoulder joints again. A stark contrast to the soft and light fabric of her Kapon uniform. *The things I do for my pack.* Colonel Harlem had insisted she wear an Interstar uniform, so she sat in her chair on Gold 1, which was actually well suited for a Holdren, trying to get it comfortable. Sundale said it would settle faster if she left it alone, but despite her best efforts to do so over the last three months, she couldn't help tugging at it. Not yet, anyway.

Thankfully, Kapon soldiers were well trained to maintain focus through almost anything. One time, they'd even poured hot syrup on her during a combat simulation. It took an hour to get it all out of her fur, but Reneca had never flinched. Not then, nor any other time, just as a well-trained Holdren should. The tug of the uniform in the moment was only allowed because there was a second of calm in the current simulation.

A second was all she got, however. Reneca's screen lit up as fictional enemy contacts appeared out of nowhere. No rhyme or reason given for their appearance. They were simply there now, and she had to deal with them.

"***NEW*** contacts!" she barked. "Polaris destroyer group, forty-fighter escort, no Vipers. Bearing 1-1-3 by 0-2."

"Time to engagement range?" Colonel Harlem called from his seat.

"Seven—correction . . . three minutes." Somehow, changing over to Earth time had been the hardest part of the transition, though Reneca was finally getting a grip on it.

"Group status?"

"Four fighters down. Assault weapons at thirty percent capacity." Reneca's right side screen flashed an alert with attached data. "*Arizona* inbound; ETA two minutes."

"All ships evade. Begin damage rotation; cover each other's butts from the remaining fighters. Reneca, send the data we have to the *Arizona*. Request orders. Make sure they know we're wounded."

"Yes, sir!"

One thing Kapon had never done was capture the energy to this extent in training. In reality, the group was sitting in the hangar of the *Alamo*. Simulated images were projected onto the cockpit windows while simulated data was shown on the screens. But for all Reneca felt, she really was staring down an enemy destroyer with escorts. The longer it went, the more energetic her movements got and the harder her heart pounded in her chest. Even Colonel Harlem's scent seemed to match the fake battle. The only things missing were the weapon impacts and the force of the maneuvers Colonel Harlem was executing.

Reneca began trying to collect and transmit the requested data, but the system was giving her problems. Her console kept telling her the transmission failed without any indication as to why. Then, when a Polaris fighter appeared on her target screen, she had to abandon the attempt to get her turret in line for a defensive volley. Interstar's targeting system did its job once she got her turret on target, but keeping it there proved difficult with Colonel Harlem's erratic evasive maneuvers. *How did Yarain do this job so well?*

Colonel Harlem managed to turn the fighter in line with the enemy, allowing the full force of Gold 1's weapons to obliterate the simulated target. Reneca returned to her repeated failure to upload the data. *Why won't this . . . oh you idiot!* She couldn't help growling when she realized she had repeated an error once again.

On Kapon ships, such a transmission only needed the destination. The rest was automatic, even during combat. However, Interstar ships had to be told long range or short, encrypted or not, and many data transmissions wouldn't even be sent without the right encryptions in place. She'd been told that in her training, yet she had now forgotten it for a third time. Something that just doesn't happen with Holdrens. The wild rarely lets you repeat a mistake even once, much less thrice. As a Holdren, she should have picked up on that far faster than anyone else, yet the exact opposite had proven true. A few taps corrected the error, but she had only just completed the transmission before the simulated *I.C.V. Arizona* and her escorts arrived.

As such, Reneca got a set of orders, only to have them be canceled before she could even say she'd gotten them. When the new orders came in, the Polaris fighters were already engaged with their counterparts. The only saving grace was that the embattled Gold Group was now getting assistance from the newly arrived squads attached to the *Arizona*. Even so, more damage was taken, and the Polaris fleet was already responding to the new arrivals.

"New orders," Reneca said, still half growling at herself. "Cover the *Arizona*, fire assault weapons any time we can. Target priorities incoming. Forwarding to second seat."

"Got it," Sundale said. "Weapons hot."

"You're on fire control, Sun," Colonel Harlem said. "I'll get you a line if I can, but it's on you to fire."

"Copy that. Second seat . . ."

Sundale trailed off as the entire simulation froze. Every single element had gone still as if time had stopped. Reneca couldn't help checking her screens and controls to see if something had gone wrong. Before she could ask, a familiar alert tone echoed in the hangar, followed by PAICCA speaking on the P.A. as all lighting changed to blue.

"General Quarters! General Quarters! All hands to battle stations. Set condition 1! Details incoming. This is not a drill. Repeat, this is not a drill."

The projections all vanished as the fighter hummed to life for real. The only pause was the half-second it took for all three of them to deploy their helmets. Reneca noted with a touch of awe how perfectly the protection built itself around her head without any guidance from her. *We should ask about getting this tech for our own forces.* Reneca's screens were reset to show the real current information, which consisted of very little as of yet beyond the status of the group.

"Magazine full," Sundale said. "Combat systems on standby. Gold 1 combat ready."

Colonel Harlem's voice came next. "Group status."

"Stand by..." Reneca said. She was waiting for two final fighters. "Group is combat-ready."

"Any idea what's going on? We go dark and on our own for days, now all of a sudden, it's 'condition 1.'"

"Noth... nothing yet, sir."

As the strain of real combat hit, Reneca couldn't keep the tension out of her voice. Three consecutive simulations, and three times she'd made the same mistake. There were also other areas that weren't as clean as they should be. *I'm a Holdren, for goodness' sake! We're better than this.* Yet she was proving to be anything but. A fact that had her beginning to regret her boast about showing Colonel Harlem what a trained Holdren could do.

"Bury that too, *Captain*," Colonel Harlem said, emphasizing the Interstar equivalent rank she had adopted. "Sims or not, you've impressed me since you've taken that seat. Don't you even think of doubting yourself now. Trust yourself, trust your group, trust your ship, and trust your instincts. You *will* be fine." He leaned around so he could look at her. "I wouldn't be going into a real battle with you if I thought otherwise."

So that's why he's their first father. He had to know about her mistake, or at least know she made one. Yet his stare, his words, and by extension his aura, left no room for doubt. He trusted her with his life and the lives of his group, even after her error. Reneca ticked her ears forward, feeling the tension fall away like a soft rain rolling off of her fur.

"*AYE,* sir!" she said with a ruff.

Colonel Harlem nodded at her, then returned his focus forward. "Poke CIC. Remind them it's really hard to engage when I don't know what it is I'm engaging."

Reneca was just about to do so when her information screen finally updated. Sensor data showed what appeared to be an asteroid field the carrier group was heading toward. Behind it, orders and information came.

"Details coming in now. Stand by," she said.

Reneca read over the reports, the sensor data, and their orders. She then remembered her Kapon training, which taught her to work past the Holdren tendency for what other races considered "limited details." Still felt like a waste of time and energy, but they expected it, so they got it.

"Sundale, assault weapons incoming," Reneca said.

"Confirmed," Sundale said just as clunking on the hull made a similar announcement. "Heavy cannons being attached now."

"So, what are we blowing up?" Colonel Harlem said.

"A listening outpost," Reneca said. "We were detected by an enemy scout. Comms jammed, but he made a run for it. Two corvettes, the *Orion* and the *Cherokee*, were able to follow under cloak. He made his way to what looks like a listening outpost in a nearby asteroid field."

"Defenses?"

"Two squads of fighters on patrol. Perhaps a group on board. No other ships detected. The base itself only has two main guns, both corvette size, one barrel each, and a dozen PDCs. Gold and Eagle groups will be tasked with destroying the primary outpost. Yusi group will engage enemy fighters and provide cover. If we need reinforcements, the *Orion* and the *Cherokee* will provide fire support."

"Cannons installed and online," Sundale said. "What about our capital ships?"

"In range to assist," Reneca said, "but Admiral Redding would prefer — group reports assault weapons ready. All ships standing by. He would prefer to keep them out of the field. He wants to limit how much trace we leave behind."

Colonel Harlem sighed. "I guess I can see that. Asteroid fields may not be as close as some movies like to suggest, but big ships could still leave a trail."

"And a destroyed outpost won't?" Sundale said.

"Not enough to tell them much. Even a cruiser carries assault cannons for their Scorns. They'll have no way of knowing if it was three carrier groups, a group of Scorns, or anything in between that did the deed. We have an ETA on engagement?"

"Five minutes to launch," Reneca said.

"All right. Gold 1 to all fighters: everybody sit tight. If you need a drink, or you need to go, do it now."

Reneca tilted her head in confusion, then remembered the phrase was human slang to suggest urinating or defecating. Feeling a minor need, she allowed her body to empty its bladder. Though the fighter had a back-up toilet just in case, the system in her uniform managed to absorb every drop and expel it through a connection in the seat. *Definitely need to get this tech for our forces.* Kapon had a similar system, but it wasn't as seamless, effective, or irritation-free. Interstar even had a system for cleaning up after defecating that wasn't nearly as uncomfortable. She'd been unsure when briefed on it, but after using it a few times, she now hoped she could find a way to never, ever go back.

Five minutes felt like five hours after that. The information was straightforward, and *Alamo*'s CIC had already done the work of providing target lanes. The group was so well trained, nothing more needed doing. Secretly, Reneca couldn't help being intimidated by it all. Thirty-five ships, one hundred and five soldiers, and it was like they were all tuned into each other. Even those few who hadn't been with the group for long required little attention. Despite Colonel Harlem's confidence in her, Reneca's tails still managed to tuck under the seat a little. It had become painfully clear over the last three months how good a soldier Yarain had been. Now it was time to see how well Reneca would fill that role for real.

At last, after confirmation that surrender had been offered and rejected, the alert came; "Prepare for launch." The landing area cleared of support personnel, and all fighters lifted off their pads. At almost the same time, the called-upon ships floated over into the runways and turned to face the hangar doors. Those doors soon opened, with red lights above them and along the walls, making sure no one left early. Reneca held the controls, keeping her eyes on her screens. Her ears were up, her chest filling with every breath, and her mind waited for the first challenge. *Let the hunt begin.*

Yellow lights flashed.

Yellow.

Yellow.

Green!

The hangar bay emptied in seconds as every ship followed the one in front of it out into the stars. The three groups formed up around each other, while the rest filtered through the carrier group just in case any Polaris fighters tried to be an idiot. The Vindinsa fighters from Yusi group flew ahead of the Scorns, already splitting into squads to engage the enemy fighters.

Reneca could now see the asteroid field farther ahead. Like most, many of the rocks weren't much bigger than a Scorn or two, though there were plenty of larger ones here and there as well. A binary star cast a sharp light over the field and the combatants while a ruby gas giant loomed in the far distance.

The enemy outpost was built into the biggest of the asteroids, with only a small amount of infrastructure, aside from the turret emplacements, sitting on the outside of the rock. A small portion opened to allow the rest of its fighters to come to its defense while the usual particle shielding covered her hull.

"All ships, listen up," Colonel Harlem said, "I don't care how easy this looks, assume it's not. Keep your wits, check your targets, and *do not* show off. I want the entire group to enter engagement range of the outpost at the same time, no matter what. Let the Kapon fighters cover you, but don't depend on it. Hold your lines, make good choices, stay alive. Let's get this done."

Reneca sent her sensor data and target orders to Sundale, who promptly tuned the assault cannons in preparation for their first bombardment. From her screen, Reneca was able to divide her group among the targets given to them. To her surprise, there didn't seem to be any resistance to her directives. The moment a line was given, the squads adjusted to follow them.

"Sun, you're on fire control," Colonel Harlem said. "I'll get you what lines I can. Do we have enough power for bomber mode two?"

"Yes," Sundale said.

"With or without cuts?"

"Minor cuts only. Only combat system we'll lose is the cloak."

"Barely counts at this point. Gold 1 to group, Mode Beta-2. Repeat, mode Beta-2. Watch your heat levels."

Reneca got acknowledgment pings from the entire group at almost the same time. Seconds later, she felt herself growing lighter as the fighter's gravity was reduced to conserve power. While the assault cannons had their own power cells, they still drew power from the fighter, so other non-essential systems had to be shut down to provide power for everything else. Most of the internal lights, gravity, waste, and even a portion of life-support were shut down or reduced. Among the cuts were half of Colonel Harlem's Gatling cannons, but all that power was being sent into the fighter's shields, engines, and assault cannons. Their job wasn't dogfighting today. Just attack.

The first flashes drew Reneca's ears up as the Kapon fighters engaged the Polaris fighters. Seconds later, a squad of five Polaris fighters that got past them came straight for Gold 1. Reneca turned her turret, put it on target, and joined her group in furious defense against the enemy squad leader. She didn't get more than a burst before the Gold Group scattered, yet stayed together all at the same time. Ships stayed in squads of five everywhere she looked — when she was able to look away from her target screen anyway — no ship ever being close to alone.

The Polaris fighters kept after Gold 1's squad, but that left them vulnerable. While Gold 1 evaded, two other Scorn squads came in. Then, all at once, Gold 1's squad flipped around and joined a charge straight into the enemy fighters. With their shields already thinned by the peppering they'd taken; the enemy squad was split apart in a hail of weapons fire within seconds of the turn.

The Scorns flipped back on target without a word between them. Reneca's screen noted some minor changes in shield generator heat among her squad, but not enough to worry about. She double-checked her assault lines and had to send a quick reminder to other members of the group to keep their engagement range the same. A reply was received, and the corresponding ships slowed to allow the squad to catch up.

As they got closer to their target, a blip appeared on Reneca's sensors and then vanished, all in less than a second. When nothing else showed except a change in the EM field around some of the asteroids, she ignored it in favor of the changing battle.

The Kapon fighters were making short work of the Polaris defenders. A few managed to get into the Scorns, but they were immediately swarmed by the very ships they had gone after or more Vindinsas. Colonel Harlem only needed some general evasive maneuvers to avoid anything beyond minor shield damage.

The two groups of Scorns were seconds from effective range when an alert hit Reneca's screen from Gold 5. Sensor data came with it. Sensor data she could have, and should have, gotten herself a moment ago had she alerted Sundale to run an active scan. The only thing that kept her from literally biting herself was the lack of time. She'd made another error, this one for real, and that wasn't the worst of it. Had it not been for Gold 5, she'd have let them walk right into a deadly crossfire.

"Enemy frigates!" she called. "One on each flank."

"Shit!" Colonel Harlem said. "All ships scatter. Get distance from the outpost. Reneca, call in the corvettes, one per frigate, focus fire on their aft section."

"Shouldn't we—"

"Don't ask, Captain, just *do*!"

The Scorns began to split off in what seemed like random directions. From her time training with them, Reneca was beginning to see they were actually well rehearsed patterns of evasion. Even as they split from one another, all ships were turning away from the outpost, staying well out of range of their guns.

Reneca barely had time to swallow her growl before opening the link. "Gold 1 to *Alamo*. Assistance required. Repeat, assistance required. Enemy frigates on our flanks. Gold 1 requests one corvette engage one frigate; focus fire on aft section. Do you copy?"

"Solid copy, Gold 1," a male voice from *Alamo*'s CIC replied. "Plan approved. *Orion* engaging star south frigate. *Cherokee* engaging north. Gold Group, follow the *Orion* in, Eagle group, you're with the *Cherokee*. Yusi group, fill the gaps, engage any remaining enemy fighters. Stand by for full barrage engagement."

Reneca's screen saw the *Orion* added to her status screen so she could help the group cover the corvette as needed or possible. "Corvettes inbound, sir. We're to assist the *Orion* with barrage engagement."

"Copy that," Colonel Harlem said. "Sun, keep a claw on that trigger. On my mark, make a hole."

"Aye, sir," Sundale said. "Second seat has fire."

The Gold Group turned from their scattering to begin swarming around the I.C.V. *Orion*, though they made sure to give the nimble ship enough room to maneuver. Vindinsa fighters joined the outer portions of the cluster, peeling off only to engage what few enemy fighters remained. Those same ships were ordered to hang back just as the Polaris frigate came out from behind an asteroid.

The enemy ship was long, smooth, and slender, with bumps along the sides like soft, rolling hills going down her flanks. Two lines of shallow tracks along her top and bottom were both filled with weapon hardpoints. Between the tracks and the small clusters on top of the 'hills,' her weapon count could rival a destroyer. Except experience had shown that only so many weapons could be active at a time. This, of course, allowed more power for stealth, countermeasures, and engine power. Even for a frigate, they were fast. Though still not as fast as a corvette or Scorns.

The Interstar assault cluster cut a wide angle turn around some of the asteroids, using them as cover as the frigate tried to hit them at long range. The fighters and the corvette turned and tumbled around, avoiding much of the frigate's fire. Even so, the *Orion*'s generator was starting to heat up despite the Gold Group absorbing some of the smaller rounds.

A different male voice came over Reneca's comms. "*Orion* to Gold Group, stand by to engage. Punch a hole; we'll do the rest. Target data incoming."

Reneca received and passed on the data that highlighted exactly what points on the enemy ship they were aiming for. The combined force picked their way toward the frigate, which was trying her best to keep her broadside aimed at the Interstar ships. A small cluster of drones was collected around the Polaris frigate, but Reneca already had PAICCA assigning targets to the Gold Group and the *Orion*.

As the enemy frigate began to increase their barrage, the order came from the Orion, "Engage, engage, all ships engage!"

"Engage enemy!" Reneca repeated. Even though it went out on active comms, habit from her Kapon training kicked in and triggered it anyway.

No one commented or reacted, however. The corvette and the group hit max acceleration almost instantly. In seconds, they were in optimal range and firing. Turrets from the *Orion* and more turrets plus Gatling cannons from the Gold Group stripped away the thin drone cover before they could fire a shot. The assault cluster held speed until they were quite literally staring down the aft of the enemy ship.

Then came Colonel Harlem's voice. "Weapons free!"

Sundale, "**WEAPONS** free, aye!"

Reneca, "All ships, **FIRE** at will! **FIRE** at will!"

Thirty-five fighters, each one carrying two heavy cannons, opened up with everything they had. The *Orion* fired as well. A cloud of weapons fire turned the enemy shields almost solid white as they tried to repel the barrage. They didn't last but a few seconds before they were stripped away, allowing the enemy armor to suffer the barrage next. The frigate tried to turn and run, but the Scorns and the *Orion* twisted with her, holding their position just aft of the ship.

The enemy aft section started eroding under the combined assault. Her engines didn't last long. Secondary explosions were like bubbles in a lava field as the ship was picked apart like an artist chiseling at a sculpture. She couldn't even turn anymore, and her guns were falling silent as well. Reneca kept her turret on target while watching her screens to be sure she didn't miss anything else. A few generators were getting warm, but otherwise, there were no threats left. The other Polaris frigate wasn't doing any better.

Soon after the enemy frigate started listing out of control, the outpost remembered it could fire, or the battle had drifted into range. Either way, her main guns tried to pick off a Scorn or two. All they did was remind Interstar they still had work to do.

To that end, Colonel Harlem had orders to give. "All fighters, finish the kill, then converge on the outpost. Reneca, ask the *Orion* if they want us to take point."

"Aye, sir. Reneca to *Orion*. Who do you want to take point against the outpost?"

"We'll lead the way, Gold 1," the *Orion* replied. "Stick close; punch a hole for us."

"Gold 1 copies."

The chipping of the Polaris frigate reached their power core. A few more shots found the same banks of crystals Interstar used for power. Several rounds landed in the right place, and the result was also the same. The crystals shattered, causing all of the stored energy to detonate. The blast lit up the cockpit of Gold 1 in blue light and erased half of the remaining frigate from existence. The rest was mostly burning wreckage that was itself breaking up in places.

"That got her," Colonel Harlem said. "What's our answer?"

"*Orion* will take point," Reneca said. "They want us to make a hole for them."

"Copy that. Pass it on. Let's get this done."

Reneca checked to make sure the entire group had received the orders. She then turned her turret forward as both assault clusters began converging on the outpost. The base's main guns and PDF turrets fired in defense, but even the corvettes were able to avoid most of the fire. The rest didn't do enough to matter. The *Orion* led the way, but the Gold Group was close by, waiting to get in range.

"All ships, burst fire on your cannons," Colonel Harlem said. "Second seats have fire. Weapons free, but save your missiles. We won't need them."

"Group acknowledges," Reneca said. "***BURST*** fire ready, missiles on reserve."

The two prongs of the attack moved in under a continued futile effort to repel them. Reneca couldn't understand why they wouldn't surrender, given the impossible odds they were facing. The task force had sent three groups of fighters and two corvettes and were effectively unchallenged. Every Polaris fighter was gone. Both frigates were new asteroids in the field. Why throw their lives away?

Whatever the reason, they didn't relent, so neither did Interstar. The Kapon fighters filtered into the ranks, ready to add their fire to the assault. A few seconds more saw them enter optimal range, and the response was delivered. The Scorns fired both barrels of their heavy cannons at the same time instead of alternating. The corvettes followed suit, and all ships continued the charge.

They held at maximum turret range, and Reneca joined her group mates – a phrase that still felt odd to use – in firing her turret on the enemy base. The outpost's shields flared so much it almost vanished between the two sides of the assault. That is, until the shields couldn't keep up anymore. Then, the barrage turned into a long-range drilling operation. Any surface technology was obliterated, silencing their defensive efforts. The rock was pulverized as the barrage bore down into the corridors beneath. The holes on both sides got deeper and deeper until, once again, a round hit the power core in the right way. Instead of simply breaking, the crystals once again shattered. Another, much brighter blast of brilliant blue light covered the area, causing visual screens and windows to go almost entirely black to prevent eye damage. A projected display over the sheath maintained visuals for flight, though the EM field created a small amount of static. When the blast cleared, there was nothing but dust left of the outpost.

Reneca checked her scopes one more time. She did not want to be caught off guard again. When it, and the sensor data from the *Alamo*, showed no signs of any remaining combatants, she allowed herself to ease into the fact that the battle was over.

The call of "scopes clear" was in her throat, but it got stuck when her ears heard Colonel Harlem breathing hard. Unlike simple exertion, this reminded Reneca more of the couple of times she'd been near a human who, a few seconds later, went looking for something to vomit into. When she looked forward, there was a hanging stillness to him that made her certain he wasn't about to do the same. However, that left her wondering what he *was* doing and if she needed to do anything about it.

"Colonel?" she said. "Are you well?"

His voice was quiet, distant, and heavy. Things Reneca did not associate with him. "I'm all right."

Calls of clear scopes flashed across Reneca's board, which triggered her training. "Scopes are clear, sir. Area secure."

Colonel Harlem gave a soft sigh, then seemed to regain almost all of his composure. "Copy that. Gold 1 to *Alamo*. With respect, we should pick up any Polaris survivors. I doubt they'll get help any time soon, and we don't want them talking."

Admiral Redding's voice came over the comms, firm and confident, yet still slightly reserved. "Agreed, Gold 1. We're already sending ships. Return to carrier. You've done your job today."

"Aye, sir. Gold Group is condition four."

Reneca repeated the order to the group, just in case, while the combined forces turned back toward the carrier. Only the corvettes stayed behind to provide security for the recovery efforts. As they made their way back to the *Alamo*, Reneca could see other fighters coming in to relieve them, as well as transport ships and utility drones to recover survivors.

Yet the comms remained oddly quiet. There were a few messages of congratulations and "nice flying" being passed around, but for the most part, Interstar seemed unexcited about the victory. The recalled Kapon ships did the traditional Haaj'kar victory maneuver; a half roll to one side, then the other, then back to their original orientation. Interstar, however, did nothing. Inside the cockpit of Gold 1, even Sundale continued his duties as if nothing had changed.

Though Colonel Harlem had returned to normal breathing, there was a heavy scent coming from him that Reneca hadn't found before that had her equally worried. With nothing else to distract her, she hit the only source she had for answers.

"*Sundale,*" she said, "*is Colonel Harlem well?*"

"*He is,*" Sundale said.

"*Are you sure? Neither his breathing nor his scent seems right.*"

"*You needn't worry. It happens to him sometimes when a battle ends as abruptly as this one did. It'll be gone by the time we land.*"

"*But what is it?*"

"*I don't know. He never talks about it. I only know it never seems to last.*"

That wasn't exactly reassuring, but Reneca didn't have much choice. If Colonel Harlem didn't talk about it, there was nothing she could do about it. Sundale wasn't worried, so at least for now, she could accept the idea that she didn't need to be either. *Though perhaps I should pay more attention to his scents from now on.*

Reneca stood to the side of the screen in the briefing room with her ears up once more. A vote of confidence from Colonel Harlem after they landed silenced most of her doubts. Though it took her until the debriefing was almost over, she soon learned that only seven members of the group even noticed the energy signature. Of those, three looked deeper, and only one made the extra effort to have it checked out. There was a lot of shifting and withdrawn looks as she brought it up, which left her feeling quite pleased to have hit the mark so perfectly. *This is what a Holdren should be doing.*

It got better when Colonel Harlem gave her a smile that she was beginning to recognize as approval mixed with a touch of deviousness. "Well," he said, "I see we have some training to reinforce. Or perhaps just a lesson in 'never relax, even on an easy one'? Captain Tanner, I suspect you'll be leading it since you were the only one awake today."

A head of blonde hair that walked right up to the regulation length limit and gave it a kiss nodded. "I think I can handle that, sir."

"I'm sure you can. The rest of you, we're on stand-down, at least until tomorrow. So, get some rest, check your fighters, and keep your ears up. This little joy ride is just getting started. Remember, we're still at EMCON Alpha, so I'm afraid your friendly games with the other crews will have to wait."

One soldier in the back spoke up. "Sir, we just blew away a Polaris listening post. Aren't we past EMCON?"

"Hardly, Lieutenant. As you'll learn with time, such strikes, when done well, only tell the enemy that *something* happened. Not exactly what, how, by whom, or where they went. They'll be on alert, but the *Alamo* isn't the only carrier to suddenly vanish from the field, and they'll all be making noise in their own ways. Not counting the ones rotating in and out like we are with the *Rhine* and *Ardennes*. And before you ask, no, I don't know the mission any more than you do. That's never a good thing. So, keep your fighters clean, yourselves sharp, and if you believe in something, might be a good idea to participate. I have a feeling when we know the mission, it ain't gonna be an easy one. Anyone got anything else to add?" No one spoke. "Very well. You've got a few hours to yourselves. I suggest you use them. I understand the flag ready room is hosting a movie marathon tonight."

"Dark Galaxies?" One soldier asked.

"We're not that lucky."

"Troy?"

"Ronnie Yultz."

The room groaned in unison. Apparently, whoever or whatever "Ronnie Yultz" was, it was not a favorite of the group. Reneca had only recently begun to try a few of these human "films" and other such media. So far, she had yet to understand their appeal.

"If you go," Colonel Harlem said, "remember, you gotta clean up your own mess. Good work, Gold Group. Dismissed."

The mutterings continued as the group broke up, and many began to filter out of the room. Some seemed to be settling in to use the ready room for its secondary purpose: a lounge and relaxation area for the group. Tables rose out of the floor to allow members to gather around for games or simply to provide a more comfortable place to spend time with one another.

Reneca couldn't help watching the transformation in confused awe. Kapon ships only used a briefing room for briefings, a lounge as a lounge, and so on. The idea of rooms serving two, sometimes three, purposes seemed unnecessary. She had asked about it once and been told, "Space on a warship is at a premium. If you can save an inch, you save it because that means the ship is that much more efficient in terms of what it costs to build and move. When your fleet numbers in the tens of thousands not counting fighters, those savings add up real fast."

The counter she'd never offered was, "Doesn't seem to be a problem for Kapon." Though, at the same time, she could understand the idea of saving materials wherever possible in a ship's design. With Kapon's last major war being so long ago that no one alive even knew someone who had been in it, there wasn't much need to worry about materials. Humanity, however, had been at war with Marcalla for forty years, as well as another ten to twenty years before that spent at war with itself. That much time spent in conflict would drain a society's resources. *Even so, surely a couple more dedicated relaxation spaces wouldn't have cost them* that *much.*

Like so many times before, Reneca watched in confusion for a short time, then gathered herself to do something else with herself.

However, this time, a voice stopped her.

"Reneca? I just wanted to tell you that you did quite well out there today, ma'am."

Reneca looked up to see Captain Tanner, the third seat on Gold 22, as the source. The woman stood almost as tall as Reneca did, and every curve of her face and body was sleek and smooth, like she was born to run.

She had also been beyond helpful in helping Reneca get used to her new duties, which is why Reneca's ears couldn't stay up.

"I should have done better," she said.

Tanner waved the comment off. "You mean the frigates? Posh. As you yourself pointed out, a lot of other people missed 'em too. Hell, even the *Alamo* missed 'em. Don't be so hard on yourself."

"I almost let—"

"With all due respect, ma'am, stop right there. Almost is a far cry from did. There's a reason Scorns never fly alone. Yarain *has* missed things like that in her time, too. Like her, learn from this encounter, and be better next time."

Reneca managed to tick her ears forward, though they didn't exactly stay up. "I will. Thank you."

Captain Tanner just shrugged. "Don't mention it. In the meantime, I am dying for a steak. Care to join me? I'm sure we can get you one fresh off the bone."

Reneca couldn't help a single ruff of amusement. "No."

"Too bad. I would have liked the company. Oh well. Maybe after the next battle. Till then, take care of yourself."

Captain Tanner walked off with several of her crew mates without another word or salute.

For Reneca, it still felt strange to have things so lax. Off duty or not, Kapon soldiers would *never* walk away from a superior officer without salute or use their names without rank. Yet with Interstar, such instances were not just frequent, they were a constant. Though at the same time, it never seemed to become disrespectful. Or if it did, it was not tolerated.

Captain Tanner was a prime example. True, she had interrupted her, but Reneca could still see a look in her eye that spoke of attention. As if Tanner were making sure she wasn't overstepping or was watching for a reprimand. It was an oddly Holdren thing to see, and Reneca was only surprised more by how much she actually liked it. It spoke of a familiarity and trust that wasn't found in Kapon's military. Here, she was included, a member of a whole rather than just another cog in the larger military machine. This, too, was commonplace in Interstar. Everyone seemed to know where the boundaries were and were capable of operating within them without crossing them.

Much like a pack.

The thought came out of nowhere, yet it felt right. In the heat of the battle, the group's dedication, attention, and professionalism had been perfect. Outside, in the times of calm between, jokes, play, and simple times of being together abounded. "Sir" and "ma'am" held far less weight when off duty, to the point of times like just now where basic protocols were outright abandoned. It wasn't uncommon to see a colonel playing a game of cards with a private and for that private to spend the entire evening giving that colonel 'a hard time,' as the humans put it. Something one would never, ever, even when drunk, see in the Kapon military, or anywhere for that matter. You wouldn't talk like that to a political leader, much less your superior officer. The contrast between the two fleets had Reneca's mind swimming. Half of her couldn't get her head around it at all. The other half was quite rapidly growing fond of the idea. One small part of her was even wondering if, perhaps, Tanner might soon become a friend.

She was about to reconsider Captain Tanner's offer when Colonel Harlem broke into her thoughts.

"She's right, you know." Reneca perked her ears toward him. "As good as Yarain is, she wasn't perfect. But she learned well from her mistakes and made sure the group did, too. What happened out there? That's her doing. She missed that once, and she immediately drummed it into every third seat in the group. I'm rather embarrassed to see that only one of them actually made good on her efforts."

Reneca's ears again fell. "It would seem *she* was the trained Holdren I spoke of."

"As you will be," Sundale said.

Colonel Harlem nodded. "I agree. You didn't let it get in the way, and you made a lot of POSNs very uncomfortable in our debriefing. I doubt they'll be making that mistake again any time soon. That's a strong start. Take the next step, and you may yet make good on your boast."

I'm a Holdren. I should already be there. Yet deep down, Reneca knew she wasn't. She had a lot of learning yet to do. True, being a Holdren meant it would come quickly, but it still wasn't coming quickly enough.

As Gold 1 took their turn to leave, Reneca thought about Tanner's offer, only to brush the thought aside. Downtime was not to be wasted, and she didn't intend to do so. Instead, she excused herself from her crew, though she didn't leave without a quick rub with Sundale. She then headed for a conference room so she could work on training scenarios for the group, using lessons learned from her own mistakes to ensure they were not repeated by anyone.

PART 3:
NO MATTER THE COST

CHAPTER 15

A VIOLENT HOUSE CALL

B*ring your scars.*
Jason played the line from the message over and over in his head. Half of him didn't want to know what it meant, while the other wanted to know what to prepare for. It didn't help that the meeting would be full of group, squad, and starship commanders and that the *Troy* and *Rhine* carrier groups had recently arrived as well. Whatever was going on, this was almost certainly the purpose of the current operation. The only good part was that they were finally going to find out what it was. The rest had Jason tighter than a ball of rubber bands.

Being the only group on stand-down, Jason's crew had no reason not to be early, and General Manster had apparently asked to get their opinions out of the way before the main briefing. So, Gold 1 headed for the primary ready room on the star base soon after they got the message. Jason didn't like the lowering of Sundale's ears, however brief, when the bit about scars was read. Yet he also didn't feel comfortable pressing him on it. It didn't seem to be a major problem, at least not yet, and Jason wanted to get all the details he could about his mission before the room filled with leaders all talking amongst each other.

However, when the doors to the ready room opened, he was hit by something else.

"It's a suicide mission, and you know it!"

Jason stopped in the doorway while Reneca and Sundale looked over his shoulders to see what they could. Aside from being a little bigger with larger screens up front, the room was the same as any other ready room. The room itself was configured for mission briefings, with Marshal Garmon, Admiral Redding, General Manster, and Councilor Goodheart all standing near the main display. Jason soon realized it was Goodheart's voice that had met them at the door. The guy had somehow managed to stay on the base for the last three months as some kind of United Systems representative to see how the two nations were working together. It felt thin, yet it also seemed to work. Not that anyone understood why.

Regardless, none of the soldiers had kind looks for Goodheart. When Marshal Garmon folded her arms in one slow, smooth motion, Jason didn't need to see her to know her glare could vaporize planets.

"I don't agree, Councilor," she said.

"Then you're more short-sighted than I thought," Goodheart said. "You launch this attack; you are condemning these good soldiers to death for nothing!"

"Maybe we should wait outside," Sundale said.

Jason thought about it until Marshal Garmon looked their way. Her eyes thankfully grew in size, though they were still plenty narrow. *Yup, full-on planet-killer glare.* Jason wasn't about to risk her wrath shifting to them, so he swallowed his heart back into place and then led his crew up to the gathered group. Gold 1 snapped to attention with salutes, waiting for it to be returned before dropping either.

"Gold 1 reporting as ordered, ma'am," Jason said.

Goodheart raised an eyebrow like a bully ready with a tease. "Volunteering for death, Colonel?"

Jason barely even blinked. "I go where I'm ordered. Even when I don't like it."

"Well then let me make it easy on you. Marshal, *I* am ordering *you* to call this mission off."

"Did someone hear a fluttering coat?" Garmon said.

Sundale gave an amused ruff while Jason and Admiral Redding had a similar smile. It was a well-known dig soldiers often made about suits so full of hot air they made their coats flutter when they tried to give orders. Having it be directed at Goodheart made it all the sweeter. As for the councilor himself, he leaned around General Manster and Admiral Redding, who promptly backed out of the line of fire.

Marshal Garmon just glared back. "Don't forget I wear leaves, Councilor."

"Vice President," Goodheart countered.

"Not yet you're not, and even if you were, it changes nothing. We are in a state of war. These soldiers are *mine* to command. *Not* yours."

Goodheart shook his head. Looked more insulted than mad. "You really going to pull rank on me, Marshal?"

"Yes. Unless you'd like to test yourself, Mister Goodheart."

Jason didn't know what she meant, but it drew some color from Goodheart's face. Years back, he had heard something about them having it out by some definition, though he never got any details. Being four parts rumor, two parts imagination, and one part "I hope it went like this," a grunt like him didn't have a chance at learning the truth. To say nothing of the coin-flip rookie he had been at the time.

Goodheart tried to swallow his fear. His pride seemed to go instead. He stood and relaxed in a way that had Jason thinking of how a Holdren might tuck their tails.

"You can't send them there. You'd be throwing their lives away for nothing."

Wow. Almost sounds like he cares. It did give Jason a chance to get some answers, though.

"Excuse me, sirs, ma'am," he said. "What's this all about? First thing I hear is General Manster wanting to get our thoughts out of the way before the briefing. Next thing I hear is talk of a suicide mission."

"Didn't they tell you, Colonel?" Goodheart said.

"Nothing specific. Just come for a mission briefing, be sure to bring my scars. With all due respect, that last one has me worried."

"You and me both, Jason," Sundale said. Jason didn't like the waiver in his voice, though for once, his ears didn't move in the slightest. *That's progress . . . I think.*

Councilor Goodheart used a console to zoom the main display in on an area of space. The section was right on the edge of where Polaris and Marcalla met south of the Norma arm of the galaxy. Very close to reference star Butterfly M2-9, a holographic image of a space station big enough to be considered a colony came up. Surrounding it appeared to be a sphere of asteroids and other debris clumped much tighter together than normal, which also seemed to be several meters thick, if not more.

Goodheart stood tall as if trying to reclaim his pride.

"Remember the transports we tried to intercept a few months back? We followed them to this facility. We've learned a lot about it since then. Interstar's scouts have been"—he seethed for a moment, though Jason couldn't say why—"highly effective."

"Sounds like good news to me," Jason said. "So, where does the bit about scars come in?"

"Embellishments by my messenger," Admiral Redding said.

"Pretty accurate, I'd say," Goodheart said. "This debris field makes a standard assault plan impossible. The facility is armed like Fort Knox. There's no telling what kind of fighter or ship support they have. It's not worth it."

Jason tapped at a console to bring up a sensor readout of the base while Goodheart ranted. It wasn't any better. Shield generators, heavy weapons on the base, extensive point defenses, even more weapon emplacements buried in the rocks surrounding it, a planetary-grade satellite sensor network to feed the main guns . . . The place was armed for a brawl. To make matters worse, Polaris had found a rare debris field that really was dense and had somehow found, or created, a void in the middle of it big enough to house their fortress. Only strike craft and *maybe* corvettes could get through with any ease, and none of them had the firepower to take on a base like that. Add in the likelihood of other surprises hiding in the field, as well as the inner rim of it still being in range of the base's main guns, and this sphere of debris was almost like a second shield around the base.

Jason finished looking it over just as Marshal Garmon finished a reply he didn't catch.

"I have to agree with Goodheart, ma'am," Jason said. "We'd need four carrier groups to have a chance. Half of them wouldn't return. That's what your messenger meant by 'bring my scars.' They've taught me a lot. They say this isn't worth the thousands of lives it would cost to destroy it."

At Marshal Garmon's direction, Admiral Redding did his own tapping to enlarge the facility so they could get a better look at the place on its own. Many parts of it formed a sort of two-dimensional lattice of structures all connected to one another and made it seem somewhat fragile. All were rounded, though some were larger and more bulky than others. Still others were more like long tubes, curved or otherwise, with one big sphere in the middle. However, the connections were well fortified, with multiple weapon emplacements scattered all around the many sections. And despite the varying parts, the longer you looked, the more the parts somehow managed to form a near-perfect circle of a complex.

Admiral Redding continued to tap at the controls, highlighting sections of the base as he went.

"Twelve shipyards and repair bays. Enough barrack space to house a full division, maybe more. A portion we're certain is a machine shop big enough to build tanks. Research labs. Communications systems powerful enough to reach both Earth and the jantan home world of Marcelis in real time. That's just what we know of, Mister Harlem."

And this is supposed to make me feel better how exactly? "With respect, it's the unknown that worries me the most."

"What we do know, Colonel," General Manster said, "is we now have a chance to strike a crippling blow against their infrastructure. Think of it. We take this base; they may never recover."

"We fail, and *we* may never recover," Goodheart said. "The vixen voiced concern about our lines before? Just think how weak those lines would be if the assault team didn't come back."

Marshal Garmon just kept nodding. *Good things never come from that.*

"I understand, Councilor. It *looks* like a modern D-day. Those that go will be knee-deep in blood in less than an hour. Anyone who fights deserves a commendation. Anyone who lasts a few minutes deserves a medal. Anyone who survives deserves several."

Sundale half barked his first word, which seemed to silence the debate for a moment. "**WELL**, sounds like business as usual for the Gold Group, doesn't it?"

Now, it was Jason's turn to shake his head. After so many years, he couldn't think about when he stopped thinking about it. They did have an annoying tendency to attract insane missions. *That's what I get for escaping Jals' flagship so early in my career.* Such things get you noticed, and each time the missions got worse, his group rose to the occasion. Business as usual? Forget that. After defending Holdre 4, this felt like a cakewalk.

"He's got a point," Jason said. "We have made a reputation for doing the impossible. That said, ma'am, I don't like the odds of an assault on that place. Brutal would be putting it mildly."

Marshal Garmon nodded again, but it was Admiral Redding who spoke first. "Why do you think they called us, Colonel? We need the best to pull this off."

"You won't be alone either." General Manster said. "The Kapon senate gave permission for the assault when this operation began. Which includes—"

"Are you mad?" Councilor Goodheart said. "Thousands of lives, hundreds of ships, *a god damned marshal*, are you really going to throw them all away?"

General Manster looked about ready to plant him in the deck plating. Jason would have enjoyed that except for once, he agreed with the councilor.

Admiral Redding beat him to the reply, though.

"I have faith in my forces, Councilor. They're born for things like this. They'll get the job done. Then they'll come home to do it again somewhere else. As for Marshal Garmon, I tried to remind her that marshals aren't supposed to *be* on the front lines. She pulled rank on me, too."

"Then if you'll excuse me," Goodheart said, "I think I'll hitch a ride with the *Rhine*. I understand her group took too much damage to continue. I think I'll go home. I'll live longer." He headed for the door but stopped beside Reneca. "Don't worry, Captain. Earth will be in good hands with me around. Be seeing you."

Jason waited for the doors to close before he allowed a breath of fire. *Gosh, I hope not.* "There are times I hate that man. Yet I have to admit, ma'am, I agree with him. I can't see any normal assault working. We'd be shredded before we got close."

General Manster grinned evilly. *I think I preferred Garmon's nodding.* "Who said you had to, Colonel?"

Reneca and Sundale perked their ears, then all three members of Gold 1 added a slight head tilt, which drew an amused huff from Admiral Redding.

"What do you mean, sir?" Reneca asked.

Another grin from General Manster sent Jason's hand tensing for his sidearm. The general replaced the image of the base with one of a ship Jason had never seen before. It looked as thin as a Scorn fighter, though Jason acknowledged that it could just be the graphic. Otherwise, it resembled a manta ray, though the wings didn't go all the way down the body, and it had two thick rods trailing out the back.

General Manster kept working with the controls. "I give you the Ja'kel-class artillery ship. A new breed of starship like none ever seen."

Got that right. We'll see if that's a good thing or not.

Aloud, Jason said, "If I may ask, sir, what's so special about her?"

General Master tapped, and the graphic changed to zoom in on the ship. On the underside of the vessel were, from the middle out, two cannons a little taller than the ship, vertical stacks of two smaller weapons on each side, and another vertical stack of four even smaller weapons on either side again. Each grade of weapon hung the same amount below the craft's wings and fuselage.

"They fill a niche never before seen in interstellar combat," General Manster said. "The ability to hit targets with energy weapons at extreme range."

Sundale leaned in as if he could sniff at the image. "How long a range?"

General Manster worked his console again. "Let me check the conversions here. The main cannons have a maximum effective range of . . . just over two hundred thousand miles."

Jason's eyes bulged so much it felt like they'd tripled in size. Beside him, Sundale's ears were equally as straight.

"Two hundred thousand *miles*?" Jason said.

"Yes, Colonel." General Manster said. "Much like you, we'd need a spotter ship to cut through Polaris ECM for more precise targeting, but with your cloaking technology, that won't be a problem. Against a stationary target, we believe their target range can match the base's effective range."

"And if enemy ships close to engagement range?" Sundale asked.

"They'll have to contend with the escort fleet and the Ja'Kel's shorter range cannons, which themselves have an effective range of a hundred and fifty thousand and one hundred thousand miles respectively."

Jason's brain still hadn't finished accepting what he'd just heard. More so after he started doing some calculations of his own. *Even the London class battleship only has a range of fifty thousand miles; our best planetary defense cannons don't go much farther, and while that doesn't account for being able to actually target anything or get the most bang per shot . . . Where the hell have these things been sitting?!*

Finally, he said aloud, "With all due respect, sir, why have we not been using these things before now? Just think what that kind of range could do in a fire-fight."

"They're a specialized craft, Mister Harlem," General Manster said. "They're slow, lightly armed and armored, and immensely expensive. The Senate hasn't felt comfortable risking them in combat until now."

Gotta love the politicians.

Sundale asked, "Why not put the guns on your warmaster?"

"The power requirements are enormous, even for the smallest of the Ja'kel's cannons. The Warmaster's frame wouldn't have room or power for much else; the extra mass would only make them even slower, and it would be even more expensive to build. As it is, the weapons on *this* ship are 70% of the cost to build it, and the main cannons alone cost the same as one of our frigates."

Okay, I guess that is a bit of a price tag.

Redding added, "The general is also glossing over a key weakness; the rounds are all interceptable. Unlike most plasmoid rounds, these need a containment emitter to keep the energy collected until it hits. You can fire through the field, and it won't do much, but if you hit the emitter in the middle, the round dissipates very quickly. During some joint drills for this mission the first time out, our test base was decimated. But it wasn't long before we keyed our PDF grid and started doing a lot better. Polaris hasn't seen them yet. So, we plan to saturate their defenses early, hopefully do some damage before they adjust."

Despite that weakness, Jason nodded as his stomach started to loosen a bit. "Well, at least we have them now. We're still talking about a shield of rocks that won't be easy to blast through. Artillery or not, it could take quite some time to punch a hole big enough for our ships. With that much facility, they're bound to have substantial reinforcements in the area or at the base itself. And we still don't know if they have any surprises hidden in the field itself . . . or do we?"

Admiral Redding shook his head. "Not that we've found. When we get close, we'll activate the sensors on the trace pod Major Torzon attached to the transport. It won't last long once its stealth is broken, but it might tell us more."

So that's what we were doing back then. Jason could only guess the transport had been tagged by Major Torzon when their barrage had broken its shields. Made sense. Interstar had toyed with the idea before, but they'd never managed a device that stayed hidden for more than an hour at best. Apparently, Kapon had perfected the design, or perhaps just the tactics. Either way, they now had an asset sitting in enemy territory waiting to be activated.

Jason finally nodded while his insides felt like they were starting to unknot themselves. "It's a bold plan, and I'm warming to it by the minute. Still a lot of unknowns, however, which, with all due respect, sirs, I don't understand. How can we know so much about the facility yet know nothing of the supporting forces?"

"Oh, we have numbers," Admiral Redding said. "But they aren't anything we haven't seen before. Further, as far as we can tell, we've caught them napping. Our scouts haven't seen a single carrier or battleship, and the base itself only has a few dozen ships, most of them cruisers or lighter. The base itself is just over a day away at fleet maximum. Now is our best chance to strike before they get reinforcements."

"A lot can change in a day," Sundale said.

General Manster folded his arms, though a bit awkwardly, as if it were a motion he was not accustomed to. "Do you have a better idea, Captain?"

"No, sir."

"Then why bring it up?"

"As a reminder, sir," Jason said. "Forgetting things like that is how soldiers get dead."

General Manster huffed with a shake of his head. "How does your fleet operate with this kind of behavior?"

Marshal Garmon only smiled. "Colonel Harlem has earned it. You said it yourself—he speaks his mind, and he's rarely wrong. I can already see how we might want to adjust our briefing."

"Then I suppose it's good we got it out of the way then. Soldiers shouldn't question their orders."

Jason couldn't help glaring, though he didn't let himself do any more than that. "I'm not questioning, sir. But I am looking out for my group. I will not let their lives be thrown away for nothing." Jason breathed out his stress, then stood at attention. "With these new ships, the plan seems workable. However, with all due respect, sir, the old combat axiom still worries me."

While Admiral Redding and Marshal Garmon nodded their agreement, General Manster gave a very Holdren head tilt. "Combat axiom? Which combat axiom are you referring to?"

All three human officers replied at once, "No plan survives contact with the enemy."

Transmission detected.
Scale fifteen encryption . . . stand by . . .
Encryption broken.
Monitors active.
Attempting trace . . .

From: COMEXTCOL
To: COMMANDER OUTPOST 1138
CC: ASSET Multi-Step
Classification: TOP SECRET Eyes Only
Message:
Operation Juno Compromised.
Begin Operation Dove Hunt Immediately.
End Message.

Transmission successful . . .
ALERT! Pings match parameters 88972 . . .
Forwarding to Office of the Prefect . . .
ERROR: Executive override active. Report blocked . . .
Attempting Contingency protocols . . .
ERROR: Executive override active. Protocols disabled . . .
ERROR: Reporting failed.

For all he felt, Jason had turned into a pretzel in his pilot seat. Even his luck wasn't this good. As the combined fleet approached the Polaris facility, they could already see a stark difference in the situation.

First off, the fleet inside the debris field was only comprised of two dozen ships, which, except for two destroyers, were all Polaris cruisers and frigates. No heavy hitters at all, though they did see a group, and probably a few squads, worth of fighters.

The thing that had his gut in knots was the debris field. Or rather, the gaping hole in it. The opening was a near-perfect circle big enough for the largest of ships to enter with an escort or two alongside. Stranger still, ships and fighters were marshaling, so they clearly knew Interstar was there. Yet the opening, which hadn't been seen before, remained. An odd sort of magnetic field seemed to be keeping the rocks from closing in, suggesting this opening was man-made.

It was all too easy, which was never a good thing.

"We reading any sign of ships on the outskirts?" Jason asked.

"Negative," Reneca said.

"Chatter?"

"None."

"I don't like it. Why leave the door open like that?"

"Could be a malfunction," Sundale said. "Or a timed protocol they can't override."

Jason shook his head. "Polaris isn't that stupid. As for a malfunction, I'd expect to see a lot more panic in the enemy fleet and comms. They haven't even sent out a distress call."

"That we know of," Reneca offered.

"That's a wonderful thought. However, if they're going to be so accommodating, might as well say 'thank you.' Just keep your ears perked."

"Aye, sir," both Holdrens said.

As if she were listening in, a message from Marshal Garmon came in the next moment.

"Attention all units: the plan moves forward. The Ja'kels will attempt to disarm the base, then we'll move in for the kill. Stand by to engage any ships that may be hidden in the debris field. Watch for traps. This feels too easy."

The fleet as a whole began sliding over so they could line up with the opening in the debris field. Jason banked his fighter, maintaining position as part of the interception cloud around the forward Kapon frigates and cruisers. Like most Kapon ships, they had a very simple design, appearing to be a not-quite circular fuselage with a block that went down each side like a row of bricks. The only difference between a frigate and a cruiser was size and the fact that the cruiser had a thick and tall tower that looked like a conning tower at its stern, though nothing overly sensitive resided there.

One advantage to these designs was it obscured their capabilities. You couldn't tell a point defense ship from an assault ship until she started firing at you. The weapon batteries were all recessed, making it difficult to detect them in scans and see in person. They weren't as well armored as their counterparts, but their shields had proven to make up for most of that deficiency.

As the fleet settled into position, they now stared down the opening so the Polaris base laid dead center of it. Jason stared at his windshield, watching the blip on it that represented the enemy base. Under it, he watched the distance tick downward. Once they hit two hundred thousand miles, the fleet came to a stop as ordered. They then separated so the Ja'kel artillery ships had a clear line of fire.

The graphic had not done these things justice. They were massive, almost as big as a Warmaster – not counting length – and they had brought ten of them. The wings of the "manta ray" now had spines that curved over much like a Holdren's tail, one over each line of weapons. Jason knew from the plan that cloaked Phantom fighters were already ahead of them, providing more pinpoint targeting data. The tracking pod had recently gone silent, suggesting Polaris had found it, so that advantage had been lost. Fortunately, Polaris did not seem to be reacting to them. At least not yet.

"Maintain position," Reneca relayed. "Keep the line of fire clear. Artillery ships will begin attack in thirty seconds."

Jason's heart beat out every second. *Here goes nothing.* He watched his screens, waiting for the other shoe to drop on this operation.

Right at thirty seconds, ten assault ships all fired both main cannons. Large spheres of blue-green energy streaked toward the enemy base at several kilometers a second. Jason's sensor display showed the rounds traveling toward the base, straight on target. Fifteen seconds later, another volley followed the first. Point defenses from the base and in the rocks around the hole fired at the first volley. Some of the spheres had their containment fields broken, causing them to dissipate. However, just before a third volley was fired, some of the first hit their mark.

Though Jason couldn't see it, the shields of the base flared as they tried to repel the immense explosion chewing at them. The second volley hit, stripping more of the shield layer away in large swaths of the enemy base. Try as they might, the generators couldn't keep up. When the third volley hit, the facility barely had a sliver of shield left, and more rounds were already on the way.

However, a mere five seconds after the first volley hit, Reneca shattered the silence of the cockpit. "***ALERT*** ping! They're transmitting an emergency signal."

"Can we block it?" Jason asked.

"Countermeasures already active. We don't know . . . ambush inbound!"

Her words had only barely faded before a fleet of Polaris ships warped in behind the Interstar ships. Interstar corvettes at the rear began spinning like tops, spraying fire and doing their best to dodge the reply. Battleships and cruisers moved through the outer portions of the ranks to solidify the "wall," while the rest of the fleet moved forward and spread out to allow everyone to maneuver.

The Polaris ships had begun firing the moment they arrived. Just over one carrier group, spread out like an umbrella over the rear portion of the Interstar fleet, poured main batteries and torpedo volleys onto the Interstar fleet. Six corvettes were torn to shreds on the onset, though they did keep the barrage from doing the same to several battleships before they could evade and reply. Several other ships took shield damage, though none of the barrage was focused, meaning only a few took any meaningful damage before the thicker ships moved in to provide cover.

Being assigned to the forward portion of the formation, Jason held his group in place for the time being. The enemy hadn't launched any fighters yet, and even if they had, him leaving would leave the tip of the spear without fighter cover. Thus, the pilot of Gold 1 could only take deep breaths to keep his gut where it belonged while he watched the fleets trade fire behind him on his sensor screen. His fingers fiddled with his controls, eager to affect the battle, but his training told him that by holding his position, he was. Not that it felt like it.

Those were loyal soldiers fighting and dying back there. Some of them he knew. He'd gone into more dangerous situations. Hell, Holdre 4 had been worse. Yet he had heard of too many disasters because zones were not maintained. So, stomach of rocks or not, he held position, even as a very small number of the heavy ships beside him had already left on orders to counter the surprise attack.

The Interstar armada had advanced toward the facility to allow new battle lines to be drawn. As they did, the larger Interstar warships began to implement a well-practiced maneuver of forming triangles with their hulls, or some going belly-to-belly, using training and tractor beams to keep them together. These formations would then rotate at surprising speed, yet never lost control. Much like when fighters did the same, it spread the damage out between them, allowing each ship's shields a second to recover before taking more damage while still allowing them to return fire.

Kapon cruisers held back, filling the gaps between these formations, while Interstar destroyers found their slots and unleashed their arsenals on the enemy fleet. The other smaller ships and fighters created a second layer of defense around the two carriers and one warmaster, who were themselves arrayed around the lightly armored artillery ships. Ja'kels continued to fire when they could, though they were now focused on the heavy gun batteries that would pose a threat if the fleet moved too far forward. Only on occasion did they still send a volley at the main base.

Though Interstar had suffered losses, the fringes of the Polaris "umbrella" had suffered far worse. While the spread of the Polaris fleet did allow them to attack en masse, it also meant no one had any cover—a fact the Interstar destroyers were exploiting with ease. Frigates and corvettes were ignored in favor of Polaris destroyers and battleships. The latter was focused on by the combined fire of the fleet. With their losses mounting, Polaris was forced to consolidate into their own battle lines, though their ships of the wall had already taken a beating.

That did not mean Interstar hadn't taken losses of their own. The tandem tactic was not without risk. If a ship were damaged too much too fast, it could, and in a couple of cases did, result in a collision that made them easy targets while they recovered from the impact. Tractor beams often prevented this, but often was a far cry from always.

Yet, as Jason watched the battle unfold on his screen, even he could tell it was going their way. An assessment further confirmed by new orders that came into Reneca's station.

"Marshal Garmon is ordering the fleet forward," she said. "We're to provide cover and engage any enemy ships that advance on the artillery ships. We will hold at the edge of the Ja'kels' third range."

Translation; time to use all the guns those things carry to finish the job.

Jason opened a line to give his own orders. "All right, boys and girls, keep your eyes sharp and your sensors heavy. The surprises may not be done yet."

The entire Interstar formation eased forward, careful to maintain their battle lines. Polaris tried to intensify their assault, but they were unable to pierce the wall. Fighters came at last, warping in along both flanks. Scorns, Phantoms, and Vindinsas spread out to meet them, some with drones flying point to absorb the initial barrage. The clouds of strike craft met, and any who strayed close to the armada were met by corvettes, PDF frigates, and drones. The spear kept moving. Artillery continued to fly, obliterating any remaining heavy cannons on that side of the debris field, as well as a few PDF positions.

As the fleet got close to the opening, the Polaris ships around the base charged forward to engage. With the outer guns gone, the Ja'kels fired their cannons at the approaching fleet. Polaris was getting better by the second at intercepting the charges, but the closer they got, the more cannons the artillery ships could bring to bear. The only saving grace for Polaris was that the churning of the fleet meant the barrages were intermittent. At times, nearly a minute would pass before even a single shot could be fired safely. Then again, that often meant those volleys consisted of a full barrage of every cannon the Ja'kel-class ships had to offer. And the ships only fired together, or not at all.

Jason squeezed his controls and waited for the order he knew was coming. *Here we go.*

"Advance and engage," Reneca called. "Class to class, but stay within range of the corvettes."

"Copy that," Jason said. "You heard the order, Gold Group. Maintain formation until contact. Watch your lines. We still have rocks to deal with."

The Gold Group was joined by a group of Vindinsas and another two squads of Phantoms as they pulled away from the Interstar fleet. Five corvettes, ten frigates, and six cruisers came behind them, with the corvettes staying close on the fighter's tails. The glow of the Ja'kel barrages lit up the cockpit with every volley, and the thick spread was proving too much for the Polaris ships to fully stop. As Jason's engagement force slipped inside the debris field, a Polaris destroyer sacrificed itself to catch an entire volley meant for the star base. The "hedgehog" shattered like a glass ball on impact.

Enemy or not, Jason had to swallow his stomach back in place. Somehow, seeing a ship go down like that made the brutality of what they were trying to do seem more real. Then, as quickly as it came, the feeling was pushed aside, though it was still there in the back of his mind.

That is until Reneca's voice echoed again. "Telemetry down! I've lost contact with the fleet."

And the day was going so well. "What happened? Are we being jammed?"

"I don't . . . **COLONEL**, the debris field has closed!"

Jason had to check his own screen before his mind would accept it. Sure enough, the debris field had suddenly reconstructed itself, sealing their engagement force behind a wall of rocks protected by an energy field. Worse yet, the Ja'kels appeared to have been stuck *outside*, leaving them on much more even terms with the Polaris fleet.

"Gold 1 to all ships, halt advance. Repeat, halt advance. Consolidate here. Reneca, I don't care what their ranks are, you tell our ships to do the same. We need to regroup."

"Already on it, sir," Reneca said.

"Sundale, find us a rally point. Preferably out of range of the base's remaining guns."

"Aye, sir," Sundale said. "Be advised, enemy ships have assumed defensive posture around the base."

"They're not still moving to engage?" Jason said.

"Negative."

"Bad and good luck all in the span of two seconds. I'll take it while I got it. Have all ships form up and start scanning. I don't want any more surprises if we can help it. While you're at it, see what you can do about reestablishing contact with the fleet."

"Aye, sir," Reneca said.

Thankfully, the captains and group leaders of the ships trapped with them were smart enough to bury their pride and follow Jason's orders. They could sort out who actually had command later. The Interstar ships formed their own mini-formation, complete with the cruisers assuming the role of "wall," while the smaller ships took position just behind them to fend off any attackers. However, Polaris continued to regroup themselves, this time around their battered and bruised starbase. Their one destroyer was even limping her way inside one of the repair facilities. For how long was anyone's guess.

Polaris had more ships, though fewer cruisers and fighters, and some had taken minor damage. All of them had retreated to the increased safety of the base. While it didn't have any heavy cannons left, it still had a relatively robust point defense grid, as well as a few remaining lighter turrets. Jason knew the Polaris ships would abuse that, which meant any attack would need to be a combined effort.

The two forces stared at each other for a couple of minutes while Interstar's group reorganized themselves. While scanners worked, Jason got on the horn with the ship captains and group leaders to sort out the new chain of command. Before he could even start, every one of them expressed their support of him taking command, despite his reminder that he wouldn't be shying away from any part of the battle. While it added weight to his shoulders, it also made it easier to bear. Their trust made him more confident in his thoughts and instincts, while the authority meant he could delegate to his heart's content.

He had just finished naming which cruiser would call out targets when Reneca came back with an answer. "Sir, the debris field and its energy shield are blocking our comms. We'll never get through with it up."

Wonderful. "What was the state of the battle when we lost telemetry?"

"Polaris forces had retreated to maximum engagement range and were attempting to separate our forces. I don't think they were succeeding."

"Still means we could be in here for a couple of hours we may not have. If even one heavy hitter is in any of those shipyards, or if that destroyer comes back out in better shape than she went in, we're dead."

"Can't we blast our way out?" Sundale said.

"The shield is rated for planetary defense," Reneca said. "Our force is too small to punch through it and the condensed debris field in any reasonable time."

Jason added, "And that's assuming Polaris was kind enough to let us hack at it in peace. No, we're going to need to fight this battle ourselves before things turn against us. Have we gotten any additional sensor data on the place?"

"Yes," Sundale said. "Forwarding to you now."

Jason read through the collected sensor data on his screen. Most of it was an update as to the base's status, though the shipyards and repair bays were too well shielded to see into. However, one thing piqued Jason's interest about the central sphere of the base. When he expanded the info, his jaw just about hit the floor.

"Remember when I said Polaris wasn't that stupid?" he said. "I was wrong. They *are* that stupid."

"What do you mean, Jason?" Sundale said.

"See for yourself. Look at their command sphere there."

A moment of silence took over as Sundale did exactly that. "Is that a panic pod?"

"Yup."

"What's a panic pod?" Reneca asked.

"A very old, very bad idea. In the early days of human space ventures, a lot of younger and more panicky officers blew their sections of the base prematurely. To prevent this, many facilities built a central hub where a commanding officer could control and approve or ignore security, lockdown, and other protocols during an attack. It was well-shielded and theoretically built to keep people out, much like a panic room for VIPs. Unfortunately, too many officers waited too long, the pod got destroyed or breached, and then the base had no commander anymore. Or worse, an enemy was able to capture the panic pod intact, something that proved far easier than it should have been, and thus take control of the base with ease. It's the main reason Interstar went away from them. Better training and better tactics did far more to fix problems than those pods ever did."

Reneca's ears had gone erect halfway through. "The entire base is controlled from a single point?"

"Every bit," Jason said. "With no secondary options. This may change things."

"How so?"

"I'll let you know as soon as I'm sure it does."

Jason tapped at his console to double-check the ships he had with him. When he confirmed that Yarain's team was on one of them, his gut did a turn at the insane plan he was about to initiate. It would not come without cost, nor was it low risk, but ultimately, it gave them a chance to improve their objective. They had come to destroy. They now had a chance to capture. Properly defended, the base would prove incredibly valuable to their operations against Polaris. This was a golden opportunity he could not ignore.

Jason sighed, closed his eyes in a second of prayer, then pushed his doubts aside. *Time to call the mother of all audibles.* "Gold 1 to all ships, listen up. In case any of you haven't noticed, that base has a panic pod. If you don't know what that is, all you need to know is if we take it, we take the base without the troops on board having any way to stop us. So that's what we're going to do. I need targeting vectors and places where our troop transport can land for Vesper insertion. I'm also open to any other ideas. In the meantime, *Appalachian*, have Major Yarain contact me. We need to talk this thing through. Everyone else, stand by for further orders."

Jason put the channel on standby so that anyone who needed to contact him still could. In the meantime, he stared at the orientation of the enemy fleet in search of his own ideas for pulling this off.

"You think she'll go for it?" Sundale said.

"She's a Vesper now, Sun," Jason said. "They live for this sort of thing."

CHAPTER 16

A FUNNY THING HAPPENED ON THE WAY TO THE TARGET

This has got to be his craziest plan yet.

It didn't matter that Yarain agreed with Jason's assessment or even that she didn't have a better plan to offer. The whole idea was nuts, even by Jason's standards. Panic pod or not, a seven-man team being sent in alone to take control of an entire military facility? Even after insisting they take WLF team as well, the chances of success had to be in the single digits.

Then again, in her time on Gold 1, it seemed like single-digit chances were when they were at their best. As Yarain had begun to truly take command of her team, it felt like she was bringing that capability with her. More so because of their unique motto;

"Victory, where defeat cannot be tolerated."

Yarain paused at her equipment stall as she said the words aloud. She was surprised, not only by the need but by what they did to her. Though her voice was barely a whisper, the words seemed to echo in her ears. The almost real vibration felt like it traveled down to her chest to the newly added Vesper Falcon among the tabs on her chest, where it filled her lungs with the warmth of certainty. Her fleet needed COB team. Success had to be achieved. So, single-digit chances or not, they were going in, and if anything, she felt lighter than one of Sundale's feathers.

With her armor settled and her own special operations rifle on her shoulder, Yarain closed her stall and walked out into Cobra's equipment room. Little more than a glorified locker room, each member had their own stall full of whatever gear they might need on a mission, as well as a few personal effects. In Yarain's case, the model of a Scorn from Phoenix Perch hung on the wall. It served as a reminder, both of her previous post and of why she'd accepted this position in the first place.

As the team finished their own prep, Yarain took a breath to try and keep that warmth from burning her from the inside. Harrison had been right behind her in being ready, which meant he saw her take that breath.

"Everything all right, ma'am?" he asked.

"*YES*," Yarain ruffed.

"You don't have to hide it, Yarain. Your first time in command is different than a temporary assignment. God as my witness, I threw up on *my* first mission as team leader twice!"

"Don't remind me," Captain Fickle said.

Fickle thrust his thumb at a soiled uniform shirt on the wall of his stall. Yarain couldn't help a slight tilt of her head, wondering why he would be so annoyed, yet keep a memento of that mission in such a prominent place.

With no time to waste on such things, she had to push the question aside for the time being. Instead, Yarain went to Lieutenant Sarson as he seemed oddly focused on the door of his stall.

"Everything set, Lieutenant?" she asked.

His voice was a hundred light-years away. "Yes, ma'am."

Yarain could see the stiffness in his shoulders, and the harsh scent of fear didn't help. "Lieutenant . . . Markus. There's no need to worry. We'll keep you safe. All you have to do is your job, just like last time."

"With respect, ma'am, last time I tangled with a Polaris base computer, 'my job' almost got us killed."

Right, wrong word choice. However . . . "And now you know the antlers you will face. You won't make the same mistake again."

"You don't know that!"

Yarain put her hand on his shoulder and waited until his eyes met hers. "**YES**, I do."

It was a soft ruff that almost swallowed the word, but she had forced it to get the exact reaction she got. It started with a smile thinner than a strand of her fur. The more she stared into him, the more the smile grew. She knew he would do this. Not could, *would*. All he needed was time and cover, and she had every intention of giving him both.

As such, she settled her own emotions, so there was nothing in her mind but that certainty. Holdren first parents did it all the time to ease the fears of their members. Yarain had slipped into the habit without realizing it and found that humans could react to it just as much, if not in the same way.

Sarson's smile was heavy, but it was still broad. Finally, he nodded with a sigh. "Kick the tires."

"Light the fires," Yarain said.

Sarson slung his pack onto his back and followed Yarain and Harrison as they led the team to the hangar. The six members of WLF team were just ahead of them in similar gear.

Being at the head of COB team, Harrison was able to speak softly enough for only Yarain to hear.

"You handled that well."

Yarain couldn't keep her ears from shifting back a little. "I almost froze him."

"Even I do that from time to time. We think we're helping when we're actually adding to their fears. You'll learn to catch it as you get better."

"What makes you so sure?"

"Phoenix Perch, Holdre 4, our daily training, what you did to that training course—if we gave out call-signs, I'd call you Fujita. You're a force of nature that is deadly to our enemies but has a calm center we can follow without question. Everything I have never been."

It was a closed hangar door, but Yarain's hand in front of him was what stopped him and the team. "Don't you start that again, Captain."

If Harrison could, he would have folded his ears. "Why hide from—"

"**LOOK** harder. See what I see."

When Harrison didn't shrink any further, Yarain marched her team inside the hangar. She felt Harrison on her tails without him missing a step. *There he is.*

Team Cobra headed for their slender, wingless transport just as a pair of Phantom fighters lifted out of the hangar. The four-man flight crew stood at the main hatch of the transport. Two wore the same heavy armor as the Vespers since they would be tasked with keeping the transport safe during their mission. All four of them were leaning against the hull of the ship until they saw the team approach. They began to salute, but Yarain waved them down before they could finish.

"Are we set?" she asked.

"Yes, ma'am," the pilot said. "Best strap in tight. Going to be some rough flying out there."

As the flight crew and teams filed in, Yarain turned to Major Tomes Salasney, commander of WLF team. The man was almost as tall as Yarain, yet a mix of stocky and sleek as if he could bench press considerable weight, then outrun an Olympic sprinter.

"Thank you for changing your mind," Yarain said.

"Don't," the man said. "I'm only here because the more I think on it, the more I see a situation we can't leave to simmer. I'd take another plan in a heartbeat, but every one I've heard is somehow worse than this one. You just make sure you make the right choices out there."

"Me? I thought you'd be taking point."

"And put my neck in the guillotine? Ha ha. Oh no. You and Colonel Harlem came up with this hair-brained idea. You can take it to the barbershop. The Wolves will be here to support you if you actually manage to pull it off."

How kind of you.

When Salasney followed the last of his team inside, Yarain huffed and did the same. It had taken some convincing to get him on board with the plan, though at least so far, they had at least acted professionally. They hadn't even commented on Yarain being given command despite her lack of experience. Though it seemed that Major Salasney was more than happy to let her bear the weight of blame if it went wrong, which even Jason admitted was a very strong possibility. On the bright side, it would let her lead the mission *her* way.

It was the only thought that helped her as she followed the rest of the team inside. No one else had said a word as they took their seats. That is until all were strapped in and ready. Then, Captain Kelly Tai started talking, soft but firm like a church reverend.

"We ride now into the abyss. We know not what we will face, whom we shall encounter, or what fate shall befall us. We know only that we ride with courage, with strength, and with honor. May whatever god be near bless our mission and protect our person."

"So say we all," Captain Fickle said. Yarain couldn't help turning her head at him in confusion, to which he smiled. "When heading into particularly difficult missions, the good doctor likes to drop a poem, line, or just a thought. He won't say where he gets them, but he always seems to know which one to use. While I can't speak for the others, it never fails to put my mind at ease."

"Ditto," Hark and Sarson said.

Shadow added a soft nod to agree as well. A couple of WLF team rolled their eyes, though two others nodded as if they agreed, too.

Yarain didn't get the same feeling from the words, but she did feel the team relaxing around her. Even Harrison, seated next to her, wasn't carrying himself as tightly. Certainty had replaced the tension from before, which *did* help Yarain to release some of her own. When she felt the ship lift off, she too felt nothing but certainty. She wasn't stupid enough to think success was the only outcome, but more than ever, Yarain did not doubt her team would find it.

However, the first thing they found was a hard jerk that tested their restraints, as well as their holds on their weapons. Another pair of jerks followed before the flight smoothed out.

"I'm up!" someone said. Curses came from a couple of others.

Yarain shook her head to clear it, but before she could ask, the pilot came on over the comms.

"Sorry about that, everyone. Gold 1 told us to launch immediately, then we had to dodge around an enemy volley. I didn't have time to warn you or calibrate the dampeners."

"All is well, pilot," Yarain said, though not without a growl. "Though remind me to have a word with Jason later."

"Copy that. Will let you know if anything changes. Cockpit out."

Salasney didn't move, no doubt fearing another sudden turn. "Colonel Harlem never pulled a move like that before?"

Yarain ticked her ears back but otherwise remained tight in her seat as well. "Only in combat, but it wasn't as harsh, and we were ready for it."

"Welcome to the commando dropship," Harrison said. "You never know what stomach-wrenching maneuvers they'll pull. That's why we rarely eat before a mission. It's not worth the risk."

"I'm glad I heeded your wisdom."

Harrison only nodded, mostly because the ship made another quick turn that threw the team against their seats. Yarain couldn't stop a growl, though she did manage to keep her weapon from getting away from her.

What a difference. Yarain had gotten used to the Scorn's relatively smooth ride over the years. With the dropship being a bit bulkier than a fighter, its inertial dampeners weren't as quick or efficient. Sharp turns and other quick maneuvers were still felt by those aboard. More than that, though, she had no idea how the battle was going. Unlike Sundale's rescue, she didn't dare leave her seat, which meant she had no information on the battle she knew was raging outside.

That, more than anything, had her tails waving. Not so much out of fear; they would get blown away, or they wouldn't. More out of the unfamiliar. For so many years, she had been a major part of keeping track of that battle. To now have zero insight into a firefight, to have no clue who was living or dying, it felt more alien than the first time she'd ever seen a human.

"Don't think on it, ma'am," Lieutenant Shillin Rad said.

Her voice snapped Yarain's ears and eyes her way. When Yarain didn't say anything further, Shillin continued. "That is not your battle. Wait for the end, or wait for landing. You can do nothing else. Stay in your brush until you are ready to pounce."

She really is getting to know me. The last metaphor was perfect. Much like when lying in wait for a prime target, Yarain could do nothing now but wait. Thinking about what she had no control over would only waste energy. And Holdrens didn't like wasting energy.

"Thank you," Yarain said.

"My pleasure, ma'am," Shillin said.

A soft whistle came from Tai. "I'd like to know your secret, Major. You just got more interaction out of her than the rest of us have in the last month combined."

"That's enough, Captain," Yarain said.

The reaction was automatic and even protective. While Yarain suspected it might have been the usual "ribbing" humans liked to do, the comment was too close to being a direct criticism, which had no place on her team, especially mid-mission.

Captain Tai apologized, and while Lieutenant Rad waved it off, Yarain thought she saw the corners of her mouth tighten as if a smile was trying to form. It was so quick, Yarain couldn't be sure. After that, the transport fell silent for good. For one thing, everyone was too busy trying to keep hold of their breakfast to say anything else.

Though it felt like hours, it was only a few minutes before the gut-wrenching turns came to an end. All except for one Yarain almost wished she didn't know was coming. Unlike Sundale's rescue, this would be during an active battle, which meant the base had its shields up. No way to punch through those undetected, so on cue, a squad of fighters made their way close enough to fire a volley of torpedoes at the base. Add in a few shots from any nearby capital ships, and the base's shields had been chipped down to the hull.

The transport pilot had seconds to land before the shields could replenish, which meant the harshest jerk of them all as he took the ship right into the wake of the barrage. It felt as if Yarain lost fur as she was pressed against her seat hard enough to take some air out of her lungs, then thrown against her restraints just as hard. A soft thump announced hull contact, followed by a hum as the transport adjusted her own shields to allow the enemy shields to envelop them. When no alarms started blaring, and the ship didn't take any additional turns, Yarain could only guess they'd made it.

A guess soon confirmed by the co-pilot's voice. "We're latched. Even managed to land on an airlock. Stand by for gravity matching."

Glad that's over.

Being designed specifically for Vespers, the transport was made sleek, thin, and low profile. As such, she had landed flush with the enemy base instead of docking like normal to minimize her signature, to facilitate being absorbed by the enemy shield layer, and to reduce the chance of being caught by stray fire. The two members of the crew in armor joined the team in the passenger compartment; then, as the teams began to unbuckle and grab their weapons, the middle section of the transport began internally rotating so that the passenger bay now matched the orientation of the base.

The first thing Yarain did was press on her armor as much as she could to lessen the pain in her left shoulder. As good as things had been, that last jerk had not been kind.

"Does that get better?" she asked, hoping it wasn't a bruise.

"Not really," Harrison said. "In time, you learn how to carry yourself. I can try to give you some tips, but it's different for each person, and being a Holdren, it'll be even more different for you."

"Worth trying. Let's get set. Hark, you're up."

Lieutenant Maureen Hark slapped her hands together with a rub. "With pleasure, ma'am."

I still worry about her.

Hark opened the inner door, then began setting very carefully planned charges on the base's airlock door. While in one way less subtle than hacking, with careful timing from the fleet, it was actually more subtle in others. Rounds would be landing all around them at the same time, hopefully making Polaris think their insertion was combat damage. Granted, it counted on quite a few ifs, but *if* successful, the teams wouldn't have to worry about facing the entire base defense force. At least not right away.

Once set, the charges began scoring the airlock door just enough to provide a crack to exploit without setting off the hull breach alarm. While they did, Team Cobra and Team Wolf clicked their rifles to bullet mode. This provided them the best chance at stealth. Plasma weapons were like firing flares, and even the best lasers couldn't guarantee a one-shot kill through body armor. Even if they could, there were still several ways it could reveal their presence.

However, Interstar had continued to research bullets. They had reached a point where coil gun technology, combined with well-placed materials, created weapons that were so silent even Yarain's ears didn't hear the shot. Such weapons wouldn't work on the thick shields and high maneuverability of modern starships, but when it came to infantry, a good bullet could still kill. Especially Vesper bullets, which were designed to cause as much damage as possible while minimizing the chances of them coming back out. Yarain had managed to get good enough to qualify, though mastery of these weapons would take time. As she checked her weapon to be sure all was ready, she could only hope her current skills would be good enough.

Before those doubts could even form, Hark raised a thumb to suggest the charges were ready. With their mission imminent, there was time for only one thing.

"Lock and load," Yarain said. "Prepare for breach. Cockpit, advise the fleet we're ready in ten."

"Copy that," the co-pilot said. "Take a round, Cobra."

I'm not sure I'll ever get used to that. "Salasney—"

"We know the plan, Major. Let's see it happen."

Yarain swallowed a sigh, though she did flick an annoyed ear only a Holdren would recognize.

The same technology that went into the new standard issue uniform had allowed for the Vesper armor to have their helmet simply retract onto the back of their armor. At the push of a button, the team and crew now deployed their full helmets, complete with ear pockets for Yarain. Much to her delight, they had managed to find the perfect balance between form-fitting over her muzzle and not driving her whiskers crazy. Even her tails were covered in thicker armor than the base layer, though still comparatively thin, while the tips were uncovered at the moment. She barely felt the rest of the bulk, thanks to the intensive training she'd imposed on herself and the three months it took to earn her Vesper Falcon. She clicked the safety off on her rifle and waited for the timer.

It was only a minute later when her HUD alerted Yarain and both teams; Interstar had managed to push inward enough to prepare another volley on the enemy base. Rifles raised, personal shields were activated, Yarain's ears perked despite the pockets, and somehow, for the first time, she didn't even feel her heart. In place of the usual thunder, there was only tension in preparation for the hunt. Her first as a first mother, at the head of a full pack, in many, many years.

The second the rounds from the fleet hit, the charges on the door went off. The airlock was blown open, and Team Cobra burst through before the echo had faded.

They opened the inner door to find the corridor empty and alert lights blinking along the walls. Yarain took point, perking her ears to check for enemy soldiers. Her eyes found them first as three unlucky Polaris soldiers stopped in the doorway. They lived long enough to confirm it was enemy soldiers they saw before three shots put them down for good. While Yarain and Harrison covered the corridors, Cobra took the time to carry the bodies back to their ship. Then they moved onward like ghosts toward their target. WLF team was close behind, splitting off on a different route to the same target.

Now inside, their passive scanners were able to get a deck-by-deck layout, allowing PAICCA to put them on the fastest path to the command deck. Fastest did not mean best, however. Though they carried sensor jammers to hide their presence, those were not foolproof, and even the blue combat lighting meant Cobra had no way to camouflage this time. As such, they could only move forward soft and quick, using Yarain's ears to help them avoid detection. Thanks to dedicated sensors in the ear pockets, she didn't have to retract the armor around her ears in order to listen for the approach of more enemy troops, though that didn't keep them from perking anyway.

Team Cobra took several detours to avoid damage control parties, flight crews, and shifting platoons running down the corridors. Each time they ducked for cover, Yarain kept her ears up, waiting for any sign they'd been detected. Thankfully, she only heard P.A. announcements of armor damage and one call for damage control parties to a weapon battery. A call that was soon canceled. *Nice shooting, Jason.*

Diverted or not, Cobra moved with calm precision, taking cover when they had no choice, ducking into rooms when they could. Only once did they meet resistance and even that was taken down without so much as a single round being fired back. They managed to hide the bodies in empty quarters, though a second blood stain meant it was only a matter of time before they were discovered. Even covered with a masking agent Rad carried, the blood of the fallen would not go unnoticed forever.

The team marched on unopposed, slowed only by the need to hide from more patrols. They went up flights of stairs, rounded corners, and advanced down corridors without a word between them. Yarain heard some soldiers talk about missing comrades, and others swearing they saw something elsewhere, yet they pressed on. At this point, they would either succeed, or they would die. There wasn't much room for other choices.

At last, they reached the inner core of the base. Roaming troops became less and less frequent, and soon, they had eyes on the doors of the command deck. Yarain contemplated checking on Salasney's position, only to see them on the far side, already set up for an assault. He lifted his rifle up a moment to show he saw her, to which she did the same.

Yarain then took stock of the entry to the control room. It was a tunnel maybe six feet long that was all stairs. Four guards in heavy armor stood at the door, while half a dozen more were scattered around the sides. The walls themselves were far too thick to do anything with. The only way in was through that door, and if those inside knew they were coming, they could lock things down enough to cause problems.

"We need to thin the herd," she whispered.

Rad gave a smile that chilled Yarain's blood. "Permission to take point on that?"

Yarain swallowed, then nodded approval.

"Hold position no matter what you hear," Rad said.

Rad pointed at Yoda and Tai, then led them down the corridor away from their position. Yarain perked her ears despite the pockets as they vanished without a sound, then waited with fidgeting fingers on her rifle. Her gaze was on the guard at the door, with glances across the way to be sure WLF team was still there and ready.

A short time later, the base shook from more impacts, then a very loud thud echoed down the corridors that Yarain could feel in the floor. Right behind it came loud yells of pain from Tai, followed by Rad's voice.

"Ah, shit! Help! Help! We need weight lifters down here, fast!"

Hark gave Yarain a worried look the Holdren shared. Her own heart had skipped two beats at the racket, but the gambit was in play. Nothing to be done but hug the walls and pray Rad's plan worked.

To her shock, one of the guards looked down the line, to which one man told them to go. Four of the guards ran down the corridor Rad's voice had come from. They rounded the corner, and then all was silent for a minute. Then Rad's voice came back.

"Don't yell at me! It was this idiot who was pulling something he shouldn't have been pulling alone."

For a second, Yarain swore she had become telepathic. Rad's voice sounded utterly natural and in place, yet was just loud enough for Yarain to hear. In that instant, Yarain knew Rad had subdued the guards, and Yarain's mind clicked into the plan as if she had come up with it herself. The feeling grew stronger when the guards spread out to cover their missing members, yet didn't weaken the lines any further.

However, it also meant they were perfectly positioned for the finishing strike.

Yarain looked toward Salasney. She lifted her rifle again and held it. When he did the same, she tapped the top of her rifle, counted up to three, circled her finger pointing down, counted again, then pointed at him. Salasney repeated the gestures, though he flipped the circle and the point back at her. Yarain dropped her rifle to confirm before going to her own team. Before she could speak, they were eyes to their sights, already lining up their shots.

Yarain let pride wash over her for a moment, then looked back at WLF team. She waited with a knot in her chest until, at last, Salasney again lifted his rifle. He tapped the top of it, tapped his ear, then pointed at her. She did the same, except she circled her finger down at the floor again.

My call when to fire.

The knot jumped to her throat, but she worked it down so she could focus on the mission. She looked over at her snipers, who held still and tracked their targets as they moved. She lowered her rifle to signal her side was ready. Salasney did the same soon after, which left Yarain watching the guards as they moved and shifted. She had a finger on her radio. Though risky, one message *should* go undetected long enough for them to make their strike. *As if we needed another "if."*

At one point, all six remaining guards paused in their wanderings and head turns. It was their best chance, and Yarain pounced.

Her claw hit the button, and she said firmly but quietly, "Send."

Her claw hadn't left the button before six rounds were fired, and six kill shots were perfectly landed by both teams. The guards fell without a sound, and both teams sprinted for the door. Even Rad's group joined the rush forward. There was no time to hide those bodies, which left little time to prepare.

Yarain motioned for WLF team to guard the entrance, then she faced the door of the control room. The second she did, Hark pulled out another charge.

"Hard or soft, ma'am?" she asked.

Yarain took a moment to consider. Sheer luck had seen them make it this far undetected. A soft entry would give them a chance to extend it... but no. They needed control of that room, and they needed to obtain it the moment they walked in. Even half a second could be enough time for the base commander to lock it down. There was only one way to do this.

She pulled a flashbang from her armor while exposing her lower jaw. Before she could say the word, Harrison and Fickle pulled out the same while Hark prepped her charges. Rad, Sarson, and Tai maintained overwatch at the top of the stairs. Each member got into position, ready to spread their ordnance across the room inside. Harrison and Fickle stood on one side of the door while Yarain stood at the other. Once the charges were set, Rad, Sarson, and Tai turned around to aim their weapons at the door. All of which happened without a word from Yarain or among each other.

Yarain couldn't help taking another moment to admire their bond and skill. They knew the plan, and though she had been with them only a short time, they were already anticipating her orders. Yet, even as they did, she still noticed the slightest of sideways looks her way just to be sure. *Just like a pack checking with the first parent.* Something she hadn't seen since Sundale was a cub. If there had been any doubt left, that simple gesture would have chased it away for good.

With everyone in place, Hark held up her detonator and focused her attention on Yarain. Cobra's commander pulled the pin on her flashbang, ticked her ears forward, and then half a second later, dipped her muzzle at Hark when she remembered that her ears were covered at the moment. *We'll have to look into changing that.*

The other pins were pulled while Hark nodded. She then started a three-count on her free hand.

3...

2...

1...

Boom!

The blast door was blown open, and three flashbangs were tossed in before the smoke had stopped spreading. Three loud bangs announced their detonation, and Team Cobra rushed in to take advantage. Guards in heavy armor were peppered until they dropped. Officers at their posts held their ears, many on their knees. One soldier seemed only slightly dazed, but with the many duty positions clogging the line of fire, he didn't risk firing, and neither did Cobra. Any one of the consoles could be the one they would need to complete the mission.

Yarain dropped her rifle and ran at this man on all fours. She weaved around the unarmed officers like a dog on an agility course. The enemy soldier held his fire until Yarain was in the air, heading straight for him. What few shots that hit were glancing blows easily brushed off by her shield. Yarain charged her energy matrix around her muzzle, deploying two short blades that ran along each side.

When her hands and paws landed on the man's chest, her jaws latched onto his neck. This triggered an automatic response from the blades. They thrust themselves down along her muzzle into the man's neck. As good as his armor was, the thin layer around his neck couldn't withstand the plasma-tipped edge of the muzzle blades. They sliced deep, severing main arteries and spurting blood over Yarain's jaws. They hit the ground with a heavy thud, where the man tried to pry the predator off him. Yarain held her jaws in place until the soldier stilled beneath her.

Yarain turned to face the room and found that any who still lived had wisely surrendered. Team Cobra was already gathering them against the wall, being careful to ensure no one was hiding any weapons or trying to use the computer for anything. WLF team had moved inside the doors for even better cover while Rad, Tai, and Fickle oversaw the prisoners, and Sarson got to work on the computers under the watchful eye of Hark and Harrison. Though some of the enemy were glaring defiance, all had their hands on their heads.

Yarain stood and walked toward Harrison, slowing only to catch her rifle, which Rad tossed back to her. She flicked an ear inside its pocket at Sarson, already hard at work, then turned to Harrison.

"Status?"

"We have the room," Harrison said. "We've disarmed everyone here, but I give it five minutes tops before they realize something happened. From there, maybe another five before we have company. No more than ten after that before we're facing half a division."

"Aren't we optimistic," One of WLF team said from their position.

Yarain ignored them. "Any way we can help you, Sarson?"

The hacker gave a soft shake of his head. "Not unless you can pry an access code from our guests. Even a janitor would get me past the main firewall."

"I'll see what I can do."

Yarain went to stand in front of the gathered survivors. She gave them a short growl that drew color from several faces.

"Who is in command here?" she asked.

One very young officer raised a hand just high enough over his head for him to point two fingers at one of the others. This one had jet-black hair that had to be pushing the limits for regulation length. Her face was long, hard, and narrow, much like Jason's in many ways, though far more weathered.

Yarain glared at this woman, even though she knew the officer couldn't see it through her helmet. "And you are?"

"Captain Bradley," the woman said, almost growling, yet she also seemed to sway a little as she spoke.

"Give us a valid login code."

"Or what? You're Interstar. You don't torture your prisoners."

Yarain growled and knelt in front of the woman. She let her lips part just enough to show her fangs, still wet with blood. The armor on her muzzle dripped as well. Captain Bradley's eyes grew by the second, though she held her ground. That is until Yarain jerked her head forward, snapped her jaws, and added a harsh ruff for good measure. Bradley flinched so hard she almost fell over. Many of her comrades gasped and/or twitched as well.

Yarain's growl remained, though it was much lower now. "After what you did to my **SON**, I wouldn't be so sure of that."

Captain Bradley's face lost any color it had, though her eyes went to Tai. "Y-y-you don't expect me to believe this? Ev . . . even if it wasn't a bluff, you wouldn't let her."

Tai didn't miss a beat. "Let her? Girl, if we weren't talking about her cub, I'd do it myself. Then again, after what I saw on Phoenix Perch?" Tai made it a point to draw his combat knife. "I'd say it's time we bent some rules. Now, let's see. Why don't we start with . . . you!"

He pointed his blade at a younger man, though one with a few scars on his face that suggested he'd seen serious combat. However, even he went wide-eyed at the idea. He tried to shake his head like he didn't believe it, but his fast breathing suggested their ruse was working.

So Fickle kept it going. "Hold on, Lieutenant. You said it yourself. Yarain's son is the one they brutalized. She should get first crack."

Encouraged by more wide eyes among the group, Yarain gave her head a soft tilt while ignoring a concerned stare from Salasney. "Thank you for the thought, but I'm more likely to kill than maim. He's all yours."

Tai nodded his thanks, then gave his blade a twirl. He didn't even take a step before another voice spoke up.

"Henry Chase," the voice said. "Sierra Alpha 2-2-7-8-4. It'll get you in."

The members of Cobra turned their glares toward the man's voice. "No tricks," Tai said, "or nothing will save you."

"No tricks. You have my word."

"Sarson?"

"Got it!" Sarson said. "Seems valid. Don't see any secondary protocols in effect."

Captain Tai walked over so he could wave the blade in the man's face. "For your sake, it had better stay that way."

He sheathed his blade and retook a guard position over the group. Yarain turned to watch Sarson work his magic. *Times like this, I wish I had Jason's faith.* Being able to pray to something might help her not feel tighter than a balloon about to pop. As it was, she risked dropping the armor from her ears for comfort's sake.

Except they soon turned back when they caught whispers from behind.

"You'll face a court martial for this, Commander," Bradley said.

"Ma'am, with all due respect, you don't know Vespers or Holdrens like I do. Trust me; after Phoenix Perch, I don't think they were bluffing."

"At least the research project isn't in there. She'd kill us for sure if she knew."

Yarain turned around in one fluid motion. "Knew **WHAT**?"

Captain Bradley's face managed to lose even more color, and for a second, her lungs seemed to stop cold. When she swallowed, she was breathing like she'd been underwater for too long. The commander wasn't far behind, though she at least was keeping her breath.

Tai glanced back and forth between them. "Ma'am? What is it?"

Yarain again knelt before the officers. "These two mentioned a research project."

"They did? How did . . . Right. Fox ears. You'd think I'd know better by now."

"Jason still forgets. Tell me about this project." When neither spoke, Yarain aimed her outside tails and fired a short burst millimeters from Bradley's ears. The woman took a gasp that was more like a convulsion, though to her credit, she didn't faint . . . yet.

While Salasney moved closer with growing concern, Yarain's growl threatened to push Bradley over the edge. "I asked a question, Captain."

Captain Bradley gave the commander a sideways glare, then let out her fear in one great exhale. "Deck 14. Room XRT-1-1-6. You'll . . . you'll find . . ."

"Yes?"

"You'll find captive Holdrens that . . . that we've been using for . . . for . . ."

She didn't have to finish the sentence. Yarain's growing growl made it clear. She knew the rest. There were Holdren POWs down there that were being used for research. It didn't take a genius to guess how well they were being treated.

Tai cringed hard. "Oh, when Colonel Harlem finds out about this."

"He'll have to get in line," Yarain said. She retracted the front of her helmet so she could give Captain Bradley a glare that could have sliced the base in two. "How well guarded?"

Captain Bradley had refound her breath but little else. "Only a . . . sm . . . small security team. No . . . no more than four soldiers. The rest are . . . are nothing . . . nothing more than scientists and doctors."

"They don't deserve the term," Tai said.

"They don't deserve to live," Yarain said.

Captain Bradley's face lost color again, but Yarain was already making her way to Lieutenant Sarson. Before she could say a word, he held up one finger, then went back to typing. No more than ten seconds later, he dramatically punched one last button, and his screen changed to show a user interface similar to the one on the consoles, yet it seemed simpler and reminded Yarain of the first time she'd ever seen a computer screen.

"We're in!" Sarson said. "Can't believe Polaris left the old protocols in place, but they're all there in all their glory. We have the base! . . . mostly."

"Mostly?" Salasney asked.

"It doesn't give us everything, but we've got access to a great deal of the protocols and commands."

"Enough to lock it down?" Yarain asked.

"Not in detail. As it is, I've got PAICCA working on interfacing the current operating system with the old one. Right now, I can do some general commands, maybe some zone-by-zone things, but more is going to take a while."

Salasney offered, "How about you start with silencing the base's guns and finding a way to keep their infantry from rolling over us."

"That I can do."

A few inputs later and Yarain snapped her head toward the blown door as emergency bulkheads further down the corridor slammed shut. Softer thuds all around them suggested that was not the only bulkhead to close.

"What *did* you do?" Salasney asked.

"I triggered every emergency bulkhead on the base. You now have an entire facility full of soldiers, totally cut off from one another. The guns should be nice and quiet now, too."

"Can't they just blast their way through?" Harrison asked.

"They could, but that would take a lot of ordnance and a lot of time. Assuming, of course, we don't do some mean things like, oh, vacate the air in that section or drop the temperature down to thirty below zero. Things like that."

This team scares me sometimes. Yarain said aloud, "What about transporters?"

"That's going to take a lot more work. Those systems are largely independent. It could take an hour to make them ours."

Harrison added, "Besides that, it could take that long to finish off the enemy fleet. Our ships don't dare weaken their shields until they do. Even using the transport would be too great a risk."

Yarain couldn't stop a soft growl of annoyance. She had hoped to get some reinforcements for the next task at hand. Unfortunately, their emergency transponder was all they had, and that was designed for an emergency evac, not full-scale use. That meant COB and WLF Teams were still on their own for the next hour, and that was time the Holdren POWs might not have. Thus, Yarain found herself making the riskiest of decisions.

"See what you can do about keeping that destroyer in drydock," Yarain said. "And make sure the inhabitants understand their new situation. Fickle, break radio silence. Tell the fleet that we have the base and advise our transport we're likely here until we get reinforcements. PAICCA, find that room and plot us a path. Tai, Rad, Hark, get ready to move. WLF team stays here and guards the room."

Rounds of acknowledgements came from COB Team with each order while WLF Team glanced at their leader. Once they stopped coming, Salasney nodded at his team, then gave Yarain a hard look. "What are you planning now, Major?"

Yarain turned to face him. "Those Holdrens may not have an hour."

Harrison spoke up. "Permission to speak—"

"Always."

"You're letting your emotions make your decisions. The base is not secure, and despite Sarson's efforts, we could still wind up staring down a Polaris battalion. We can't risk it."

"I have to agree," Salasney said. "I'm already wondering how in control you are after how far you took things just now. I get that these are your people, but you can't help them if you're dead and we get overrun."

While Yarain tried to find the right words, Tai spoke up. "With all due respect, sirs, I'm with Major Yarain. If they're treating those Holdrens the same way they treated Captain Sundale, they may be in dire condition."

"Assuming they're in any danger. I can't believe they'd keep working during a battle. An assault could put them in danger they're not in."

"Or we stopped them mid-experiment, and the Holdrens need medical care they aren't going to get. Quite frankly, sir, I refuse to sit on my hands wondering if they're dying slow deaths I can prevent."

"Agreed," Rad added forcefully.

Harrison stared at Rad like she'd said something profound. He then sighed like he had a galaxy on his back. "Why do I get the feeling that I'm going to be feeling like this a lot in the coming years?"

"Like what?" Yarain asked.

He hesitated until Yarain perked her ears. "Like I wish I hadn't given up my command. When you have the position, it doesn't matter if you're outvoted. The pins on your shoulders mean your vote equals those below plus one. Been a long time since I was on the other side of that."

"I thought you insisted she take command," Salasney said.

"And right now, I'm starting to wonder if I shouldn't have."

"It's the right decision," Yarain said.

"I suppose we'll see. In the meantime, we'll hold the fort here. You just make sure you come back so we can debate whether or not it really was the right decision."

"Deal."

They shook hands just to lighten the mood.

Salasney, however, remained grim. "For the record, I still think this is a bad idea, but I'm willing to go with the judgment of your team.

Just watch yourself, Major. Don't lose control, not even for a second, or you won't save anyone."

"Understood, sir."

They too shook hands, then Yarain redeployed her full helmet and headed for the door. Rad, Tai, and Hark were right on her tails while all four switched their weapons to plasmoid mode.

"Clear the way for us, Sarson!"

"Already on it, ma'am. Take a round!"

All four leveled their rifles on their way into the corridors. They didn't even break stride as bulkheads opened before them and closed behind them. PAICCA had the path plotted, and this time, stealth was not a concern. This proved unfortunate for one Polaris squad, who were mowed down when the door to their makeshift prison opened, and they foolishly went for their weapons. Yarain thought about warning the base's crew not to resist, but such a warning could also allow them to prepare for it. To say nothing about how it might endanger the Holdrens they sought to rescue.

Thankfully, the encounters were rare, and only two groups tried to fight back. The rest were unarmed or had their hands up when the doors opened. They were told to stay silent and behave themselves, had any comms gear removed, and then the team moved on.

Yarain's fire team moved with careful precision through empty corridors, downstairs to the appropriate deck, and along their path to the research station. With no resistance encountered, they held position outside the door. Yarain perked her ears, hoping to hear some indication of who was inside.

What she heard sent her hackles spiking.

"I said hold her down, Sergeant!"

"I'd like to see you do better."

"How hard can it be to hold down a tied-up fox?"

"Why don't you come over here and find out? *Urgh!* Corporal! Get her hind paws, will you?"

"Just keep her neck still. I only need a moment, and then we'll see what happens."

You won't get the chance.

Yarain hit the panel to open the door. Four vespers burst inside before it could fully open. Two guards standing over a table were cut down before they knew who had come in. Everyone else wore only lab coats, and they were smart enough to throw their hands up the moment plasma started flying. A quick glance around the room found it otherwise empty.

A half dozen lab techs and "doctors" were forced to face the wall so they could be checked for weapons or other threats. Yarain held vigil over them all, though she also scanned the room to take in its horror. There were four tables in what otherwise might have been called a medical bay. Each table certainly had all the readouts, but they were clearly modified to restrain Holdrens in either form, complete with buckles for the tails.

The walls, however, were more telling. The instruments held there were medical but also appeared to be variations on tools meant for construction, ship repair, hazardous materials, or other things Yarain didn't even recognize. On the far wall near a door, two Holdrens lay dead, their blood and organs strewn about the floor. They had been dissected and discarded like waste meat. Seven tails, each with a different fur pattern, hung on the wall above them. Two of them matched the bodies on the floor, and Yarain realized the innards there accounted for more than just those two.

Yarain's snarl grew with each depravity. It filled the room when she noticed the instrument still held by one of the technicians. It looked a lot like a plasma torch, but the emitter seemed thinner than any she'd ever seen, and it had a tiny spike in the middle that made no sense at all. When he was checked for threats, Yarain had Tai give it to her. When she couldn't make sense of it, she retracted the face of her helmet so her snarl could be heard, seen, and felt.

"What does this do?"

The man was surprisingly calm in the face of still bloody fangs, though facing the wall might have helped. "Find out for yourself, bitch."

"Wrong answer!" Tai said.

Yarain "rewarded" the man by twirling him around, then latching her jaws onto his throat. She bit down enough to press on his windpipe, though she stopped short of breaking the skin. For now, at least. He tried to claw her away, but all he got was armor until she pinned his hands to the wall with her own.

With Yarain's jaws full of neck, Tai took over questioning. "I know what you're thinking. She's Interstar. She wouldn't do it. You would be wrong because, I remind you; Sundale is her son. And she saw firsthand what you Pols did to him. Considering you were about to do something similar to this vixen, you're lucky she didn't snap your neck like a twig. As it is, I figure you only get one more strike before you're out . . . permanently. So, let's try this again. What does the device do?"

The man remained defiant. "You'd never allow—"

"Oh yes, I would. And I'd enjoy every minute of it."

The man only seethed until Yarain bit down harder. Faced with having his throat literally ripped out, he finally stiffened against the wall. "Okay,

okay! It's a radiation syringe. We were going to see how she responded to radioactive material delivered directly into her bloodstream."

Yarain snarled through her bite. Only Salasney's words echoing in her mind kept her from snapping his neck where he stood.

Meanwhile, Lieutenant Hark shook her head. "I'm sorry, but even from a psychopathic point of view, what could that possibly do?"

"Holdrens have a natural resistance to radiation because of their energy matrix. Delivering radioactive material directly to the main conduit for that matrix might help us understand how it works. It could lead to all kinds of breakthroughs."

Yarain's snarl only grew. For a moment, she wanted to rip out his Adam's apple so he could look at it as he died. However, despite everything Tai said, Salasney's words again reminded her: she *was* Interstar. They made a big show, sometimes pushed the limits, as she had already done, but in the end, they were better. No matter how much they might want to not be.

She withdrew her fangs, though she didn't leave without glaring straight into the man's eyes with her snarl. That finally drew color from his face when he realized just how much she wanted to tear him apart like she would a moose. She then turned away to assess the situation.

Her ears were drawn up by an opening door in the back. Growls came soon after, followed by more grunting. She gave a snarl of her own when she saw another bound and muzzled Holdren being carried in by his paws.

"I vote for sedation," one of the guards said. "I swear these things are getting . . ." He trailed off when he realized he was staring down the barrels of four Vespers. "So that *wasn't* the battle outside we heard."

"Well, look at that," Tai said. "The man has eyes."

"Though his ears are suspect," Hark added.

"Put him down," Yarain said, "Gently."

The guard nodded and began to do just that, though the Holdren's shoulders wound up landing in front of the guard's ankles. "Okay, no problem. No need to shed any more blood here. I know better than to risk—"

As the man's hands reached the floor, three Holdren beams burned holes through his head. While the other guard threw up his hands, Yarain glanced back to find the female Holdren had been freed, and her tail tips were still glowing.

"*EXPLAIN* yourself!" Yarain barked.

"He was reaching for a weapon," the Holdren said.

"How do you know that?"

"He did the same thing once before. He used a captive as cover then, too."

Rad was already advancing toward the dead guard, though her rifle was trained on the other. This one wisely kept his hands up the entire time, allowing her to kneel and examine the kill.

"I can confirm that he *was* reaching for a sidearm, ma'am," Rad said.

"Take in the other guard," Yarain said. "Then guard the door. Name, soldier?"

"Commander Ulina, ma'am," the female Holdren said.

"Commander Ulina, grab a weapon and take charge of the others. Tai, help this male out of his bonds. Check him for injuries."

"Gladly," Tai said.

While her orders were put into action, Yarain went up and grabbed the dead guard by the back of his shoulders. She found enough grip to lift the still leaking body up so it could be seen.

"Do I need to worry about anyone else?" Several heads shook, save for two that were trying very hard not to puke. Yarain let the body collapse on the floor. "**GOOD**. Now, are there any other POWs on this base?"

Surprisingly, the tech from before answered without a shred of his former defiance. "No, ma'am. They're all through the door there. The guards have—had—fobs that will unlock the cells."

"Any still wounded?"

"No."

"Any more guards?"

"No."

With the male Holdren now free, he shifted to his finesse form so he could claim the rifle of one of the dead guards. Shillin, meanwhile, had secured fobs from the guards, glanced at Yarain for another check, then ordered the male Holdren to follow her through the door so they could free the others. Yarain let her go without reaction, instead trying to decide what to do with the horror she was staring at.

The two bodies didn't bother her beyond the disrespect they represented. Had they simply been dead, it would mean nothing beyond arranging for someone to make sure they were collected once the base was secure. But they hadn't just been killed. They had been brutalized, subjected to dreadful, painful experiments that might have been worse than even Sundale's treatment. Then there were the tails. Tally marks, trophies, body count, untainted DNA samples for reference—no matter how she saw them, they turned her stomach and sent her hackles on end. The men and women still standing would answer for it, but she wanted to do something about it now. Unfortunately, she could do nothing but stare and keep herself under control.

She had decided to simply leave when her comm. link chimed to life. Somehow, she knew it wasn't good news before Harrison had said a word.

"COB 2 to COB 1. We've got a new problem."

Of course we do. There's always that one more thing on missions like this. "Report."

"It would appear Polaris is smarter than we thought. Someone has managed to reach the computer core. They're trying to undermine our efforts."

"How? The panic pod has the protocols."

"Which are still stored in the main computer. If they can sever the connections going in, they can simply do what we did, and it'll be *us* on the wrong end of the lockdown. It's one of the many reasons the pods were abandoned. COB 5 managed to put some firewalls in, but once they kick him out, it won't be long until they take the base the same way we did."

The captive Holdrens exited the cell block, along with a few humans and haaj'kar. Yarain had Shillin secure the Polaris techs in the same cells. "What can we do?"

"We'll have to take the core, ma'am, and it gets worse. We have strong indications that there's a sizable Polaris force down there."

Yarain tried to growl, but it came out as more of a sigh with a touch of a whimper. As if the day hadn't been hard enough, now they had this to deal with. For half a second, Yarain suddenly wanted to curl up and nap anywhere that wasn't here. The next half-second saw her eyes meet those of several of the other Holdrens. More than humans ever could, they were able to pick up on her feelings as if they could read her mind and she theirs. They, in turn, held up the weapons they had claimed from the guards or made their tail tips glow. Though only a few Holdrens still wore their uniforms, the message was clear; they were ready to fight.

However, Yarain's ears fell when she thought about forcing these soldiers into action so soon and with so little to work with. Few had weapons; none had armor. They might be willing, but how could she possibly ask them to walk out of this horror into another one?

One of the humans spoke up. "Something wrong, ma'am?"

Yarain huffed out another sigh. "Polaris is trying to retake the computer core. If they do, we could lose the base."

"Then let's get moving," A haaj'kar said.

"You've been through enough, and you have no gear. I can't let—"

The human called out, "Protect and serve!"

The other humans from Interstar besides Cobra replied, "Honor and uphold!"

The Holdrens added, "My life for the pack."

The haaj'kar soldier said, "We don't have a phrase, but we too pledge our lives to the cause."

It was a united front. No hesitation, no fear, no choice left for Yarain. Not that she fought it. The unity before her had filled her with a burst of energy that wiped away all traces of doubt or exhaustion. There was only tension filling her body, waiting to be let loose upon her next kill. Her body felt light and fresh, as if she had just woken up from that nap she wanted.

She wasted no time using it. "COB 2, have COB 5 clear us a path to the core. Do what he can to keep it clear."

Harrison was surprisingly calm on the other end. "Yes, ma'am. I'll send down COB 3 to assist."

"No need, and no time. We have POWs here that can fight. Just keep the doors open."

"Understood! Take a round. COB 2 out."

As the group scoured the guards for any remaining weapons or took sidearms from the Vespers, Yarain addressed Ulina. "Can you give me a head and weapon count?"

"Fifteen Holdrens, eight humans, four haaj'kar," Ulina said. "We have four rifles and eight sidearms besides your Vesper weapons."

"How many can still fight?"

"All of us," a human said.

Yarain glanced over her group to try and get a feel for them before making adjustments. "Two Holdrens cover our six with rifles; keep your ears perked for ambushes. haaj'kar in the middle, two rifles and two sidearms. The rest is first come, first served, spread yourselves among the formation. Use your tails sparingly. Rad, you're on point with me. Tai, Hark, at the rear. Hark, watch your care packages. Check your targets if you can for surrendering forces, but don't take chances you don't have to. In the core room, watch your fire. We need the core intact. Keep together, keep to cover, don't ask for clarification of orders. Questions?"

A unanimous "No, ma'am" echoed in the room.

"Follow close."

Despite its size, the group flowed out of the lab like a snake slithering on its way. Their formation filled the corridor, yet no one ever lost a step. They only stopped once, and that was because Rad pointed out a door with the word "armory" beside it. It was a stroke of blind luck Yarain did not hesitate to take advantage of. Though it would cost a few precious minutes, she could not pass on the chance to properly equip her new assault team with weapons and armor.

The two men inside gave them zero trouble from the moment the doors opened. The group went to work fitting the humans with full armor and the haaj'kar and Holdrens with basic combat vests. Everyone without one grabbed a rifle, and a few grabbed grenades. Yarain tried and failed to find a portable combat shield while the Polaris soldiers were restrained. Then, the group flowed back on its way.

Each step saw the thunder in Yarain's chest grow stronger. Lieutenant Sarson could lose the battle at any moment, or they could march right into an enemy battalion, either of which would end their mission then and there. She didn't question the choice, but she still worried that equipping the team took time they didn't have. Yet they couldn't just run either since that would increase their chances of being caught off guard themselves. All they could do was keep moving, keep their ears perked, and hope like crazy their timer didn't run out.

They rounded the corner for the core and were driven to cover by a fierce volley of weapons fire. The only hits taken were glancing blows, most of which were absorbed by armor. Yarain's force returned fire, with Rad laying down behind cover to do what she did best.

Harrison's "sizeable force" turned out to be that battalion she had been dreading for so long. Worse yet, they were a well-equipped battalion, some of whom seemed to be sporting armor very similar to the Vesper's. They were hiding behind the same combat shields Yarain had hoped to find in the armory. *Probably took all there were.* There didn't seem to be any snipers, though Yarain didn't expect any to last long with Rad already set up.

The two forces traded fire that only sparked off of the walls and support columns. No one was landing any meaningful hits. Truth be told, it seemed as though only Rad was landing kills, and her position quickly became a favorite target of the enemy barrages. Good as she was, Rad had to spend a lot of time taking cover instead of firing.

With a timer on the engagement, Yarain was forced to take a radical risk.

"Stand by for a full barrage. Holdrens, on my first bark, sling your rifles on your back and sprint on your hands and paws. Hug the walls, fire your tails on the enemy positions as you run. When you hear a second bark, retake cover."

The group managed to adjust themselves so that most of the Holdrens were upfront. Bursts of rifle fire streaked over their heads, but none were hit. They continued to trade fire while Yarain watched the enemy lines as best she could. Though their firing patterns were random, she did notice a sort of cadence developing. A flurry of shots, more, then less, less again, more, more, less, more, less, less, more. It was subtle and rare for a military to allow it to happen, but there it was. She waited for the downbeat to begin her plan.

Right on pattern, there was a minute drop in the enemy barrage. Yarain gave the order, and every allied weapon fired down range. The enemy fire stopped as they all ducked behind cover. It lasted but a second, yet it was all the time she needed.

Yarain let out a sharp bark. Every Holdren, including herself, slung their rifles on their backs, and two lines of them tore down the edges of the corridors as fast as their hands and paws could carry them. Most were firing with a middle tail. The rest managed to hold stride while using their outside tails instead. Their comrades behind them fired over their heads to keep the enemy pinned down. However, the Polaris soldiers were able to return fire even so. Shots went past their heads and between their ears, yet no one slowed. A member took a hit in the leg; he went down, and the line flowed right over him. Another took a direct hit between the eyes. Still, the charge continued.

They were only thirty feet away from the enemy lines, but Yarain knew that she'd used all the luck she dared. She let out another bark, and the foxes all plastered themselves to the walls just before a counterattack peppered the paths they had been on. *Cut that one close.* The Holdrens still didn't stop moving. Though many were panting from the sprint and tail use, they retrieved their rifles and continued their assault with almost no delay.

Now closer, Yarain could confirm the presence of Polaris special forces. She had yet to hear a name for them, but their armor was as distinct as her own. Her ears ticked forward in approval when she saw two long rifles on the floor and four bodies beside them. *Nice shooting, Shillin.* However, Polaris had a full team there, with several more soldiers wearing frontline armor.

They didn't have time to fight this out, nor did she expect to win it without significant casualties. Once again, Yarain had to adapt to her new situation.

"COB 1 to COB 5. What would happen to our situation if the core were damaged?"

"Right now? We'd have a hard time locking down that destroyer," Sarson said. "But the base would remain ours. Do I want to know why you're asking?"

"***NO.*** COB 1 out. Everyone, rescind my earlier limits. ***NOT*** you, Hark! Take them out by any means necessary."

Three grenades were thrown at the Polaris position only a second later. A pair of Stiletto micro missiles blew an enemy apart soon after. The allied fire intensified as Yarain's group no longer cared about stray shots damaging the core within. Yarain peeked around a corner so she could continue to add to the exchange. With the limitation lifted, their volleys were starting to claim soldiers.

During one exchange, a burst of fire peppered Yarain's position. Before she could retreat to cover, two rounds landed on her right cheek. Shock, pain, and surprise drew a screeching yelp from Yarain as she twisted backward into the wall. The impact knocked the wind out of her lungs. Her body went limp, and she collapsed onto the floor.

Yarain stayed down while her body tried desperately to reboot her lungs. She felt herself being pulled against the wall, but she felt nothing else for what felt like an hour. Her cheek stung from the impact, and she had no idea if it was a minor burn or a gaping wound. Her back didn't like hitting the wall either, which only made it that much harder to regain her breath.

Finally, slowly, Yarain managed to breathe again. It began with a few heaves, then some coughs joined them, then at last, she was able to start panting like she'd been running for days. Each breath shook her body as it worked to recover from the shock. As her lungs managed to regain their function, her perception improved as well. She could hear the firefight still raging around her, including calls for targets, the yelps of others clipped by fire, and the vibration in the floor when they went down.

Someone touched her cheek, and she again cried out, though more in surprise than pain this time. Yet it also triggered her instincts. Her jaws opened in preparation for a return bite, only to hold when she realized it was Ulina checking on her wound. This reaction rebooted her brain. Aside from still being a little winded, Yarain suddenly felt herself back to normal, as if someone had flipped a switch within her.

"Are you well?" Ulina asked.

Yarain took a moment to confirm her surroundings, then ticked her ears forward. *"Yes."*

Yarain rolled over, retrieved her rifle, and rejoined the line. She found many of the Polaris forces dead or wounded, with fewer of hers than she'd feared down for the count. Many had taken hits to their arms, legs, tails, bodies, and vests, but only five appeared to be out of the fight. Of those, three were still breathing.

She pulled a flashbang off of her armor, tossed it to another Holdren, then pulled off her last one. *"On my mark, count three, then throw. Prepare for another sprint."*

Several ears ticked forward in understanding. Yarain waited for the cadence but found it gone. So, she simply waited until it felt like the smallest of lulls in the enemy barrage came.

The moment it did, she let out another sharp bark. *"Now!"*

Yarain counted in her head. 3 . . . 2 . . . 1 . . . both flashbangs went out at the same time. Hers landed too short to do much, but the other bounced off of a helmet. It went off right in the middle of the remaining enemy forces.

No order was needed. The second the flash was gone, every Holdren was already on their hands and paws. Rifles were abandoned. Fangs were bared. When the enemy managed to recover enough to return fire, most of their faces went chalk white.

Half of the survivors felt the full force of Holdren tails. As the Holdrens poured into the room, fangs and claws dug deep into necks and faces. Screams echoed in the computer room. Gargles and hacking soon replaced them as throats were torn open. Yarain herself used her muzzle blade to cut into the neck of a Polaris special forces soldier, but his armor couldn't stop the sheer might of her bite. His neck snapped before they even hit the floor. She pointed each tail at a different target and killed three more. Polaris tried to regroup to counter, but those who stood their ground were killed by fang and claw, while those who ran for cover died by tail fire or Shillin's aim.

In less than a minute, the entire Polaris force was dead or surrendering. Even those who had been typing away the entire time abandoned their chairs. The open computer core room fell silent, save for the snarls of the Holdrens daring anyone to try anything stupid. Only two Holdrens lay injured, neither seriously.

The rest of the team soon joined them to confirm everything was secure. Polaris was disarmed and gathered against a wall while Captain Tai approached Yarain to check on her wound.

Yarain knew him well enough to know it would take less time for him to check than it would to convince him others needed him more. She even fully retracted her helmet so he could get a better look. The burn was maybe an inch in diameter, though there was still enough to blister. Part of it had already popped, adding a tiny bit of her blood to the blood of her prey on her muzzle.

Tai gently pressed one finger on the burn, drawing a soft whine from Yarain. He then hummed as he pulled out a spray applicator. "That's gonna sting for a while. So will this, but it'll keep things from getting worse until we can get you better treated." He sprayed the wound, and Yarain whimpered with a sharp cringe as the substance burned like he'd set it on fire. He covered the wound in a layer of white medicine before turning her muzzle to check his work. "Sorry, Major. Combat medicine is rarely gentle."

Yarain knew that, but it didn't make it feel any better. "I'll live."

"Yes, you will. Now if you'll excuse me, I have other foxes to save."

Tai left to check on the other wounded while Yarain turned to check the damage to the core. The walls and terminals had taken several hits, with one console utterly destroyed. Yet the panels over the core itself seemed to have done their job. The consoles on the sides remained active despite the damage. Ulina was even working on one to make sure no programs had been triggered.

Then came her comms again.

"COB 5 to COB 1, whatever you did worked. I'm not reading any further threats."

Let's hope that lasts. "What about the base personnel?"

"They're taking my threats seriously. We're getting offers of surrender from all over the base. Hang on . . . more good news. The Polaris fleet has surrendered. I say again, Polaris has surrendered. The base is ours."

Yarain suddenly felt half her weight fall off when she realized that the battle for the station was well and truly over. While the surrender might not include the fleet outside the rocks, call it an honest assessment or blind confidence, she knew it had gone no worse out there. It wouldn't be long before she could shed all the pressure and, with any luck, get that nap she wanted.

Unfortunately, the worried tone in Ulina's voice made the weight jump right back on. "Ma'am? I think you'd better take a look at this."

Yarain gave a soft growl, then walked over to check the display Ulina was sitting at. "What is it?"

"Their shipyards show four ships in dock. The damaged destroyer and three ships under construction. One is a Polaris frigate, but I don't recognize the other two."

A small diagram of each ship appeared on-screen. One of the unfamiliar ships was more or less a giant saucer with a thicker rim around the sides. Yarain had seen this Raider "battleship" before. They were surprisingly effective despite their design, though they were no match for a *London*-class battleship. Really, their main claim to fame was a very thick, very deadly point defense grid that even Scorns didn't dare test unless they had to. The rare times they got into knife-fight range, they could do a number on capital ships, too. Their main guns weren't nothing, they just couldn't match the power of Interstar warships.

The other, however, Yarain knew only too well. It was long and slender with a thicker, half-circle-shaped bow and curved spikes running the length of the hull along the sides. The spikes ended where three sets of wings resembling Earth battle axes sat at the stern of the ship. The moment she saw it, she remembered Reneca's question of whether or not the Marcallan ships at Holdre 4 had been 'real.' It would appear they had their answer, though Yarain's ears ticked back for just a moment while her mind contemplated what to make of it.

"What's wrong, Yarain?" Rad asked from behind.

Yarain let out a soft huff of amusement. *She is one quiet human.* "They were building a Marcallan heavy cruiser."

"They what?" An Interstar soldier asked. "Why are the Pols building a Jant ship?"

"There's more," Ulina said.

She worked with the computer to bring up what looked like records of communications and orders. Most of it was the usual operations of a military, though a message from someone under the code name '1-18-7' was incredibly encrypted. Strange thing about that one was it was received only a few hours ago, followed by a massive spike in activity. Whatever that message was, it had put the base on high alert.

They knew we were coming. Somehow, someone warned them about our assault. The thought did nothing for Yarain's stomach, though until Sarson could crack the message, she could do nothing about it for now.

Besides, she had something else to think about. Among the activity, one file was marked as having been activated earlier that day. At Yarain's request, Ulina managed to find an attached communication so new it hadn't been fully decrypted yet.

From: $%#^^
T¢£μμ*^##1
##: %^&ET M*@$i-S~#%
Classificati%$$#^& TOP SE%*@(@)@$#nly
Message:
Ope~@#$@^%^ has been compromised.
Begin Operation Dove Hunt imedi%$#&*.
End me%^#@$

Yarain stared at it for one second to be sure, then hit her comms. "COB 1 to COB 5. We need contact with the *Alamo*, **NOW**!"

Harrison replied first. "COB 2 here. COB 5 is a bit focused trying to unlock the transporters right now. What's going on?"

"Polaris was warned of our attack, they were building a Marcallan heavy cruiser *and* a Raider battleship, and they just began something called 'Operation Dove Hunt.'"

"Right. I'll refocus him."

CHAPTER 17

YES, IT CAN GET WORSE

Jason couldn't help keeping his hand near his sidearm. The battle was so recent, some ships were still on fire. Yet here he and his crew were in a flag conference room. They didn't know why, only that Marshal Garmon had made it clear; now meant an hour ago. So, they landed fast, walked fast, and now they had to wait to find out what the heck was going on.

Finesse form or not, both Sundale and Reneca had settled onto the floor, with Reneca seemingly learning how to groom his feathers. Jason smiled as he watched, though, in the back of his mind, he knew that members of the same blood pack tended to do similar things. That amusement wasn't enough to keep him from pacing, however. He didn't doubt Carter's ability to lead without him; he just didn't like being pulled from that responsibility without good cause. Except he didn't even have bad cause. In fact, he had nothing, which only made it worse.

It didn't get better when Marshal Garmon finally arrived … along with Admiral Redding, General Manster, Captain Torzon, and Yarain still in her armor.

Jason turned to ask what this was all about, only to stop cold when he saw a bandage on Yarain's cheek that did not cover all of the burned fur.

While Jason got his breathing under control, Sundale spoke first. "Yarain. What happened?"

"I took a hit on the mission," she said. "Before you ask, Jason, I'm fine. You have nothing to worry about."

Sundale didn't flinch. "Not with this much brass in the room."

Captain Torzon put a hand on her hip. "And since when are you such a pessimist?"

"I know trouble when I see it."

"As do I," Jason said. "With all due respect, sirs, ma'am, I'd like to know what I'm doing here."

The rest of the group took seats around the table while Marshal Garmon worked with a console on the table. "You're here to finish what you started with the Marcallan Prefect. Take your seats, Gold 1."

The crew did so, though even Reneca's tails were starting to wave. More than ever, Jason's hand remained primed and ready to draw his weapon, though he wasn't really aware of it until he had to adjust his arm around the chair. Once all were seated, Marshal Garmon activated a holo-projector in the middle of the table. An image of a Raider "battleship," a Polaris frigate, and a Marcallan heavy cruiser appeared in the air between them. *This isn't good.*

"What I'm about to tell you is so top secret, this meeting is not even showing in the ship's log," Marshal Garmon said. "As far as the computer knows, this room is empty."

"Not making me feel better, ma'am," Jason said.

"Trust me, Harlem, it's only going to get worse. These three ships were all under construction inside the facility we just captured. Records we've dug out of their computer suggest it's not the first Raider ship they've built, and based on the intel Reneca gave us, it's not the first Marcallan ship either."

While nice to have full confirmation of things, this wasn't exactly an earth-shattering revelation. Simon had already told them the Raiders and Polaris were one and the same, and Reneca had already presented data suggesting Polaris had been building Marcallan ships. As major as this revelation was, it didn't feel like it warranted this kind of secrecy or attention.

"What else did we find?" Jason asked.

"Isn't that enough?" General Manster said.

"With respect, no, sir. Not for this kind of treatment. There's another shoe here."

General Manster huffed. "Do any of your soldiers respect the chain of command?"

"Lieutenant Colonel Harlem has more than earned it," Admiral Redding said. "His instincts are good, and the more time I spend with him, the more I like how little regard he has for bullshit."

"Discipline keeps a military running, Admiral."

"So does trust."

"Sirs, please!" Captain Torzon said. "We can argue about our differences until the cows come home. We don't have time for that."

"Indeed not," Marshal Garmon said. "Tell me, Colonel, do the numbers 1-18-7 mean anything to you?"

Jason's head snapped up while Sundale's ears gave a similar perk. He almost kicked himself for not keeping control of it, but when Marshal

Garmon smiled, he realized that Yarain probably told her everything they knew.

"For the record, I don't blame you for your caution," Garmon said. "Though the General and I had quite the argument about withholding information, even he had to admit; you had to be sure before you could trust even me. However, we believe we have a way to assure you that you can trust everyone in this room. Admiral Redding?"

Admiral Redding leaned on the table with a bounce of his folded hands. "Ever since the communique that led us to Holdre 4, I've been looking into who this '1-18-7' could be. A random thought sent me digging into ancient codes, which led me to Nazi Germany. After that, I realized they hid their code in plain sight. During World War Two, Nazi forces would often use the code '88'. This stood for 'H-H' or . . ."

"Hiel Hitler," Jason said when he was gestured to.

Admiral Redding gave him a nod of approval. "I began to suspect that whoever this operative was, he was using the same code. A bit obvious, but hardly helpful even if broken."

"Surely a broken code can still be of use," Reneca said.

"Depends on the code," Captain Torzon said. "We know that someone using the code '1-18-7' warned Polaris that we were coming, but all that really gets us is the initials 'A-R-G.' There are over twelve *billion* humans in the United Systems Republic. Of those, just under four hundred *thousand* have those initials."

"But whoever it is knew where we were going," Sundale said.

Jason nodded. He knew where this was going even before Torzon spoke again. "Two carrier groups, additional support and assault ships, scuttlebutt that we couldn't control, and we're still looking at just under a thousand individuals who could be our man or woman. It's going to take days, maybe weeks, to fully clear each one. We don't have days or weeks."

"You keep saying that," Jason said, "but I've yet to hear why we're so pressed for time. If this is all so important and secret, why am I the only captain or group leader here? With all due respect, I'm still waiting for that second shoe."

Admiral Redding chuckled with a glance toward General Manster. "See? No tolerance for bullshit. You and your crew are here, first and foremost, because none of you have those initials. There are still a few within the fleet here that do, so the fewer people involved, the better. Second, when the jantans came to Earth for peace talks, of all the people in the escort fleet, Prefect Colark asked for *your* crew to meet him on his ship. This provides a direct connection to him we may need and quickly. Reneca may not have been there at the time, but she is your crew now, so she could hardly be left out. As for your second shoe, it's called 'Operation Dove Hunt.'"

"I hate it already."

"Just wait. That heavy cruiser Polaris was building? As Reneca's data indicated, she's not actually Marcallan. There's just enough Marcallan tech in her to fool sensors, but aside from that, she's entirely human-built. Probably explains why we haven't found any jantans on the base. We're still sorting out exactly how, but they were going to use it to assist with a coup of the Marcallan leadership. A coup that is going to begin in just a few days."

I'm sorry I asked. "Oh boy."

Jason's head fell into his hand. The idea of a coup, assisted by Polaris, just about turned his stomach to ice. The tide had turned against Polaris, but at a high cost and hardly to the point of sure victory. If the jantans were to join them in full, even with Kapon, he had to wonder if they could hold the line.

However, just as fast as his blood had chilled, Jason's body sparked a fire. They couldn't let it happen. They were so close to ending it. So close to beginning an era without bloodshed, without funerals, without casualty lists. It was only a matter of time before Prefect Colark brought about a truly lasting, living, permanent peace. They couldn't let Polaris take it all away.

The fire grew in Jason's chest until it became a single coal hotter than the center of the Earth. His hand dropped, and he glared forward at no one in particular. "What are we doing? And don't you dare tell me we're doing nothing."

General Manster leaned back while folding his arms like a disappointed dad. "You don't get to give orders, *Lieutenant Colonel*."

"Do you want me to beg, sir? I'll beg. I'll get down on my knees and kiss your boots if I have to. We can't afford to sit by and do nothing. We need to stop this." Jason surprised himself even more than the others when he started to breathe heavily, like he was close to panic. "We have to. We've buried too many friends already. If we let this coup happen, we'll be burying a lot more in the coming years. Prefect Colark is our last, best hope for peace. We can't let him fail."

Never mind a pin; for a moment, everyone heard every strand of fur that hit the floor. Even General Manster had turned to stone with eyes weighed down by thought and emotion. The longer things were silent, the more his stare fell on nothing. Jason could only breathe and try not to faint. There was too much hope in Prefect Colark. They had to defend it. They had to.

A minute passed like a thousand years. Then, slowly, Marshal Garmon's smile returned. "*That* is the other reason you're here. No one can doubt your conviction. Your crew is known for coming up with the impossible and making it look easy. If we're going to stop this coup, we're going to need that kind of thinking. None of us have come up with anything short of a full-blown assault. We've tried to contact the Prefect, even using the protocols he gave you, but we've received no confirmation he's gotten a single message. In short, Mister Harlem, I'm asking you for ideas."

Right, no pressure.

Jason blew out his stress while staring at the three ships represented above the table. His mind covered the galaxy, touching on all the many places and histories the next few days would affect. So little time, so much to protect, and they were expecting *him* to come up with the solution? *I'm not paid enough for this.*

And yet, his gaze never really drifted from the heavy cruiser. He saw it there, floating above the table, and the simplest of ideas seemed to be written on her holographic hull.

"How ready is that Marcallan ship?" he finally said.

Admiral Redding waved him off. "Forget it. First thing we thought of. We're getting her prepped just in case we can use her, but we don't know the codes, counter signs, anything that would get us past the checkpoints. Never mind the fact that there is no way to fake hundreds of jantan soldiers. Not unless they had a trick we haven't found yet."

"We don't need to. You said it yourself, there isn't a jantan anywhere near here. I doubt Polaris would give up the location of a base like this even to an ally. I know we wouldn't." General Manster cocked his head but remained silent. "That suggests that they're *expecting* it to be crewed by humans. All we have to do is mask any Holdrens we take with us, and we should be golden."

"We'd still never get all the way to their home world undetected," General Manster said. "Security would be too tight."

Captain Torzon bounced a finger toward him "Perhaps not. If they're expecting Polaris to be crewing the ship for a coup, they may have intentional security deficiencies in place to allow them passage. All we have to do is go through the motions of the plan."

"Until we break from it. Once they realize it's not Polaris on that ship, they'd blow it apart."

"So, we don't let them know," Marshal Garmon said. "If we need shock troops, we can call in FLAREs. The *Andes* has a contingent on board. This wouldn't be the first time they had to land on an extraction ship without being seen."

Yarain's ears and hackles shot up. "As long as my team is out of it. We've given all we can to **THIS** mission."

About time she showed up. Jason watched her with a bit of pride warming his shoulders. How many times had he told her she'd make an excellent leader? How many times had she doubted him? Now here she was, standing firm in defense of her team. Jason fully agreed with her. One need only see the wound on her cheek to realize that COB team had done their share of the work. It was time for someone else to carry that burden.

General Manster gave a huff that was close to a growl, but before he could comment, Marshal Garmon spoke first. "I would never ask you to do more, Major. You can ride home with me. You need to let that wound heal, and if you'll forgive me, Vespers are too much of a scalpel anyway. If things go south, we're going to need the brute strength FLAREs can provide."

General Manster glared at Marshal Garmon, though Jason couldn't tell why. "And what is a 'flare'?"

"Field Logistics Assault Recon Echelon. They're the best-trained, best-equipped soldiers we have. They take on the missions even Colonel Harlem wouldn't try. They may be just what we need to complete this mission successfully."

"Assuming we can get enough of the plan to play the part," Reneca said. "We'll still have to convince any jantans we meet that we *ARE* Polaris."

Yarain ruffed a soft chuckle. "Lieutenant Sarson should have that in about five minutes."

Admiral Redding rose slowly. "In that case, with your permission, Marshal, I'd like to make sure I have a crew ready to go the second we do."

Marshal Garmon bowed her permission. "The cruiser should be ready to go by now. Colonel Harlem, load your group for assault and get them transferred to the cruiser. Tell them nothing beyond the absolute minimum they need. We'll have a full plan for you by the time you leave."

Jason and his crew stood as one. "Aye, ma'am."

Preparations went in a blur. All Jason really remembered was twenty minutes later, he was once again landing his fighter on a Marcallan ship of his own free will. Two hours after that, Admiral Redding gave the order, and the fake heavy cruiser *Hulio* jumped to hyperlight on a direct course for Marcelis, the jantan home world.

CHAPTER 18

THE SEEDS WE SOW

Admiral Solez couldn't peel himself from the window of his office. His eyes were picking apart every road, building, tree, and car he could see. All of those people, *his* people, their fates were about to be decided. He could only rub his wedding band while trying to keep himself together.

"Sir," he finally said, "with all due respect, I don't think you understand how much of a disaster we have on our hands here. Outpost 81 is firmly in the hands of Interstar, and I don't see a way to dislodge them without weakening our lines to the point of breaking. On top of that, I am quite sure that Operation Dove Hunt has been compromised. The plan has *failed*!"

Somehow, his brain told him he could hear the grand marshal smiling over the comms. "No, Admiral. Plan *B* has failed. Plan *A* is still in play and is fully capable of fulfilling itself."

Now, Admiral Solez spun around to stare at his computer. "What? What are you talking about? There was only ever one plan."

"I will explain when I feel it is appropriate, Admiral. For now, I can only say that the war has achieved what it needed to and will continue to do so. My way to the presidency is paved. We need only stay the course, and I will be where I need to be to end the wars for good."

"Achieved what it . . . Our lines are crumbling, our soldiers are dying, now we've lost a base *INSIDE* our territory—"

"That is enough, Admiral! You will follow your orders, and you will make it work! Nothing will stop my ascension! I will lead humanity to where it belongs in this galaxy! Stay . . . the . . . *course*, Admiral!" The marshal took a breath Solez could hear, which covered his own muttered curse under his breath. "Operation Dove Hunt has been shifted to still work in our favor. I have seen to that. All you need to do is wait for my orders and follow them. A great sacrifice will likely be needed, but it *will* achieve our end goal. I will be in touch. Goodheart out."

The console indicated the connection had been closed. Admiral Solez might as well have become a wax figure in his own office. Only his eyes and lungs were moving. *What the hell is he planning? How can this disaster possibly lead to victory?* His mind raced around like a carnival ride at five times the safe speed. Try as he might, he couldn't find any possible way.

He spent the next few hours trying to lead the disaster as best he could. There wasn't a lot to do that day that hadn't already been done, though he didn't know what else to do. That is until his mind replayed every step, every word, every order from the grand marshal. Blocks he never knew were there fell away, allowing him to realize the truth of the marshal's plan. When he remembered the marshal suggested there were different versions of the plan, despite Solez himself only ever knowing of one, his heart outright vanished. *No wonder he kept the plan going. It fell in perfectly with his own.*

Solez didn't give another order for close to an hour. He was too busy confirming what his heart already knew. Eventually, he looked up from his computer screens at his few pictures while rubbing his wedding band. Then, with a moon in his throat, he sent instructions to his agents. *I need to be sure, then I can act.*

Lieutenant Tua later found the admiral again gazing out his window at the masses below. Tua snapped into a perfect salute, which Solez returned weakly.

"At ease, Lieutenant," Solez said. "Did you bring everything I asked for?"

The young man handed him a clip-com, then glanced at the console as it started beeping. "Yes, sir! Every file we have is there, and Corporal Chang should . . . have . . . uhm . . . are you sure you don't need to answer—"

"Quite sure, Lieutenant. It's nothing important. Now then, you were saying something about Chang?"

Grand Marshal Goodheart glowered at the station in his office, or rather at the tense man sitting at it.

"What do you mean he's not answering?"

The middle-aged man dressed in an Interstar dress uniform threw his hands up with a sigh. "I mean I've been pinging him every way I know for an hour. He's not responding."

"He is the supreme commander of our forces. How can he not respond?!"

"I don't know! Sir, I don't know. I only know what I just told you."

Goodheart seethed. Of all the times for his most important piece on the board to go missing. He couldn't believe the man was ignoring him. He wouldn't be that stupid. But it didn't change the fact that forces needed to move, and the man who could move them was incommunicado.

"Try his aide, Lieutenant Tua," Goodheart said. "Gustov, try to get a hold of Roland. If Admiral Solez can't be reached, we may just have to give the order ourselves."

The man at the computer looked back at his leader. "Sir, won't that expose us?"

"Interstar is too busy chasing other tails to worry about anomalous messages from God knows who using channels no one knows exist. Even if they notice, they won't dig deep enough to find out the truth."

"And if they do?"

"Then we'll switch to plan C. Nothing will stop my ascension. Nothing."

Kor'Agel Colark remained still with all four arms in the air as if he were about to clap a bug. As the incense burned out in the shrine in front of him, his lower body remained coiled under him, with his upper body held straight up in the middle like a snake displaying a threat. He let the sun warm his naked, grey, carapace-like skin to help keep him relaxed. The layer of antennae lay relaxed on his head as the last wisps of the incense floated in front of him.

Kor'Agel Colark blew the four candles out one by one. The ritual left him feeling more comfortable than he had in days. There wasn't the slightest hint of a headache for a change, nor any tension anywhere.

A far cry from his first anniversary address, where he had to fight past his head feeling like it was splitting in two. Then again, he had learned well from that first time.

His speech was written and planned. He knew what to say and how he planned to say it. Every detail had been set in place days ago. He also had more support from the military than he had that first time. He knew some of it to still be shrouded in their own agenda, but at least they were keeping appearances, which he preferred over the barely veiled glares of threat and contempt he'd gotten before.

His prayer complete, Kor'Agel Colark left his shrine room and entered his main quarters. Like most places of high status, the walls were primarily dark violet, though there were accents of silver here and there that always appealed to him. While hardly a man who craved such opulence, he did like how the designers had made an effort to ensure the light appeared to move down the walls, as if the light itself were instead water flowing along the curves and lines. The carpet, a lighter shade of purple, provided the extra cushion on top of the soft elastic surface below. The walls were otherwise bare, save for a shelf that held awards, commendations, and letters of pledge from those who served on his personal guard. Two of these lay on their faces, a reminder of those who gave their lives for him on Earth. Highly adorned doors led to his sleeping chamber, his social room, and others beyond, while his black, crescent-shaped desk sat in front of a window looking out over the city below.

Kor'Agel Colark went to this window first and looked out over the city. Winding spires like twists of rope filled the skyline, with several arches dotting the ground level. The curved and beveled windows made sure the glare of the sun went in all directions, allowing the light of their star to spread Galla's favor to all. He felt some of this favor penetrate the window and warm his naked body even now. As always, it put him at ease within seconds. He felt as if he might be able to float as he absorbed the sun and sights outside.

Streams of shuttles and air cars went along carefully plotted lines to ensure only a few lines of the cityscape were blocked by traffic. In the distance, he could see the Yunilin temple. A great dome fashioned in the brightest of silver, carved to resemble the eye of Galla, which even Colark had to admit was nothing more than a jantan eye, at least visually. Though that did not mean it was unimportant. Indeed, he had grown up in the temple, and it, in turn, had helped him on his journey to the office he now held. He could only pray that the all-mighty Galla would help him do what had to be done to preserve his nation.

The chime of his door brought the kor'agel rushing back to the moment. He let a ruffle pass through his antennae, then turned to hit the answer button on his desk. "Identify yourself."

"Auro Jals, sir," a familiar voice said. "You asked me to make sure you were preparing at this time."

I know myself too well. He had once again lost himself in thoughts of his people. "Thank you, Auro. I will be out in a moment."

Another ruffle went through the kor'agel's antennae. They rattled for a second, then settled down as he accepted that he did indeed have work to do.

Kor'Agel Colark walked over to where his royal attire was waiting for him. Unlike the simple clothes he wore when meeting Gold 1, these held meaning. He walked on top of them so he could slip his many legs into the lower robes, which were a bright violet adorned in silver clasps with green braids running between each clasp. The kor'agel tightened the clasps so the robe hugged his body, then lifted the main portion onto his torso.

The green cords continued to run all the way up the clothing until they became a green collar that held everything in place. The rest of the upper portion hugged his form tighter to allow movement and to show his own personal power, or so the theory went. His arms were bare, a symbol of status reserved only for the highest of officials, or by those in the service that required them for one reason or another. His chest held a layer of silver cloth decorated with patterns that showed moments in his family history. Battles won and lost, people who mattered, those who didn't matter at all, birth, death, and in the middle over his lungs, etchings of himself, with the eye of Galla over him, blessing his ascension into the kor'agel's office.

What a joke. As he again tightened clasps around his body, Colark found himself again laughing at the whole idea. Even the kor'agel was seen as a sign of strength and power. A message proclaiming, "Behold! The great leader of the glorious Marcallan people. The rightful rulers of the galaxy." While he had no doubt Galla had helped him achieve his position, the idea that it made him some being worthy of so much awe and wonder threatened to coil his antennae into a mess worse than matted fur. *Perhaps in time, I can change that too.*

Now clothed, Kor'Agel Colark pressed the call button again. "Hisuto, please have the auro join me."

"At once, Kor'Agel!"

Almost immediately, Auro Jals entered the kor'agel's chambers. He cupped his hands around his heart in a jantan salute with tight antennae, but he only held it for a moment. His social armor had thin plates of protection around his vital organs, while the rest of it was the same military dark purple. His had more green accents in it than silver since he, more than the kor'agel, was in charge of actively fighting for the people. He wore a simple pistol on his top hip, the only weapon such a uniform allowed.

Kor'Agel Colark placed his left hands over his heart with a smile. "At ease, Olon. There's no one here to impress but me."

Auro Olon Jals chuckled. "It is hard to break old habits. That robe triggers my training more than anything else."

"'This robe' is why I need you. I can never reach the clasps behind my shoulders. Could you get them, please?"

Olon again smiled while gesturing for the kor'agel to turn around. He did so, allowing Olon to pull the rest of the upper portion tight around the kor'agel's top shoulders. Having done this before, Olon knew how tight to make it. Once all were secure, the top portion of the robes now moved like a layer of skin over Colark's body. The two of them flicked the cords around so they flowed and hung like they were supposed to, and then Colark nodded victory.

"Thank you. I suppose it's time."

"It is," Olon said. "Are you sure you want to risk it? We still don't know who is a part of the conspiracy."

Collark shook his head dismissively. "No. If I don't appear at this, the people will wonder, and that will weaken my position. If I am going to affect change, I am going to have to be the all-mighty leader tradition expects of me." The kor'agel adjusted his collar and some of the clasps under his arms, then slumped with a sigh. "Do you remember when all we dreamed of was building a spire that touched the clouds?"

"Every day," Olon said. He handed Colark a green and silver necklace that held nothing but the silver eye of Galla, outlined by the purple threads of life, time, self, and soul. "But as Galla once said, sometimes one must sacrifice their dreams to ensure the dreams of others can be made true."

A soft rustle came from Colark's antennae. Not because he disagreed. Indeed, he knew that in order to save his people from themselves, he would probably never again see an architect's table. But just because he had accepted that trade did not mean it hurt any less to lose the dream that had, in fact, gotten him here in the first place.

However, the rustle lasted only a moment. Colark then accepted the necklace and strung it around his neck to complete the outfit.

"Majestic, my lord," Olon said. Colark's glare said death, but his still antennae said otherwise. "You look perfect. Shall we go?"

"Not yet."

"What's missing?"

Kor'Agel Colark returned to his window. "I don't know. Them, maybe. One last change to my speech. Perhaps nothing but my own contempt for what this position is supposed to represent."

"Or . . . a secret desire to not go through with it?"

Perhaps. Colark stole one last look out the window, breathed in the glow of the spires, then shook his head. "Come on, Auro. Let us begin the festivities for our . . ."

A furious beeping from the desk drew both of their attention. This wasn't a usual announcement. This was a fast-repeating alert signal that announced an emergency communique being sent directly to the kor'agel. Such things were rare and were even less often good news. Olon seemed stunned by it, while Colark wasted no time checking to see if the news was good or bad.

"Identify yourself."

"Prefect! Thank God we got through. You and I need to talk, just us, with zero chance of being overheard, *now*!"

It was the voice of Lieutenant Colonel Harlem.

Bad news.

CHAPTER 19

CAESAR'S PALACE

Jason almost fainted when the prefect told him where they'd be meeting. His idea of a private conversation had entailed about thirty encryptions that were constantly changing. Instead, he was taking a Marcallan shuttle down to the surface to meet the man in person. One human and two Holdrens, all in full armor and weapons, heading into the presidential palace of the Marcallan government! This was insane, even by Jason's standards.

Yet there he was, flying what to him was little more than a purple burrito with a large, vertical triangle on each side serving as wings. The weapons and armor were actually the prefect's idea in case of trouble, though that did little to calm Jason's nerves. *I can only imagine how his personal guard feel about this.*

Insane or not, he had no time to offer a better plan. So, Jason followed the landing pattern precisely, hoping the sensor scramblers were doing their job without attracting other attention. The FLARE soldier who put it in told him it had never failed before, but it only takes once to get them killed. Thankfully, no sign of detection was ever seen. Jason eased the shuttle into a bay just big enough for it, set her down, and led Sundale and Reneca out a side door into the bay.

Two guards were there to meet him. One of which was a familiar, very round face Jason remembered from the last time he had landed on a Marcallan heavy cruiser. Though it took him a moment longer to remember the Marcallan equivalent for the rank of full lieutenant in Calnav.

"Araf Malook, I believe?" Jason said, a bit surprised himself at how happy he sounded to see him.

Araf Malook bowed, though his eyes remained heavy. "I am honored you remember me. How ironic that I am once again here to lead you to the pre . . . fect . . . wings?! And who is she?"

Jason glanced at the Holdrens as Malook pointed at them, then chuckled. "Fate likes to give us the same job sometimes, and those are long answers we don't have time for. But I assure you, she can be as trusted as Yarain, so please lead on."

Malook ruffled his antennae, then turned and led the way while the other soldier fell to the rear of their group. They marched at a quick pace through incredibly adorned and vibrant corridors, some of which held pieces of art that would put many Earth artists to shame. All seemed to capture individuals wearing the same robes of violet, silver, and green, which led Jason to theorize that these might be past prefects. Malook never lost speed, even when he rounded a corner. Jason wondered if they shouldn't just make a run for it, but then he realized that fast walking could be explained away. Jantan soldiers, with Interstar soldiers between them, running through the halls of such a place was more likely to cause outright panic, followed by a firefight.

Thankfully, Jason was able to keep pace without long strides, though Sundale and Reneca did drop to their hands and paws so they could trot better. The entourage encountered no one on the mad dash toward a pair of large doors with even more intricate carvings of jantans and other things Jason didn't have time to absorb. Malook hit a panel on the side without even looking at the honor guard.

The doors opened, and Gold 1 was led inside a massive space Jason couldn't ignore. It was filled with purple carpet, silver mats on the floor, and slight-green accents everywhere. The walls were full of drapes holding a vast array of symbols and insignias, all in variations of the same three colors. Displays on the far wall made Jason think of an Earth living room, while another space on the opposite end looked like a small kitchen, though he couldn't quite find something he could recognize as a sink or stovetop. The roof itself made a dome that had to be at least ten feet above Jason's head and was comprised of something that looked like marble.

As the mission at hand finally broke through the awe, Jason found the prefect standing in front of a set of windows wearing the same robes as those in the paintings. *Theory confirmed.* Auro Jals stood right beside him while half a dozen personal guards dotted the walls.

Half training, half to break the tension of the moment, Jason first gave a salute his crew echoed. The prefect bowed with a slight erection of his antennae, though he did sneak a long look at Sundale. No doubt for the same reason as Malook.

"Skip the protocol, Colonel," the prefect said. "What is this about?"

Here goes nothing. "Sir, we have confirmation that your life is in immediate danger."

"What? What kind of danger?"

"No time for that. We need to get you to a secure location."

"Make the time, Colonel! I won't run and hide without details."

"Sir, with all due respect, the longer I'm here, the more danger you and I are in."

"Only my personal guard, Auro Jals, and Hilashan Forin know you're here. No one else would dare scan this palace hard enough to find you. Now explain this danger to me!"

And to think I admired his stubborn streak not that long ago. "Polaris was working with the Marcallan conspiracy to have you killed here, *right here*, and put the blame on Interstar. With you dead, your successor would rally the people in a campaign of vengeance against us. Now that part of the danger has passed because a couple of days ago, we captured . . . what the?"

The roof gave a loud thunk, and then the dome began to slowly open up like a giant door. The dome became two halves that retracted into the sides of the floor, exposing the room to the open air. A loud crackling met them that triggered Jason's home instincts because it sounded like a thousand rattlesnakes. He then realized that it was, in fact, Jantan antennae. A lot of them. Jason looked out and saw platforms and stands that seemed to stretch for miles full of jantans. *Oh, holy mother of shit.*

The crackling quickly faded in favor of the familiar murmur of voices as people realized the prefect was not alone. He could only imagine the many calls being made to their equivalent of 9-1-1 to report that their prefect was under attack by Interstar soldiers. *Great. What's next?*

It was the prefect who spoke first however. "Who opened the canopy?! The speech wasn't due for another thirty minutes."

Jason slowly drew his sidearm while glaring at Auro Jals. "I suspect one of your loyal subjects had a hand in it."

A hard voice from behind sent Jason whirling around to aim at it while he deployed his helmet. "Incorrect, Colonel."

Sundale and Reneca had also taken up their rifles, as had the entire personal guard. However, they were staring down the barrels of six heavily armored, heavily armed Marcallan special forces. Behind them came Hilashan Forin, also in heavy armor. His lighter complexion made him almost glow as the sun hit his features. Yet there was no light in his smile or his eyes. The personal guard moved to stand in front of their prefect while Gold 1 stood between them.

"Stand down!" the prefect said. "These soldiers are no threat to me or our people."

Hilashan Forin only scowled. "No, but *you* are."

Jason's mouth fell open in a silent gasp. Of all the people on his list of suspects, this guy had to be down in the fifties. Back on Earth, he had shown very tight signs of loyalty to the prefect. Even backing down when confronted without a word. *The perfect traitor.*

"Wow," Jason finally said. "Talk about a change. Loyal campaign manager to—"

"I was never loyal to this grishta!" *I don't think I want that translation.* "My campaigns were my own! I was doing what we must to ensure the future of our people. To see that Vultoo's vision was made true."

"*Vultoo's* vision?" Jals said. "Vultoo was mad. The only prefect to have his image stricken from our halls, and for good reason."

"He alone saw the truth. He saw our future. Our destiny. He saw a mighty empire, second to no one, feared by all, the owners of Galla's creation."

"And how many have died in pursuit of it?" Reneca said. "How many *more* will die?"

Hilashan Forin's antennae rattled, though a couple of his soldiers did glance his way. "You speak as if you were there, but you are new to their crew. They are hardly innocent. Their fleets flattened *three* of our colonies."

"Your fleets destroyed **TWENTY** of ours," Sundale said. "You killed millions of innocent civilians in Polaris."

"Rightful penance for their crimes and yours! You should understand that better than anyone. Do you not wish vengeance for what they did to you? What they did to your world?"

Sundale gave an odd breath that was equal parts sigh, growl, and stress relief. Jason risked a look his way and found his ears back, but there was no shudder to be found.

"Not if more have to die for it," Sundale said.

Hilashan Forin shook his head with another rattle. "Weak. Pitiful. This is why you need to be under our rule. You have no sense of right. You have no honor!"

A buzz from behind again triggered Jason's instincts. He flinched but held his aim as Jals' voice echoed behind him. "You are the one without honor, Forin! Galla has chosen the leader of our people. *You* are the one who ordered assaults without permission. *You* were the one to break treaties. *You* are responsible for the deaths you claim to want vengeance for."

Well, that explains a few things. Jason had the sudden sense that Forin had had more direct control over Jals than anyone ever knew. In the span of a second, Jason's mind went over his many encounters with the jantans. Jals had been there for the assault on the Golain outposts, but so had Forin. Come to think of it, all those years ago when Jason had been a POW himself, when Jals had given the order to try a brainwashing technique on him, Jals hadn't looked too happy about it. And of all the engagements reported, not one reported anyone ever having the chance to fight for their lives in a sword duel. *Have I been wrong about him all these years?*

As much as Jason wanted to explore that thought, the present held a bit more urgency. Hilashan Forin's antennae had gone straight up like a layer of spiked hair. Jason had seen this before, only once, when he'd managed to get Jals absolutely pissed.

"You go too far, Auro. I was willing to spare you, but now I see you are as demented as he is. This has gone on long enough. To all of you, this grishta is no leader of ours. We deserve better. We *are* better. Stand aside, let this come to an end, and help me wage a campaign that will see our people achieve our rightful place in this galaxy." Every member of the personal guard moved as one, closing ranks even tighter around their prefect. "So be it. You will die with him!"

Forin drew his weapon, and Jason also shifted into the line of fire. He stood between two members of the personal guard, providing an extra layer of armor over the seam in theirs. Several of Forin's men glanced his way while the crowd outside began to murmur. This seemed to stop Forin before he could fire. His eyes went out to the masses beyond, and his weapon lowered slightly.

"Forgot about them, didn't you?" Jason said. "I'm guessing this wasn't even a contingency plan."

Forin scanned the crowd he could see for a moment, then his eyes narrowed, and he retook his aim. "It changes nothing. They cannot hear what is being said."

"And why does that matter?" Reneca said slowly.

Jason laughed when the Hilashan gasped silently. "Not sure the masses would agree with you, Hilashan? They may not have ears, but they have eyes. Clearly, they can see what is going on, and do you know what they see? They see *you*, aiming *your* weapon at *their* prefect. And they see an enemy soldier standing in defense of him."

"It won't stop me," Forin said. "I have plans to deal with those who don't fall in line. The only thing I can't control is *him*."

"Then what? Will you wait around for them to seek vengeance on you? Your plan is falling apart here, Hilashan. Why not quit while you're ahead?"

"I would think after our many engagements, Colonel, you would know, I don't quit until I am victorious."

Jason knew his armor would never hold up. He would be the first to fall, and almost certainly before he got to fire a shot. He thought about firing first, but then an idea struck him. If he was going to toss a wrench into Hilashan Forin's plans, he could borrow an idea from those ancient TV shows he loved so much. *Perhaps today is a good day to die.*

Jason stood straight, retracted his helmet, and extended his arms. "Then go ahead. Fire. Inscribe our names in history."

The murmur outside only grew. Both Holdrens growled. Some of Forin's men fidgeted with their holds on their weapons. One seemed to rock a little as if unsure if he should move or not. Forin held his aim for an eternity, and Jason stared him down, hoping things wouldn't hurt so much this time.

Hilashan Forin smiled, but before he could fire, a bleating dual tone began to echo throughout the city. The crowd murmur grew to a roar while a device held by both Forin and Jals' belts went crazy. Forin growled, pretty close to a Holdren actually, and answered his device.

"Report!"

"Interstar signatures detected!" A voice from the device said. "Interceptors are up, but they've already breached the atmosphere."

"What?! How did they get past our perimeter sensors?"

"Unknown, sir."

"Where are they..."

He trailed off as a deafening hum came from overhead. Both Holdrens pinned their ears back with a soft whine as it seemed to settle right above the estate room. Eyes went up, but none found a thing. Not until two holes appeared to open in the air above them, followed by a pair of six-legged machines, each standing four feet tall, with an armored twin-barreled PMG turret on top, thundering onto the floor right between the prefect's line and Hilashan Forin's.

Forin had just enough time to turn and run before the walkers opened fire. Half of his men tried to follow while the others fired futilely at the walkers. Those that stood their ground were sliced apart, while two of the sprinters were caught halfway down the corridor, though Forin was not among them. The 'engagement' lasted only a few seconds before all was quiet aside from the crowd outside, and the still bleating tones in the city.

Admiral Redding's voice came from a speaker on one of the walkers. "Our fighters managed to pull off their first responders, but it won't be long before they realize where they came from. Prefect, we believe you should come with us."

"I will not abandon my people!" Prefect Colark said.

"You won't be," Jason said. "Forin said it himself; the only thing he can't control is you. So long as you live, his coup can't happen."

Before he could reply, Jals put a hand on the prefect's shoulder. "He's right, sir. Your government lives so long as you do. We don't know what else he has planned. You are not safe in our space."

"He can't harm me here," Prefect Colark said. "Not anymore."

"With respect, sir, you are wrong," Reneca said.

She was pointing to the horizon. When Jason followed her finger, he could see four tiny spheres, Jantan fighters, heading their way. He knew the Gold Group was on board their captured ship, but he realized that if Forin was willing to commit fighters, one ship from orbit would be all he needed to erase the prefect from the surface. Worse, once he realized they had come in the ship Polaris built, he could even use it to turn public opinion back to his side. Maybe not forever, but for long enough.

"Prefect, you have to trust us," Jason said. "You won't survive here. Not until you can be sure who else you can trust."

Prefect Colark glanced in every direction. His guard, Jals, Jason, the still scattering crowd outside. His breathing got faster by the second, and Jason didn't blame him. Things had gotten really complicated really fast. In his place, Jason wasn't sure he'd be taking it half as well.

Finally, the prefect said, "I cannot abandon my people."

"You're not," one of his guards said. "You are ensuring the traitors have no way to win. The people saw what happened here. So long as you live, Forin cannot lie enough to change that."

"Even if I did run, I can't escape on an Interstar ship."

"Good thing we didn't come in one," Admiral Redding said through the walker. "It's a long story, but we came in a ship that looks very much like a Histmar class heavy cruiser. They still don't know it's us, but we need to leave before that changes."

The prefect held the side of his head for a moment, then nodded. "Very well."

The hum above shifted to the end of the room. A hole again opened up, this time in the shape of the side hatch of a commando transport. Reneca and Sundale were sent inside first, followed by the prefect, his guard, and Auro Jals. Jason went last and strapped into a seat once inside. The jantans had to hold onto bars above their heads to ensure balance since none of the seats would accommodate their physiology. The transport closed its hatch and hovered over the estate room. Thrusters from below the walkers propelled them into the bays they had come from, and then the transport blasted into orbit with all speed.

"We'll need to make a detour," Jason said. "We can't go straight for the ship if they know we're here."

"Don't worry, sir," the pilot said. "We do this kind of thing every other Saturday. Just sit back, relax, and enjoy the ride."

The ship made a hard bank that thrust everyone into their seats or, in the case of the jantans, left them pulling on the bars for dear life. Once his stomach crawled back into place, Jason shook his head to keep his last meal from coming up. *Who knew you could miss your own ship in a matter of seconds?* Scorns were fast and nimble, but they were built with that in mind, which meant that the same maneuvers weren't nearly as hard on the body. Transports and dropships on the other hand, were only fitted with enough inertial dampeners to keep the crew alive. Comfort wasn't anywhere in the design. Though at least he had a seat, so he could hardly complain.

The occupants had to endure half a dozen more hard turns before a soft thud announced their landing on the *Hulio*. Jason didn't trust that until the pilot announced, "We're down! Transport is locked and secure."

Every Jantan released the bar so they could rub shoulders that were no doubt sore. Jason unbuckled his straps and chuckled when he was rubbing his own shoulders for different reasons.

"Sorry about the rough ride," Jason said.

"We've faced worse," one of the honor guards said.

"I don't doubt it. Come on. Let's get you into more comfortable quarters."

"Colonel Harlem, I insist that I meet the ship's commander first," the prefect said. "He saved my life. I want to thank him in person."

Jason thought about refusing given the situation, but he had his doubts that the prefect would take no for an answer. "Very well. Follow me. Sun, make sure Gold 1 is hot, just in case."

"Copy that!" Sundale said.

Jason led Prefect Colark, Auro Jals, and, after some negotiating, only two of his honor guard down the corridors for the nearest lift. Despite being built by humans, the ship still had the same rubbery flooring that always looked like metal to Jason, despite how it felt. Polaris had spared no detail, copying the same violet on the walls that turned darker in the hangar, as well as egg-shaped doors. Lighting strips tucked in the ceiling were barely visible, yet their light reflected down the squarer corridors enough to brighten nearly every inch. Green lights oscillated along the walls to announce the ship was under combat status, which is a detail Jason had to remind himself every time he passed one.

The lift itself wasn't all that different than Interstar's, though it was a little longer. *Makes sense. Jantans are naturally longer than we are.* They rode the lift up two decks and walked through a few short, though well-guarded, corridors into the Marcallan bridge. Jason had to stop and take a moment to reset his mind. He'd never seen a Marcallan bridge intact before, much less been on it while it was in operation.

The pause came more because for the most part, it wasn't that different from the CIC on the *Alamo*. More a large oval than a square room, but otherwise the same. Stations lined the walls while one wall had four large displays full of information. The only real difference came in the middle of the room. Two human chairs—a detail Polaris *had* spared—sat dead center of a platform that was raised five inches above the rest of the floor. Multiple duty stations sat in a ring around the platform, but they faced out instead of in so the commander could see their screens for himself. Green alert lights dotted the ceiling, casting a soft green glow over much of the room.

Admiral Redding stood on the platform, along with a woman with red hair and a soft complexion who was almost as tall as Redding. Jason recognized her as Redding's XO, though he'd never interacted with her outside of the briefest of moments when receiving orders. Even then, it had been pure business, which was the only thing he knew about her.

She barely acknowledged their arrival, while Admiral Redding needed only a second to make his way to them once he saw them. He shook the prefect's hand cordially enough, though his scowl the entire way suggested another feeling entirely.

Whatever his feelings, his voice betrayed none of it. "Welcome aboard, Prefect. I'm Admiral Mason Redding. I'm sorry we have to meet under these circumstances."

"As am I, Admiral," The prefect said. "Please do not blame Colonel Harlem for my presence here. I didn't give him a choice."

Wow, he is good. And thank you, by the way.

"I see. I suppose it's just as well. At least I get to meet the man we're all trying to save."

"And I thank you for doing so. I only hope it did not cost you many soldiers."

"Didn't cost us any. Our fighters only went in enough to get the attention of your first responders. Once space was made, they disengaged just as fast."

"Something I will have to address when this is all over," Auro Jals said. "I thought I trained them better."

Admiral Redding nodded with a humorless laugh. "I didn't say it was easy. But I train my troops hard."

Jason gave a chuckle of his own. *That he does.* "If I may ask, sir, what's our status?"

"We're on course for the border. We should be hitting United Systems space in two days. So far, no one knows we're not a Marcallan ship. Not sure how long we can keep that up, however."

"I can help you with that," Jals said. "If I may?"

He gestured toward the center chair, and Admiral Redding stood frozen for a moment. Jason could see the same thoughts in his eyes that were going through his own mind. *Are we sure we can trust him?* A ridiculous idea he couldn't pry himself away from. They had just stood together in the face of certain death, and yet he still didn't trust the man? Then again, there was that scar on Jason's left side, right at the armpit. A reminder of all of the things Jals had put him and his crew through. One doesn't just forget all of that. To his credit, Jals didn't move so much as a single antenna. He only held his pose, waiting for a reply.

After a minute that felt like months, Admiral Redding huffed out a breath. "I'll take all the help I can get."

He gestured for Auro Jals to proceed, and the two of them headed for the center station. Jason couldn't even form a theory as to their plans, so he didn't try. He instead watched them go until a sigh from the prefect drew his attention.

"I sometimes wonder if there's any chance," the prefect said.

"Chance of what, Prefect?" Jason asked.

"Peace. As I said, I don't know everything, but I do know you and Auro Jals have faced each other before many times. It's clear your people still hold him in contempt, and I suppose I would as well, were I in your place. I might be able to stop my people, but how do we overcome that much blood?"

"By giving it a chance to dry. Hilashan Forin was right about one thing; we're not innocent. We may not have gone as far as you . . . as some of your people, have, but we've done some pretty nasty things in our time as well. There is blood between us, and there will always be blood between us. The only way to overcome it is to stop the flow. So long as that blood is still wet, there will never be peace. That's why we're doing this, Prefect. You are the best chance we've ever had to put an end to the bloodshed."

"What if I can't stop it? What if Hilashan Forin can't be stopped. What if my attempts are the wrong—"

"Stop there, Prefect. You can't think like that. Once you do, you defeat yourself. You try your best, you consider where things could go without dwelling on them, you make the best choices you can, and you let things fall where they will. In my experience, it's better to be confidently wrong than hesitantly right. Once a choice is considered and made, you follow it through. The moment you lose yourself in 'what ifs,' you lose any chance of making the right choice."

Prefect Colark's eyes seemed to brighten almost immediately. He soon nodded. "Thank you, Colonel. I hope to be worthy of that trust."

"Prefect, more than ever, I have no doubt of it."

CHAPTER 20

I SHOULDN'T HAVE ASKED

Yarain winced as the bandage came off. No fur this time, but the wound was still a little sensitive. Thankfully, the haaj'kar doctor was far more gentle than Sundale had described. The male, with dark-tan skin and a head like a diamondback, very carefully pressed his gloved hand along the burn. The touch hurt so little that Yarain didn't even change her ear position.

"Very nice," he said. "You should stop feeling it by tomorrow. It'll take another two or three days for the fur to start growing back, but it *will* grow back. You have my assurance on that. By the time I'm done with you, there won't be any sign you were ever wounded. Until then, don't lick or scratch it, and you'll be fine."

A matter of perspective perhaps, but Yarain appreciated the care all the same. The burn and subsequent care had created a bald spot on her right cheek just over an inch long and maybe half an inch wide. She didn't like seeing her own skin so prominently exposed. The only saving grace was that it still matched her fur pattern, so at least she didn't have this glaring space of pink standing out against the white and gold of her fur. She also couldn't really hunt since the biting force required made the wounded area hurt too much to be worth it, though that, too, was already much better than it had been.

The doctor grabbed another instrument from the table. "Now this will sting slightly, but it will heal the wound and help your fur follicles rejuvenate themselves. Are you ready?"

Yarain ticked her ears forward. The Haaj'kar, having worked with Holdrens as long or longer than Jason, recognized it and proceeded to apply a clear gel to the wound. It did indeed sting, but only enough to cause a slight wince from Yarain. She held still while the wound was covered, followed by a new bandage that covered the wounded area entirely. The application was done with more care and attention to her physiology than any human, aside from Marcy and Doctor Blount, had ever taken. *Never thought I'd be glad to see a haaj'kar doctor here on Earhart.* The station had seen an uptick in Kapon members coming in and out, so naturally, they had wanted their own doctors to be on staff. They had also brought some of their expertise with them, which meant Yarain's treatment was more effective than anything Interstar could provide.

"And we're done here," the doctor said. "I want to see you again in three days to check it, but if I'm right, that will be the last time you need to see me for a long time."

"Thank you," Yarain said.

She slid off the bed and headed out of sickbay. Harrison and Shillin were leaning on the wall, waiting for her.

"Well, you don't look dead," Harrison said.

Yarain huffed a soft chuckle. "I'll make a full recovery."

"That's good," Shillin said. "How do you *feel*?"

Yarain put her hand up to the bandage. "Uncomfortable."

"I can imagine," Harrison said. "Those things drive me crazy, and I only have skin. I can't imagine fur making it much better."

"I'll live. Any details yet on our next mission?"

"Yeah, there isn't one. Mission got scrubbed. The operation that was to pave the way got paved over. We're on standby for the time being."

"At least we get to rest."

Alert lights and tones filled the corridor, followed by PAICCA. "Set condition 3! Repeat, set condition 3! Stay alert! Major Yarain to flag intel. Repeat, Major Yarain to flag intel."

Harrison glared at Yarain. "I blame you."

Yarain growled, but it was more a play growl than an actual one. "Follow."

The three of them made their way to a lift, took it to the center of the station, and headed straight for a small room off of the main command deck designated for intelligence. Two opposite walls were covered in screens, with more stations situated below one of the walls. A holo-table sat in the middle of the room while the far wall was loaded with clip-coms, data storage devices, and two communications stations. Marshal Garmon stood looking over Lieutenant Sarson's shoulder at one of the communications stations. The rest of the room was a buzz of chatter, both in the room and over comms.

With her team on standby, having one of them used for his particular skill set made *some* sense. Calling Yarain in at the same time made none at all, unless things were about to go very bad.

Marshal Garmon waved them down the moment she saw them arrive. "Skip the salute, Major. We may have bigger fish to fry."

That's never a good sign. "May I ask what this is about, ma'am?"

"We've been seeing a lot of comms traffic on channels that don't exist, if you get my meaning, over the last couple of days. More than can be explained, and it's all been directed at Polaris space."

"Spies?" Harrison asked.

"That's what I'm trying to figure out," Sarson said as he worked on his terminal.

Yarain's tails started waving. "Why is that grounds for condition 3, ma'am?"

"Because the activity just spiked to near triple," Garmon said. "With just as many return signals. All coming and going from Earth itself."

That's not a good sign, either. Though Interstar had managed to capture a great many Polaris assets, no one believed they'd gotten them all. Not yet, anyway. The idea of assets still active on Earth, with access to the kinds of channels that aren't listed *anywhere*, explained a lot about the marshal's caution. As well as why Yarain had been called. Without saying so, Garmon had shown she considered COB team above suspicion. If an asset needed to be silenced, she would need such a team. *So much for rest.*

Yarain had just finished alerting the rest of COB team to stand ready when Simon came in with clip-com in hand. "Sorry I'm late, ma'am. I—"

"No need, Lieutenant," Garmon said. "I know. Maybe you can help us cut through the encryptions we're seeing."

"I'll do what I can, but I don't have anything left to offer."

"I somehow doubt that. Come close. Sarson, are you getting *anything*?"

"Just what we know so far," Sarson said. "Still the same code name; 1-18-7."

A tech at the other terminal looked up. "Ma'am, Vice President Goodheart is demanding to know why his comms are down."

"Tell him we'll tell him when he needs to know," Garmon said.

Simon gave an almost Holdren head tilt. "Goodheart?"

Harrison answered first. "Alistair Goodheart. He was a councilman until the vice president was killed on Phoenix Perch. President Priolozi appointed him as the new V-P."

"Heh, guess the name is popular among politicians."

Yarain perked her ears and turned to face the young man. "What do you mean?"

"That's the same name as our grand marshal."

Several heads turned toward him as the room fell silent. Even Sarson snapped around to look at him from his station. To his credit, the young man didn't shrink, though he did swallow hard.

Garmon spoke slowly and with intent. "Do you happen to know if his middle name begins with an R?"

"Yeah . . . I think it does. Why do you—"

"Sarson—"

"On it—"

"Tracking Officer—"

"Working—"

"Yarain—"

"***READY!***"

Simon's head snapped around as the conversation bounced back and forth around him. When his head finally stopped moving, he took a breath to settle himself. "What am I missing here?"

Marshal Garmon only held up a finger, though a moment later, she did look back to nod at him with a tiny smile. Simon still glanced around the room, looking for an answer. Having little to do but wait, Yarain put her hand on his shoulder.

"We need to be sure before we explain, and we need to get sure quickly."

Simon nodded with a heavy breath. Then they both watched the flurry of activity as stations were worked and information passed between them. Too much for Yarain to keep track of, though her mind was also swimming with the possibility.

In the time between, Yarain tried to break the tension with Simon while also satisfying her own curiosity. "Any reason you never mentioned this before?"

Simon smiled and shrugged. "I had never heard of this guy before now. I don't generally pay attention to politicians. I can't even tell you who most of *my* political leaders are. The grand marshal has been everywhere, though. Almost impossible to not at least know his name. Even if I had, it wouldn't be the first time I'd met or heard of someone who shared an unusual name with someone else. Not something I would think worth reporting."

Yarain ticked her ears forward to agree. The more she thought about it, the more both arguments made sense. Even Jason tended to not give a lot of thought to politicians until he had to. And while a first and last name combination was rare, Yarain had also seen cases of it happening. Between the two, how many would see it worth reporting?

Even so, part of her tried to think back on anything she could have missed from Goodheart. Any clue that would have warned her. Those thoughts quickly died, considering she had barely had any contact with the man. She didn't know him well enough to see anything. The only item might have been his reluctance to let the assault proceed, and she hadn't been there for that. His cover had been too deep and too good. Though how ironic that, if it was indeed him, it had just been shattered so easily.

After eternal minutes, Sarson let out a breath as heavy as a carrier. "It all correlates. Every instance, every message, every clue we've got. It even lines up with periods where he fell off the grid for a bit. Quite honestly, ma'am, I think we have enough to be one hundred percent sure; Goodheart is an enemy asset."

Yarain was already tapping her wrist comm. to alert the rest of COB team to suit up. Meanwhile, Marshal Garmon turned to a wall station. "Do you have him?"

"Yes, ma'am," the soldier said. "He's in Bunker Seven. By all accounts, he's adamant that he not be disturbed."

"Now we know why. This much activity is definitely a set of orders. We can't just go after him until we know what he's planning."

Simon hummed and rubbed his chin. "From what I remember, much of Operation Juno relied on misdirection and destabilizing Interstar from within. Our assets were meant to cause chaos and prevent you from fully mobilizing."

"But that all collapsed when their attempt on the prefect failed," Yarain said.

"At which point the grand marshal ordered us to attack anyway. Just before I defected, I did hear a couple of officers talking about how the marshal had a bigger plan that not even my father knew about. I didn't think anything of it since my father was our supreme commander. Now I have to wonder if they were right."

"What bigger plan could the man have?"

"I don't know."

More silence fell on the room as everyone seemed to withdraw into themselves to think. Yarain certainly was, and her mind couldn't find anything. As vice president, Goodheart now had a lot of access to a lot of things. He could use it to cause a lot of damage, but with how the war had been going, it seemed unlikely he could really turn the tide of anything. Though, if Marcalla joined their side, it might tip the balance. Except with Kapon now allied with United Systems, even Marcalla was unlikely to be enough.

"We need more information," Yarain finally said. "Some tiny trail we can follow."

"I agree," Garmon said, "but we don't have anything to offer. All we've got is him yelling at us for blocking his phone, and that's not exactly telling since he's been yapping at us for a while now."

"Has he asked for anything specific lately?" Shillin offered.

"Nothing out of the ordinary. Protection, protocols, updates on the war. All stuff the previous V-P often asked for as well."

Simon lifted a heavy finger. "Wait . . . didn't Goodheart ask for Priolozi's recent itinerary?"

"Yes, he did. He said he wanted to . . ." Yarain could see the almost literal click in Garmon's mind that was echoed in her own. "Ah, shit! PAICCA! Emergency alert! Attack on the president is inbound. I say again, the president is under attack. Alert his security detail."

"Copy that, Marshal," PAICCA replied. "Alert pings sent. Any other details?"

"None available."

"Copy that."

Harrison's eyes glazed as things clicked into place for him, too. "This was the plan all along. It's why they attacked Phoenix Perch. It wasn't about the *Enterprise*. It was about the V-P. No one was surprised when Goodheart was appointed. If he could take out the president next—"

"A Polaris asset would be in command of the Republic. Major. Assemble your team, bring the bastard in, *alive*."

COB Team had already begun to move out. They only paused long enough to hear their specific orders.

Transmission detected.
Scale fifteen encryption . . . stand by . . .
Encryption broken.
Monitors active.
Attempting trace . . .

From: COMEXTCOL
To: EXTCOL 1315
Classification: TOP SECRET Eyes Only
Message:
EMERGENCY ALERT!

> Primary target has entered maximum security. Initiate contingency attack plan CS-21. Destroy target at any cost. Asset 1-18-7 is now threatened. Extraction order 010 activated. Divert all assets required.

End Message.

Transmission failed...
Repeat transmission detected...
Transmission successful...
ALERT! Pings match parameters 88972...
Forwarding to Office of the Prefect...
ERROR: Executive override active. Report blocked...
Attempting Contingency protocols...
ERROR: Executive override active. Protocols disabled...
ERROR: Reporting failed.

A familiar shudder woke Jason from his nap. He had taken a rare time when things seemed to be less dangerous to steal some sleep in the quarters that sat right off of the main hangar. He'd even managed several hours, but the moment he felt the ship vibrate under him, he knew exactly what had happened. He'd felt that same shudder before during the sleeper escort that became anything but. He tried to tell himself it could be any number of other things or that it was just another storm. No part of him believed either one.

Further confirmation came when his crew was once again called to the *Hulio*'s bridge. His crew got to the lift just behind a haaj'kar that looked like a crocodile with a much shorter snout and another Holdren of almost solid orange aside from a white underside. They were the lead pilots of the two Vindinsa squads they had managed to squeeze aboard the cruiser. *Not getting better here.* The strike craft commanders marched onto the bridge together, though not a single Holdren tail was still.

Prefect Colark and Auro Jals were already there, both huddled around what Jason had come to identify as the communications station. The soldier in the chair kept shaking his head at them. Each time he did, the antennae on both jantans rippled.

When no one even noticed their arrival, for the first time in his life, Jason abandoned all protocol. "All right! Somebody tell me how bad it is."

Admiral Redding doubled over in silent laughter. "How I wish General Manster had been here for that. Over here, Colonel." Admiral Redding directed them to the large displays on the wall. One image showed the Marcallan border that had a dotting of stations and outposts all along the stretch. It also showed a grey field that covered a lot of territory that had been behind them. The grey field got brighter near the border and ended right where their ship now sat.

"It would seem that Hilashan Forin has a larger reach than we thought," Redding said. "We thought we were heading through friendly lines, but the border's HL inhibitors have been activated. Very cleverly, I might add. He's overlapped their fields so that any ship coming or going can't jump to hyperlight, but they won't be forced out of it until they're several minutes into the field. The outposts know we're here, though. We know that first because the force-out range has been extended since we dropped out of hyperlight, and second because we've already got enemy ships shadowing our movements along the border."

Jason could feel his blood turning to ice. "How many?"

"That's the one saving grace. Our little incursion on Marcelis drew a lot of the fleet inward, looking for us. We're facing only three frigates and fifty Jantan fighters in our immediate theater. But Forin's forces won't be far behind, nor will other patrols. We're trying to make contact, but so far, the ships and stations are ignoring us, are under radio silence, have false orders, or who knows or cares? The point is, they aren't talking."

Jason stared at the sensor display. He saw the contacts of the enemy fleet as well as the inhibitor field. It would take hours to get out of the field's range at sublight. The border itself was lightly defended compared to normal, although the jantans knew by now they were only looking for one heavy cruiser. The ships alone were an even match. Add in even the weakest of outposts, and the odds got a lot less favorable. They could fly "up" over it, but the ships would just match and buy time for reinforcements to join. If they just sat there too long; other patrols would likely converge on them, assuming Forin's forces didn't find them first. If they turned back the way they'd come; they would almost certainly run into ships loyal to, or fooled by, Forin before they could reach hyperlight.

Even if they didn't, what then? Run around until they stumbled into loyal ships? Hope they gave up and shut down the HLS inhibitors? Spend the multiple hours, if not a full day, it would take to get out of range of the pulses that traveled for light-years? Assuming they didn't run into more overlapping outposts casting the same pulses. The list of choices started at horrible and got progressively worse.

Auro Jals and Prefect Colark soon approached the gathered group. Both of them had limp antennae and heavy eyes.

"We've tried everything," Colark said. "My heart won't accept anything other than their being loyal to Hilashan Forin. The other possibilities hurt even more. Whatever the reason, they won't listen to either of us."

"So, what can we do?" The orange Holdren said.

"I don't know," Auro Jals said. "We're both out of ideas. If we could take out even one of the outposts, the inhibitor field would drop dramatically. Enough for us to push our way through to the other side. But such an attack would demand extensive losses."

"Can't we get the Prefect out on a Scorn?" The haaj'kar pilot asked. "Once he's passed the line, the jantans will care more about him than the rest of us."

"Good thought, but impossible," Redding said. "The border outposts have sensors that can penetrate even the best of our cloaks. Even enemy ships are likely to spot them, thanks to the inhibitor field. At best, a cloaked Scorn would just be hard to target until it got close, but she'd never make it …" Admiral Redding slowly turned to face Colonel Harlem. Jason met his eyes, and he could see the light vanish from them. "I can't possibly ask that."

"I don't see another choice," Jason said.

It came without doubt or hesitation. He knew exactly what he was signing his group up for. He also knew that no one would turn it down. They knew what was at stake. If the prefect died, so would any hope for peace. They had all buried so many friends over the years. If they could put an end to those funerals, any one of them would give their lives without being asked.

"Ask what?" Prefect Colark said.

Admiral Redding stared at Jason for minutes that felt like days. His gaze soon shifted to the sensor screen. Then, he closed his eyes, took a deep breath, and faced the gathered pilots with even darker eyes than before. "Man your ships! You'll get your orders before you launch. Set condition one! Prepare to engage."

As alert tones and green lights filled the room, Admiral Redding called after Jason to stop him. "Colonel! Volunteers only. I won't order this of anyone."

Jason only smiled at him. "If I know my group, you won't have to."

CHAPTER 21

CHAINS OF COMMAND

Seeing Vespers running in full gear is never a good thing. When they are doing so without any call for condition 1, you know two things; something really bad is going on, and somebody, somewhere, is about to have a really bad day.

Yarain could only hope her team would be on the delivering end of that bad day as she led her team sprinting through the halls of Bunker Seven. One of many emergency command and control points on Earth's surface, this one was built specifically to house and protect any high-ranking officials in the area during an attack. That also meant defense against the very type of incursion they were conducting. While many such countermeasures had been taken from Goodheart's control, that did not mean he didn't have access to any, to say nothing of his own security team. They couldn't risk alerting them for fear that they were his own men, but Yarain had a bad feeling that if they didn't act soon, things were only going to get worse. Hence the charge down wide halls toward their target.

With no engagement in progress, the base only held a skeleton staff. What few soldiers were there managed to clear the way for COB team, though some had to hug the wall once they heard barks and yells from the team. They quickly reached an inner part of the base, and thanks to Marshal Garmon's clearance sent ahead of them, they were able to walk right through heavily fortified doors. The walls changed to having a rougher texture since this area was designed to be even more fireproof, as well as built to withstand attacks from ships and infantry. They passed by the CIC area, also sparsely manned, deeper into where the estate quarters were. Goodheart was confirmed to still be there, having met with generals only an hour before. A fairly common occurrence for such bunkers as the facility held robust communications equipment, and it gave the staff an excuse to test a few things.

When they reached the doors of Goodheart's suite, Marshal Garmon's codes ran out of use. Not even a Marshal could override the locks on these rooms, though the doors themselves weren't anything special. If the enemy was able to get this deep, another armored door wasn't likely to stop them, so the concern was more about privacy than defense. What was normally an annoyance was now a barrier to a high-value target.

Yarain gestured for Lieutenant Hark to prepare a direct way to open the doors while Sarson tried to use his skills to do so less violently. She then hit the door chime to see if neither method would be required.

"Who is it?" a gruff voice asked.

"Major Yarain, commander of the COB Team. We're here to take Vice President Goodheart into protective custody."

A different, smoother voice came on. "This is Vice President Goodheart. I think my personal guard can handle things, Major."

"With respect, we don't agree. They sent Vespers for a reason. The area is **NOT** safe. You need to come with us, now."

There was a long pause. Long enough for Yarain's tails to start waving. Sarson shook his head, suggesting his efforts were failing. Hark squatted by the door with her finger hovering over the button on the breaching charges.

Right as Yarain was about to give the order, Goodheart came back on. "Very well. But you'll need to wait a minute. I just got out of the shower, and I would like to make my escape in something more than a bathrobe. I'll be out shortly."

The panel changed color to suggest the connection had been broken.

"We're not that lucky," Captain Fickle whispered.

Yarain had to agree. She had no doubt taking him in wasn't going to be that simple. However, they couldn't be sure how it would get complicated until it did. For now, all she could do was perk her ears to see what she could catch from within.

At first, there were a lot of loud voices. Goodheart and his men seemed to be arguing about something, or perhaps orders were being shouted. Despite her ears, the walls were well sound-proofed, which meant she couldn't quite catch any words. After a pause in the shouting, there came one last shout that sounded very much like an order, followed by a sudden gathering of voices right at the door. Yarain tilted her head in confusion, then her eyes snapped up when she realized what they were up to.

She reached down, grabbed Hark by the collar, and heaved them both to the side of the door. They hit the floor just as a flurry of weapons fire tore through the door where they had been. Sarson and the rest of the team hugged the wall to ensure they stayed out of the line of fire. A couple of charges were destroyed by the barrage, though having not been armed, they fell harmlessly on the floor. Every helmet was deployed without anyone having to say a word.

"Flash and pop!" Yarain called out.

"Fire in the hole!" Hark said.

A command adopted from Harrison himself, Yarain's order was put to use the moment the remaining breaching charges blew the door open. Two flashbangs were thrown in, followed by the hard advance of Fickle and Rad. Their weapons, though set for stun, still flattened the four soldiers who had tried to ambush COB Team. The men managed a sharp yelp before they all hit the floor, out cold. Team Cobra filled the room, spreading out into the wide-open, well-furnished main room. Yarain led two others toward the back rooms while the rest searched the other rooms for any more resistance.

Yarain, Rad, and Tai marched into a bedroom bigger than Jason's quarters on the *Alamo*, with a king-size bed that had sheets more expensive than Yarain's weapon. Tai moved into the bathroom while Yarain and Rad went into a large back room. While no bigger than the living area in standard quarters, the furniture was again highly adorned and pressed. *Anything for a suit.*

Her attention was drawn to the far back wall as it seemed to close like a door. Yarain tilted her head in confusion, then perked her ears when Shillin rushed right up to the same wall. Two men tried to pop up from behind the couch and fire, but Yarain and Shillin were able to fire their stunners first. Both men hit the floor without a sound.

Shillin began to examine the wall as the team reported in.

"Back rooms clear," Harrison said over comms.

Fickle. "Main room clear."

Sarson. "Kitchen clear."

Tai's voice echoed from the bathroom. "Bed and bathrooms clear!"

Yarain. "Private room clear . . . I think. Converge on my position."

The team quickly joined her in the back room while Rad pressed on the back wall. She pulled on a latch of some kind, and the back wall opened up to expose a narrow tunnel that went into the wall for several feet, then turned out toward the outside of the base.

"I should have remembered this," Shillin said. "Many of these high-end suites have a secret escape run that is incredibly classified."

"How did you know about it?" Harrison asked.

"My mother was a diplomat who worked for President Hugo. I don't remember much about those days, but I do remember the one time we had to use it. This will lead to a bay that houses a single escape ship rated for at least HLS 16."

"We talking a corvette?" Fickle asked.

"More like a large Scorn."

"Single file then," Yarain said. "Check your corners—"

Alert tones echoed in the room ahead of PAICCA. "Alert! Set condition 1! Unknown forces have breached the base! All hands, report to inner bunker. Hatchet is on station. Repeat, Hatchet is on station."

"Oh, that's just perfect," Sarson said.

My sentiments exactly. Bad enough the base was apparently under attack, but their little warning had sent President Priolozi — call sign "Hatchet"— right into the middle of it. Or, more likely, the base was under attack *because* he had been sent there. Exactly which it was and why it happened were questions for later, though. Right now, Yarain had two missions and only one team.

"So, what now?" Tai said. "We go after our HVT, the president is staring down who knows what with a skeleton contingent of Terrines. We defend the president; our ex-*vice* president gets away to cause God knows what kinds of havoc."

"We do both," Yarain said. When all eyes turned her way, she stared them down with straight ears, helmet or not. "Rad, you're with me. Harrison, take the team, defend Hatchet at all costs. Hark, we need two Stiletto rounds each."

"Ma'am?" Harrison said. "With all due respect, you can't go in there without back-up. You don't know what you're facing."

"Neither do they." Yarain tapped at her wrist-com, and her armor pigment changed to match the color of the tunnel within. She then mounted her Stiletto rounds on her rifle while Shillin did the same to her armor. "You have your orders, Captain. Rad, on my six. **MOVE!**"

Yarain vanished down the tunnel with Lieutenant Rad hot on her tails.

Look harder.

The words echoed in John Harrison's mind as he led the remaining portion of COB Team toward the second suite. Major Yarain had said that to him so many times, and now more than ever, he would have to do exactly that. He still had no idea what she saw in him, but she had trusted him with this mission, and he wasn't about to disappoint her. Though that vow did nothing to pierce the cloud of doubt rolling in his head about how to actually make things happen. *Step by step,* his instructor used to say. *Check each thing off like a to-do list. Keep it simple, stupid.* While not exactly helpful, it was a start.

The first step was making contact with President Priolozi, which proved to be quite easy. PAICCA had already confirmed that he was unharmed and on his way to the second suite. By the time the rest of Cobra arrived, several Terrines were already there in full armor. Some were tight against the door, some behind support beams along the corridor, still more behind portable combat shields. Their weapons took aim, but fire was held once Cobra was seen as friendlies. Harrison went straight for the gunnery sergeant in charge of the gathered troops. She was the very picture of "average." Average height, medium build, middle-toned brown hair, smooth complexion.

"Captain Harrison, COB Team. Affectionately called the Cobras."

"Gunnery Sergeant Jules, 403rd, third company."

"What do we know?"

"Twenty soldiers, heavy armor, five confirmed power suits. They aren't hiding who they are. The troops are definitely Polaris. Armor, weapons, everything is consistent. They used a standard troop transport to get within our perimeter, then boom! Hit the outer guard before we knew what happened. General Zhou got caught in an armory outside the inner bunker. Old man didn't go down easy, but he still didn't last long. I haven't heard anything from anyone higher ranked."

"Hatchet?"

"Should be here any second, and he is *definitely* their primary target. One of our squads stuck outside heard the enemy directly order, and I quote with some offense taken, 'Forget the Terrines. Find Priolozi. We aren't leaving without his body.' We've called for reinforcements, but I don't know if our signal got through. We're dug in deep here. It's not a great plan, but I figure our best shot is to hold ground here."

Not against power suits. They weren't a common sight in the field because too many things could go wrong and turn them into target practice, but combined with an infantry unit, power suits could pose a significant problem in tight quarters like this. While Lieutenant Hark always carried a few Stiletto rounds just in case, the more Harrison thought about it, the more the idea of facing them head-on felt like a sure way to die. There was also the possibility that what the squad overheard was just smoke to distract them from the real objective, though given the intel they already had, the chances of that were low.

That left him with his mind swirling around all the many choices. Stand and fight. Run. Buy time for the president. Each one carried amazing risks, and any deaths doing it would be on his head. His commands would decide who did or didn't survive this engagement.

So many choices. So many tactics. So many lives depending on him. How could he choose? How could he make that choice?

Look harder.

She wasn't even there, yet Major Yarain was still glaring into him. Harrison closed his eyes and breathed for a second. Gunny Jules asked if he was okay, but Harry Fickle told her to just give him half a minute. Harrison took every bit of it he could to force his mind to settle down. *Just make a choice. Even if it's wrong, it's better than standing here doing nothing. You are a leader. You just have to look harder.*

Harrison's eyes snapped open when that thought dominated the swirl. How hard would the enemy be looking? Did they know about the tunnel? Even if they didn't, what if they did? What if they thought their target had made his escape? It was a huge risk; it assumed a lot of things not fully proven, and it was exactly what Major Yarain would do.

Harrison had decided to take that chance just before a call came down the corridor.

"Pan!"

Harrison responded with the counter sign, "Spoon!"

Not the cleverest of codes, but then again, who would believe any military would use something so ridiculous? Especially when it was only used by high value assets such as the president, and the counter sign wasn't anywhere near as intuitive.

Two men in front-line armor jogged down the corridor just ahead of a clump of more men. In the middle was the tan-skinned President Priolozi who had almost no hair on his head, though not even his eyebrows were gray. Two more soldiers came behind them, which brought the entourage count to ten plus Priolozi. *I'll take everybody I can get.*

As the group moved past the fortifications, Harrison stepped forward to meet their charge. "Mister President. Good to see you well, sir."

"I wouldn't call dodging plasma 'well,' son," President Priolozi said. "But I thank you all the same."

"Just stick with us, sir, and we'll make sure things improve. Speaking of which, I'm going to need your help in our defense."

"My soldier days are long behind me, Captain. I doubt I can help you at all."

"If you'd follow me, sir, I'll explain how you can. Cobra, on me." Harrison led the combined group into the back room of the suite that, aside from the entire floor plan being flipped, was identical to the one they'd just left. "Sir, I need to know how many secret escape paths are in the room, where they are, and how to activate them."

The president's gaze turned grave. "You've been watching too many war movies, son. There aren't any secret passages here."

"Sir, with all due respect, we don't have time for this. My sniper's mother worked for President Hugo. She remembers having to use one once, and Vice President Goodheart just used one to make his escape. So, I know that they *are* there, sir."

President Priolozi nodded with a fraction of a smile. "Very well. There's only one—right on that wall. I can show you the latch needed to open it."

"No others?"

"No others."

Okay, that makes that easy. "Fine, we'll make our stand here. Hark, I need you to disguise charges at the doorway to this room and in the bedroom. Assume they'll gather in the bedroom itself and maybe just outside. Get creative. The enemy cannot know they're there. Fickle, organize the Terrines. I want a token defense in the corridor; the rest will hide in the kitchen and back rooms. I'll brief them in a minute. Sarson, we need control of the lights. On my mark, black out the suite."

"I'll have to take down the whole base," Sarson said. "No way I'll gain access to just this room in time. The V-P messed with the command codes before he left."

"I don't care how you do it, just make it happen. And don't say you can't. I know better. Tai, stay with Hatchet. He is not allowed to die. Move Cobra!"

Harry Fickle was grinning from ear to ear. "Welcome back, John. We're on it!"

As the team scattered to carry out his orders, Harrison turned to face the president. "Sir, I realize this doesn't make sense, but trust me, it will. I need you to open that tunnel then follow it until you find the first bend. Once you're out of sight, don't go any farther. I don't trust them to not have anti-air waiting for you."

"That's all fine," Priolozi said, "but what about you and your men? Shouldn't you come with us?"

Harrison made a point of lifting his rifle. "Don't worry about us, sir. If my plan works, you'll be seeing us again real soon. Now get going. Captain Tai here will keep you breathing."

"Be safe, Captain. And thank you."

All part of the job.

While the president left as instructed, Harrison went to work setting his trap. He had portable shields mounted at the tunnel entrance, then had their only two PMGs attached there to lay down cover fire. Lieutenant Hark managed to hide half a dozen charges all over the bedroom. A tossed pillow here, a charge in a drawer there, another in a broken light fixture, yet another behind a table just outside the bedroom, and so on.

Priolozi gave Sarson some tips on how to blackout the base before he went to his cover position. A few minutes later, Sarson announced that at Harrison's order, the suite, and the entire base for that matter, would go dark. Harrison explained his plan to the troops, then had them take their places. Each Vesper loaded a Stiletto onto their rifles, switched to lethal on their weapons, took their places with the Terrines, and waited. Harrison himself was tucked against the wall in a room opposite the bedroom. He'd have a clear view of everything, provided he didn't peek too much to be seen. *God, I hope this works.*

A few eternal minutes later, the firefight outside began. Light arms at first, then heavier cannons carried by the power armor. The terrines outside did their jobs well. They held for a short while, then retreated inside. Sadly, only five of the eight had made it that far. Harrison had to swallow his heart back into place as they made a running retreat into the back room. *They knew the risks, and they knew what had to be done. You did the best you could.* Hollow words, just like all the times before, but they would have to do for now.

As hoped, the Polaris soldiers followed them right into the bedroom. Though some watched their six, the force still ignored the rest of the suite in favor of the perceived main threat. As expected, the slightly taller power armors remained in the middle to provide suppressing fire. While little more than thick armor along the lines of medieval knights, the large bulk, glowing visor, and heavy weapons on the arms still projected an imposing figure. They also carried combat shields thicker than most infantry, though still easily cut through by sustained fire.

That last part was the biggest risk Harrison's plan would face. Their Stiletto rounds wouldn't penetrate those shields in one volley. So, they would have to punch a hole and then finish the job. Their only hope was that the enemy would be too confused to mount a proper counterattack.

When the PMGs opened fire, Harrison listened to the calls of the enemy. As he'd hoped, they believed that President Priolozi was making his escape. He also heard one of them yell out over their comms.

"HVT has transport. Watch for enemy shuttles leaving the area, but *check your target*! Our assets may use the same means . . . Yes, he has a strobe. So *be careful*! We'll make sure they don't double back. Out!"

It's nice to know my gut is still good. However, that same gut did a twist. It was time. He adjusted his rifle in his hand, then nodded at Harry.

"Kick the tires,"

Captain Fickle nodded with an evil chuckle. "And light the fires."

"COB 2 to COB 5; drop the wool."

Three seconds later, every light went out. One second later, explosions ripped through the enemy lines. Several screams announced direct hits, and the shields on the power suits flared. Before the blast had fully faded, flashbangs went in. The second they popped, every Terrine and Vesper opened up.

Stiletto rounds were fired the moment a power suit's shields stopped flaring. Each hit saw the bulk collapse onto the floor with a mighty thud. The enemy did a lot of yelling, both in pain and attempts at communication, but not a lot of firing back. The Terrines managed to move into position without tripping over anything, while the Vespers used their helmets to see perfectly in the dark. After thirty seconds of fierce fire, the room fell silent.

"Lights!" Harrison ordered.

Sarson reactivated the lights to reveal a carnage of broken, charred, and blasted-apart bodies. Many parts of the bedroom were still burning, though the fire suppression system was already fixing that. The power suits all had several holes in them, with their occupants sporting similar bloody craters. The floor and walls were littered with debris, ash, and blood. Everyone remotely intact was checked to be sure, but no life was found inside the kill zone.

"I don't think we're getting our cleaning deposit back," a Terrine said.

A soft laugh rolled through the group, but Harrison only sighed. "We're not done yet. The enemy had support outside. Mount up. We need to find them and take them out."

"What about the vice president?" another Terrine asked.

"Pity him."

Jason had already sent the order ahead for his group to gather around Gold 1. He had a feeling how this was going to go, but he also owed them the chance to prove him wrong. Truth be told, he half hoped some or all would accept his offer. It would mean a much smaller funeral.

He let those thoughts fall away the moment he entered the hangar. With Sundale and Reneca right behind him, he cut through the assembled group to stand at Gold 1's hatch, then turned to face them. *Here goes nothing.*

"We have a plan, but it won't be easy. Third seats should be receiving details shortly, but here is what we have so far: We will be attacking one of the outposts with the intent of disabling the hyper-light inhibitor. Our group will ride our cloak as much as we can, then at maximum detection range, we will break and attack. The *Hulio* may or may not join us in the engagement, but disabling the inhibitor will be up to us and us alone. Here's the other shoe . . . We won't be coming back. Now, the *Hulio* will try to draw as much attention as she can, but the fact is, it's highly unlikely any of us will survive this engagement. As it is, it'll take every bit of our training just to accomplish our objective.

"This is a volunteer-only mission. Many of you have families, homes, lives. I wouldn't blame any one of you for backing out, and I *will not* tolerate anyone thinking less of you should you wish to do so. Knowing you might die is one thing. There's always that chance of meeting death every time we put on the uniform. We live with it, we accept it, even as we try our best to avoid it. This is different. This is walking right up to death and giving it a hug like an old friend. This is charging into a mission, knowing that you *will* die. I cannot, and *will not*, ask that of anyone here today. You all know me. You know I mean what I say. There is no shame in shying away from this one, so if you want to walk away from this line, you have every right to do so. You will not be called a coward, not on my watch.

"Therefore, I now ask: Those of you who will not be joining the assault—"

A soldier Jason didn't even remember the name of called out, "Protect and serve!"

Every single soldier, without hesitation, responded with a booming voice, "Honor and uphold!"

There was Jason's answer. The call wasn't a pressure—quite the contrary. It was a way of polling the squad. If any had been in doubt, their call would not have been as firm. Jason hadn't heard any hints of that from anyone. It was one voice, unified in its vow.

Jason nodded while his chest felt close to bursting with pride. "No matter the cost." When no one so much as wavered, Jason went on. "Very well. We stand united on the beaches of peace, and I say to you, we shall make good on that vow today. Our blood will end war, our lives will put a knife in the heart of tyranny, and our names shall be *carved* in the halls of victory! Mount up, Gold Group! The enemy awaits its end."

The squad again responded as one, "Yes, sir!"

The men and women of his group scattered to their fighters. Gold 1 entered theirs to bring her up to combat status. As the ship hummed to life, Jason checked his information panel.

"Reneca, do we have particulars yet?"

"Just came in, Colonel," she said. "On mark, Gold Group will launch behind Fusa and Ino squads under cloak. We will proceed to designated target and engage. *Hulio* will bombard the base at maximum range while Fusa and Ino squads provide cover for her. *Hulio* and her squads will try to draw enemy defenders, but Admiral Redding expects Marcallan fighters will be able to intercept no later than engagement range with target outpost."

"Should be enough to pull the frigates at least."

"I'll take what we can get," Sundale said.

"Amen to that. Sun, we'll need target points and any power you can throw into the heavy cannons. Reneca, watch your screen like a hawk. I don't want any surprises."

"Aye, sir," she said. "Third seat will have eyes."

"ETA to launch?"

"Ten minutes."

"Gold 1 to all ships, if you pray to anything, now's the time. Godspeed."

As they waited for their order to engage, Jason couldn't help one of the few lines of Shakespeare he knew popping into his mind.

"Now, if these men do not die well, it will be a black matter for the king that led them to it."

Thanks a lot, Picard.

CHAPTER 22

HUNTERS

One thing the escape tunnel did was provide amazing acoustics. Yarain could hear every word spoken by those at the end. They knew she was coming. They were expecting Vespers. They also weren't sure how much coverage outside she had. That last one seemed to be causing quite the disagreement on whether or not they could launch. *Good. Maybe their own fear will keep them grounded.*

However, the narrow tunnel was designed to give the defenders every advantage. It was only wide enough for two people, and Lieutenant Rad confirmed that the end opened right into the bay, which meant no cover for the attackers. They only had one advantage; their armor was able to match the color of the walls quite well, and the lighting was dim at best.

As they got closer to the bay, Yarain realized that the lighting was also exposed. Further, the last run of the tunnel came after a sharp bend and was long enough for them to see the bay at the end, but not be seen by the men standing guard. *Guess I'll have to make a note of these things for the designers. They missed a few things, or they got lazy.*

Whatever the cause of the flaws, they left Yarain with a risky but plausible idea. "Can you take out the lighting from here?"

"Easily," Shillin said, "but they might start shooting."

"Stay close to the bend, stay low, take cover if they do. I'll get the lights here."

Rad laid herself on the floor, then clicked her rifle to the solid round mode. Yarain did the same, took aim at the lights, and fired shots into the single strip of lighting overhead. She had to search for the right spots, but she managed to sever the power line to each strip. Shillin began her work at the same time, hitting the right spots with much better accuracy. Bit by bit, the entire run of the tunnel went dark. The men at the end fired bursts at them, but every shot was aimed high. Shillin could easily roll behind the bend while Yarain was already there for just that reason.

When the enemy fire ended, Shillin continued her work. After the third time she came back from cover, the enemy didn't bother spraying fire anymore. All they did was gather their troops at the entrance behind pop-up points of cover. They shined flashlights down the tunnel, but Shillin's aim made short work of those long before they found her. One man screamed, and Yarain was able to hear the others say that the round caught his elbow.

That wasn't all her ears caught.

"It's a damned Vesper sniper."

"Stay behind cover. They can't hit you there."

"Did you miss what I said? A *Vesper* sniper. Whoever it is could literally take your ear off if they wanted."

"Take cover to the sides. They'll have to come out to get to us. Even a Vesper can't shoot around corners."

We could if I'd thought to bring the right gear.

Goodheart's voice came above the others. "Just stand ready. And check the men outside again. We need to know what assets they have out there."

"Sir, with respect, we may have to risk it. Vespers are not to be underestimated. Especially Major Yarain's team."

"She's nothing but a fucking fox! If she tries anything, you put her down like the dog she is. Now stand ready. Wait for them to make the next move."

He'll pay for that one.

The other soldiers continued the debate.

"We should launch now. You don't sit and wait against Vespers."

"You also don't go out into an unknown situation. If Interstar has ships out there, we won't make it into orbit."

"So, we don't wait. We power her up here, spin the HL drive, then jump the second we're out."

"Do you realize how many things we could hit along the way?"

"You got a better idea?"

Goodheart again. "That's what sensors are for. Make it happen."

"But, sir—"

"I said, make it happen!"

You won't get the chance.

With the tunnel now completely dark, Rad and Yarain were able to slink their way forward. They pushed their luck as far as they could but stopped just ahead of where the light from the bay leaked into the tunnel. Rad wasn't wrong about the bay or the ship. It looked exactly like a Scorn, except she was painted black, she didn't have wings, and she seemed to be about three meters longer. The turrets were set in the middle of the ship, and Shillin had said a matching pair was on the bottom. Everything else about the ship seemed to be the same, right down to the main engines.

Yarain thought about trying to disable the ship, but the Stiletto rounds had a low chance of doing enough damage. Even if they could, they would have to land hits in precisely the right spots. While Rad might be able to do so, Yarain didn't like the odds of her staying safe after the first round, and the chance of one round being enough was in the single digits at best.

Then again, her next idea wasn't exactly a stroke of brilliance either. As the hum of the ship powering up filled the bay, she had Rad retreat with her back to the bend so she could discuss it safely. Even if every bit of power was diverted to the hyperlight coils, they still had a few minutes before the coils could receive power and then spin up, but they still needed to move soon to prevent Goodheart's escape.

"Get ready to throw a flashbang," Yarain said softly. "I'm going to sprint forward, draw their attention, then when the flashbang detonates, I'll be in a position to assault their points of cover."

Lieutenant Rad slowly turned her head to face her. "With respect, ma'am, that's suicide. You'd never make it."

"I will if our timing is right. The flashbang has to detonate a second before I exit cover."

"You'd be running blind. Whether from the flashbang itself or your helmet's defenses against it. There must be a better way."

"I'm open to ideas."

Even through the helmet, Yarain could sense and smell Shillin's stress. For good reason. Yarain herself saw the plan as something even

Jason would have scoffed at. She also didn't see an alternative. Their comms weren't getting out of the base, Harrison was no doubt neck-deep in enemy forces, and Goodheart had a plan that wasn't nearly as dangerous as his men thought. Like he had said, a good sensor sweep would find them an easy lane to jump through, and they would be long gone before any HLS inhibitors could stop them. They had to be stopped here and now, or they wouldn't be.

But for this to have a chance at working, Yarain would have to be running as fast as her paws could take her. That meant hitting close to twenty-five miles an hour – double that if she took her primal form – and as Shadow said, she'd be blind for one or two seconds of it. If she wasn't able to stop or steer well enough, she could be the first soldier to have 'high-speed collision' on their service record without a vehicle being involved. That's assuming their timing was right, or that her personal shield could protect her from any fire she took, or that she didn't miss a step anywhere in her path.

Rad eventually sighed with a shake of her head. "I'm sorry, ma'am, I can't. I can't be put in that position. If my timing is off—"

"It won't be," Yarain said.

"You don't know that. If I'm off by half a second, you're dead."

Yarain could feel the tension in Rad's body. She understood it. A lot rode on her throw. Not just timing but aim. It was a lot to ask of anyone, Vesper or not.

Yarain retracted the face of her helmet so she could stare at Shillin. Much like she had done before with Sarson, she centered her own thoughts and feelings into a certainty. Yarain tried to find Shillin's eyes through the helmet so she could somehow infuse that feeling into them. The longer she held her stare, the weaker Shillin's scent got. Shillin soon began to breathe lighter, and her shoulders eased themselves down even faster.

"How do you do that?" Shillin said.

Yarain tilted her head. "Do what?"

"I've served on three different teams, and I have never felt the confidence I do with you. You defend us better than any armor, yet even when under fire, you're as gentle as your fur when we need it most. It . . . it reminds me . . . never mind."

Oh no you don't. Not this time. "Go on. Reminds you of what?"

Yarain could almost feel Shillin's scent change. "Of . . . something I haven't felt since . . . since I saw President Hugo die."

She was there for that? Had to be as a child, given her age. President Hugo had not died easily or peacefully. It was the only time a United Systems president had been killed while in office. A Marcallan assault team had managed to get to him, and unlike most instances, they took their sweet time ending his life. No doubt they had wanted to "send a message" to the United Systems Republic. Instead, they were taken down by a Vesper team, and those they didn't have the time to kill went on to inspire the masses that much more.

Many blamed Hugo for going that near the lines in the first place, and Yarain often agreed with them, but she'd never considered the effect such an event would have on those around him. Shillin had said her mother worked for him. No one ever spent the time to report on the other casualties on the mission. They were too busy mourning or blaming Hugo.

If Shillin's mother had been among the dead, which Yarain now suspected she was, it would explain a lot. Humans didn't process things the same way Holdrens did. She had heard of similar events becoming repressed, even as they changed the person's personality. Yarain had to wonder if that event was why Shillin was so distant. Though she couldn't say exactly how one caused the other, what she knew of humans told her that it could be the source of everything she had sensed from her.

More than ever, Yarain tried desperately to find Shillin's eyes. She held her stare, and Shillin continued to relax. When neither fear nor pain could be found in her scent, Yarain ticked her ears forward in approval.

"You asked how I do it. As a first mother, it's instinctual. My pack lives or dies by how I lead them. But I never ask anything of them I don't think they can do. Which is why I can say to you, without a doubt, you will do this perfectly. Not you *can*. You *will*."

Shillin let out a heavy sigh but also nodded. "Maybe. But I have to ask, ma'am, are you sure you can do this without getting yourself killed?"

Not in the least. "Yes."

"All right. Let's do it."

Yarain took a moment to program a one-time command with PAICCA. When she charged her matrix behind her eyes in a certain way, the system would trigger the helmet's defenses against flashbangs for exactly one second. She tested it three times to be sure the command worked, then abandoned her rifle so she could assume her primal form. Combat would have to be done with her tails, though thankfully, the personal guard had thus far been lightly armored.

With her helmet redeployed, Yarain took her position at the end of the straight length of tunnel while Shillin got as close to the opening as she could. Once there, she primed a flashbang and held up a hand. Yarain sank onto her legs, ready to unleash the growing tension in them. With the timer adjusted on the ordnance, Shillin began a countdown on her hand.

3 ... 2 ... 1 ... GO!

All four legs let loose for all they had. Yarain's body bounded with each step as she gathered more and more speed. As the opening rushed at her, she tried to choose her path as best she could. As far as she could tell, the bay barely had enough room on either side of the ship for two men, if that. She only saw two panels of armor for cover, though she knew more were on the sides. The ship itself was recessed just enough for the hull to be flush with the floor, though there was still a tiny gap between the rear hatch and the engine nacelles.

Half a second after her sprint started, Yarain decided to try a blind leap over the armor panels at the point of detonation. If it worked, she could spill out along the side of the ship to slow, turn, and fire. If it didn't, she'd lose at least a little speed before hitting whatever she wound up hitting.

Just as Yarain was approaching Shillin's position, every light in the bay went out. The dim emergency lights were barely enough for a human to not trip over something, and only after their eyes had time to adjust. Yarain's eyes didn't need time or adjustment while Shillin, in one fluid motion, tossed the flashbang behind them, hit the night vision on her helmet, and turned to join the charge. Both soldiers emerged from the tunnel at the same time.

Yarain braced her sprint against one of the armor panels and leapt right into the thick of the enemy position. The flash from the tunnel drew their attention, allowing her to land the full force of her paws on the first man's chest. He grunted as they landed, and his head hit the ground so hard Yarain could feel the impact vibrate up his body. Only his helmet kept it from being fatal, though he was still down for the count. Two other men turned in an attempt to find her, but her tails were already curving over. She fired an extended burst until both men collapsed, out cold.

Despite the growing hum of the ship's hyperlight coils, she heard the deep tones of stunner fire and knew without looking that Shillin had taken care of the other emplacement. In an odd moment of instinct, Yarain barked twice toward the ship, somehow knowing it would convey the order to Shillin while also drawing out those inside. Then, as easy as it was to walk, Yarain slid through the tiny space in the floor into the repair area below the ship while Shillin made herself vanish behind another cover point along the far wall. They were both gone from vision seconds before the main lights came back on. Soon after, the rear hatch opened, and four men with the same thin armor and rifles emerged.

"We should just launch," one man said. "This is stupid."

"We'd never make it," another said. "Those Vespers could easily disable the ship from the outside. If the grand marshal is going to make it out, we've got to find them."

"Or delay them long enough," another said.

Or none of the above.

The men started by taking up guard positions close to the hull of the ship. Having only a clear shot on two of them, Yarain decided to save her energy matrix for the time being. She retook her finesse form, then reached up, grabbed a man by his ankles, and pulled him down under the belly of the ship. He yelped as he fell, was stunned by his face hitting the floor, then was put in a choke hold until he fell limp in Yarain's arm.

The others cried out his name. One fired into the hole. Neither tactic got them anywhere. Their man was gone. A second later, another man fell to a stunner shot only Yarain's ears could catch over the hum of the ship. The remaining guards whirled around to fire at a couple of random shadows. They never came close to where Shillin was already hidden behind cover.

Yarain was already moving. She found an even smaller gap along the side of the hull, and though it took slightly more effort, she was out and climbing on top of the ship in half a heartbeat. Her paws moved slow and silent, inching her closer to her prey. The remaining men were still searching for any sign of a target both along the walls and below the ship. They had also left the rear hatch wide open. To get the jump on everyone, Yarain would have to move fast, move quiet, and trust her instincts were right about Shillin. She went down on all fours, more rolled than slid off the back of the ship, and darted inside without even turning an ear to the others. She heard them yell, then heard more deep tones as they both went down before they could fire a shot.

The interior of the ship remained very much like a Scorn. The panels on the side of the mini corridor still allowed access to the ship's systems, though the longer length meant a dedicated space for passengers had been added. While hardly comfortable, it would allow several people to escape on the same ship.

The cockpit had two additional stations along the wall as well, but all were empty save for the two pilot seats up front. Yarain drew her sidearm, took aim with it and her outside tails, and started growling.

"Shut it down," she said.

Two men in thin combat vests jerked to look at her. The younger of the two reached for a weapon and felt a shot from Yarain's tail before his hand ever touched it. He slumped in his chair while former Vice President Goodheart only glared at her. She marched forward, yanked his harness off, and tossed him out of his chair despite some rather vile insults being thrown her way. He started to say more until Shillin cleared her throat from the entrance.

Yarain shut the ship down, made sure the pilot was well and truly unconscious, then turned to face the last man left awake. "By order of Marshal Garmon, you are under arrest."

Goodheart laughed as he collected himself to his feet. "This changes nothing. I shall still be the emperor humanity deserves. And you? You shall be my little—"

Shillin stuck the barrel of her weapon into the man's cheek. "I suggest you choose your words more carefully unless you'd like to be dragged out of here on your face."

For a second, Goodheart's eyes widened in fear. He then seemed to literally swallow it down, though Yarain could still smell a hint of it on him. "Fine. Enjoy your pale victory. Once Forin kills his prefect, Marcalla will join our side. We will destroy you, then I will return as grand marshal of the Confederacy. I will rise to assume the presidency, and with the combined might of Polaris and Interstar, we will put an end to the Jantan threat once and for all. I will lead humanity to its rightful place as ruler of this galaxy."

Yarain ticked her ears back, the Holdren version of shaking her head in disbelief. "Except the Gold Group is already there to stop them."

"You underestimate our reach, Major. If they try, they will die, and good riddance to them."

"No, you underestimate Colonel Harlem."

Despite her words, a part of Yarain's heart sank at the very real chance that Sundale would not be coming back this time.

CHAPTER 23

THE GATES OF VALHALLA

An odd sort of calm had fallen over the cockpit of Gold 1. The enemy outpost lay ahead just out of view, with fifty Marcallan fighters and three frigates floating around it. As expected, the frigates and fighters hung outside the base's effective range. Either the battle would drift into range, or they would damage the incoming enemy too much to be a threat. A risky, though effective, tactic. The Gold Group stayed on course for their target. Every crew had their base armor deployed. With everything powered to a minimum, they'd get just past the frigates before they could be more easily targeted. At best, they'd have enemy fighters only seconds behind them, then all hell would break loose.

And in the cockpit, at least for now, a gentle calm. Not quite enough to hear a pin drop, yet still silent. It was as if a chill had taken over, but the kind that you want while sitting by a fire with your favorite cup of tea on the table and a book in your hand. In this moment, there wasn't anything. There was just life.

Jason chuckled at the thought. He wasn't going to be alive for much longer, but that did not keep the here and now from making his body relax as if he were about to fall asleep. He wasn't anywhere close to it, of course, not with combat only minutes away. Yet he enjoyed the thought while he had it.

He got to enjoy it a few minutes more until the enemy base and defenders finally came into view. Just dots at first, but Jason had seen them so much that his mind constructed them from memory. The Marcallan fighters, literal spheres with "wings" like battleaxes forming an X pattern on their hull. The outpost itself was a large sphere as well, though without anything breaking the smooth contour of the hull aside from the weapon emplacements. This allowed the base to have a free field of fire from almost any angle, and it wasn't unheard of to see them rotate in combat, however slowly. Then three frigates, which looked like blocky, diamond-shaped ships with a large sphere in the middle. *Jantans do like their geometric shapes.*

He knew them well. He knew how to fight them. He also knew how hard they were to take down. Not the fighters. Those things were nimble but couldn't withstand the firepower of a Scorn. The frigates, however, were tough nuts to crack. To say nothing of the base itself. Just getting close was going to be an adventure.

That's why they pay us the big bucks, Jason thought. With a sigh that triggered his 'switch,' he set about making good on that trust.

"Sun, do we have targets yet?"

"Yes," Sundale said. "Plotting now."

It only took a few seconds for a diagram of the base to come up on Jason's target screen. Narrow channels leading into the hull of the base allowed for the energy wave of the inhibitor to scatter far out into space unhindered by the base's structure itself. While hardly a threat to the base itself, the right damage to those channels would disrupt the flow of that energy and neutralize the effect. A sustained barrage on bare armor could reach the generator and take it out, but the chances of them being able to do that were pretty low. So, the plan remained: get in close, target the channels, pray like crazy they would last long enough to make their mark.

With engagement range only minutes away and communication too risky this close to the enemy, Jason had nothing left but his rare ritual. A common, static prayer he only used on the eve of high-risk combat just in case he didn't survive it.

But before he could start it, one of the Marcallan frigates and ten of their fighters suddenly activated a small portion of their running lights. Literally the next second, Reneca's station went nuts, as did Jason's own comm panel.

"Report!" Jason said.

"Just this," Reneca said.

A hard-toned voice came over the comms. "Galla has shown us the truth. We now stand with the righteous. *Kezil Harage Var!*"

A phrase Jason knew to roughly translate as "Glory to the ancient blood." *That can't be good.*

With just over a minute until engagement range, Jason's eyes froze open as those same Marcallan ships began firing on their own. The no doubt stunned ships were slow in returning fire. A number of fighters were taken out before they could even start, and one of the other frigates found itself having to rotate fast to keep her shields up.

"Ooook," Jason said. "We getting any updates here?"

"Yes," Reneca said. "IFF tags are being updated. Aggressing Marcallan ships now marked as friendlies."

Sure enough, Jason's sensor screen had changed to show the one frigate and ten fighters as allied ships. While he wondered if it could be trusted, this broke the plan wide open. With such a major change in numbers, Jason took the risk of tossing out the entire battle plan. *Admiral Redding can court martial me if I live.*

"Gold 1 to all units. This mission just became survivable. On engagement range, Gold 2, take second and third squads—help finish off that frigate. Fourth Squad, cover the allied frigate. Everyone else, engage enemy fighters. Pair up for damage rotation. Do your jobs, hold your lines, accomplish the mission, but don't be shy about your eject handles. Let's get this done."

Reneca reported squad-wide acknowledgments. As the last seconds to engagement range ticked down, Jason snuck in that prayer even so.

"As I lay me down to sleep, I pray the Lord my soul to keep. If I should die before I wake, I pray the Lord my soul to take. AMEN!"

Right on engagement range, the Gold Group decloaked as one. Ten Scorns took a hard line on the embattled "enemy" frigate. The *Hulio* was hot on their tails with her own fire to further pressure the enemy ship. Jason meanwhile paired with Gold 8 as they engaged the enemy fighters. They each split a Marcallan fighter in half with their combined main and turret cannon fire. They held each other's wing as the two groups of fighters began scattering to engage each other.

Jason managed to get on the six of another ship, but the darn thing was bouncing around like a pinball. Reneca and Sundale had to turn their turrets in defense, so they were unable to assist with the chase. Jason finally predicted a jerk correctly and managed to land a full barrage of cannons and missiles. The small sphere became a slightly bigger fireball.

He then had to flip, turn, and run like hell as three of the fallen fighter's friends came screaming in for revenge. Worse yet, the two frigates were still intact enough to add their PDF turrets into the mix. Even through his dunking, Jason saw one of the other Scorns succumb to the combined fire. He wasn't doing much better. With three spheres on his tail, his shield generator was having a hard time keeping up. Gold 1 and Gold 8 were managing to rotate around each other, but they were still taking a lot of fire, and their turrets were only able to claim one of the pursuers.

An allied sphere came charging in between them toward their attackers. When the chasers turned their attention toward the newcomer, Jason wasted no time. He and Gold 8 flipped on their backs, and two more enemy spheres felt the full brunt of a Scorn's weaponry.

"All Scorns, engage frigate one, focus command sphere," Reneca called. "Vindinsas will buy time."

Not much. But the order had been given. He could only hope the Kapon pilots would prove as effective against Marcallan spheres as they had against Polaris Comets and Vipers.

Every Scorn turned toward the still-spinning frigate. She had taken hull damage, but her weapons and engines remained online enough to keep her a threat. Though the Gold Group had taken losses, they were still a cloud of weapons fire that began pounding on the enemy frigate's central sphere. With the allied frigate managing to hit the same place, the shields didn't last long. Missiles and torpedoes streaked toward the unprotected armor, shattering it like panes of glass. Their weapons tore into the hull beneath, then deeper through exposed corridors into the heart of the ship. Their rounds soon found the ship's main power core. With the layers of armored shell breached and containment components ruined, the micro singularity within flashed out for a second to consume most of the engineering section and then collapsed on itself into nothing. Soon after, the ship began drifting through space without any way to power so much as a flashlight.

Yet there were plenty more to deal with.

"***BANDITS***," Sundale barked. "Nine-o'clock sharp!"

Shit. "Scatter and engage!"

The Gold Group spread out to avoid getting caught together. The enemy fighters tried to bunch up on Scorns, but that left them somewhat exposed.

Unfortunately, Gold 1 found herself facing four more spheres alone.

Jason tried to duck under, but they were able to get off a sustained barrage that tore through their shields. Sharp vibrations spoke of hull damage. An alarm at Sundale's console spoke of worse.

"How bad?" Jason asked.

Sundale was already removing his buckles. "Shield feed took a hit. I need to reroute the system manually."

"How long until we lose shields?"

"Minute tops."

And the day was going so well. "Reneca, we need cover. Sun, work fast."

Reneca tried to request cover fire while Sundale attached an overhead lattice to his uniform. Though not perfect, it would keep him from slamming into a wall or the roof during a hit. Jason then heard one of the panels open up behind him. All he could do was pray and twist Gold 1 into every evasive pattern he could make up on a vector away from the main battle. Two of the pursuers had been taken down, but two more remained, and they were proving hard to shake.

Come on, Sun, come on. Jason knew better than to say anything out loud, but they desperately needed to regain shield use, or they'd be dead very, very soon. All he could do was dink, dive, slide, and flip to avoid as much enemy fire as he could. An alarm on his panel warned of imminent shield failure. His eyes warned of an enemy fighter coming straight for him.

"Hold onto your fur!"

Jason yanked the fighter hard in a sideways sliding roll. Some of the enemy fire actually hit their own ships, but it soon caught up with him, and Sundale's minute was up. More rounds hit the armor; then, a single missile impacted right over Reneca's head.

The blast knocked Gold 1 into another roll while the explosion inside sent Jason's ears ringing over hull breach alarms. The sharp pings of jetted metal echoed in the cockpit while Jason's right shoulder twitched for some reason. While auto force fields sealed the hole almost immediately, he heard the clanging of metal right before a pained yelp came from Reneca's seat.

Jason would have been surprised how frantic her cry had made him if he wasn't busy sliding his ship between two Scorns coming to his rescue. "Reneca?! Talk to me!"

He heard a hard ruff first, more metal, then her voice. "Third seat operational, sir."

Oh, thank God.

"Shields back up," Sundale called.

Even better!

The ship status screen showed the same, though warned of the hull breach. Without hull plating to cover, the shields wouldn't work there. Thankfully, Sundale was well trained and experienced. Seconds later, he was able to attach an emergency plate under the hole. Little more than a stiff sheet of tin foil, it did seal the breach and provided a conduit for the shield layer to cover.

There was a soft tinking sound coming from Sundale's seat for a moment, but before Jason could wonder what it was, Sundale's voice cut him off. "Hyper-light and transporter are down. Starboard magazine is damaged. It now only has ten rounds available. Reneca, be careful of your turret. The heat sinks may have taken damage. Debris shields engaged."

A thin force field now covered each seat and their consoles. Worthless against pretty much anything, including shrapnel, it would at least keep the crew and their systems safe from the bits of metal strewn all over the cockpit.

With emergency repairs complete, Jason turned Gold 1 back into the fight. He first got to play chicken with another enemy fighter. Tough as Marcallan spheres were to hit sometimes, Scorns had more firepower. With no evasion from the enemy pilot at all, he took the full force of Gold 1's barrage, and his ship broke apart like a shattered egg.

Jason managed to find Gold 8 in the middle of the melee. They reformed their pair and started chasing after the remaining enemy fighters. The other enemy frigate, meanwhile, had taken damage to two of her engine clusters. That meant no more spinning, which meant the *Hulio* and their frigate ally got to focus their fire on one side. The enemy frigate didn't last long after that.

With the scopes clearing fast, Jason knew it was time. "All right, boys and girls, get ready for the fun part. Reneca, any word on how our new friends plan to help?"

"Admiral Redding on the line to explain that," she said.

"Redding to all ships, listen up. The frigate *Jaria* is going to provide cover. Once optimal assault range has been reached, fighters will break cover and attack. Flight lines and target points being sent now. Godspeed everyone."

Once Jason's info screen changed to show target and flight data, he joined the remainder of his group in tight formation to keep the *Jaria* between them and the base. He ordered the group into bomber mode, though he felt a literal twinge in his heart when he saw fewer Scorns around him than there had been before. There weren't as many Vindinsas out there, either. The irony was not lost on him since, a few minutes ago, he hadn't expected anyone to come back at all. *Is this favor not big enough for you?* Time would soon tell.

He didn't like hiding behind another ship for his benefit, but orders and the patched hole over Reneca's head kept him in place. He could see the shields of the frigate flaring ahead of them, but the ship maintained speed despite its usual spin tactic. In only a few minutes, the bulk of the station loomed over them.

That's when Reneca started barking the same order he heard over the comms. "***ENGAGE! ENGAGE!*** All fighters begin attack run!"

The remaining ships flowed past the frigate like a fog rolling over a hill. Every fighter flipped and rolled to avoid the field of PDF fire as best they could. Any ship not under fire unloaded its full arsenal onto a chosen point. Not just one of the channels—this was the closest point to the main HLS inhibitor generator. This made the plan painfully clear; they were going all in on disabling that generator. A risky endeavor, but one Jason agreed with. Without enemy ships to harass them and with additional firepower, they had a better chance of forming a hole they could maintain and take advantage of.

But they were losing fighters, the frigate was starting to take armor damage, and they had yet to do any meaningful harm to the base. As

Jason had to roll over the corpse of the last allied Marcallan fighter, he took a rare breath that heated his entire body, and he glared as if his eyes could bore the hole for him.

"All ships, Pure power to weapons. Punch through!"

Sundale: "Pure power to weapons, aye."

Reneca: "All fighters, Pure power to weapons! Pure power to weapons!"

If we live, mention she doesn't need to repeat those orders.

Every watt, every volt, every scrap of power that could be found was thrust into the fighter's weapons. All light besides the consoles went out, Jason felt his body tug against the straps as gravity faded, and life support failure warnings sounded. Aside from a few key systems, the entire ship's power output had been shunted into her firepower. The results were immediate.

The heavy cannons had their rate of fire almost doubled; all Gatling cannons spun like turboprops, and this effect was echoed by every Scorn still standing. The shields of the base became solid white for ten seconds, then her hull began erupting like fireworks. This became a volcano when scores of missiles streamed in, as well as several laser batteries melting their way through the hull. PDF turrets tried to defend the base, but there were too many ships remaining to fend off. On top of that, the *Hulio* had risked joining the cause to lend her cannons to the barrage. She took fire, but not enough to penetrate the thick shields of a Histmar-class heavy cruiser, even a Polaris-built one.

Jason kept turning and evading while holding his bombardment as best he could. That generator *had* to go down. His panel screamed at systems reaching their literal melting point, yet he held fire. One of Reneca's guns flew apart from overheating. Its power was fed to every remaining weapon. Two Scorns were blasted apart in front of him. No one so much as flinched. Their only movement was evasion of fire and the frigate moving way too close to the enemy base.

"Reneca, any idea what the *Jaria* is doing?" Jason asked.

"No, sir," she said. "Admiral Redding is asking them the same thing. So far—"

Sundale cut in. "**FIELD** down, **FIELD** down! Inhib field is down!"

Jason wasted no time. "Total Defense. Scram! Scram! *Everybody out*!"

Sundale confirmed, "Total Defense, aye!"

Reneca repeated, "All fighters, Total Defense and scram. **VACATE! VACATE!**"

The barrage ceased as every remaining ship turned and weaved their way toward the retreating *Hulio*. All the power that had gone to weapons now went to the shields and ECM systems. While this would strain already hot generators, it only had to last long enough to escape. Even so, the PDF fire chased them well out of range, but a large number of fighters made their escape. A couple took fatal damage on the way, but the cockpits were ejected to serve as flying life-pods. Intact Scorns covered the pods as best they could on the group's way out of combat range.

However, one ship was oddly missing.

Jason hit his comms. "Gold 1 to *Jaria*, mission accomplished. You can bug out."

The same hard tone from before came back. "Negative Gold 1. I will not chance them finding a way to threaten the mission. We give our lives so that the Kor'agel may live. Remember us, Lieutenant Colonel Harlem. Remember us, and continue what you have started. May Galla continue to bless you."

The channel was closed. With his fighter now out of range, Jason couldn't help it. He flipped Gold 1 around to see for himself what was going on.

The *Jaria* had made hull-to-hull contact with the enemy base. Sparks and fires erupted from where the two hulks met. The base's shields couldn't reform through the frigate's armor. Only a few guns could land hits. Then, the frigate vanished in one brilliant flash. A self-destruct method seen all too often on the battlefield. Every missile, torpedo, charge, or anything else that could be had been detonated. The ship's core had been intentionally breached. The combined blast was so bright it would have blinded Jason had the windows not activated their light shielding system. Even so, the glow filled the cockpit and surrounding space like a new sun.

As the glow faded, the aftermath became clear. Close to a quarter of the base was now missing. The edges of the damage were filled with fire and floating chunks. The base itself was actually listing away from where the frigate had been, no doubt pushed out of place by the blast. Jason's sensor panel read a massive reduction in power output, though he had a feeling the base still had some teeth left.

Despite that fact, the *Jaria* had succeeded where their combined fleet likely could not have. Even at full strength, their barrage would never have been able to disarm the base so effectively. The base might have a few potshots left in it, but the *Hulio* could now make her jump in safety. The cost was high, but it had not been in vain.

"Kezil Harage Var, *Jaria*," Jason said. "May God greet you on the other side."

An order soon came in for all ships to dock with the *Hulio*. As Jason turned back around to comply, he decided to see who else was meeting God today.

"Reneca, did they train you how to do a Gold Group roll call?"

"Yes," she said.

"Please start it then."

"Aye, sir. Gold 1 to all units. Begin roll call. Report ship and crew status."

While Jason landed his ship in the hangar of the *Hulio*, Reneca read off the responses tailored in their own specific way. It wasn't protocol, but no one cared. It was a tradition established long before Jason was named group commander.

"Gold 1: active. No losses. No wounded."

Barely.

"Gold 2: active. No losses. One wounded."

"Gold 3: active. One loss. No wounded."

"Gold 4: destroyed. Three losses."

"Gold 5: destroyed. No losses. No wounded."

"Gold 6: destroyed. Three losses."

Jason leaned against his chair. It didn't matter that it had been a suicide mission a little while ago. His group had lost soldiers. Good soldiers. Lives he couldn't save.

"Gold 12: destroyed. One loss. One wounded."

"Gold 13: active. No losses. No wounded."

"Gold 14: destroyed. Three losses."

"Gold 15: destroyed. Three losses."

On and on it went. Men and women he knew well. Men and women he didn't know at all. His command. His orders. His responsibility.

"Gold 20: active. No losses. Two wounded."

"Gold 21: active. Two losses. One wounded."

"Gold 22: des . . . destroyed . . . Three . . . three Losses."

Jason couldn't help an amused huff. *I see Miss Tanner made an impression on you. She did for me, too. Even put her in for a promotion a few days ago. Guess I'll be giving the pins to her brother instead. As well as her medal for fighting this one.*

"Gold 33: destroyed. No losses. One wounded."

"Gold 34: destroyed. No losses. No wounded."

"Gold 35: destroyed. Two losses. No wounded."

"Roll call complete. Gold Group accounted for."

What's left of it.

He had kept track in his mind. He couldn't not. Thirty-seven were dead. Twenty-three more injured, some of them no doubt permanently. Some of the Scorn escape pods, little more than the ejected cockpit with tiny retractable wings, were still landing around them. Of the ten Vindinsa fighters sent out, he could only count four, though one of the Scorns came in towing two Kapon escape pods behind her. Medical personnel were rushing between the ships in a desperate bid to save any still clinging to life.

A lot of bloodshed to protect one man. Yet despite feeling like an oak tree was in his heart, Jason felt a voice in the back of his mind saying, "It was worth it."

He actually agreed. More than ever, Prefect Colark was their only hope of a lasting peace. If their lives meant no more would be lost, then those lives meant something. That said, one of the arriving crew was already having a sheet draped over him in the hangar bay. Many more likely would never be recovered. Worth it or not, volunteers or not, it had still cost a lot of lives.

With Gold 1 powered down, Jason slowly dragged himself out of his seat. He had no idea where he was going. He just wanted to be somewhere else. He started walking out just as the other two stood themselves.

He stopped cold at Sundale's seat. He could almost feel his blood drain from his body as if his feet had sprung a leak. Half a dozen holes had been stabbed in Sundale's chair. One of them dead center of the headrest. Just to the side, shards of metal his helmet would not have stopped. That tinking sound from before...

Sundale had been pulling those shards out of his seat. Had he not been making repairs...

Jason looked away. He didn't want to go there, not again. But the shocks weren't done. Sundale had the medical kit out. He was treating a shallow cut on the back of Reneca's head just below the base of her skull. Like all head wounds, it was bleeding like crazy but wasn't actually serious. His own feathers had blood on them from cuts at the leading edge of the wings. These too looked far worse than they were.

Not that Jason's heart cared. His best friend had been that close to death. Now, as it turned out, his new friend hadn't been that far from it herself. Even through her helmet, the debris from the hit had wounded her. A little more one direction, or a little deeper, and it might well have been fatal! As it was, her uniform had a streak of blood down the back from that wound. Had that missile hit the center of the cockpit, or more dead on the starboard nacelle, odds were high they'd all be dead.

It was all too much. Jason couldn't feel his own heartbeat. He couldn't hear any words spoken. His legs seemed to move at the direction of another. Through the chaos of the hangar, he made his way to his temporary quarters just across the way. He sat on the bed and saw nothing. Felt nothing. All he could perceive was the sensation that all of his blood had been lost, and yet his head still managed an odd pulsing that kept him from thinking.

He heard the door open, but it felt like someone else had told him about the sound. Yet it was enough that he didn't jump out of his skin when a paw-like hand touched his. Though Holdren paw pads could never be called "soft," this touch was, and it felt like it was infusing blood back into his system. He looked at it and was surprised that the fur was a slightly darker shade of sandy gold. Further, when he followed the arm up to the head, there was no white there, and it had orange where he didn't expect it.

Reneca stared into his eyes, and all at once, his body was full of blood again. Everything that had – apparently – been tense all this time released into a heap of calm. Thoughts and feelings he couldn't perceive spread through him until a rush of pain coursed through his veins like a jolt of electricity.

For the first time in his life, Jason's switch didn't work. His heart felt like it had split in two. He clutched the front of his chest while slowly bending over. Though tears never came, his eyes were closed all the same. He breathed like he had been punched in the gut, even as it felt like he didn't have one.

And through it all, there was Reneca's hand. She didn't say a word, didn't make a move. All she did was sit, stare, and let him breathe.

They sat together for what felt like months. Slowly, Jason's breathing eased. His world rebuilt itself until at last, he could actually see things again. He still didn't like the blood on Reneca's fur and uniform, but at least he could see it and understand it again.

Finally, Jason took a long, hard breath. "I need to be out there."

Reneca spoke with her usual confidence, yet soft like Yarain often did. "The group has Sundale and Captain Gomez. You need to lick your own wounds before you can help them with theirs."

"I'm not wounded – OW! . . . what?"

On his right shoulder, barely an inch from his neck, Reneca had pulled out a tiny piece of metal. In a flash, some part of Jason remembered flinching when they took their missile hit. But there had been nothing else there. His own uniform had blood on it. That blood had trickled down his chest, run along the silver sash, and continued to drain down the side of his hip. Yet he hadn't felt any of it . . . until now.

"How did I . . ." Jason couldn't even finish the question.

"I admire your dedication, Colonel," Reneca said. "But you will do your pack no good if you don't keep an ear turned at yourself. You can't carry that burden alone."

"I'm their commanding officer. Their lives are *my* responsibility."

"And what good is that if you're dead? **THIS** could have been much worse for you. You once told me to swallow my pride. Now you need to swallow yours. Care for yourself and share the burden, or your pack will lose a lot more than they did today."

My pack lost thirty-seven members today! He wanted to say it aloud, but as Jason turned to glare at her, a twinge of pain from his wound drew his attention there and to the blood continuing to stain his uniform. The anger instantly turned to lead weight in his chest. His hand touched the hole, and he cringed at the pain. She had a point. An inch or two was all that stood between him and death. Just like last time.

Jason's hand went to his other armpit. He touched where the scar lay beneath his uniform. A couple of inches further in, and his duel with Jals all those years ago would have been fatal. It would have been anyway, had

Sundale's bluff not given them the chance to escape. Had Carter and Marcy not gotten him treatment in time. Ironic that it wasn't long after that Sundale and Carter started ragging on him about "ignoring them." While he still didn't understand why they wouldn't let him be the unit leader he was, he had to admit that he wouldn't have become that leader without them.

"You don't fight fair," Jason finally said.

"No one ever should." Reneca tossed the shrapnel aside and stood. "Shall we get that wound checked?"

Jason chuckled before standing. "Only if you do. You might have a concussion, you know."

"I doubt it."

"You getting prideful on me, Captain?"

"It's not pride if it's an honest assessment."

Debatable, but I'm in no mood to argue.

Chief Tillman tried to not bang his tan, hairless head on the console while he worked. Part of him wondered if this really was the best way, but experience had taught him that it was the quickest way to replace the relays, if not the easiest. For him, at least, a little more effort was worth shaving as much as two hours off the job. *Who knew a simple console would need so much work?* He complained to vent, but he actually loved the challenge. Plus, he didn't often get the chance to enter the station's command deck, much less work on something this important. Doing both at the same time felt darn good.

It soon came to an end as he managed to attach the last of the new wires to the power feed. "Try now," he yelled from beneath.

"Still nothing," the lieutenant said.

All right. When in doubt, violence. Tillman gave the main connectors a hard smack with his wrench. The space lit up, followed by the usual even beeping of the sensor console.

"That's got it!" The lieutenant said. "She's up and running now . . . uh . . . I think."

"You t'ink?"

Chief Tillman extracted himself so he could look at the display himself. He instantly understood the man's confusion. It was reading a Marcallan heavy cruiser approaching at high HLS, seemingly escorted by Scorns and Vindinsas.

"I don' understand it. It shouldn' be doin' that."

Commander Austin, a short man with no more hair than the chief who commanded the base, joined them. "Problem Lieutenant?"

"I don't know, sir," the lieutenant said. "We got the relays fixed, but this is the readout we're getting."

Commander Austin tried tapping on the console himself, hummed, then turned toward the comms officer. "Have the boys in intel check their screens."

"Aye, sir! Stand by." Everyone watched the comms officer, waiting for the answer. "Sir? They confirm our reading. One Marcallan heavy cruiser, with Interstar and Kapon fighters in escort . . . sir . . . they are definitely on an intercept course!"

"What the hell? Set condition 1! All hands to battle stations. Alert the *Scorpios* and *Leo* to prepare for fighter interception but to hold fire until my order. Chief, seal that console, then get to your station in the hangar."

"Aye, sir!"

Chief Tillman came close to literally diving under the console to get at the innards he had been working with. Considering combat might be imminent, he rushed as much as he could without neglecting standards. *I ain't gonna be blamed for something goin' boom.*

He reattached the panel and slid out just in time to see the aforementioned ship and escorts arrive on one of the monitors. Chief Tillman had never seen a Marcallan cruiser in person before, but he instantly recognized battle damage on her armor. Some of the fighters showed similar signs, including one Scorn that was missing a wing. *What in the hell is going on?*

His curiosity beat out his training, and he lingered while the comm officer spoke up.

"Uh, sir? We're being hailed by Admiral Redding."

"I won't say no to reinforcements," Commander Austin said, "but I think we can handle a beat-up cruiser."

"Sir, he's *on* the cruiser."

"*What*?!"

The lieutenant at the sensor station added, "And I'm getting IFF tags identifying those Scorns as the Gold Group."

Commander Austin went still with an open mouth, but his eyes had gone blank as if his brain had crashed like a computer. Chief Tillman wasn't far behind. Like everyone else, he couldn't figure out what the FCO of the *Alamo* carrier group was doing on a Marcallan cruiser.

Fortunately for Commander Austin, it only lasted a moment. He then shook his head and gestured at the main screen. "Put him on."

This should be interestin'.

One of the screens flickered on to show Admiral Redding, Colonel Harlem, and a jantan in VERY nice clothes, all standing on what appeared to be the cruiser's CIC.

"Commander, I realize this is highly unusual," Admiral Redding said, "but you can stand down. There are no hostiles here."

Commander Austin blinked slowly, no doubt trying to get his brain to fully reboot. "You'll forgive me if I don't take your word for that, sir."

"I do. You should be receiving IFF confirmation codes now."

Austin checked with his comm officer, who confirmed not only reception of said codes but also their validity. "Okay, with all due respect, Admiral, I think I need to know what's going on."

"I agree. What's your name, son?"

"Commander Austin, sir."

"Well, Commander, I'm sure you know the colonel here, if only by reputation. And this is Prefect Giller Colark. We'll be granting him asylum for a little while until he can connect with loyal sects of his government and sort things out. In the meantime, we'll need to arrange for reinforcements to keep him safe."

"Sir, with all due respect, this is my command, and I need to know *everything* before we do *anything* that could jeopardize this station."

"I understand. I'll transit over to explain all of that in person. While I do, our fighters took a beating. They need repairs."

"Forgive me if I have them shadowed, sir. This entire situation is highly unusual."

"Commander, you don't need to apologize for doing your job. Take whatever precautions you see fit. I'll see you shortly. Redding out."

You could have heard a pin drop from the deck below. Yet Chief Tillman was already heading out the door. If allied fighters were going to need care, especially those fighters, he was not going to let anyone else oversee them. While some may have doubted things, he didn't. *No one would be stupid enough to try an' fake Colonel Harlem. Nor could they an'way. There's no fakin' his special kind of tired.*

CHAPTER 24

MY LIFE FOR THE PACK

Admiral Solez had to take a deep breath to settle himself. The council was not in a good mood, and he didn't blame them. So many things had gone so very wrong. The Grand Marshal had been captured, the Marcallan prefect defended, and instead of Marcalla joining Polaris, it seemed more likely the conspiracy was going to spark a civil war, assuming it hadn't already. With Goodheart unobtainable, they were looking for someone to blame, and Admiral Solez was their first choice.

He had his own pound of flesh to offer, but he wasn't about to give more than that. So, when it came time for his report, he took the center stand in the chambers without hesitation or fear. His only act of contrition was to avoid glaring death at the well-dressed men and women surrounding him.

"Honored council, I understand your feelings, but we must face the truth of this matter. Our plans to destabilize the United Systems

Republic have met failure after spectacular failure. In my opinion, continuing the war will only see us lose more. We must declare peace so we can regroup, reset, and make sure we don't lose anymore."

The council argued over each other, many incensed at the idea of making peace with United Systems. Solez had taken some time to stomach the idea as well, even if he fully intended to break it when the time was right.

"You were in command, Admiral," one of them finally said. "Any losses are on you."

Not entirely. "I accept that my efforts were less than successful, but I remind you that Grand Marshal Goodheart had executive command of the operation. I will accept responsibility for my hand in those failures, but as you will see in my report, Grand Marshal Goodheart dug our grave more than I ever could."

"Tread lightly, Admiral." President Markus said. "You're talking about one of our best assets."

"Respectfully, sir, I am not. In fact, it is my belief that his true intentions were to subvert *our* plan for *his* personal, treasonous goals."

"Do you have proof of this?"

"While largely circumstantial, I have enough to bring his motives into serious question. However, even if I were wrong about his plans, there are a few things he himself ordered that I believe led to our failure."

"Such as?"

"Item one: moving forward with the operation as planned when the first two phases failed in spectacular fashion, and then again when we lost a vital forward operations base that severely hampered our ability to repair and resupply our ships in the field, which led to several more missions failing. Item two: The attack on the civilians of Phoenix Perch, an act he admitted—not in so many words—was an act of vengeance that only inspired Interstar more. Further, I have it on good authority that it was a direct factor in their presence at Holdre 4. Speaking of which... Item three: the attack on Holdre 4. We knew it was controlled by an outside force, yet we went in anyway to secure it as an ally or to create a new base for ourselves. Instead, our forces were intercepted by Interstar, and they were able to buy enough time for Kapon forces to arrive. Because of our attack, Kapon wound up joining Interstar in their war against us. Item four: experiments on Holdren POW's."

"Didn't you yourself torture a Holdren POW?" The Vice President said.

Don't remind me. "I did that to gain information that could have and would have helped us salvage the operation. Grand Marshal Goodheart ordered brutal scientific tests, almost all of which would have told us nothing about how to better combat Holdrens in the future. They are war crimes of the worst kind that did nothing but galvanize United Systems *and* Kapon even more. And that is just the beginning. I direct your attention to reports my aide and my s..." *Best not admit where some of it came from. They'd never accept it.* "My top remaining asset managed to procure. I think you'll find them most disturbing..."

Jason stared out the window at the gold-colored planet that was Holdre 4. Seeing it there brought a sense of calm, but also a bit of weight in his chest. A lot of good men, women, and foxes had died protecting it. Then, many more had died in the months after. It seemed odd to be there, yet not even at condition 3. Almost like he expected a Polaris fleet to appear out of nowhere and begin the war all over again. Standing on the decks of the *Berlin*, light-years from his own fighter, created a sense of near nakedness.

But there would be no ambush today. No call to battle stations. Heck, they weren't even at war anymore. Mere days after they rescued the prefect, Polaris had called for a ceasefire. They'd even gone so far as to promise a full removal of all forces from captured territory. In exchange for Interstar doing the same, but still. It caused quite a stir throughout the fleet, with opinions flying more fiercely than a barrage from a destroyer.

Jason joined those who didn't expect it to last. For one thing, it wasn't even an armistice. Just a ceasefire, and no one, not even Polaris, tried to admit it was anything but tenuous. Though the lines would fall silent for now, he fully expected Polaris to remain a thorn in their side for a long, long time. Simon held out hope change would come after Goodheart's actions came to light. Marshal Garmon had even arranged to let the young man get Yarain's report of Goodheart's confession, among other damning information, to his father. But Jason knew better. Even if peace did take hold, it wouldn't come for several years.

For one thing, some didn't even want the ceasefire. Members of Kapon and United Systems were outraged that the treatment of the Holdren POWs was going to go unpunished outside of Goodheart. To say nothing of the attempt on President Priolozi and their planned involvement in the Marcallan coup. Many questioned why such a nation should be allowed to sit and rebuild after such acts, even if the acts had been ordered outside of the Polaris leadership. More so because there remained a legitimate question of how many acts Polaris leaders ordered or at least knew about without stepping in.

All of that said, Jason found a great deal of wisdom in the decision to accept. While the tide had turned, it still wasn't firm, and earning it had come with a heavy price. Many battle groups—including Jason's own group—were in pieces, more than a few bases were damaged or destroyed, colonies like Phoenix Perch were still rebuilding their defenses, and the dead were long past six digits. While Prefect Colark had managed to find loyal troops to take over his defense, there were already reports of skirmishes between sides within Marcalla. It seemed likely a civil war was brewing, and rumor had it even the Polaris negotiator admitted that the situation had his leaders worried about eventual spillover. If nothing else, one side or the other might well take vengeance on the group they believe triggered the whole thing.

Besides, Kapon was already in talks to share technology. While such decisions had generated their own tensions, it meant that the time to rebuild and re-tool might actually be worth the risk for Interstar as well. Now that Polaris was a known threat, new base construction and fleet deployment changes had already been implemented. With the lines silent—for a while at least—those changes could go into full effect before the next war started.

Thus, Jason got to have a happier day. After what they went through saving the prefect, the entire *Alamo* carrier group had been granted some extensive leave time, as had other units here and there in the combined fleet. The Holdrens involved had wasted no time arranging to be taken home, and Jason was thrilled to be there to see them off. Sundale tried to get him to go home himself, but once the *Berlin* was done off-loading her Holdren passengers, she'd be heading for Earth at maximum HLS. Marcy wouldn't have to wait long to see him again. So, he insisted he be there for his favorite foxes first.

Still, seeing the world he had risked so much to save did threaten to reopen some old wounds. Some of which weren't so old. Half of him wished he could head down himself, to be in the purity that was the Holdren mindset. He then wondered if it would be worth the stress and strain of living wild, though it did not make him opposed to trying it if he could.

An announcement from PAICCA broke into his thoughts. "Attention all Holdrens, we are ready to begin transit. Please report to your designated rooms. Enjoy your leave!"

You can count on that.

Jason headed for Sundale's quarters, then waited just inside for Sundale and Reneca to stretch themselves out of a nap. Neither wore anything beyond their fur. Technically, it was a bit premature, but with the ceasefire in place, no one was going to enforce that rule. The two foxes traded a playful nip, then trotted along to join Jason at the door.

"Need a moment alone?" Jason teased. "I wouldn't mind."

Sundale gave a single, amused ruff. "No. Thank you."

"Very well. Let's get you two home."

Jason saw Sundale take a breath, but before he could check on it, Reneca was already licking his cheek. Whatever had been there instantly vanished as he gave her a soft nuzzle in reply. When neither said a word, at least that *he* could hear, Jason decided to let it be. He saw no reason to spoil the moment now.

They walked together through the corridors to transit room three, which would be servicing the section of Holdre 4 that their pack lived in. Jason noted with a warm heart that both of their tails were more relaxed than they had been in months. Though there was a little bit of sorrow there, too. Yarain had arrived a few minutes ahead of them on another ship, and Harmus had made the same trip shortly after the battle to secure it. That meant it was just going to be him and his wife. *And Carter, when he finds out we're having her casserole*, Jason thought with a chuckle.

"Going to be strange not having any of you around back home," he said.

"I'll miss you too," Sundale said.

"I could always send down some of Marcy's casserole."

Sundale panted a soft laugh, though Reneca spoke first, "Thank you, sir, but I prefer a fresh kill."

Jason stared at her for a moment. "Are you ever going to call me 'Jason'?"

"No."

Sometimes, I forget how blunt Holdrens can be. "We'll see about that. In the meantime, you two take care of yourselves down there. Home without you, I can adjust to . . . I think. Gold 1 without her foxes? Not a chance. I'd never survive being Carter's only target."

"Don't worry, Colonel. We'll be fine."

They walked into the transit room, and Jason told the operator where they were going. As the pad was tuned, Sundale flicked an ear. "You should come down with us, Jason."

Reneca went straight-eared towards him. "*WHAT*? Why?"

"It would mean a lot to him to see what he saved without the pressure of impending combat."

Reneca's ears shifted back, then fell. "Sundale, we can't keep Holdre 4 wild if we start allowing guests."

Sundale turned an ear up in her direction, though he didn't quite look at her. "Isn't Karol a guest?"

"No, she's our contact with Kapon."

Oh boy. While Jason certainly wanted to see the planet without the fog of war, it sounded like his presence would cause more problems than it was worth. He didn't want to be the beginning of a bad precedent, nor did he want any special treatment for any reason at all. He knew Holdrens too well to risk that.

"Look, Sun, I appreciate the gesture, but I'm okay," Jason said. "This is your home, not mine."

Sundale gave him his full attention. "That didn't stop us from sharing your territory. If nothing else, you deserve to actually **MEET** Karfen."

Didn't realize how much I needed leave until now. Jason didn't know what to say or what to do. His brain wouldn't work at all, perhaps because he *did* want to properly meet the first father of Sundale's blood pack. He had heard good things about the fox, and he wanted to see them for himself. But he worried about what his presence might cause, while at the same time, he didn't want to disappoint Sundale.

Thankfully, Reneca gave a sharp sigh to break the stalemate. "If he comes, he must leave technology behind. That includes your sidearm, Colonel."

She knows me better than I thought. Jason slowly drew his weapon, holding onto it as if he might not see it again if he left it behind. "Are you sure about this?"

"***NO***," Reneca ruffed. "But we can speak with Karfen. Let him decide."

"What about blade and uniform? I don't have fangs or claws to defend myself with or fur to keep me warm."

"Take them for now, but Karfen may insist you leave them as well."

Jason had more reservations about this than he had about the assault on the Polaris base, but it seemed like it might work. He just prayed it didn't cost anyone anything, including their lives.

He left his sidearm and wrist com with the techs, made sure his combat knife was where he liked it on his back, then joined his crew on the pad. A sparkle and a flash later found them once again on the surface of Holdre 4. This transponder sat on the edge of territory claimed by Sundale's pack. From there, Jason couldn't see any sign of the battle fought to keep it. Even the mountain used as a bunker still looked like rock at their distance; though the forest as a whole had had a few months, and help from Kapon, to recover.

At least it wasn't too warm or cold, and the very light breeze only served to rustle the leaves of the trees. Even Jason's weak nose could find sap on that wind, though he chuckled at the thought of what his crew found on that same wind.

Then Yarain's voice had him nearly jumping out of his uniform.

"Is something wrong, Jason?"

Jason snapped around while his hand reached for his sidearm, even though it wasn't there. He breathed relief when he saw Yarain standing there with Karfen and another Holdren he didn't know.

"No," Jason said. "I'm here on an invitation to see that which I helped to save."

Karfen's hackles rose ever so slightly. "Who gave you this invitation?"

"I did, Karfen," Sundale said. "I thought it would mean a lot . . ."

He trailed off when Karfen started growling. *I know that sound.* Jason quickly fell to a knee and lowered his head. Sundale's ears fell in much the same way.

"You overstep," Karfen said.

Jason acted on his first thought and prayed it wasn't wrong. "I'm sorry. If you don't want me here—"

"***QUIET!***" *Shutting up.* "Sundale, what made you think you could do this without asking me first?"

Sundale hugged the ground with his tails tucked beneath him. "I'm sorry. I didn't think it would be an issue."

"Then you were not taught or did not learn the dynamics of the pack well enough. Colonel Harlem, the fault is not yours. As it is, the issue is resolved, for *I* wanted to meet *you*."

Every ear that could perked toward him, but Jason spoke first. "Then I think I am honored. If I may ask . . . why?"

"I wanted to try to understand how a *human* could attain the position of first father in the hearts of a *Holdren*."

Reneca's ears went straighter still while her eyes bulged. "***WHAT***? I don't understand."

"Harmus has spoken of how he, Yarain, and Sundale all thought of Jason as their first father before they came here."

"He is the first father of their combat pack, but that doesn't mean—"

"He meant as if they were a *blood* pack."

Thank you, and I think I'm in trouble. Jason turned his eyes to Yarain in search of help, yet she only offered ruffs of laughter. "You don't need to worry, Jason. You're not in danger, nor is Sundale if he learns well from his mistake."

"Of that, you can be sure," Sundale said.

"Well, that's one worry down," Jason said, "but I have to ask; did all three of you really think of me that way? I thought you were your own small pack."

"Why do you think we always came to you during leave?" Sundale said. "You, Marcy, and even Carter brought a dynamic that our pack lacked."

"You spent a few leaves away, too, Sun."

"As did you."

While Jason hummed his acceptance of the point, Reneca stared forward as if she didn't see anything. Her ears were frozen in an odd, outward-facing middle point between perked and falling. Jason could only guess what was going through her mind. He also doubted he'd be anywhere close.

As for Jason himself, all he could think was how this whole thing was going nothing like any of the possible scenarios he'd come up with.

"Sooo, what now?" he said.

Karfen stepped forward so they were eye to eye. "If I take you to my pack, will you defend them with your life?"

"Yes."

"If I tell you to die for me, or them, or any reason, will you follow my command?"

"Yes."

"If I tell you to do something that does not make sense or to do nothing at all, will you do it?"

Jason had to almost literally swallow that one. He knew well that there were times when a leader must stand and watch another die. That did not make it easy to agree to, however. Yet the fact that Karfen was even asking meant more to him than any medal. It showed a willingness to trust that Jason had not expected from a wild first father.

"Not easily, but yes."

"Then follow."

The assembled group made their way through the forest at a slow, distance-eating pace that Jason had no trouble maintaining. He appreciated the gesture since he knew that the Holdrens could easily leave him in the dust without breaking a sweat. No one spoke during the jog, though some of the ear changes he saw in Reneca and Sundale made him wonder if they were having a conversation. The changes eventually stopped, but Reneca's tails seemed stiffer than before. Jason worried about what it meant but felt it better left untouched. This wasn't his pack, after all. Nor would he really know where to start or if anything was even wrong.

When Karfen slowed to a stop, Jason could see a clearing not far away where the rest of the pack seemed to be gathered. Either Karfen's pack had split, or some of their members were out on a hunt. Jason only saw five or so members, not counting those who stood with him. A lot of heads and ears turned his way, but otherwise, the pack appeared to be mostly milling about. Some were playing, some sleeping, some simply sitting or lying in the sun or shade. Only two came toward them when they didn't move closer, and Jason knew one of them all too well. This Holdren's orange lay on the tips of his ears, as well as the leading edge of his hip and shoulder joints, with an additional strip of orange along the top of his muzzle from his nose to just behind his ears. His white undercoat covered his entire face without a single speck of grey.

There was a lightness to Harmus' trot that Jason couldn't remember seeing before. At least, not very often. Though he called himself crazy, he thought that his fur was smoother and cleaner than it had ever been. Or maybe it was simply fuller. Regardless, Jason felt quite sure the gruff father of his best friend was more comfortable out here where he belonged.

After both gave Karfen a quick greeting rub along the cheek glands, Harmus went straight for his mate, while the other Holdren, who Jason now remembered was Milsol, went toward Sundale. Harmus and

Yarain nearly tackled each other as they rubbed, licked, and nuzzled each other. *Not unlike the times I come home to Marcy*, Jason thought. Milsol and Sundale exchanged a similar greeting, though nowhere near as energetic. When he came to Reneca, though, his energy waned, and his head tilted.

"What's wrong?" Milsol asked.

"I am suddenly conflicted," Reneca said.

"About what?"

"Many things."

She walked toward the clearing with even stiffer tails. Sundale, Milsol, and the other Holdren that had been with Karfen followed, while Harmus and Yarain were stopped by a ruff from Karfen.

"I think you will be of help," he said.

Both ticked their ears forward and laid together just off to the side. When Karfen did the same, Jason took the hint and sat on the ground himself. *I hope they don't expect me to lie down as well. Not as comfortable a position for us humans.* Thankfully, none of them so much as flicked an ear at it.

"May I ask why we're not joining the pack?" Jason said.

"You are not of them," Karfen said. "This keeps them from worrying about us without disrupting them."

Translation: pack members only. This way, they can see you enough to know I'm not killing you, and they get to live out their wild lives in peace. "I see. Well, you said you wanted to understand how I earned the position of first father with these three. I have to be honest . . . I don't know either. I never knew they thought of me that way."

"We always deferred to you," Harmus said.

"Yarain and Sundale did, but I was their CO. Those instincts never really turn off. Heh, just look at Reneca. Even off duty, she still calls me

'Colonel.' It felt like you and I spent more time snarling at each other, so to speak."

"I'm not surprised," Karfen said. "He's a good necker, but he still has the will and heart of a first father. I suspect much of your tension came from him trying too hard to keep his pack safe."

That would explain a few things. "I suppose so. Though if you'll forgive me . . . necker?"

"What you might call a beta or enforcer," Yarain said. "They hold the pack together and settle disputes if needed."

"I didn't realize you guys had 'disputes.'"

"Even wild wolves will have internal arguments. A necker keeps the pack from tearing itself apart when the blunter—what humans often call an omega or defuser—can't calm things down."

Jason had to hold a hand up. His mind was swimming with too many new terms and aspects of Holdrens for him to handle. Karfen tilted his head, confused, until a barely audible bark, more like a sharp whine, from Yarain brought his ears forward. No doubt she was explaining the gesture, for which Jason felt eternally grateful.

"I'm sorry," Jason finally said. "I was getting too much too fast there. I didn't think my comment would trigger an info dump."

"It's a distraction anyway," Karfen said. "Perhaps my questions can be answered . . ."

Every ear and head snapped toward a loud screech echoing in the distance. *I know that sound.* A Holdren was in distress, and this close to a meeting area, the chances of it not being a member of the pack were almost zero. Jason jumped to his feet along with the entire pack. Much like Jason, they appeared to be getting a bearing on the sound.

"Mind if I join you for this?" he quickly asked.

"*NO*," Karfen barked.

The pack sprinted toward the sound in unison at a second bark from Karfen. Jason tried to keep up, but they were gone in seconds. Even so, he held course in the direction the cry had come. Rumbles, an odd roar, and tail fire helped confirm that he was on the right path.

He saw some of the pack ahead, every one of them in finesse form with their tails curved around. *That's trouble.* He reached for his sidearm but found only the empty holster. *Damn you, Reneca. I really need an equal weapon.* He drew his combat knife instead as he caught up with the pack. He didn't feel too confident when he saw two Holdrens land off to the side, and not on their paws, nor gently.

What are they facing out there that could – GOOD GOD!

As Jason dodged around a tree, even his "switch" couldn't keep him from stopping cold. What had been a large figure in the shadows quickly cleared into what he could only call a monster. Whatever this creature was, it had eight legs like a crab with pincers to match. However, there were four pincers, and they were attached to an upright portion topped with a head closer to an eagle than anything else. It had a tail like a scorpion to finish the terrifying image, and it had to be *at least* nine feet tall at the head. It seemed to be standing over a small kill of some kind, though Jason was too busy with other things to tell what.

"What in the name of . . ." He couldn't even finish, partly because the creature let out a deafening, deep-toned roar. "What *is* that thing?!"

"It's a jesween," Yarain said. Her voice held a fear Jason had never heard in her. Not even close.

Despite his initial horror, Jason's combat training was already kicking in. His mind was taking note of every joint, every bit of edge on the pincers, and the environment around him. They were in a somewhat thick patch of trees, though the leaf coverage overhead was fairly thin. One of the two members who had no doubt been thrown was limping away. Several feet behind the jesween, he saw Reneca and another adult standing their ground in finesse forms with snarls but their ears pulled back. Two more adults lay motionless behind her, as did two very terrified-looking juveniles. Members of the pack were giving a bark-howl call that even Jason recognized as a rally. He saw two members try to circle around, only to have the jesween match their movements, keeping itself between them and Reneca.

That's when Jason's mind connected the dots. This thing had pinned Reneca's party for the kill, but it didn't want to finish them with the pack barking challenge at it. It also wasn't about to let help reach her, and he doubted they could escape for the same reason. *I really wish I had my P-mag right now.*

"Okay, so how do we take this thing down," he asked.

"We can't," Karfen spoke heavily.

"What? You've got half a dozen healthy Holdrens here. Carve him up like a steak with your tails!"

"Its hide is too thick. We need the full pack to have a chance, and half of them are out hunting."

"Okay, we've still got six sets of fangs and claws, plus my knife—"

"It's too **DANGEROUS**, Colonel! You saw what it did already. If the others don't arrive in time . . . we may have to watch them die."

Over my dead body. Jason snapped around, paused a moment, then sheathed his blade so he didn't wave it around at the pack's first father. "Look, I know what I promised, but I can't just let them die! There's got to be a way we can . . . What the . . . Sundale! *Captain*! What do you think you're . . . Yikes."

Sundale had been the only Holdren silent the entire time. While everyone else had been snarling, he hadn't made a sound. Instead, he was watching, very carefully, how the jesween moved. Every time it fended off help, he noticed how it seemed to over-commit to the one direction and thus be slower to turn the other way. While he couldn't tell if it was physical or mental, the tendency remained, and he intended to use it.

While Jason argued with Karfen, Sundale saw three of the pack try to circle around to at least steal away a cub. He knew he only had seconds to act, and so he did. He turned around, drew Jason's blade off his back, then sprinted forward as fast as his paws could carry him. With the Jesween turning to face the others, it couldn't turn back the other way fast enough to catch him. He slipped past long before its tail could catch him.

Sundale reached Reneca with ease, but he wasn't done. He knew a determined hunter when he saw one, and he knew there was only one way to end such a being; death. As such, he stood his ground in front of Reneca and the others. There, every hair went stick straight, his wings spread out as far as they would go, the energy veil extended further to almost double their size, his ears remained forward, his tails spread out though still pointed behind him. His snarl rang inside his own ears, showing every tooth and fang he had.

He faintly heard something from Jason, but Sundale's focus was on his prey. The jesween gave a toned roar at him with another thud of its pincers. Yet, at the same time, the creature wasn't advancing. If anything, the back set of legs seemed to retreat, almost as if bracing. While not quite fear, the creature wasn't ignoring him.

When the beast took a quarter step back, Sundale sprinted forward. Reneca protested, but he would not be deterred. This beast threatened his pack. That had to change.

At a mere twenty feet away, he leapt into the air with a flap of his wings. Sundale added his flight to his sprint, aiming his blade directly for the jesween's head. Though two pincers went low, one came up toward him. Sundale only just managed to bank in time to avoid a direct hit. However the pincer caught his arms enough to force a roll, and he lost hold of the knife. His right arm ached, but he ignored it as he gained altitude.

It's too fast for a direct approach ... or is it? He remembered the time he'd tried firing at it before anyone told him its hide was too thick. One beam had struck a leg, while another had hit the back of the neck. The Jesween had rubbed the leg, but it seemed unable to get a pincer on its own neck. This led him to decide on an outright insane idea. *Jason would approve.*

Sundale flapped his way into the air, firing a couple of shots from his middle tail to keep the jesween's interest. Once he had gained enough altitude, he tucked his wings, limbs, and ears and stooped into a steep dive. The air rushed over his fur and feathers as he sped at the jesween. He tilted just enough to stay on target while priming his hands for the catch. The jesween roared at him, yet he held course.

With only seconds to spare, he spread his wings to slow himself. The joints of wings to body felt as if they popped out of their sockets; yet they had, in fact, absorbed the burden without harm. The jesween swiped at where he would have been had he been going full speed. His remaining momentum carried him past the missed arms right past the creature's neck. There, he dug his hand claws deep into the creature's neck. Most of his remaining forward motion stopped, while the rest was used to swing him around the back of its neck. He latched on with his jaws, finding the flesh surprisingly soft despite its thickness, though it served only to keep him in place. His hands got more purchase, however. He found the bulge that was the jesween's windpipe, and he was able to pinch it between his hands.

Blood started running down his arms, yet his hold remained. The jesween tried to sting him with its tail, but it seemed unwilling to risk stinging itself, and thus, it never reached him. His paws and jaws held him there, and his wings fluttered and flapped to help him stay in place. Meanwhile, his hands continued to pinch despite searing pain from his right arm. The jesween began to wheeze and buck, trying to breathe or kick him off. Its pincers tried and failed to reach him. The beast rolled on the ground twice to brush him off, but its own bulk created just enough of a pocket for Sundale to escape injury, though not all of the pain.

His arms ached, his paws stung, and his hands were going numb, yet Sundale refused to let go. This threat to his pack would end, and it would end now. As the jesween started to stumble, the combined pack rushed forward. They split themselves between the pincers, the tail, and what legs the remaining members could get. Even Jason had his hands wrapped around the tail just below the stinger. With no way to defend itself or move, the jesween wheezed and pulled to no avail. Finally, it slumped to the ground as the loss of air took hold. Soon after, the upper body thundered onto the ground; it gave a few futile convulsions, and then it fell still at last.

Sundale held on long enough to be absolutely sure the thing was dead before letting go. His arms were stiffer than when he had been uncuffed in the Polaris mess hall, his right arm hurt like it had been split in two, but aside from a bruise or two on his back, he had escaped harm. While he let his arms loosen up again, Sundale leapt off of his kill to check on Reneca's party.

The pack was already caring for the wounded adults. The injuries were varied, but none seemed to be fatal, though one had apparently been paralyzed by the jesween's venom. He'd be down for a while but would recover—or so Karfen said when Jason asked about it. That let Sundale check on Reneca. Her concerns from before miles from his mind, he only cared to see if she was wounded.

"Did it hit you anywhere?" he asked.

"No," Reneca said.

"Good." Sundale's ears ticked up at more noise but relaxed when he saw that it was just the hunting party arriving. "I'll take the cubs home."

Before he could even turn away, Reneca said, "Why did you risk so much for me?"

Sundale didn't hesitate. "My pack stood threatened. I defended them as any member would."

"I see modesty runs in the family," Jason said. Sundale hadn't noticed him come close, though he did notice that he had already retrieved his blade. "I've known you a long time, Sun. I have *never*, *ever* seen you look like that. Now maybe that is your natural response to defending your pack, but of all the times you defended me, *that* never came out. Not even close."

Sundale gave a soft growl of annoyance. *Now I see why Yarain hates the phrase so much. I didn't do anything I wouldn't do for my pack.* Though he did have to admit, this felt a little more personal than it ever had before. Funny thing is, though Jason would probably never believe him, it had nothing to do with Reneca. Members of his pack were in danger.

He saw only one way to end that danger, so he did what he had to in order to end it. Nothing more.

"Think what you will, Jason," Sundale said. "I'm going to rest."

Jason chuckled. "I'd say you earned it. We'll handle things here."

Sundale huffed more annoyance, then fell on his paws as he took his primal form. He yelped in pain as his right leg gave out and erupted in agony. He slumped to the ground before he could catch himself on his other legs. Reneca and Jason were kneeling beside him just as fast.

"Easy, buddy," Jason said. "That didn't sound good. What happened?" Sundale whimpered as he tucked his leg. He then panted with a slight tremor as the pain shot up his leg. Jason hummed while gently squeezing it. It only took two before Sundale whined in pain again. "Ah, that's what happened. You broke it, you stubborn fox. Why didn't you say anything?"

"I didn't realize it—" Sundale yelped in more pain as Jason quickly set the bone like an expert. "Smooth."

"Marcy taught me well. That's gonna sting for a while, but once we get you up to the *Berlin*, you'll be hunting like new in no time."

"He's not going," Karfen said. Jason glared at him, which caused Karfen's hackles to rise. "He was wounded in the wild and will heal in the wild."

"Karfen, his leg is broken clean through. I'm astonished he was able to hold on. That bone needs to set and stay set."

"And it will. The pack will make sure of that. But this is our way, Colonel."

Jason started to protest, but Sundale cut him off. "***JASON***. For once, let me stay wild."

Jason sighed with a shake of his head, then sighed again as he stood. "All right. It's your call. Karfen, I'm sure you still want answers, but I think under the circumstances—"

"I have all the answers I need," Karfen said. "Thank you for coming, but it is time you left for your own territory."

In an odd way, it didn't feel as dismissive as the words sounded. Maybe because his tone was somber, almost regretful. Maybe he knew what it meant for Jason to be leaving them behind. Regardless, Jason nodded with an honest, pain-free smile.

"Thank you for letting me be here," Jason said. "I'm honored you trusted me enough."

"You earned it," Karfen said.

Jason gave another nod, then pointed at Sundale. "You heal up. Gold 1 wouldn't feel right without you."

"I'll be back," Sundale said. "Count on it."

Another chuckle, then Jason, after finding someone to help him find his way, headed for the nearest transponder. Sundale started to stand, careful not to put any weight on his injured leg. Reneca insisted she walk beside him, and he wasn't about to object.

Though she took her primal form, she never left his side. Any time he wavered, her body was there to catch him if required. Any time he stopped, she stood with forward ears to watch for how he might need her. Feeling her there, knowing he didn't stand alone, made every bruise, strain, and broken bone feel miles away. Though it didn't quite keep him from panting in response to it.

He found a thick tree in the meeting area to lay under. The one leg took extreme exception to being touched but complained less once he was down. Reneca dashed off, only to return with some kind of bulb the size of his paw in her jaws.

She dropped in front of it and spoke in the Holdren's natural language. "Break it up in your jaws before you swallow it. It will help the pain." Sundale did so, then retched when juice from within was more bitter and foul than anything any human had ever given him. It got so strong it felt like his tongue had literally melted from it. "Fight past it. You'll be glad you did."

It took considerable effort and a few more dry heaves, but Sundale did manage to break the bulb into smaller pieces before swallowing them. His mouth still felt like it was dissolving from the remaining taste, though Reneca brought a tiny bunch of yellow berries the size of peas she had him chew on next. These silenced enough of the taste to make it bearable. By the time it began to fade, he realized the pain was significantly less. Still not gone, and things complained about movement, but at least he and Reneca could lay together in peace without him panting and shaking now.

The pack finally joined them with the rest of the wounded, as well as hunks of meat from the jesween. Yarain and Harmus circled by to check but went to help the others when they saw him as well as possible and under Reneca's care. Many of those wounded were brought similar plants, though at least one didn't keep the bulb in his mouth the first time. *I don't blame him.* Didn't seem like anyone else did either, though they did urge him to keep trying.

Now well and truly surrounded by the pack, Sundale leaned over to rub against Reneca. He had meant to only offer his thanks, but an instinct caught him by surprise, and he found himself seeking to put his cheek gland against hers. Before he knew what he was doing, she answered with a rub of her own that saw their energy matrices meet.

He wasn't aware of much for the next few seconds. Unlike when Karfen had claimed him, when Reneca's energy matrix touched his, it didn't stop at the surface. Their energies felt like they were merging, and the moment they did, he felt her in ways no human could understand.

Sundale could feel every part of her. Her tails, her ears, even her claws. It was all there as if they were a part of him. So too could he feel her essence inside of him, touching every part of his own body. He felt things about her he could never put into words. It was like he suddenly knew her biology right down to the DNA. Karfen's signature was there in the background, but it felt like the soil beneath a thick coat of grass. A base from which the rest formed. He could feel her body, its strength, its certainty, and the few small wounds she held. So too could he feel her touching the same parts of him.

When the rub ended and they separated, Sundale could only stare at her with straight ears and a body that felt lighter than a cloud. "What was that?"

"The pack," Reneca said as if it was obvious.

"I've never felt that with Yarain and Harmus."

"That's because they were never an option. They always had each other."

"Don't tell me you're changing your mind about me."

Reneca's ears flicked back. She sighed and watched as another of the wounded eased herself into a resting position. "I don't know. There's a lot about you that worries me."

Sundale tilted his head. "Like what?"

"You're still tied to Colonel Harlem and to Gold 1. Your wings may make you more vulnerable to other predators. You're brave and devoted, but you're also willing to take risks you don't need to. You didn't need to kill that second bilark or fight the jesween like you did."

"I couldn't let it remain a threat to my pack."

Reneca's ears shifted in thought. Forward, back, out, they couldn't settle for some time. Sundale could only watch with his ears up. Finally, she snorted and rubbed against him again. "Just be more careful. I don't want to lose you before I know for sure how I feel."

"Like I told Jason, I'm not going anywhere."

She ruffed a soft laugh and allowed her cheek gland to meet his once more. This time, he didn't resist it. Though it didn't go anywhere near as deep, he still felt their energies mix on the surface once more.

Later, after eating some of the meat from his latest kill, Sundale would drift to sleep with Reneca beside him. He finally understood his curiosity, if only in part. He also felt like his entire being was lighter than it had ever been. He could feel the pack around him, keeping him safe. He could feel Reneca there as a resource until his leg had healed. For a time, he even managed to forget that there were other nations out there among the stars. There was only him, his pack, his territory, and a future that was quite uncertain. But, at least for the moment, that too was unimportant.

THE END ... FOR NOW.

GOLD 1 AND HER CREW HAVE MORE
MISSIONS AHEAD OF THEM.
STAY TUNED.

GLOSSARY OF TERMS

MARCALLA RANKS

Araf: Marcallan military rank that is equal to an Interstar full lieutenant in the Calnav (U.S. Navy rank structure).

Auro: Marcallan military rank that is equal to an Interstar four star general/admiral.

Hilishan: Marcallan military rank that is equal to an Interstar five star general/admiral.

INTERSTAR TERMS

Calnav: Branch of Interstar focused on interstellar fleet operations. Not to be confused with a "navy", which is a solely water based unit, they govern all starship operations, often with their own fighter units used for defense or attack missions. They use the same rank structure as the real world U.S. Navy.

Calor: General term for a soldier in Calnav. Much as soldiers in the U.S. Navy are called a "Sailor".

PSC: Precision Strike Command. Branch of Interstar focused on strike craft, bombers, and precision special forces operations. While PSC fighter units will often hitch a ride on, or be stationed on, Calnav ships, they will also be sent on missions on their own, sometimes without starship support. Calnav fighter units by comparison will almost never be sent on missions without a mother ship in play, if only as a home base. They use the same rank structure as the real world U.S. Air Force.

Cosman: General term for a soldier in the PSC. Much as soldiers in the U.S. Air Force are called an "Airman".

Terrine: Branch of Interstar focused on infantry or mobile ground forces. While best known for ground assaults, they are often called on to attack or defend bases and ships during boarding actions. Thus they claim, "Be it grass, rock or the metal of a hull, point us at the target, and we'll plant our flag there." They use the same rank structure as the real world U.S. Army.

Vesper: Name of the PSC special forces arm. Used for missions requiring high precision and/or stealth. Best known for information gathering, exact strikes on enemy targets, and rescue missions. Often considered "the scalpel" of special forces, as they are often scent on missions requiring a narrow, specific target/focus in their mission.

FLARE: Short for "Field Logistics Assault Recon Echelon", they are the Calnav special forces arm. A highly trained unit using hyper advanced equipment, some of it so classified, no computer record exists of it. Best known for missions ranging from various behind the lines assault or recon missions, to clearing a landing zone for incoming troops, to deep infiltration or retrieval. Often considered "the sledge hammer" of special forces, as they are often sent on highly secret and/or dangerous missions that require large teams and high end equipment.

AESO: Active Engagement Systems Officer. Often called "Second Seat". Oversees active sensors, targeting, and status of ship systems and magazine on a Scorn Heavy Fighter. Is required to be flight rated.

POSN: Passive Operations Systems and Navigator. Often called "Third Seat". Oversees passive sensors, communications, information flows, and navigation on a Scorn Heavy Fighter. Does not need to be flight rated, but many are anyway.

FCO: Fleet Commanding Officer. The person in charge of a fleet of ships. Usually an admiral. Most often seen commanding carrier groups or large task forces.

Laney PSC Base: A large PSC base used for training various high end tactics, most notably where Vespers are trained, located in *CLASSIFIED*.

Target Range: The distance at which you can begin to somewhat reliably target an enemy, This can vary based on the duel between ECM and ECCM systems, and does not guarantee accurate targeting. Fighters close to enemy ships can transmit targeting data to allow for higher accuracy at longer ranges, sometimes allowing one side to out range the other.

Effective Range: The distance at which weapons are actually effective. Being plasma based, eventually, each round will begin to break apart and dissipate, thus reducing their damage significantly. The larger/more powerful the round, the further this range can extend. This range is often greater than "Target Range", especially for higher caliber weapons.

Engagement Range: The distance at which no amount of ECM can prevent accurate targeting. At this range, both sides can easily target the other with pinpoint accuracy.

GENERAL TERMS

ECM: Electronic CounterMeasures. Various systems used to jam enemy targeting and communications efforts. Often these systems are trying to cut through enemy ECM, though those are usually called ECCM, or Electronic Counter-Countermeasures.

EMCON (Insert level): A state in which transmissions and emittance of energy signatures is highly restricted to reduce detection. Level "Bravo" is highly restricted, but not a total blackout, while level "Alpha" is essentially "be as absolutely quiet as you can!"

HL or Hyper Light: The common term for faster than light travel.

"PAICCA": Personal Artificial Intelligence Combat Computer Assistant. While not a "true AI" (though many sometimes wonder), it is a *highly* adaptive computer system that operates ships systems. It can respond to requests and queries, and sometimes even anticipate them once it "learns" about a person. It will often shift it's behavior to better match the person it is interacting with once it has learned about them.

"PAIA": Personal Artificial Intelligence Assistant. PAICCA's civilian version. Much of the functionality is the same, though it's not as adaptive or as capable.

PDF: Point Defense Fire. Weapons/systems design to target enemy fighters and/or incoming ordinance. Usually low in power and range, but high in accuracy and rate of fire.

"Pencils": A slang term for micro-missiles that can be fired from infantry rifles. Little more than more potent grenades, they can still threaten unshielded targets.

PMG: Personal Mini Guns. A small scale Gatling gun with a very high rate of fire. Can be used for infantry based point defense, suppressing fire, or in some cases, wearing down the shields/armor of larger targets.

"Shells": A slang term for torpedoes, so named since they have a stacked burst of energy fire, followed by a shaped kinetic charge. The intent being the energy portion chips through the shields enough for the shaped charge to send streams of shrapnel into the ship, causing damage to internal systems and/or crew.

SMT: Shoulder Mounted Torpedo. A missile that can be fired by infantry that can potentially damage tanks, fighters, or even transports and ships, depending on how well shielded they are.

Strike Craft: A blanket term covering fighters, fighter bombers, and other small attack craft.

ACKNOWLEDGEMENTS

This book has been a long time coming, and it wouldn't have happened without those few who have stuck with me through thick and thin. Though it's frustrating that I cannot thank many of them by name, as a computer glitch fried some of my records, and when I went to restore from my back-ups, my back-ups weren't there! So my deepest apologies to those I want to thank by name, but cannot find the name to thank you by.

Though I have to start with my family, who remain my best cheerleaders, sounding boards, and prodders. They don't sugar coat things. They tell it how it is, and while the deliver things gently, it remains honest. They don't sugar coat. Just offer it constructively, in a way I can actually hear the feedback given.

To Laurel, whom I still call my first fan, and also remains a source of drive when I am at my lowest. I'm not sure she'd forgive me if I stopped. To the late James Montenegro, who gave me hope I could have a stellar book trailer, and then to Jeremy, who actually made it happen when James was taken too soon to see it finished. And to Postmaster Paul, a man who continues to support and assist me in so many ways.

To my beta readers, whose names are among those that were eaten by the computer glitch. Your insight helped me plug some holes, and make the story that much better. Same with more than a few who offered tactical and technical insight to my battles and technology, and a few neat ideas to Polaris ship designs.

There are also those who chose to remain unnamed, who still gave me help when I needed it most. A technical person who plows snow and can't stand the desert. I gotta get you down here in the winter sometime. A gun slinging, cute dressing, lover of pink and purple, horse girl. Remind me to stay on your good side. And a "crazy Finn", whatever that means. Hey, don't look at me! He said to call him that! Though I think it's safe to say, he's no more sane than I am.

There are certainly more that I am forgetting, and I cannot apologize enough. Some I simply forgot because of Dysgraphia, others that were lost when my computer threw up. But none of my books would happen without all of you. I don't have a publishing house behind me. I only have me, and you.

So in many ways, YOU are my publishing house. And for that, I cannot thank you enough.

www.ingramcontent.com/pod-product-compliance
Lightning Source LLC
LaVergne TN
LVHW041736060526
838201LV00046B/830